A WAR APART

Dakotah Gumm

THE BUBBLY BOOKWORM, LLC

Copyright © 2024 by Dakotah Gumm

All rights reserved.

Paperback ISBN 979-8-9860157-8-1

Library of Congress Control Number: 2024914087

No portion of this book may be reproduced in any form without written permission from the publisher or author, except as permitted by U.S. copyright law.

Cover design by Selkkie Designs selkkiedesigns.com

Author website dakotahgumm.com

Published by The Bubbly Bookworm, LLC

For Delanie

The first to make my imaginary friends her own

CONTENTS

Content Notes		1
1.	Barbezht	3
2.	Five Years Later	12
3.	Tsebol	26
4.	Consequences	34
5.	Grief	46
6.	Aftermath	52
7.	Writing Home	61
8.	Back to Tsebol	66
9.	Borislav	75
10.	Meeting the Tsar	85
11.	A Stranger's Body	99
12.	Becoming Sofia	113
13.	Setting Out	122
14.	Raising Support	132
15.	Idesk	141

16.	Radomir, Prince of the Blood	149
17.	Miroslav's Court	160
18.	Betrayed	169
19.	Gathering an Army	176
20.	Complications	187
21.	Battle Joined	194
22.	Miroslav's Return	202
23.	A Mission	209
24.	Training	224
25.	Drakra	234
26.	A Night Off	243
27.	Ethics of War	255
28.	A Compromising Position	265
29.	Traitors	275
30.	Discontent	285
31.	Surrender	296
32.	Attainted	304
33.	Breach of Ethics	312
34.	Allies	319
35.	Survivor of Barbezht	324
36.	March	332
37.	Last Chance	341
38.	Borislav's Arrival	350
39.	Reunions	361

40. Before the Storm	369
41. Battle	376
42. Confrontation	386
43. Disinheritance	395
44. Execution	408
Epilogue	419
Acknowledgements	428

CONTENT NOTES

A War Apart contains content some readers may be sensitive to. Your mental health matters. If you find any of the following topics triggering, you may want to consider finding another read.

Ableist language
Attempted genocide
Forced amputation/loss of hand
Marital infidelity
Medieval style warfare
Miscarriage/stillbirth
Murder and attempted murder
Physical assault
PTSD (not diagnosed)
Racism
Slavery
Sexual assault
Traumatic birth experience

For more specific questions regarding triggering content, please email contact@dakotahgumm.com. If you or someone you know is facing a crisis and need someone to talk to, call or text 988 in the US.

1

BARBEZHT

Han

One more minute. If I could survive one more minute, I'd be able to go home. My heart pounded, muscles aching with the exertion of the battle. Just one more minute.

I'd been telling myself the same thing for what felt like hours.

"Watch out, Han!" My friend and commander, Benedikt, shouted a warning, and I turned just in time to block an ax aimed for my head. I cut the man down with a blow to his stomach and dodged past him, stumbling in the blood-soaked mud.

"Thanks," I shouted.

Benedikt jerked his head in acknowledgment, pushing sweaty strands of hair from his dark brow. Then his brown eyes widened, fixed on something behind me. Sharp pain shot through my head, and the world went black.

I drifted in and out of consciousness, hearing the clash of metal on metal and the screams of dying men. Unable to move, I lay in the mud, waiting to die. The face of my betrothed appeared in my mind, her soft, brown skin, the twinkle in her brown eyes when she laughed. *Mila...* I hoped I would see her in the next life.

Eventually, the sounds of battle faded, and I regained control over my limbs. They were stiff, weighted down by something that lay atop me. I opened my mouth to call for help, and a foul-tasting substance dripped on my tongue. I moaned.

A muffled voice came through the darkness. "Got a live one back here!"

The weight on me shifted, and I blinked in the sudden brilliance of sunset. Sunset. I'd been out for hours. Long enough for the battle to be decided. I looked up into the faces of my rescuers.

On the peak of their pointed iron helmets, they each wore a black-and-red flag. Miroslav's men. My stomach turned to iron as they dragged me to my feet and pushed me toward a row of wooden cages, cursing when I stumbled.

"Enjoy your stay." One of the men laughed as he pushed me into the first cage.

Several people sat inside the makeshift prison. As I fell to the ground, I heard a familiar voice.

"Han?"

"Benedikt!"

He helped me to my feet and embraced me. "I thought you were dead."

I pulled back and took stock of my body. Aside from a few scrapes and a bone-deep ache, the only injury I seemed to have was a gash across the back of my head, deep and tender but no longer bleeding. The blood was matted; it would be next to impossible to wash it all from my tightly coiled curls. I'd have to shave it all off. I wondered, briefly, if Mila would still find me attractive without my hair.

Time enough to think about that later, after I'd survived this. After I made it home to her.

I licked my lips, wetting them to speak. "I'll survive. What happened?"

"We lost." Benedikt's voice was flat, as though he didn't quite believe it yet.

"The tsar?" I didn't want to know the answer, but I had to ask. Had to know if Borislav was alive.

Benedikt's face grew grim. "Gone."

My throat closed. Impossible. Borislav was supposed to save the tsardom. He couldn't be dead. Couldn't leave us to his brother Miroslav, whose paranoia and reckless ambition would drive the country into the ground.

"Sit down." Benedikt gestured to a bare patch of ground between a grizzled, black-skinned soldier and a pale beardless boy not older than thirteen. Another man sat in the corner of the cage, sandy hair swept over his brow and a haunted look in his eyes.

"How did we lose?" I asked. "I missed the end of the battle, but I thought we were winning."

He shrugged, taking a seat across from me, between the young boy and the man in the corner. "Reinforcements. Miroslav's allies from Vasland arrived just in time to prevent his men from retreating. The tsar... Tsar Borislav must have been killed in the confusion."

Silence hung thick in the pen, broken only by the sounds of revelry coming from Miroslav's nearby camp. After a moment, Benedikt cleared his throat. "We fought like hell, but after Vasland showed up, we were hopelessly outnumbered. They slaughtered us. There's about three dozen of us in these pens," he said, gesturing to the row of wooden cages, "but I'd say that's all of us that survived. They hadn't brought anyone else for a couple hours before you came."

I blew out a long breath. Of all those hundreds of men that had taken the field for Tsar Borislav, less than forty had survived. It was a massacre.

But at least I was alive. Whatever came next, I could manage it, if it meant I could go home to my Mila.

"What do you think they'll do to us?" I asked. Execution was possible, though unlikely—after the massacre his men had just committed, Miroslav could hardly be eager for more bloodshed. Would he imprison us, or have us beaten and sent home?

The man in the corner gave a humorless bark of laughter. "You're a fool if you think we're getting out of here alive. If we're lucky, they'll hang us one by one, but most likely they'll use us for sport. I've heard the Vasland army travels with a giant white bear, makes their prisoners fight it bare-handed. They take bets on how long each prisoner will last."

The boy flinched, his freckled face a mask of terror. "They wouldn't take us prisoner just to kill us, would they?"

The sandy-haired man grinned. "No one will expect you to last more than a minute, boy. The bear's massive, a single paw twice the size of your head. One swipe—"

"That's enough, Boris." Benedikt threw a protective arm around the boy's shoulders. "Most likely they'll ransom us back to our families."

The words didn't comfort the boy, whose lip quivered. "My mama'll never be able to pay a ransom!"

"There's no need to worry about it now," Benedikt soothed. "Try to get some sleep now."

The boy swiped the back of his hand across his eyes and nodded, curling up on the ground and tucking his long coat over his feet. The patches on the coat spoke of years of use. His older brother's, perhaps, or his father's?

The old soldier to my right nudged me, his long gray locs brushing against my shoulder as he leaned close enough to speak. "Yakov's father was killed in the tsar's service when the war first broke," he muttered. "As soon as he could, the boy signed up to follow in his father's footsteps."

I matched the man's volume. "You knew his parents?"

"No, he's in my unit. We're out of Tsebol, but he came from Selyik, a small town not far from there."

I looked down in surprise to where the boy's coat shook with silent sobs. "I'm from Selyik." Yakov. The name wasn't familiar, but I didn't know everyone in the town. Mila would probably know who he was.

"Are you?" The old man raised a bushy gray brow. "Maybe if we get out of this alive, the two of us can see him home safe." He leaned back against the pen and closed his eyes.

The sandy-haired man had settled in as well. "You should rest, Han," Benedikt said, turning deep-set eyes toward the camp. "I'll stay awake in case anything changes, but they're drunk on victory. They'll be passing around drinks and women until dawn."

I nodded. "Wake me in a few hours, and I'll take the second watch. We should all be rested for whatever happens tomorrow." I pulled my collar up and shut my eyes for a fitful sleep.

I woke to the distant sound of cheers. In the dim moonlight, I saw Benedikt craning his neck between the slats of the pen, looking toward Miroslav's camp.

"What is it?" I scrambled to my feet as the others started to stir.

"Miroslav," Benedikt spat. "I guess he wanted to get an early start greeting the troops. Middle of the night and he's out there soaking up all the praise. He probably figured they'd be too drink-sick in the morning to cheer for him."

I peered toward the camp, but I could see nothing through the tents but the glow of their fires. A tall soldier walked toward us and barked something at the two sentries who slept near the middle pens. They leapt to their feet.

The newcomer thrust a long rope into one sentry's hands and gestured for the other to open the pen. The prisoners—my fellow soldiers—stood against the wooden slats of their cage as our captors tied them wrist to wrist, linking them together. They repeated the process in each stall, forming a chain of prisoners.

When they reached our pen, they bound me between Benedikt and the boy, Yakov.

"What are—" Yakov began, but a sharp blow to his cheek cut him off.

"Shut up," the tall soldier ordered.

With prods and pushes, they shepherded us toward the camp. As we approached the tents and Miroslav's soldiers caught sight of us, they jeered. A rock hit my temple, but the pull of the rope kept me from turning to look for the source. Not that it mattered. There was nothing I could do in response.

The further we walked, the more men surrounded us, until at last we reached the center of the camp. We stopped moving, and I looked around at the tents, all in various shades of gray, illuminated by the fire in front of us. On the other side of the fire, a large man lounged in an even larger chair.

The soldier who had collected us spoke. "You are in the presence of Tsar Miroslav Vyacheslavovich of the Blood, Heir of the Sanctioned and rightful ruler of Inzhria."

Miroslav might claim to be our rightful ruler, but I would never accept him. He was a monster. Benedikt swore, and someone behind us kicked him.

Miroslav stood and clapped his hands together. He had straight black hair, like his brother, but that was where the resemblance ended. Borislav was tall and muscular, his bearing that of a lifelong soldier. Miroslav, on the other hand, was short and stout, better suited to a feast table than a military camp.

"Welcome, welcome!" he said in a honey-sweet voice, much higher than I expected. "I apologize for the accommodations, but you understand. Perils of war and all that." He walked around the fire, gold glinting around his fat stomach and arms. "I have a proposal for you, sirs. My brother, Borislav, once the Grand Duke and pretender to the throne, is dead. Now, a wise man knows when his cause is beaten. I'm prepared to be merciful." He gave a warm smile that turned my stomach. "Renounce your ties to the pretender. Kneel before me, and all will be forgiven. You can return to your homes and families."

He paused and looked at us, gauging our reactions. "If, however, you will not kneel, the punishment will be...severe."

The threat hung over us like a cloud. Further down the line, someone knelt.

"Traitor!" Benedikt shouted. "You should burn for that!" He yanked on the rope that bound us together.

"What an intriguing idea." Miroslav's sweet voice dripped with venom. He snapped his fingers and held out a heavily jeweled hand.

Benedikt stopped struggling and eyed the velvet-clad man. A soldier handed Miroslav a long, black staff, which he caressed.

"'You should burn for that,'" Miroslav repeated. He stalked toward us, his movements surprisingly smooth for a man of his size. I took an unconscious step back as he passed me. "Shall we see what that looks like?" He stopped in front of Benedikt and touched his staff to my friend's head.

Benedikt burst into flames. He fell to the ground, screaming. The rope binding us together burned, releasing me from my friend. I scrambled back, desperate to avoid his fate, as the flames licked my arm.

After a moment, the screaming stopped, and there was only silence and the acrid smell of burning hair and flesh.

My stomach roiled as I watched Benedikt's body burn. What was I going to tell his wife? Their son was only two, and they had another baby on the way. He'd been fighting for them, to make the country a safer place for his children, but what would happen to them now that their father was gone and a monster ruled the tsardom?

"Kneel," Miroslav said in a sickly sweet voice. "Kneel, or face the same fate."

I had to make it home to Mila. I had to survive for her. Her face flashed before me, her warm brown skin flushed with worry, umber eyes full of unshed tears. We were supposed to marry this fall. What would she do if I didn't come home to her?

Bile filled my mouth, but I knelt. All along the line, other prisoners knelt as well, until we all bowed before the vile creature who had slaughtered our army and murdered Benedikt.

"You will never again take up arms against me." Miroslav turned and spoke to the guards. "Remove their sword hands before you release them."

2

FIVE YEARS LATER

Han

"Going to be a hot day," I said to no one in particular. It was just past dawn, but already the smells of dirt and sweat mingled in the air.

"Can't handle the heat, old man? If it's too much, I'm sure you can take the day off."

I cast a withering look at the freckled face of Yakov Aleksandrovich, my tenant and best friend. "And miss the chance to make you buy me a drink? Not a chance. First to the end of the row, as usual?"

Pyotr Vasilievich, an older tenant with red-brown skin and a forked gray beard, shook his head. "I remember the days when the landowner was a man of dignity. He didn't stoop to childish competition with his tenants."

"But it's so much more fun this way." I grinned at him as I buckled the sickle to my wrist. "Ready?" I asked Yakov, who had finished buckling the sickle to his own wrist.

"Go."

We swung the blades with practiced ease, letting the wheat fall to the ground. Some of the younger boys who lived on the land trailed behind us, gathering the fallen stalks and binding them into sheaves.

As I worked, my mind wandered back to the battle at Barbezht and the night I first met Yakov. I had taken it on myself to see Yakov home alive and safe—or as safe as could be expected for a marked traitor with a dangerous wound. After tending to our injuries as best we could, the two of us, we'd made our way home together.

On our return to Selyik, I'd brought the boy into my home. My fiancée, Mila—now my wife—and Yakov's mother had nursed us back to health. As owner of a large farm with several tenancies, I'd offered Yakov and his mother a house and a field on my land. In the five years since the battle, we'd learned to live without our sword hands, and we'd developed a friendship from our shared tragedy and the work we'd done to overcome it. Yakov had grown, too, until I no longer considered him a child to be protected, but an equal.

An equal who was going to win our competition. I swung my blade faster.

"Keep up, old man," Yakov tossed over his shoulder.

"'Old man.'" I scoffed. "Twenty-eight isn't old to anyone but children. Which, I suppose, you are. Maybe you should be gathering the wheat instead of cutting it."

The heat and grueling work made conversation difficult, so we worked in silence to the end of the row.

Yakov, finishing first, wiped sweat from his brow and reached for his water skin. "You owe me a drink."

"Day's not over yet," I replied. "Most rows by the end of the day? I'll throw in one of Marya Ivanovna's apple pirozhki if you win."

"Deal."

By midday we were tied, a whole row ahead of the rest of the men. A loud, clanging bell rang, signaling the dinner break, and everyone dropped their sickles where they stood. I unbuckled the belt around my own sickle, rubbing where the leather had chafed my skin. I'd have to ask Mila for some of her salve later.

Yakov shot me a grin. "Tired yet?"

"Not really." I was exhausted and sore, but I wouldn't admit that to him, just as I knew he wouldn't admit how much the red skin around his wrist pained him. "You?"

"Better than them." He jerked his thumb over his shoulder at the rest of the men.

Yegor Miloshovich, a tenant since my grandfather had owned the land, furrowed his brow and frowned at us. "Not all of us are as young as you two."

"But you have twice as many hands as us," Yakov said.

Pyotr Vasilievich snorted. "And what good is that, when the sickle only needs one hand? Or none, apparently," he added, nodding at my arm. "No, this work was made for young people. It doesn't cause you as much pain to be in the field all day."

Kyril Kyrilovich, my steward, stood in the shade of the trees near the field as we approached. "Does it matter who works hardest, so long as the work gets done?"

"Yes," Yakov and I said in unison.

The steward shook his head, smiling with fatherly affection. He'd been my father's steward before mine, and he had known me from childhood. "The water bucket's freshly filled. We'll take a half hour."

I took a seat in the shade and lifted the cloth on top of my dinner basket. Marya Ivanovna, our housekeeper, had overpacked it, as usual. Smoked fish, black bread, and enough apple pirozhki for everyone. I passed around the pirozhki, to a chorus of approbation.

"Mary Ivanovna's making her apple pirog for the harvest feast next week, right?" Yakov spoke through a mouthful of food.

"She always does. You'll have to fight Mila if you want to get any, though. She's been craving apples, and you know how she feels about sweet things." I grinned. Despite the fact that my wife was six months pregnant, I had no doubt that she could beat Yakov in a fight, especially if he came between her and her food.

Yakov turned to Yegor Miloshovich, who sat a few feet away, deep in discussion with Kyril Kyrilovich. "What's your son's wife making for the feast?"

Pyotr laughed. "Don't you think of anything but food, boy?"

I frowned at Kyril and Yegor, who hadn't looked up at Yakov's question. "What has you two so serious?"

Yegor's dark face was grim, the wrinkles streaked with dust. "The soldiers in Tsebol."

"Ah." The tsar had stationed a large portion of his new standing army in the nearby city, and they had been a source of constant trouble for the locals. "Any news?"

Kyril shook his head. "No, and I hear they're getting restless."

"Restless." Yakov spat on the ground. "That's just how these shits are. They think the world belongs to them just because they won the war."

Yegor Miloshovish pursed his lips. He'd chosen not to fight—with the baron out of the country, our region hadn't been called to arms—but he was a traditionalist, of the opinion that the oldest son should inherit, no matter how cruel or incompetent that son may be, or how close in age the next son was. I didn't agree; Borislav, the tsar for whom I'd lost my hand, had been only a couple hours younger than his twin brother Miroslav, and both kinder and more competent. Their father obviously agreed. On his deathbed, the previous tsar had named Borislav his heir, leading to the war which had culminated in Borislav's death on the field at Barbezht.

But the war was over now, and there was no need to cause tension over past battles. "Have the soldiers done something lately?" I asked, hoping to forestall an argument—or worse—between Yakov and Yegor. Yakov was quick to take offense and quicker to respond with his fist. Despite his age, Yegor could most likely hold his own in a fight, but I preferred not to have to deal with the consequences, no matter who won.

"They burned down a cooper's shop over his head two days ago," Kyril Kyrilovich said.

"Bastards!" Yakov swore. "What for?"

Kyril shrugged. "Rumors being what they are, it's hard to say, but I heard he'd refused to let them use his daughters for entertainment."

I shuddered. The soldiers were growing bolder. I said a silent prayer to Otets that they would leave soon.

"I'd have killed them with my bare hands for that," Yakov said, clenching his fist. His light, freckled skin was red with anger.

"You've only got one hand, *durachok.*" I elbowed him in the ribs, then fixed him with a stern look. "We'd best pray you don't meet the tsar's men. You'd get yourself hanged for fighting them."

Yakov ignored me. "What does Miroslav want a standing army for, anyway? The war's over."

Yegor picked up a piece of grass and chewed on the end. "Probably planning to drive out the Drakra once and for all." The previous tsar had waged several wars against the Drakra, a race of gray-skinned people living in the east, and it would come as no surprise if Miroslav continued his father's crusade. "Either that, or there's a foreign threat we haven't heard about."

"I doubt that," Kyril said. "He's always been paranoid. Remember when he fled the country, thinking his father was going to have him assassinated? He's probably built the whole army for another one of his delusions."

"That story's nothing but fiction, made up by Borislav's followers in order to discredit the rightful heir to the throne."

"Oh!" Pyotr Vasilievich let out an awkward laugh. "Speaking of stories, you'll never believe the tale Ulyana's betrothed told us the other day."

Grateful for the change in topic, I leaned back against the tree and glanced at him. "Is she getting married? I hadn't heard."

Pyotr's chest puffed out with pride. "To a baker in Tsebol, Konstantin Anatolyevich. He's a good man." He winked at me. "A bit of a gossip, though, and places too much stock in rumors. He told us Borislav was alive."

"*Da*, I saw Borislav at the inn last week. He decided being tsar wasn't the job for him, so he's working as a blacksmith." Yakov rolled his eyes. "Where'd he hear nonsense like that?"

"Some friend of his. Another survivor of Barbezht." He nodded at me and Yakov in acknowledgment. "All nonsense, of course."

"Borislav died at Barbezht," I said. "We would have fought to the very last man if we'd thought he survived. Nearly did, in fact."

A solemn silence fell over us at the mention of the massacre. I took a deep breath, blocking out the memories of that awful day.

After a moment, Kyril Kyrilovich stood and stretched. "The wheat won't harvest itself. Best get back to work." He picked up the bell and clanged it, calling everyone back. We rose, abandoning talk of soldiers and politics in favor of the backbreaking work of the harvest.

Mila

I followed the fragrant smell of roasting chicken through the house, my hand resting on my swollen stomach. Half the afternoon had disappeared while I was napping; the new life growing inside me sapped all my energy, and Marya Ivanovna had finally insisted I lie down and rest before Han returned from the day's harvest. I caught a glimpse of myself in the hall mirror; despite my nap, dark circles bruised the warm brown skin beneath my eyes. When would the exhaustion finally end? Never, if what Anna and Marya Ivanovna told me was correct. I sighed and walked on down the hall, leaving the mirror behind me.

At the entrance to the dining room, I nearly collided with Han. He'd just come from the field, I could see from the dust and sweat that covered his face and neck, darkening his naturally brown skin.

"There you are!" He swept me into a kiss, heedless of my clean clothes. "How are you feeling?" he asked, tucking a stray lock of hair beneath my simple kokoshnik, the pointed headdress I wore.

"Mm." I pulled back, my lips tingling from his kiss. "You're in a good mood."

He grinned. "I won."

I rolled my eyes, hiding a smile. Han and Yakov could turn anything into a competition. It didn't matter to either of them who won—though they'd vehemently insist otherwise—but the challenge was good for them. They kept each other sharp. Having each other to compete with kept them from dwelling on what they'd lost in the war.

I brushed a bit of dirt from the tight black curls on top of his head. "What does he owe you this time?"

"A week's worth of drinks. I think I'll take him to Tsebol with me, make him pay while we're there."

"Are you sure you can keep out of trouble?" I teased. "I don't think I trust you two alone in the city."

He waved me off. "We'll be fine. I can keep him from doing anything too impulsive."

"And who's going to keep you from it?" I asked, a hand on my hip.

He grinned, leaning in to whisper in my ear. "You'll just have to make sure I'm too tired to get into any trouble while I'm gone."

"You're incorrigible." I laughed, rolling my eyes again. "Aren't you too tired from the harvest?"

"Too tired for you? Never." He pulled me close and nuzzled my ear.

"Not now, Han." I pushed him away. "I'm starving!"

He sighed. "I suppose I can wait a couple hours."

I pressed a quick kiss to his cheek. "Go clean up. Supper should be ready soon."

I stepped into the dining room, where Anna Ilinychna, Yakov's mother and my closest friend, was setting the final dishes on the table. She was dressed in her second-best sarafan, the rich green of the dress setting of the pink tones in her light skin and the blue-green colors in her eyes.

"You'll have Marya Ivanovna in a fit," I said. The housekeeper was a stickler for ceremony. Anna and Yakov were staying with us for the week of the harvest, and Marya Ivanovna refused to let them help with any of the household chores.

"Yes, she was in the process of scolding me when Kyril Kyrilovich stepped into the kitchen. I took advantage of her distraction."

I laughed, taking a seat at the foot of the table. "I'm sure you'll hear about that later."

"Evening, Mama. Mila." Yakov came into the room and took a seat, immediately reaching for a piece of rye bread. His mother swatted his hand.

"Wait for blessing!" She sat down next to him, shaking her head. "I swear, you're worse than a Drakra sometimes."

Han came in as she spoke. "Who's worse than a Drakra?"

"My son," she said, scowling at Yakov.

"Ah." Han took a seat across from me and snatched a piece of bread as well, taking a bite. "I completely agree."

"And you!" She pointed an accusing finger at him.

Han set the piece of bread down on his plate, looking abashed. "My apologies, Anna."

"Blessing," she said. *"Then* you may eat."

Han took a drink, then bowed his head. "Divine Otets, we ask you to bless the food and drink of your children, given to us by your gracious bounty. So shall it be."

"Let it be," we responded.

As we finished praying, Marya Ivanovna bustled into the room carrying a roast chicken. Her lips were tight with disapproval, and I had to smother a laugh as I caught Anna's eye.

We were silent as we filled our plates and mouths. Marya Ivanovna had had the foresight to prepare extra food in anticipation of the men's increased appetite. And my own, I realized, serving myself a generous helping of chicken.

"How was the harvest today?" I asked Yakov, watching him spoon a third serving of stewed beets onto his plate.

His freckled face darkened as Han laughed. "I didn't eat enough breakfast. I'd have beaten him otherwise."

Han chucked a chicken bone at his head. It bounced off, landing on the table. Yakov tossed it back, and it clattered to the floor.

"Boys!" Anna scolded. "Can we not have a peaceful meal without the two of you throwing things at each other?"

"Han started it," Yakov said, as Han ducked his head and started shoveling food into his mouth. Anna and I shared a wry smile.

When we had finished eating, Han stood and stretched. "I should head to bed. Another early day tomorrow." He offered me his hand. "Milochka?"

I hesitated. "I slept half the afternoon. I ought to get some work done." It was too late for gardening, but I still had the baby's gowns to finish. I could sew by candlelight.

Marya Ivanovna came into the room just in time to hear my remark. "You'll do no such thing!" she scolded. "Up to all hours of the night, and with child, no less! I'll hear nothing of it. Head you to bed and rest yourself. I've enough to do without worrying you'll overwork yourself."

I knew better than to argue with the motherly housekeeper. I didn't object as she shooed me out of the room and up the stairs with Han.

"I'm really not tired," I said as we reached our bedroom. "There's no sense in me going to bed. I slept until supper."

He caught me by the waist and kicked the door closed. "Well, if you're not tired..." he whispered, looking at me with heavy-lidded eyes.

"Marya Ivanovna wouldn't approve, you know," I whispered back. "'A gentle lady subjected to such goings-on when she ought to be resting! And with child, no less!'"

He trailed kisses along my jaw, sending a rush of warmth through me. "'Such goings-on?' Well, if Marya Ivanovna wouldn't approve, we shouldn't." He untied my apron and let it fall to the floor, kissing further down my neck.

He knew how to make me melt with a single touch. "That's not fair." My voice came out breathy as he tugged at the string of my skirt. In a moment, the skirt joined my apron. The room was cool, and I wore only my long shirt and kokoshnik, but my skin radiated heat. He guided me to the bed and untied the ribbon that fastened my kokoshnik, setting the headdress on the bedside table. Then he unbraided my hair and combed the tangles out, each touch lingering.

Once my hair fanned over my shoulders in long, black curls, he pressed a kiss to my shoulder, letting his hand trail down to the hem of my shirt. He caressed the swell of my stomach—I said a silent prayer of thanks that the baby was restful for the moment—and moved to my swollen, sensitive breasts. Letting out a whimper of need, I turned and wrapped my arms around his neck, pressing my lips to his.

Some time later, we lay together in bed, breathing hard. A trickle of sweat rolled down my stomach, and I pulled away from Han's sweltering touch, fanning myself with a hand.

"Warm, are you?"

I glared at him. "Well, it's certainly not my fault if I am."

He touched a finger to the tiny black freckle at the corner of my eye, then trailed a path down my cheek. "Yes, it is. Your fault for being so beautiful." I rolled my eyes, and he laughed as he went to the window and opened it. "Better?"

The slight breeze that came through the room was divine. I laid my head back and sighed. "Much."

"Good." Han sat down on the bed and ran his fingers through my hair.

The combination of the breeze and his touch was almost enough to lull me to sleep. I closed my eyes. "Was there any interesting news in the field today?"

"Not really." His voice was tight, though. I opened one eye, looking up at him in question. He sighed. "More problems with the soldiers in Tsebol."

"I wish you wouldn't go next week." After the harvest, he'd travel to the city to sell the wheat. His missing hand marked him as a survivor of the battle at Barbooht, and I wouldn't put it past any of the soldiers to target him because of it.

"I've been going to Tsebol my whole life, Milochka. This isn't any different."

"It hasn't been crawling with soldiers your whole life, though." All the news about unrest in the city had me on edge. I wished we could do all our business in nearby Selyik, but the harvest wouldn't sell well in our small hometown.

"It will be fine," he soothed. "No one's going to look twice at a farmer in the crowds."

I caught his hand in mine. "Just be careful, *da?*"

"I will." He pressed a kiss to my hand. "I have too much to come home for."

"And Yakov?"

"I'll keep him out of trouble."

"Hm." I wasn't sure I believed him. Yakov was more likely to draw Han into trouble than Han was to keep him out of it.

He squeezed my hand. "We'll be fine, *dorogusha.*"

"I—oh!" My words were lost as the baby kicked me, hard. I placed Han's hand where I'd felt the movement.

The scar on his head, a remnant of his first battle, wrinkled as he frowned in concentration. We sat in silence for a moment, until the kick came again.

Han's eyes widened. "Was that him?"

"That was him." I smiled. "I think you woke him up."

He stared at his hand on my stomach, his eyes bright. "My son," he said, his tone wondering.

Typical. *"Our* son."

"Our son," he agreed. "Or daughter."

"No, definitely a son. I've got a feeling." The baby kicked again, slightly lower, and I shifted his hand.

"I'll be happy either way." He pulled me onto his lap and pressed a kiss to my lips. "As long as I have the two of you."

3

TSEBOL

Han

Travelers filled the market in Tsebol, buying and selling their summer harvests. Pockets full of the profits from our own crops, Yakov and I pushed through the crowds that stopped to admire the goods at each table. Catching Yakov's eye, I gestured to the blacksmith's tent.

"Looking for a new sword?" my friend asked.

I rolled my eyes. My skill with a blade would never be what it had been, even if I could buy a sword. Following the battle at Barbezht, Miroslav had decreed that anyone selling weapons to the traitors would be summarily executed. Most smiths wouldn't sell weapons to anyone missing a limb, for fear of the tsar. Regardless of my skill, I'd never own another sword.

"Need a new ax, *durachok*," I said, my teasing tone belying the insult. "I told you that on the way here."

We skirted around a stall filled with kokoshniki and povyazki, headdresses decorated with brightly colored beads. I made a mental note to stop by before we left and buy a new kokoshnik for Mila. She didn't really need a new one, but the harvest had sold well. I could buy her a new one for the harvest feast.

We kept a healthy distance from the tent marked by the metallic smell of magic and a checkered banner. The tent of a traveling Blood Bastard, an illegitimate descendant of Otets. Blood Bastards' reputations were as formidable as their prices were high. Only the desperate sought their services. The desperate and the rich.

Just before we reached the blacksmith's tent, a table full of woodwork caught my eye—specifically, a ring the size of my palm, with various animals carved into it. I didn't know what made me stop, but I picked up the ring and turned it over.

"It's a teether," the old woman behind the table told me. "Babes love the soft wood on their gums when a tooth is coming through. It's rubbed with beeswax to keep the splinters down." She didn't look up as she spoke, but continued carving a design in the edge of the mug she held.

"How much?" The baby wouldn't be born for a few months, but it sounded like a practical thing to have. Not that I knew what babies needed.

"No charge for you."

I looked up at her with raised eyebrows and saw she'd noticed my missing hand. I looked back at the ring, turning it over again. What I'd thought were butterflies carved into the edge were actually tiny letter B's placed back to back. For Borislav?

The woman grabbed my hand and wrapped it around the teether. "For the true tsar," she said in a low voice.

I stared at her, unsure how to respond. A hand grabbed my shoulder.

"There you are!" Yakov said. "I turned around and you were gone."

"Something caught my eye." I held up the ring, glancing back at the table. The woman was busy carving her mug again as several more market-goers browsed her wares.

"Huh. Bit big for you, isn't it?"

"It's not for me, *durachok*. It's a teether." At his blank look, I explained. "They chew on it when their teeth are coming through. Makes them feel better."

"Oh." Yakov nodded sagely. "Of course. Well, if you're finished searching for trinkets, can we continue shopping? I thought you wanted to be home tomorrow."

By the time the market closed, we'd finished our purchases. We loaded up the cart and made our way to an inn brimming with the after-market crowds. Pushing through the room, we found an unoccupied pair of stools, and I waved over a frazzled barmaid.

She had to shout to make herself heard. "We've got shchi and kvass, but if you're looking for pirogi and vodka, you'll have to find somewhere else. The army's been through our whole supply."

"Soup and kvass is fine," Yakov shouted back.

She fiddled with the end of her long braid, smiling at him. "Be right back."

While we waited, I looked around. The smell of cabbage and rye filled the air, along with the overpowering scent of spilled vodka. A group of drunken soldiers, distinguished by their red-trimmed black kaftans, sat in the corner playing dice. Their laughter and shouts drowned out the chatter of the other customers.

"Town's busy this week," I said. "I think we made twice as much as we did our first year back from the war."

Yakov opened his mouth to respond, but the barmaid returned with her arms full. As she set the dishes on the table, a soldier staggered over, leering down at us.

"Shouldn't be serving these types, girl," he said, just loud enough to be heard.

"Beg your pardon, sir?" I laid my hand on Yakov's arm to forestall any rash reaction. There were at least ten soldiers in the inn, and attacking the tsar's men was a hanging offense.

"I'd heard there were some Barbezht survivors in this part of the country." He nodded at our arms and spat on the ground. "Traitors."

Yakov jumped to his feet, fist clenched. "Say that again."

"Ooh, look at this, boys!" he told his companions, who had joined him. "The cripple thinks he can take on the tsar's men."

The whole room had gone silent, watching the scene.

I stood and grabbed Yakov by the collar. "Let's just go," I muttered. Louder, I said, "We are loyal supporters of Tsar Miroslav, and we meant no offense. We'll leave you to your supper." I steered my friend toward the door but found our path blocked by one of the other soldiers.

The first man sneered at us. "Miroslav should have hanged you all."

Yakov's fist connected with the man's nose.

The room erupted in shouts, and Yakov disappeared under a pile of soldiers. I dove into the fray, swinging wildly at anything in reach. Something hit my lip, and I tasted blood. I grabbed a mug from the floor and smashed it over the head of the nearest soldier. He turned on me, too drunk to see straight but still flailing his fists.

Yakov stumbled out of the mass of bodies, breathing hard. I grabbed his arm, and we ran for the door, momentarily unobserved.

As we rushed down the street, the inn door opened behind us. We ducked around a corner into a dark alley in time to see several of the soldiers run past.

I waited a moment to ensure our pursuers were out of sight before turning to my friend.

"Home."

Yakov nodded, pinching his bleeding nose.

I didn't draw an easy breath until we left the city gate. As we pulled onto the moonlit road home, I looked at my friend.

"What were you thinking?" I hissed.

He crossed his arms, leaning back against the wagon seat. "They were asking for it."

"Do you have a death wish?" His temper was going to get us both killed. "You'd best pray they don't find us, or we'll both be hanged. And that's nothing compared to what Mila's going to do when she finds out." She'd already been worried; if she found out I'd been in a fight with some soldiers, she'd lose her mind.

"What was I supposed to do, just take it?"

"Yes! That's exactly what you're supposed to do!"

"Maybe you can handle being treated like scum, but I can't."

I sighed. Sometimes it was easy to forget how young he was. "I hate it, too, but Mila needs me. I deal with the abuse so I can go home safe to her."

He didn't respond, scowling down at the horses' heads in front of us.

"Let's just go home," I said. "You can stay with us tonight. There's no need to wake your mother."

It was late, well past midnight when we finally made it home. Not wanting to wake anyone, we left the wagon fully loaded in the barn, stabled the horses, and crept into the dark house.

I left Yakov to find the spare room by himself, making my way to my own room. Mila must have been warm; she'd left the window open, and the breeze coming through the room chilled me. I closed it, stripped off my clothes, and climbed into bed with my wife.

She rolled over, frowning. "Han?" Her voice was slurred with sleep.

"I'm sorry, *dorogusha*," I whispered. "I didn't mean to wake you."

She sat up and rubbed her eyes, the moonlight from the window illuminating the beautiful curves of her body. "Why are you here? I didn't expect you until dinner tomorrow."

"We decided not to stay." There was no need to worry her with the real reason. Not in the middle of the night, at least. Doubtless she'd wring the truth from me in the morning. I pulled the quilt up and wrapped my arms around her. She leaned in for a kiss, and I bit back a hiss of breath as she brushed my split lip.

She pulled back. "What happened?"

"It's nothing," I said. "Let's go to sleep. I'm exhausted."

She sat up, lighting a candle and holding it close to my face. "Han! *What* happened?"

"Just a scuffle in the inn." I didn't meet her eyes. "It was nothing."

"And Yakov?" She pursed her lips.

I shrugged. "A few bruises, same as me. Could have been worse."

"Who started it?"

"Yakov, but he was provoked." She raised a brow, but I held up my hand. "Truly! We tried to leave, but one of them blocked us. Yakov threw a punch, and we ran off."

She took a handkerchief and the jar of salve from the bedside table. "He punched, and you ran? Then how did you get this?" She scooped some flowery-smelling ointment from the jar and used the handkerchief to dab it gently on my lip.

"We did run. They attacked—"

"They who?"

No avoiding it now. "A few soldiers," I mumbled.

The handkerchief fell from her hand. "Soldiers? Han..." Her eyes filled with tears, her mood shifting in an instant. "I knew it was a bad idea for you to go."

I ran a hand over my face. "I had to do it, Mila. They jumped on him. If I hadn't pulled him out, he'd be dead."

"And if they come after you, you'll both be dead," she snapped, wiping at her eyes.

I pulled her close again. "It's fine, Milochka. We'll be fine."

"But what if they find out who you are? What if someone recognized you and told them where to find you? Han, they'll hang you!" I could hear the fear behind the anger in her voice. Her hands clenched my shirt.

"Shh," I whispered into her long, loose curls. "They won't. We're not important enough to chase around the countryside. As long as we stay away from Tsebol, they won't come looking for us."

"I'm scared."

My heart twisted. Mila didn't often admit her fears, even to me. I brushed a curl from her face and kissed her brown forehead. "I'll keep you safe."

She shoved me halfheartedly. "I'm not scared for me, idiot. I'm scared for you."

"Nothing can keep me away from you, *dorogusha*. Not war, not soldiers, not Miroslav himself." I kissed her, long and slow, until she relaxed under my touch. "I'll always come home to you," I said, resting my hand on her belly. "To both of you."

"You swear?"

"On my father's grave." I blew out the candle and said a silent prayer that I'd be able to keep my promises. I didn't believe the soldiers would hunt us down—most of them had seemed too drunk to remember the fight, and even if they did, finding us wouldn't be worth the effort. Still, as I fell asleep, I couldn't help thinking Borislav would never have allowed the country to come to this.

4

CONSEQUENCES

Mila

A week after Han's misadventure in Tsebol, I had the house to myself except for Marya Ivanovna. Han and Kyril Kyrilovich had gone into Selyik for the day on business, and I planned to take advantage of the solitude by working in the garden.

I stopped in the kitchen for some bowls, accepting the baked cabbage pirozhok Marya Ivanovna pressed into my hand and grabbing my gardening knife from its hook by the door. Stepping outside, I took a deep breath. The air was crisp and cool, a light breeze signaling the end of summer. Behind the house, in the sun, would be the perfect place to spend the day.

I stepped through the garden gate, scanning my plants for signs of unwelcome intruders. No bite marks were evident on any leaves, so the rabbits and deer hadn't found their way in yet. I set down the bowls and knife and bent down to pull a stray weed that had taken root near a patch of comfrey. I groaned as I did; if I grew much larger, I wouldn't be able to bend over at all. Marya Ivanovna would have to take care of the garden, or we'd have to hire someone from town. Otets knew what a tragedy that would be. I didn't doubt someone else could do the work, but I was protective of my domain. The garden was the one realm of the house Marya Ivanovna would let me exert myself. "A lady's hobby," the housekeeper called it. "It's not right for a lady to do the housework, but a bit of gardening to soothe the mind and make beauty creams is perfectly genteel." Nevermind that I was a farmer's wife. As a relatively wealthy landowner, Han was firmly in the category of "gentility" in Marya Ivanovna's estimation.

I refused to be confined to beauty creams, though. Taking a seat in the dirt, I pulled a small book from my apron pocket. The cover read *Tonics and Remedies for the unSanctioned: a Collection of Blood Bastard Writings*. Han had bought it for me before he left for the war, and it was my most prized possession. I opened it to a recipe titled "For the Reduction of Pain in Childbirth." The tonic was relatively simple to make, and I had almost everything I needed growing in my garden; Han had collected the final pieces for me in Tsebol after the harvest.

Chamomile flowers, rosebuds, raspberry leaves, and leckozht needles. The leckozht plant was my prized possession. Small and hardy, it had been cultivated by Blood Bastards to help combat outbreaks of Moon Fever throughout the country. It had proven ineffective against the plague, but its pain relief properties had made it highly desired. I used it sparingly—it was too expensive to use for every bump and bruise—but a childbirth tonic seemed a reasonable use for the precious plant.

Once I had gathered all the supplies for my tonic, I moved back to the rosebush. I was running low on rosewater, and I wanted a large supply to get through the winter. I took the most suitable blossoms and placed them in a bowl, then turned to the comfrey. With all the injuries Han formed wrestling with Yakov or working in the field, I was always in need of more comfrey ointment.

Hoofbeats sounded nearby. I looked up, frowning. It wasn't even midday yet. Han couldn't be returning from Selyik already. Likely it was travelers stopping in for a drink. Marya Ivanovna would give them what they needed and send them on their way. I went back to my gardening.

A moment later, I heard a knock, followed by voices at the front of the house. A few moments later, the door to the kitchen opened behind me.

"Mila Dmitrievna?" I turned to see an unusually flustered-looking Marya Ivanovna. "There's a few men here asking to speak to Han Antonovich. A nobleman and two soldiers."

Soldiers. My heart leapt to my throat. They couldn't be here because of the fight in Tsebol. Could they?

"I'll be right in," I told the housekeeper, keeping my voice measured despite the racing of my heart.

I stopped in the kitchen to clean myself up, taking deep even breaths to calm my nerves. They couldn't know it had been Han and Yakov in the inn. There were dozens of survivors of Barbezht. They had to be here for some other reason.

I adjusted my kokoshnik and walked into the sitting room.

Two of the men, both short and stocky, wore red and black kaftans. Soldiers, like Marya Ivanovna had said. The third man was taller, his clothing made of expensive silk, though dust and sweat stained his shirt. His hair and beard were orange, and his heat-reddened face was set in a scowl. I twisted my hands in my skirt to stop them from shaking and made a bow.

"Can I help you, my lord? Sirs?" Thank Otets, my voice sounded almost calm.

The nobleman looked me up and down. "Where's your husband?"

"My husband is in Tsebol for market until tomorrow," I lied, praying Han would stay in Sclyik until they left. "I'm sorry you missed him."

The two soldiers shared a doubting look as the nobleman cocked a brow. "Is that so?"

"Yes, but I would be happy to tell him you called. I'm certain he'll contact you as soon as he returns, my lord of...?"

"Arick." He took a seat on the divan without being offered. The two soldiers remained standing. "I take it he didn't tell you of his criminal activity the last time he was in the city."

My mouth fell open. He knew about the fight in the inn.

This couldn't be happening.

I closed my mouth and swallowed hard. "I—I beg your pardon, my lord?"

"Your husband is one of the traitors of Barbezht, yes?" When I opened my mouth to answer, he waved a hand. "Don't bother to lie. He's lucky I wasn't in Tsebol that night. I arrived the next day, and I've had a hell of a time trying to find him since. He attacked the tsar's men. You're aware that's a hanging offense?"

I had to stop him from finding Han. Thinking quickly, I said, "My lord, I—" I let a few tears leak from my eyes, a task which didn't take much effort, given the fragile state of my emotions. "I didn't know. He's been gone for over a week. He—" I shook my head. "Please forgive me for lying, my lord. When he didn't return from market last week, I assumed he was in trouble, but I had no idea he'd done something so heinous." *Please, Otets, keep Han away from the house until they leave.*

The nobleman watched me impassively, tugging at his beard. "Is that so?"

I nodded frantically. He had to believe me. "If you'll leave your address, my lord, I'll be sure to contact you if he returns."

He stood, and I held my breath. Would he believe me? He stepped closer, holding my gaze.

He smacked my face. I tasted blood.

No. No. He hadn't believed me. Ears ringing, I touched a hand to my stinging cheek. "My lord?"

"Lying bitch. Do you honestly think I'm stupid enough to believe that shit?"

"Mila Dmitrievna?" Marya Ivanovna stood in the doorway, looking between me and the nobleman.

"Where is he?" he snarled.

I glanced nervously at the soldiers, who had both stepped closer. "I told you, my lord. I haven't seen him." This was getting out of hand. I had to get them out, before he turned truly violent. My chin quivered, but I raised my chin and looked into his eyes. "I believe you need to leave."

"I don't believe I will. It seems to me you and your husband both need to be taught a lesson."

"You are no longer welcome here. Leave my home this instant, or I will be making a complaint to the baron." I realized, belatedly, that I didn't know this man's title. For all I knew, he could outrank Lord Ilya.

The nobleman grinned, baring his teeth. "Oh, I hope you do. I would relish the opportunity to expose Ilya Sergeyevich for the traitor he is."

Marya Ivanovna stepped forward. "My mistress has asked you to leave."

"Shut up," he snapped.

She moved to stand in front of me, eyes fixed on him. "Mila Dmitrievna, why don't you go on to visit Anna Ilynichna until these men have gone?"

He grabbed her headscarf and shoved her out of the way. "Shut her up," he barked at the soldiers. They each grabbed an arm, and one of the men put a hand over her mouth.

The nobleman turned back to me. "Now, I'm going to give you a choice. You tell me where I can find the traitors of Barbezht that attacked my soldiers, or I'll kill your housekeeper."

Marya Ivanovna shook her head, eyes wide in warning.

"What's it to be, girl?" He drew a dagger from the sheath at his side.

My heart raced. Marya Ivanovna's life or Han's. An impossible choice.

Han wouldn't thank me for protecting him. Not at the cost of someone else.

Stomach in knots, I hung my head. "He's in Selyik," I whispered.

"What was that?"

"He's in Selyik," I said, louder. "He'll be back this evening."

He nodded. "Good." He turned to Marya Ivanovna and sliced the dagger across her throat.

I screamed, bile filling my throat. The housekeeper's body fell, blood pooling across the floorboards.

He ignored my scream. "I'd rather not spend all day waiting for your husband to return. I've already spent enough time hunting the bastard down. He has to be punished, of course, but I'm not wasting the rest of my day waiting to arrest him. I'll just have to send him a message instead."

He took a step toward me, and I backed into the wall, hands over my belly. The baby. I had to protect the baby.

He grabbed my shirt in both hands and tore it, baring me down to the waist. I jerked away, scrambling to cover myself, and my foot caught on the rug. I slipped, landing in Marya Ivanovna's blood as he kicked me.

I curled up into a ball. Keep the baby safe. That was all that mattered. I couldn't breathe. Couldn't scream. I looked up at the soldiers, silently begging for help, but they watched with hostile grins on their faces. One yanked my kokoshnik off and dragged me to my feet.

"Please," I gasped. The nobleman smacked me again, knocking me onto the divan.

The two soldiers tugged and tore at my clothing until I was naked before them, bruised and bleeding. I curled into myself again, shielding my stomach. They could hurt me, but not my son. *Otets, shield him.*

"Now," the nobleman looked down at me with hatred in his eyes, "I'm going to show you what happens when you defy the tsar's men."

Gone. They were gone.

Everything hurt.

Han would be back soon. He couldn't find out.

I struggled to my feet. I needed to burn my clothes. I couldn't let him see. He'd blame himself.

The kitchen fire was still burning from earlier, when Marya Ivanovna had made our breakfast kasha. I added the wood and put my torn sarafan on top. The dress caught quickly, despite the blood-soaked fabric.

Clean. I had to clean the sitting room. Han couldn't see the sitting room.

The muscles in my stomach clenched, making me cry out. I had to be more careful how I moved. I didn't want to hurt the baby.

I stepped into the sitting room. Marya Ivanovna. What would I do with the body? Han couldn't see Marya Ivanovna's body.

I'd have to drag it outside. Back to the garden. Kyril Kyrilovich could do something with it afterward. He loved Han. He wouldn't let Han find out.

I grabbed an arm and dragged the body through the kitchen. It was so heavy. My stomach clenched with the movement, and I doubled over. It hurt so much. They must have bruised something in my stomach.

The muscles relaxed again, and I pulled my load harder. I had to get it out before Han came back.

Too slowly, I made it to my garden. He wouldn't look out here. I pushed the body out the door and turned back.

A trail of blood led through the house. I had to clean it. He couldn't see the blood. He'd know something had happened.

Marya Ivanovna had left the dishwater in the big wooden tub. I upended it on the kitchen floor, turning the crimson blood pink.

Rags. I needed rags. Where did we keep the rags?

I found a pile in the corner. They weren't clean, but they would have to do. I started scrubbing the floor. Han would be home for supper. I had to finish before then.

A sound came from the front of the house. Han? I froze. He couldn't find out.

A scream, then a pause. A trembling voice asked, "Hello?"

Not Han. Yegor Miloshovich's grandson. He worked in the stable twice a week. What was his name? I couldn't focus.

"Is anyone here?" the boy called.

I opened my mouth to answer, but my stomach clenched again. The words became a scream.

Quick footsteps sounded, and the boy came into the kitchen.

As the clenching stopped, I realized I was naked. I needed to cover myself, not let the boy see me naked, but I had to finish cleaning before Han returned.

"You're hurt!"

"Not my blood." I kept scrubbing. I had to finish.

The boy stood in the doorway, eyes wide and face ashen. "Han Antonovich is in Selyik, right? I'll go find him."

"No!" Han couldn't see this. He had to stay gone until I finished cleaning.

He stepped closer. "You need help, Mila Dmitrievna. I'm going to get your husband."

I opened my mouth to answer, but another clench of my stomach muscles dropped me onto the ground. "Anna," I managed to gasp. "Get Anna."

He stared at me for a moment, then rushed out the door.

I lay in the puddle of bloody water, my face on the floor. The clenching was happening more often. Something was wrong.

How long had I lain here? Hours. It had been hours. Anna Ilynichna was coming. I had to stay calm until Anna came.

Anna was coming, wasn't she? The boy had gone to get her.

Boy. There had been a boy. Hadn't there?

"Mila, dear, can you hear me?"

Anna. Thank Otets. Her voice was a sip of cool water to my parched ears.

A splashing sound. Someone had stepped into a puddle. No, I was lying in a puddle. A puddle of what?

"Mila? Can you hear me?"

I nodded. My throat was raw, like I'd been screaming. Had I been screaming?

"Can you stand?"

I shook my head.

"Yakov has gone for Han, dear. He'll be here soon."

"No," I rasped. He couldn't see this. Why didn't they understand? I cried out as another clenching pain took me.

A warm touch on my stomach. A hand?

"Mila, how frequent are your pains?"

What did she mean? The clenching? I gasped for air as the pain stopped, but another one started again.

"Mila, dear, the baby's coming."

I shook my head. The baby couldn't be coming. Too early. It was too early. Wasn't it? The baby wasn't due for weeks. Months.

Another pain overtook me.

"Can you get onto your knees?"

I shook my head again.

"What about your back, dear?"

I let out a whimper as I slowly rolled onto my back. Anna propped up my legs so my feet were flat on the floor. "Now, Mila, when the next pain starts, you need to push with it. Can you do that?"

Push? That would bring the baby out. Why would she want me to do that? "Too early?" I whispered.

"Babes come when they will, dear." Anna's voice was calm. How could she be calm at a time like this? "Many babies are born early without a problem. Just push, and let Otets worry about the rest."

I couldn't do it.

The pain started again.

"Push," Anna ordered.

I pushed. I was being torn apart from the inside.

A brief reprieve. I gasped for air.

"Again."

Pain. Burning. Tearing.

Reprieve.

"Again."

Tearing. Burning.

Breathe.

"Once more, dear."

I couldn't do it.

"You can do it."

Sheer torture. Nothing existed but pain.

"I have him."

Have him? The baby? I didn't hear his cries. Was he healthy?

"One more push."

Sight, hearing, taste, smell disappeared in the face of the white-hot agony ripping me in half.

A soft hand touched my cheek. "It's over, Mila."

The baby. Where was the baby? I looked around. Everything was blurry. "My son?" I croaked.

"I'm sorry, Mila." Anna's eyes were wet. Was she crying? "He didn't make it."

Didn't make what? Before I could process the meaning of the words, I fell into blessed oblivion.

5

GRIEF

Han

I sat by the bed, holding Mila's hand. She lay naked beneath piles of quilts—we hadn't wanted to move her more than necessary, so no one had dressed her. We'd moved her as she was into the guest bedroom. I'd sponged off the worst of the blood and dirt, but she still looked awful. Her golden-brown skin was mottled with blue and purple bruises.

I'd been in Selyik with Kyril Kyrilovich, haggling with the baker, when Yakov had burst in, a frantic look on his face. "It's Mila," was all he'd said, all he'd had time to say before I'd rushed out the door.

I'd come home to find my wife naked and battered, unconscious on the kitchen floor. Anna held my stillborn son. Marya Ivanovna's body lay in Mila's garden. Blood made a trail from the sitting room to the garden, and no one knew what had happened. No one but Mila.

She'd regained consciousness several times in the three days since we'd found her, but she didn't speak. She didn't even seem to recognize us. She swallowed whatever we put to her lips—water, broth, tonics—but other than that, she lay staring at the ceiling, unmoving. The doctor had said her injuries weren't life-threatening, but he couldn't say when—or if—her mind would return.

I reached for the Blood Bastard book on the nightstand and rifled through it again. I hadn't found any remedies yet, but maybe I'd missed something. If anyone knew how to cure my wife, it would be a Blood Bastard.

I flipped past "Tonic to Speed Bone Healing" and "Salve for Broken Skin"—the latter was familiar, a recipe Mila used on me frequently. I stopped on a page that read, "For the Reduction of Pain in Childbirth," and my heart stuttered. She had mentioned it to me just a week ago, a new tonic she was planning to make for the birth of our baby. Our son.

I'd already lost him. I couldn't lose Mila, too. We didn't have the money to pay a Blood Bastard, but if she remained like this much longer, I'd sell everything I had. Anything to heal her.

I set the book to the side and took her hand again, squeezing it slightly.

She squeezed my hand back.

My breath caught. "Mila?"

She opened her eyes and looked around, her gaze landing on me. "Han?"

She was awake. Thank Otets. Really, truly awake. She knew me. "I'm here, Milochka." I blinked back tears. "Don't move. I'll get you a drink."

I poured a cup of water from the pitcher on the bedside table. Propping her head up with my arm, I held the cup to her lips. She gulped it down, then let me lean her back against the pillows.

"How do you feel, *dorogaya?*"

"It hurts." Her voice came out small, and a pang went through me.

I brushed a hair away from her face. "Where?"

"Everywhere." She coughed and cried out in pain.

"You have some broken ribs." I stroked her cheek, unable to keep from touching her. "You'll have to stay in bed until they heal."

She nodded. Then her hand flew to her stomach. "The baby?" she whispered, eyes wide with horror.

I couldn't voice the words. I shook my head.

"No." Her voice was plaintive, desperate. "No."

There was nothing I could say to fix this. I climbed onto the bed, careful of her injuries, and wrapped my arms around her. Tears fell from my eyes as her body shook with silent sobs.

I held her until both our tears were spent.

Mila

I'd thought it was a nightmare. Prayed it was a nightmare. For the first few moments after I'd awoken, before I'd opened my eyes, I'd been able to imagine it was.

Then I'd woken fully, and it had all become real.

Han was the first to speak, his voice low and thick from crying. "What happened?"

I froze.

He didn't know. Of course he didn't know. No one had seen my attackers but me and Marya Ivanovna. With Marya Ivanovna dead, only my attackers and I knew the truth.

The nobleman had intended to use me to hurt Han. He'd succeeded—nothing I said could erase the deaths of our son and our housekeeper—but that didn't mean Han had to bear the blame for it. He didn't have to know who attacked me or why. They wouldn't come looking for him again. I couldn't protect him from the pain, but I could protect him from the guilt.

"Mila?" he prompted.

"Deserters." It was the only thing I could think of to say. "They didn't know who they were. I don't know why Marya Ivanovna let them into the sitting room. I was out in the garden when they started shouting. I—" I choked on my words, remembering the housekeeper's final moments. "Marya Ivanovna was dead when I came in."

His arms tightened around me, and I clenched my teeth to keep from crying out in pain. "What did they do?" he asked.

Otets, his grip was painful. "They wanted me to keep quiet. Not tell anyone that I'd seen them. I guess they thought if they—if they hurt me, I wouldn't talk."

"Did they..."

I knew what he wanted to ask. He wanted to know if they'd done more than beat me. He wanted to know why I'd been naked on the floor when they'd found me. If they'd raped me.

"No," I lied. He didn't need to know the truth, the details. What he'd seen was enough. Too much, even.

"When are the funerals?" I asked. Marya Ivanovna and the baby would both need to be buried. Marya Ivanovna's sister would plan hers, but who would plan the baby's?

Han tensed. "We didn't know..." He stopped. "Anna saw him buried this morning. I didn't want to leave you."

I'd never even gotten to see him. My son, he was my son, and I didn't even know what he looked like. Tears choked me, grief threatening to drown me, but I swallowed hard and spoke again. "How long has it been? Since—" I couldn't bring myself to say the words.

"Three days. Do you not remember...?"

I'd been unconscious for three days? "Remember what?"

He pulled back to look at my face. "You woke up, but you didn't say anything. You didn't even move, just laid there, staring off at nothing. You don't remember any of that?"

I'd been awake? And I'd missed my son's burial by just a few hours. The tears were more insistent this time. I jerked from Han's grasp. A bolt of pain shot through my torso, and I screamed.

"Mila—" he started, but Anna rushed in.

"You're awake!" She hurried to the bedside, taking my hand. "Where does it hurt, dear? What can I do?"

I shook my head, clutching my stomach. There was nothing she could do.

Anna swatted Han's arm. "Get off the bed! You're going to hurt her more." He scrambled off, and she turned back to me. "Should I send for the doctor? Do you need anything?"

I shook my head again, fighting against the flood of tears.

"It's alright, Mila," she said, stroking my hair. "You're safe now. It'll be alright."

It wouldn't be. Nothing would ever be alright again. I nodded anyway.

"I'll go fix you some kasha, *da?* You need to eat something." She patted my hand and hurried out the door, leaving me alone with Han again.

"Mila—" he began, but I held up a hand.

"I need to be alone."

He opened his mouth as if to argue, but after a moment, he nodded once. "I'll be right outside the door if you need me."

I waited until the door had closed to let my tears out in full force again.

6
AFTERMATH
Mila

The following weeks dragged by. As the first of my bruises began to heal and frost formed on the ground outside, I was finally allowed out of bed, but only as far as the chair by the window. Han and Yakov sat with me when they weren't working, and Anna was a near-permanent fixture in the room.

They hadn't yet deemed me fit enough to relocate from the guest room on the ground floor to the upstairs bedroom I shared with Han. While Han and Anna worried that the stairs would be too much of a challenge for my injured body, I had a more personal reason to avoid the bedroom. I wasn't ready to share a bed with him again. I didn't want to be touched.

A stream of well-wishers trickled through the house as time passed. I was spared their attentions by virtue of my bedroom confinement, but I could hear their hushed expressions of sympathy from my room.

After a month of confinement, the constant hovering had begun to grate on me. That morning, I sat by the window between Han and Anna. Han stared at a set of papers—financial statements from the year, I assumed, but he hadn't actually done anything with them in over a half hour. Instead, he tapped his foot incessantly, rubbing the scar on his forehead. Whenever he thought I wasn't paying attention, he looked up at me, as though afraid I would disappear if he didn't keep me in his sights.

"By Otets!" I finally swore, throwing down the shirt I was mending—the only work I was permitted to do. Han jumped at the outburst. "Your fidgeting is going to make me lose my mind. Go. Away."

He reached out and put his hand on my knee. "I don't want to leave you alone."

I clenched my teeth. "Anna is here. Kyril Kyrilovich is working in the stables. Please. For the love of all the Sanctioned. Go away."

He let out a breath. "If that's what you want, Milochka. Yakov is chopping firewood; I can join him." Leaning down to kiss my head, he added, "I'll be back for supper. You'll send for me if you need anything?"

"Go!" I screeched, pushing him toward the door. He left with one last worried look back.

Anna clicked her tongue. "He's mourning, too, you know."

"He's treating me like a porcelain doll," I huffed, picking up the shirt I'd thrown down. "I can't handle his hovering. And he'll feel better getting back to normal. Back to work." I stabbed my needle through the cloth. "We all need to get back to work."

When I didn't hear a response, I looked up to find Anna watching me.

"Mila, listen to me. It's alright to mourn. You can't expect everything to go back to normal so quickly. You're still healing, and not just physically. I know when my husband Sasha died, I couldn't leave my bed for a week, and it took months before I could hear his name without bursting into tears. Give yourself time to process things, to cry. To be sad."

"I've cried enough. I'm not sad anymore."

She gave me a look that was half disbelief, half pity.

"Truly! I'm not sad, I'm angry. Angry at the bastards who took my son from me. I can't change anything by crying or trying to make myself feel something I don't. So I'm going to go back to a normal life. And I'm not going to be treated as if I'm made of glass." Ignoring her stare, I set my mending down and stalked out of the room.

In the hallway, I stopped and took a breath. I hadn't been out of that room in a month, and the sudden freedom was almost overwhelming. Why had I let them keep me trapped for so long? I was weak still, but I didn't need to be stuck in a single room for weeks on end. I needed industry. A task.

At the foot of the stairs, I looked around guiltily. No one was watching me.

What had happened to me? I was sneaking around my own house. The confinement had tampered with my mind. I shook my head and began climbing the stairs.

I stopped at the top, breathing hard. More than my mind had been affected, if climbing a single flight of stairs winded me. After catching my breath, I opened the door to the room I shared with Han.

The man was impossible. He'd left papers strewn across the bed. Dirty clothes covered the floor, and he hadn't thought to empty the basin of his shaving water that morning. I sighed. At least I'd have something to keep myself occupied. Someone had to clean the room.

Marya Ivanovna wouldn't approve, I thought as I gathered up the clutter. The mistress of the house shouldn't concern herself with such menial labor.

Grief pierced me, as sharp as the very first day, and I took a seat on the bed.

I hadn't lied when I'd told Anna I was angry. I'd done everything I could to protect those around me, and it hadn't been enough. Someone should hold my attackers responsible for their actions, but I knew Miroslav wouldn't give me justice. He was almost as culpable as the lord of Arick.

No one would hold them responsible. Not the soldiers, not the nobleman, and certainly not the tsar who'd torn my family apart.

It all came back to Miroslav, didn't it? He was the one who had taken Han's hand. He was the one whose army attacked innocents, who allowed his soldiers to treat the few remaining survivors of Bar bezht like dirt. He was the one who sent his nobles to execute men for a simple tavern fight.

My son's death, Marya Ivanovna's death, my pain—they could all ultimately be laid at the feet of Miroslav. Someone should make him pay for his crimes against the people of Inzhria. Not that anyone could or would.

I sighed and leaned back on the bed. My hand brushed a paper, and I picked it up. It was a letter addressed to me from Ulyana Petrovna, the daughter of our tenant. I had a flash of irritation at Han for not giving it to me. Had he been hiding my letters?

I scanned it. Ulyana sent her condolences and asked after my health. She wrote about her wedding, which I had missed, and about her new home in Tsebol and the bakery her husband owned. She shared the latest rumors—a gamayun, a legless bird whose appearance foretold the death of a great leader, had been spotted over the city, and Tsar Borislav had not only survived Barbezht but was living in the woods outside of Tsebol. I snorted at that; rumors of Borislav's survival had abounded since the battle, but I'd never heard of him being so close to home.

I finished the letter and set it back on the bed. It was entirely innocuous. Had Han planned on answering it for me, or was he just reading it before passing it on? I fumed. Protecting me physically was one thing, but I didn't need to be coddled. Reading my letters was too much.

I went to the desk and penned a reply. Thanking Ulyana for her concern, I assured her I was feeling much better and apologized for missing the wedding. I'd have to make sure to send a gift along with the letter. Doubtless Han hadn't remembered to send one the day of the wedding. He hadn't attended, either, preferring to spend the day hovering over me.

I paused, a sudden thought coming to me. If the nobleman who attacked me had been in Tsebol, his presence would have been noted. Ulyana might know who he was.

If nothing else, I could learn the name of the man who killed my child.

I heard Tsebol had an auspicious visitor recently, I wrote. *The lord of Arick, according to rumor, although you know how untrustworthy rumors can be. (Borislav living near Tsebol! I've never heard of anything so ridiculous.) Tell me everything! I am truly starved for news here.*

There. Nothing to arouse suspicion, but if Ulyana knew anything of the nobleman, she'd pass it on. I finished the letter and folded it up. I could have it sent out in the morning.

Han

I took my ax and dinner basket and found my way to the woods behind the house. Mila was right; I did need to get out. We would need plenty of wood for the long winter, and the exertion would be good for me, after spending the morning staring mindlessly at expense reports.

"Mila finally kick you out of the house?" Yakov hollered, waving his ax in greeting. Despite the cool autumn breeze, his jacket lay on the ground, and he'd wrapped his shirt around his waist. He wiped sweat from his brow with his arm.

I grinned sheepishly. "She was going to wring my neck. I'll be over here if you need me."

The first swing of the ax was a balm. I *had* needed to get out, to be alone for a while. I hadn't been alone since the day it had happened; even when working outside of the house, I'd had Yakov or Kyril Kyrilovich with me at all times, and I'd managed to pass most of my outdoor work to Kyril so I could work inside, near Mila. Here in the woods, with no one in sight and only Yakov in hearing, I felt freer than I had in a month. The ring of metal on wood, the smell of dirt and wood chips, and the cool autumn air healed me in a way I hadn't realized I'd needed.

Chopping wood one-handed had been one of the first tasks I'd learned to do after returning from Barbezht. Even now, after five years, it didn't come naturally, requiring concentration to ensure the ax landed where I intended. I was grateful for the focus today, as it kept my mind from wandering.

I didn't stop until the tree was felled and the branches were stripped. I raised the ax to begin splitting the first branch when Yakov shouted.

"Are you going to take a dinner break today?"

I looked up. It was later than I'd expected. I set down my ax and walked to where my friend sat on a nearby stump.

"I've been sitting here for ten minutes," Yakov said, handing over my dinner basket.

"And you've still got food left?" I raised a brow. "I don't believe it."

"No. I finished mine and started on yours." He took a last bite of his apple and tossed the core over his shoulder.

I rolled my eyes, reaching into the basket for a hunk of black bread. It wasn't Marya Ivanovna's pirozhki, but it was good nonetheless. Anna had been cooking for us since Marya Ivanovna's death, spending her days at our house and only going back to the house she shared with her son at night.

"It's good to get out," I said, pushing away thoughts of the past month as I took a bite of the bread.

"I'm surprised you stayed in this long," Yakov said with a sidelong glance. "I'm surprised Mila let you."

"She needed me."

He snorted. "She hasn't seemed to need anybody, from what I've seen. She's been mean to everyone since the moment she woke up."

I clenched my fist, crushing the bread. "You wouldn't understand." I stood and turned away. "It's like—like an animal caught in a trap. She's hurting so much she'll lash out at anyone nearby."

Silence met my words. After a moment, I felt a hand on my shoulder, and I turned. Tears glistened in Yakov's brown eyes.

"I'm sorry, Han. I shouldn't have said that."

"No, I'm sorry. I shouldn't expect you to understand. You've never been..." I took a deep breath through my nose. "Nevermind."

"I know it's not the same," he said, tugging at a loose string on his sleeve. "I know I haven't lost a son, and it wasn't my wife who was attacked, but if you think I'm not hurting too, you're wrong. You're like a brother to me. Mila's like a sister. Whatever hurts you hurts me. What those bastards did, they did to all of us."

I pulled him into a tight embrace. "Thank you. That...that means a lot."

His ears were red, but he grinned as he pulled back. "Just don't go hugging me like that in front of other people. I have a reputation to maintain."

"As what? A eunuch?" My throat was swollen with unshed tears, but I swallowed the lump, grateful for the change in topic. I'd spent enough time drowning in my emotions.

"As a ladies' man." He puffed out his chest, and I shoved him.

"You'd have to actually spend time with ladies to get that reputation. And no," I added, seeing him open his mouth to respond, "Mila and your mother don't count."

"Oh, shut up. Shouldn't you be working?" He grabbed his ax and stalked back off into the woods, ignoring my laughter.

As he walked out of sight, I sat down on the stump. I felt almost guilty, laughing so soon after everything that had happened. But it was like a weight had been lifted from my shoulders. The walls of the house had threatened to suffocate me, and while I was reluctant to leave Mila alone for long, even with Anna, the work and laughter were healing.

Nothing would be the same as it was before, but we could get through this.

7

Writing Home

Mila

My dearest mother...

The words swam in front of me. I'd put off writing this letter for weeks, but my mother would be expecting a letter announcing the birth soon. I couldn't put off the news any longer.

Mother had lost children herself—my older brother Sergei and I were the only two still living of the nine she had carried—but still, I couldn't find the words to express what had happened.

I pray you are in good health. To Sergei and his wife, as well as the children, I send my love.

I regret that I must tell you of a tragedy that has of late befallen our house.

I scratched through the last line and began again.

Our house lies under a dark cloud. Great Otets, in His infinite wisdom, saw fit to call to rest our son before he drew his first breath.

I crumpled the paper and threw it in the fire. Picking up a clean sheet, I bit the end of the quill, thinking.

A cough sounded from behind me. I whirled around, heart pounding in my throat. Han stood in the doorway.

"I'm sorry, Milochka. I didn't mean to scare you." He stepped closer and wrapped his arms around me.

I fought to breathe as I shrugged him off and scooted the chair back. "No, I'm fine. I didn't hear you come in." Damn my nerves! Most of the time, I could pretend nothing had happened, but some days, like this one, every unexpected sound sent me into a panic.

"Writing to your mother?" he asked in a tone of strained nonchalance.

"Trying." I turned back to the paper. Maybe he'd go away.

Instead he placed his hand on my arm. "I can tell her, if you want."

"No." I shook his hand off. His touch made my skin crawl. *Any* touch made my skin crawl. I knew it wasn't his fault that I felt like this, but knowing that didn't change my body's reaction to him.

He cleared his throat. "I talked to Yakov today."

He talked to Yakov every day. Why wouldn't he leave?

"He said he has a reputation as a ladies' man." He laughed, but it sounded forced.

"He's an idiot," I snapped. "Maybe if he spent less time thinking with his fist, he might actually find a woman."

"You're probably right."

I nearly snapped at him again for agreeing with me. Instead, I pursed my lips and didn't answer.

He brushed his hand over my hair, and I willed myself not to flinch. I hadn't bothered to cover it since the attack. No one saw me but Han, Yakov, and Anna, so I wasn't concerned with the social dictates that required married women to wear a scarf or kokoshnik. Most days it was all I could do to get dressed.

"It's getting late," he said. "Will you be to bed soon?"

I gestured at the desk. "Once this is finished. Don't wait up."

"Try not to be too long. You're still healing; you need your rest." He bent down to kiss my cheek, and I clenched my teeth.

As his footsteps faded down the hall, I let out a sigh of relief. If I slept at all, it wouldn't be in bed with him. Ever since the attack, Han took every opportunity to touch me, like he was afraid if he didn't hold me enough, I would disappear. Every touch made me want to scream.

I spent a restless night on the divan in the sitting room, tossing and turning beside the fire. At the first light, I made my way to the kitchen and poured myself a cup of kvass. Taking a large drink of the sweet, fizzy liquid, I rummaged through the pantry until I found a bit of rye bread and gooseberry preserves.

If Marya Ivanovna could see me, she'd have had a conniption. I could imagine what she'd say. "Mistress! You ought to be in bed! And serving yourself. It isn't genteel, the lady of the house fetching her own food." Of course, she'd ignore my protests that I wasn't a lady, just a farmer's wife. Marya Ivanovna had always treated us like nobility. I smiled at the thought, but a pang of grief went through me.

We'd have to find a new housekeeper soon. I rubbed my aching chest as I walked into the dining room. We couldn't rely on Anna Ilynichna forever. I could do some basic cooking, but I'd been educated as a seamstress, not a housekeeper. Yet another way I'd been a disappointment to my mother, by marrying a farmer rather than taking over the practice in Selyik. If Dobromila Nikolaevna, famed seamstress, found out her daughter was living without a housekeeper, she'd be appalled.

Footsteps in the hall interrupted my musings. Han came into the room, already dressed for the day, his face filled with concern. He leaned down to kiss me. I pulled back, and he frowned, tracing my cheek with his hand instead.

"You didn't come to bed again."

"I fell asleep writing," I lied. I took another bite of bread and stood, leaving the rest of my breakfast untouched on the table. "I need to get dressed."

"Mila, wait." He followed me out the door. "I need to talk to you."

"Can it wait? I've got a lot to do today." I didn't, really, but every moment with him had my chest tightening and my heart racing.

"It's...no." He took a step closer, reaching for my hand, and I stepped back, ignoring the hurt look on his face. "I don't want you to worry, but I need to go back to Tsebol."

"Oh." He didn't know there was no reason to worry. The soldiers had already taken their revenge. He wasn't in danger anymore. I'd taken the brunt of their anger. "What for?"

"I need to see Ulyana Petrovna's husband. Pyotr was telling me during the harvest—"

"Oh, good. It will be nice to see Ulyana. You don't mind if I go with you, do you?" It would be easier to find out about the nobleman in person, rather than waiting for letters. And being out of the house would be a relief. Away from the memories.

He frowned. "Are you sure you can handle it?"

I fought the urge to roll my eyes. "I'll be fine. When are we going? I had a letter to send to Ulyana. I'll add a note telling her to expect us."

"I've already written to Konstantin Anatolyevich—her husband—and told him I'd be there on the first of the week." He paused, looking me over. "Even with the wagon, that's a long way with you still recovering."

"I'll be fine," I said again. "We can get a room for the night. I'd like to get out." It was as close as I would come to admitting my need to get away. "I've been wanting to see Ulyana, since we missed the wedding."

He swallowed, memories clouding his eyes. "I'm sure she didn't want you risking your health being out so soon after...well, after."

He couldn't even say the word "attack." It was a good thing I'd lied about what had really happened. He'd reacted so poorly to finding out I'd been beaten; I couldn't imagine how he'd have handled hearing I'd been raped. And if he figured out who my attackers were, he'd never forgive himself.

"I'll just go and finish that letter." I turned and disappeared down the hall before he could say another word. Truly, men were incredibly fragile.

8

BACK TO TSEBOL

Han

The following week, Mila and I were bundled against the frigid autumn air on the road to Tsebol. I'd taken the extra precaution of filling a glove with dry beans and strapping it to my wrist, hoping to make myself less conspicuous. Though not as big as the capital, the city was large enough that I didn't expect to run into the soldiers from my last visit, but I preferred to be cautious.

Mila sat next to me in silence, knitting a pair of woolen socks. Despite my worries about the journey, I was glad she'd decided to go with me. I hadn't wanted to leave her at home alone. Maybe the trip would give us an opportunity to reconnect. I understood that she was lashing out from pain, but that didn't make it any easier to bear. Every time she shrank from my touch, every time she snapped at me, every night she spent away from our bed hurt a little more.

Getting away would be good for both of us. So long as we avoided the soldiers Yakov and I had fought.

I'd first written to Konstantin Anatolyevich a week after the—a week after Mila had been hurt. Discussing the possibility of Borislav's survival in a letter was out of the question, so I had asked the baker to meet in person. The day before his wedding, he had called on me at home and shared his belief that the rumors were true. Tsar Borislav was alive.

I hardly dared to think about what to expect in Tsebol. Konstantin Anatolyevich had seemed confident, but he wouldn't reveal his source. Not by name, at least. The baker had said he would introduce me to someone who could give me answers, and while I trusted his sincerity, the whole thing could be a trap to weed out traitors. Or it could be a fruitless effort, a crazed beggar's delusions taken on new life as the story spread through the countryside.

Still, after all we'd faced since the war, I had to try. We had so little left to lose. If there was a chance that Borislav was alive, was ready to take the throne, I had to join him. For the opportunity to give Mila something resembling justice against the deserters who had attacked her, to give her a better life, I had to try. She didn't deserve what we'd been through. I glanced over at her, her brown face blank as the needles in her hands flew. I hadn't seen her smile since the morning she'd been hurt. I'd give anything to see her smile again.

She looked up and frowned at me. "What?"

"Nothing." I turned back to the road in front of us. We were nearing the city, the wild countryside giving way to a more developed landscape. Houses separated mown fields, and gradually the fields surrendered their place to buildings crowded around the city wall.

Inside the wall, it was emptier than the last time I had visited. Market day had passed, and with only a month until the first snow, most city-goers were likely at home preparing for the coming long winter.

We made our way through the streets unchallenged. I sat stiff in my seat, scanning the streets for signs of a threat. We were nearing the baker's shop when Mila gasped.

My heart dropped into my stomach. "What's wrong?" I followed her gaze to a pair of soldiers on the corner.

"Nothing," she said. "I'm fine."

She'd said the men who attacked her were deserters, but was it possible she'd been wrong? My vision went red as I watched them. I rested my gloved wrist on her leg, needing to assure myself that she was there, was safe. "Mila, is that them?"

"What? No, of course not."

I glanced over to see her shake her head.

"They took me by surprise, that's all. Is this the place?" She tucked the unfinished socks back into their bag and nodded at the bakery ahead of us.

I cast a wary look back at the soldiers and took a deep breath. It wasn't them. Mila was safe.

As we pulled up in front of the bakery, Ulyana came bustling out to greet us. A faded blue scarf covered her head, and the apron she wore was covered in a dusting of flour. "You're here early!" She took Mila's bag. "I had meant to clean up before you got here."

"That's alright," Mila said quietly, stepping down from the wagon.

Konstantin Anatolyevich's large pink face peeked through the doorway. "Han Antonovich, good to see you again!" He came out and put a hand on Ulyana's shoulder. "You'll have to drive around the block to put the horses and wagon up. These tiny roads, you know. No place to stable on our own street. Here, I'll go with you." He climbed up into the seat Mila had vacated.

I looked back at my wife, but she was already following Ulyana inside. The baker kept up a steady stream of conversation as we drove around to the stable.

"I'm sure you'll want dinner soon. Ulyana has it cooking right now. We have some time before my friend is expecting us. I told Ulyana I was helping you make a business connection and that we'd be gone for the afternoon. I'm sure she wants some time alone with your wife, anyway. She doesn't say anything, but it's hard for her, being away from everyone she knows. She's glad you've come. Gives her a taste of home."

At the stable, Konstantin bounded out of the wagon and unhooked the horses before I could even climb down off the seat. "The brush is on the hook, if you want to brush them down before we go in. I'll just check that the trough is filled."

Once we finished, he led me through a door in the back of the stable. It opened into the bakery, where a young boy stood behind the counter, tending to something in the oven.

Konstantin clapped the boy on the back. "My apprentice. The guild sent him to me last year at his parents' request. Keeps me in business, he does." The boy looked down at his feet, but I saw a flash of a proud smile. "I'll have dinner brought down to you in a bit, alright? Mind the shop while we're with our guests."

"Yes, sir!" The boy turned back to his work.

"We're up here." Konstantin led me up a narrow set of steps in the corner, into a well-furnished sitting room where Mila and Ulyana sat by the window talking.

"Business must be good, Konstantin Anatolyevich," I remarked as I took a seat, "if you're able to have an apprentice."

The big man grinned. "You must call me Kostya."

It was impossible not to like the man. "Business must be good, Kostya."

"Oh, you know." He waved a large hand dismissively. "I can't say much in favor of the army, but they are good for business. The baron is generous, too. He varies his order throughout the guild, encourages local business."

"You're too modest, Kostiukha." Ulyana smiled fondly at him before turning to me. "Lord Ilya gives him twice the business of the other bakers in the city, and he's already been commissioned to provide the sweet pirogi for Prophet's Day."

"And my biggest competition was commissioned for the meat pirogi, and the rest of the bakers for the poor-breads. He's not singling me out, *dorogaya.*" He smiled at Mila. "She gives me too much credit. But how are you, Mila Dmitrievna? We were so sorry to hear of your troubles."

She stiffened. "I'm doing well. Thank you for asking."

Ulyana stood. "Dinner is ready, Kostya. We were just waiting for the two of you. Shall we eat?"

The cramped dining room was obviously not made for more than two or three people, but the food was good, and Ulyana and Konstantin had a cheerful banter that more than made up for Mila's detached silence. I was grateful; I didn't feel up to carrying the conversation myself.

When we finished eating, Konstantin stood, his head nearly brushing the ceiling. "Well, we should be off. We're expected soon."

"You'll be alright?" I asked Mila. She pursed her lips and nodded once. "Then I'll come get you once I've found us a room."

"Don't think of it." Konstantin wore an indignant expression. "You'll stay here tonight, and I'll brook no refusal. We have plenty of room." He leaned down and placed a kiss on his wife's scarf-covered head. "We'll be back for supper, *dorogaya*."

The walk to the inn was short, the air warm from the early afternoon sun. I kept a cautious eye out for the soldiers from the tavern fight, but I saw none. Konstantin chatted amiably as we walked, stopping several times to talk to passersby or to mention a piece of trivia about a certain house or store.

We finally stopped at the door to an inn, and Konstantin held the door open for me to enter. "Here we are."

I looked around as I stepped inside, blinking in the sudden dimness. The place was empty but for a sandy-haired man sitting in the far corner, slouched over his mug. He looked up as we approached, and I felt a flicker of familiarity.

The man stood, revealing a hook where his right hand should be. "You're late."

Konstantin grinned. "You know me. Never on time. Han, this is Boris Stepanovich."

"Boris?" One of the men that had been imprisoned with me the night I'd lost my hand. Their faces were burned into my memory. Yakov, young and terrified; the grizzled old warrior from Yakov's unit; Benedikt Ivanovich, my childhood friend who Miroslav had burned to death with his magic; and Boris Stepanovich, the man standing across from me.

His eyes narrowed. "Have we met?"

I removed the glove strapped to my right arm, and he relaxed visibly at my missing hand. "We were imprisoned together the night of the battle," I said. "You'll remember my friend, Captain Benedikt Ivanovich?" The smell of burning flesh filled my nose, and I pushed back the memories. Benedikt had deserved better.

His expression darkened. "I remember." He turned to Konstantin. "This is the man you wanted me to meet?"

Konstantin nodded, and Boris Stepanovich gestured for us to sit. He waved for the innkeeper and ordered a bottle of vodka.

As the innkeeper stepped out, Boris looked at me. "What are you looking for?"

"I just want to know the truth." Wherever that would lead me. I just wanted to know if there was any good left in this world. Anyone who could bring justice to me, to Mila, to Yakov and Anna.

"What truth?"

I furrowed my brow. Had Konstantin not told him why we were here? "I want to know—"

He cut me off. "I know what you want to know. What I want to know is why. You knelt. I can't tell you anything until I know you won't betray us to Miroslav."

"You knelt as well." If I'd thought there was even a chance Borislav had survived... No. It was too late to dwell on past actions. "We all did."

"I've answered for my actions."

We fell silent as the innkeeper returned with the vodka and three wooden cups. Boris Stepanovich poured us each a generous serving as the innkeeper left once more.

I lifted my cup to my lips and took a large swallow, relishing the burn of the alcohol down my throat. Then I spoke again. "I would have died for the cause. We all would have. But I believed the cause—the tsar—was dead, rotting on the field. If it had been Otets' will for me to die for my tsar, I would have done so willingly. But given the chance to go home, I wasn't going to seek martyrdom."

He raised an eyebrow. "Do you seek it now? This conversation is treason."

Treason or not, I had to know.

Konstantin cut in. "Han is a close friend of my wife's family, and loyal to the tsar. I trust him, Boris Stepanovich."

The other man's eyes flashed, but he kept them trained on me. "I told you I would meet with him, Konstantin Anatolyevich. If he wants to know, he'll answer me."

I shook my head. "If I was wrong to kneel, I need to know. If I'm given another chance to serve the tsar, to fight for justice, I have to take it. For the sake of the hundreds, thousands of lives Miroslav has destroyed."

Boris Stepanovich leaned back and took a drink. "Konstantin tells me you're a prosperous farmer, and happily married. It doesn't seem that he's destroyed *your* life."

I slammed my drink on the table, the rage I'd suppressed for the past six weeks boiling up inside me. "Don't presume to tell me what my life is like," I whispered, clenching my remaining hand into a fist. "I lost my hand and nearly my whole livelihood. My wife's family forbade her from marrying me when I returned, and when she married me anyway, her mother didn't speak to her for a full year. I can barely write my own letters, and I'll never wield a sword again. I had to relearn how to do everything at home, and I can hardly come into the city without fearing someone will attack me for being a traitor. My wife was beaten half to death by some deserters that monster allowed into his army, causing the death of our unborn son and destroying her spirit. So don't you d—" I choked on the words, tears of anger clouding my eyes. "Don't you *dare* tell me Miroslav hasn't destroyed my life."

Chest heaving, I stared at Boris Stepanovich, who watched me with a calculating look, as though weighing the sincerity of my words. Then he nodded.

"Go to the temple outside the city gate. Tell the Brothers there you've come to pray for the tsar. They'll help you find the answers you're looking for."

Some of the tension in my chest released in a silent breath.

"Thank you, Boris Stepanovich," Konstantin said.

Boris grunted, and tossing a coin onto the table to pay for his drinks, strode out of the inn.

9

BORISLAV

Han

"You are sure you want to go alone?" Konstantin asked again. "I can go with you."

"I don't want to put you in danger. If this isn't some elaborate trap, we could need men like you soon." I mounted my horse and cast a glance upward toward the house, where Mila would be sitting with Ulyana waiting for me. "Tell Mila our business finished early, so I went to the temple to pray for—for the baby's soul." A wave of grief swept over me, tightening my throat. I would find justice for him, for the family we never got to be. "By Otets' grace, I'll be back safe by supper."

"Otets go with you, Han."

The small temple outside of Tsebol was quiet and unassuming, as most people worshiped at the larger temple inside the city. I tied my horse to the post outside and entered the small wooden building, brushing my hand reverently over the red-painted doorframe.

Inside, I took off my black ushanka-hat and bowed reverently in the direction of the altar. A stocky Brother in a simple white robe and cap approached.

"How can we serve you, honored son?"

I swallowed, my skin clammy. The moment of truth. "I've come to pray for the tsar."

The priest blinked once and nodded. "Follow me." He led me to a prayer room off of the main sanctuary and shut the door. "Please kneel."

I did as I was told, heart thundering. Almost as soon as I knelt, the Brother shoved my head onto the kneeling rail and yanked my arms behind my back.

"Who sent you?" he growled, tying my wrists together. I hadn't fastened the bean-filled glove to my wrist properly; it slid off, and the rope slackened. "What is this?" the priest demanded.

I fought down my panic. It wasn't a trap. It couldn't be. The Brother was just being cautious, trying to protect Borislav. "I'm a survivor of Barbezht!" The words tumbled out of me. "Boris Stepanovich sent me!"

The Brother didn't answer but tied my hand to my belt. He placed a rough sack over my head and yanked me to my feet.

I fought to keep my breathing even. They wouldn't cover my face if they were working for Miroslav. They would arrest me, or kill me outright.

A tug on the rope made me pitch forward, and someone—the priest, I assumed—led me, stumbling, through the temple. I heard the sound of a door opening, and we walked down a steep set of stairs. The air became cool and damp, clinging to my skin. Our footsteps echoed as we walked for what felt like ages. Finally, another door opened, and the tugging on the rope stopped. A hand on my back forced me to my knees.

I should have told Mila goodbye. If I died here—

Someone tore the bag from my head. Candlelight illuminated the small, windowless room and the desk in front of me.

On the opposite side of the desk stood Borislav, rightful tsar of Inzhria.

All the air left my lungs. I'd never seen the tsar this close, but it was unmistakably the same man who had led us into the fated battle at Barbezht. His black beard was overgrown, hiding the high cheekbones that would have exposed his heritage, and his simple clothing belied his rank, but he held himself with the same unmistakable authority.

The Brother cleared his throat. "Your majesty, he said he was here to pray for the tsar. He said Boris Stepanovich sent him."

"Thank you for your diligence, but this man is no threat to me." The tsar's voice was soft but commanding. "He has suffered enough for my sake. Unless I am much mistaken, he lost his sword hand at my brother's order." He crossed the room and drew a dagger, using it to cut the rope that bound me. "What is your name, soldier?"

I stared, wide-eyed, at the royal standing before me. "Han Aleksandrovich, your majesty."

He inclined his head. "I thank you for your service, Han Aleksandrovich." To the Brother, he said, "You may leave us."

The door closed behind the priest, and the tsar and I were alone in the small room.

I had to explain, to tell him why I was alive, why I had knelt to his brother. "Your majesty, if I had known, if we had known—we would never have surrendered. We would have fought to the very last man—" I choked on the words, my eyes stinging.

"Rise. Be at peace. How could you have known? You did what you must to survive." Tsar Borislav took a seat, gesturing for me to sit as well.

I remained on my knees, placing my wrist over my heart. "Your majesty, I'm yours to command. I was wrong to kneel to your brother, and I want to swear loyalty to you, only you, for the rest of my life." I'd made a mistake before, changing my loyalties, but I wouldn't make that mistake again. I was Borislav's man for life.

The tsar nodded solemnly, and I said the words every Inzhrian knew but few ever had reason to say. "As I live in the light of Otets, I will serve only you, my lord, do you no harm, and defend and protect you against all who would harm both your good name and your person. I swear to do so from this day until I am called to my eternal rest."

Placing a hand on my head, the tsar gave the traditional response. "I accept your allegiance and swear to be an honorable judge of all your causes, worthy of your loyalty, and I swear also to provide you always with protection of your body and spirit. Rise."

I swallowed the lump in my throat as I stood. "Thank you."

He gestured again to the seat across from him. My whole body hummed with tension, but I sat.

"If we had kno—" I began again, but the tsar held up a hand.

"I have heard what my brother did to the survivors."

The memory of burning flesh filled my nose, and the sound of Benedikt's screams echoed in my ears. I shook myself, trying to escape from the memory. "My friend, Captain Benedikt Ivanovich…"

Borislav nodded. "Boris Stepanovich told me of the captain's death. He was a brave man, and he did not deserve to die like that. But while I'm grateful for the captain's loyalty, I bear no ill will toward the men who chose not to follow him to the grave. Allegiance to a dead tsar benefits no one, and you could not have known I had survived."

The tsar turned to the desk behind him, reaching for a pitcher and two mugs. He poured the drinks and handed one to me.

I raised it into the air. "To the true tsar."

Borislav bowed his head in humble acknowledgment. "Tell me, Han Aleksandrovich. Most of the survivors died following the battle. How did you survive?"

I took a sip and swirled the water around in my mouth, thinking of how to begin. I'd done all I could to forget the events of Barbezht, but they were never far from my mind.

"After your brother pronounced our sentence, they marched us out of the camp and cut us one by one. A few men tried to fight. One of them lost his whole arm. Another lost his head. There was less fighting after that." I took another drink. I hadn't told this story to anyone. Not even Mila knew everything that had happened that night. Only my fellow survivors and the men who had maimed us. "I managed to stay conscious through it all, thank Otets." Yakov had passed out, and I knew that if I did the same, I wouldn't wake back up. "I worked with a couple other survivors to bind our wounds and cauterize them." I shuddered at the memory. I'd never felt pain like that before, the red-hot iron on my open wound. I could still hear the sizzle of burning blood, smell its sickening metallic odor.

I shook myself out of the memory and went on. "I traveled with a young boy named Yakov, the blacksmith's son from my hometown. Between the two of us, we made it home—barely. My parents had died a few years before the war, so I was alone, but my steward was there. He sent for Mila, my betrothed—even though I ordered him not to—and for Yakov's mother. Between the three of them, they nursed us back to health."

I hadn't wanted Mila to see me like that, missing my hand, my face disfigured from the scar I'd received in a previous battle. I'd been furious with Kyril Kyrilovich for summoning her, but the steward had ignored my anger. "She deserves to know," he had said.

"I wouldn't have survived without Mila," I said softly. I'd done everything in my power to make her leave me. I told her I was crippled, a traitor, unable to work. I told her I didn't want her. She hadn't listened, of course. The day after I returned from Barbezht, she made me marry her in a bedside wedding. I smiled wryly at the memory. At my brave, headstrong wife.

"She sounds like a rare woman."

"She's my life." My smile faded. "She made it through that time stronger than ever, but she's changed."

The tsar frowned. "How so?"

I set down my cup and looked into the tsar's dark eyes. "My wife was attacked, your majesty, by some deserters from your brother's new army. We were expecting our first child, and the attack caused our son to be stillborn."

His face grew stormy. "You aren't the first to suffer at the hands of this abomination my brother calls an army, but I will see him dethroned and rectify the wrongs he has committed."

Mila

I glanced out the window at the street below. It was already dark, and Konstantin and Ulyana sat in the parlor with me, keeping a light conversation. I pretended not to see the worried glances Ulyana cast my way, or the slight furrow in Konstantin's brow every time a horse passed the house.

"Did Han mention when he would be back?" I hoped my voice sounded nonchalant.

"I'm sure he lost track of the time." The baker's smile was a touch too wide. I didn't know what he was hiding, but I didn't like it.

"He'll probably be back any minute." Ulyana stood. "I'm just going to make sure his supper's still warm. Can I offer you a hot cup of sbiten?"

I shook my head. My mother had always ordered the cook to make sbiten when we received bad news. I couldn't drink the spiced honey water without thinking of my sister's illness or my father's death. "No, thank you. I think I'll retire."

"Of course. Rest well."

I slipped into the small bedroom and sank down onto the bed. Where was Han? And why was Konstantin behaving so strangely? As I undressed for bed, I gnawed on my lip. Maybe someone had recognized him from the fight after the market. The nobleman—whose name Ulyana hadn't known—had seemed to consider Han's punishment sufficient, but maybe the soldiers hadn't agreed. If they'd seen him, they might have taken the opportunity to enforce their own brand of justice. I'd been so eager to get away from my house, from the memories of the attack, that I hadn't stopped to think about the danger Han could still be in.

"Idiot," I muttered to myself.

Han should have thought of that as well. Why *had* he been so insistent on coming to see Konstantin? He hadn't offered an explanation, and distracted as I had been, I hadn't asked. If I hadn't known him better, I might have assumed he was looking for information on the men who'd attacked me, but that wasn't like Han at all. He wasn't vengeful, no matter how much we'd been through.

The door behind me opened, and I turned to see him enter the room.

"Where have you been?" Anger overtook the rush of relief I felt. "We expected you back hours ago."

"I'm sorry, Milochka. I lost track of the time."

I stiffened. "Ulyana mentioned she had a plate for you, I assume."

"She did, but I wasn't hungry." He sat on the bed next to me and began pulling off his boots, a slight smile playing on his face.

"Well?" I shook with barely suppressed anger. He'd been gone all day without a word of warning, and here he was acting like nothing had happened.

"Hm?"

I stood, throwing up my hands. "Are you going to tell me where you've been all day? I was worried sick! You left this afternoon with Konstantin to meet someone, and then he came home without you and said you'd gone to the temple to pray and would be back by supper. And don't think for one second I believe you were at the temple this whole time. After everything that's happened, you disappear for a whole afternoon in a city crawling with soldiers, and you come in hours after you're supposed to be back, without so much as a hint of remorse!"

He grabbed my hand, but I jerked it back, eyes stinging. "I am sorry, Mila." His expression was open, honest. "I didn't mean to worry you. I didn't want to get your hopes up until I knew…"

"Knew what?" I snapped.

"I went to see the tsar."

In the silence, I could hear the low murmur of Ulyana and Konstantin's voices through the walls. I opened my mouth, trying to form words through my fury.

"Why—How?"

He stared at me, uncomprehending, for a moment. Then understanding dawned on his face. "No! No. Not him. Mila," he took my hand again, "Borislav is alive."

I sat down as his words sank in. "How?" I repeated.

He squeezed my hand. "He survived the battle, Mila! He's been in exile since then, but he just returned. He's raising support to take the throne. To finally defeat his brother." He quivered with excitement.

I frowned, not believing what I was hearing. "You were with Tsar Borislav? He's alive?"

He grinned. "We went this morning to meet someone who claimed the tsar was alive. It turned out to be another survivor from Barbezht. He told me where to go to find him."

I sat unmoving, too shocked even to pull my hand from his, as he recounted his meeting with the tsar.

"He's alive, Mila." He brought my hand to his lips and kissed it. "The tsar is alive. And..." His expression wavered slightly. "He wants to meet you."

Shock washed over me like a bucket of icy water. "What?" Borislav, chosen heir of Tsar Vyacheslav, wanted to meet me. "Why?"

"I told him about..." He shook his head, unable or unwilling to speak about my attack. "Everything that's happened over the past few months. And about what we went through after Barbezht. He was impressed by your bravery."

An ember of hope flickered in my breast. No one could restore my child to me, but if Borislav wanted to meet me, maybe he would help me claim the justice I deserved. The justice I'd never find in Miroslav's tsardom. I could tell Borislav the truth about who attacked me. When he took the throne, he'd see those men punished.

Han cleared his throat. "If you're not ready—"

I cut him off. "When do we go?"

"Tomorrow morning." He reached out to brush a thumb over my cheek, and for the first time in months, his touch didn't make my skin crawl.

"Good." I climbed under the covers, turning over and closing my eyes. "You should get some sleep."

He laid his hand on my head. "Good night, *dorogusha.*"

10

MEETING THE TSAR

Mila

We said our goodbyes to Ulyana and Konstantin the next morning and left the city. My stomach churned with nerves as we stopped at a small temple outside the gate.

Han led me inside. To the left of the altar was a simple statue of the Prophet, who had revealed the divine ancestry of Fima the Blessed and guided him in his conquest of the country. The statue held a scroll, head bowed in pious prayer. To the right of the altar was a statue of Tsar Fima himself, sword and head raised in victory.

The temple was empty but for a stocky brother in his white robes, cleaning the statue of Tsar Fima with a rag. At our entrance, he set the cloth down and approached.

"What can I do for you, honored children?"

"My wife and I would like to pray together before we return home," Han said.

"Follow me." He led us to a small prayer room with a wooden kneeling rail, closing the door behind us. On one wall was a giant wooden icon depicting Tsar Fima's victory over Inzhria. The Brother pulled on one side, and it swung open to reveal a dark hole. He gestured for us to go through.

Han went first, descending into the darkness. I felt my way after him, down a narrow set of stairs, until I reached a stone floor. A small click sounded, and torchlight illuminated an underground tunnel.

"We have a bit of a walk now," the Brother said, waving the torch ahead of us.

The tunnels twisted and turned. Every so often we would come to a split in the path, but the Brother knew his way. The corridors grew damper and colder the further we walked. Were we nearing the river? We had to be traveling underneath the city. A faint scent of mildew hung in the air, and occasionally, I heard a rat scurry by. I hated rats.

Han noticed my discomfort, and he reached out, offering me his hand.

"I'm fine," I said, forcing my muscles to relax. He already thought of me as weak. I didn't need to give him more reason to patronize me.

Finally we stopped. We stood outside a closed door, similar to many we had already passed, but voices came from the other side. The Brother knocked.

A deep voice answered. "Enter."

The room inside was dimly lit, an old, repurposed wine cellar. Standing at a low table strewn with papers were two men. One, an old nobleman with a long gray beard, I recognized as Baron Ilya Sergeyevich. Out of the country when Miroslav ascended to the throne, he hadn't been involved in Borislav's failed rebellion, although I'd heard rumors that he favored Borislav over his brother.

Next to the baron stood a man I'd never seen before, but his bearing and black hair and beard were identical to statues and paintings I'd seen of Tsar Fima. There was no doubt in my mind that this man was Fima's heir, that he carried the Blood of Otets in his veins. This was Borislav, the true tsar of Inzhria.

I bowed low, and Han said, "Your majesty, my lord, I present to you your loyal servant, my wife Lyudmila Dmitrievna."

The tsar stepped forward and took my hand. "Your husband told me of the trials you've recently faced, Lyudmila Dmitrievna. You have my deepest sympathies for your loss. If it were in my power, I would erase the injustices done to you and restore your child."

My throat tightened as I looked into his dark eyes, crinkled with sympathy and reflecting my grief. Tears filled my own eyes, and the tsar handed me a handkerchief.

Crying in front of the tsar. I must have looked every bit as weak as Han thought me. "Forgive me, your majesty." My voice was strangely hoarse. I wiped my eyes and tried to hand back the handkerchief, but the tsar closed my hand around it.

"There is nothing to forgive. You've suffered so much in the years since my brother came to the throne. If I could ease your pain, I would. Alas, all I can promise is to give you justice."

I nodded, swallowing the lump in my throat. "Thank you, your majesty."

"Your husband told me of your bravery following the battle at Barbezht. You must be the strongest of all my subjects, to overcome what you have."

"Bravery?" I didn't understand. Nothing I'd done in the past few weeks could be considered brave.

"To nurse a defeated soldier back to health, to marry him, knowing the difficulties you would face. To align yourself with someone called a traitor, despite the stigma it would bring you. And more recently, to survive the trauma you have and not let it break you." A sad smile played on his lips.

I didn't feel brave. I'd been cut down to raw rage and grief. But if this fury was bravery, I would channel it. During the last uprising, I'd sat at home waiting for news. I wouldn't do that again. "We're with you all the way, your majesty. Whatever it takes to bring you to the throne, my husband and I will be there."

Han put his hand on my shoulder. When I glanced up at him, pride and concern mingled in his eyes. I looked quickly away.

"My cause can only be helped by an ally such as yourself, Lyudmila Dmitrievna. In fact..." He paused, glancing at Baron Ilya. "I was just speaking to the baron of you before your arrival. We have a proposal for the two of you, but it's best if we discuss it over dinner. Ilya has made accommodations for the two of you. Please, stay with us tonight. We can dine together and discuss our plans at that time."

A muscle flickered in Han's jaw. He wasn't pleased with this turn of events. A proposal from the tsar was an honor for him, but if he could, he'd be happy to lock me away to keep me safe. Still, he wouldn't refuse an invitation from the tsar. He bowed. "Thank you, your majesty."

The tsar took my hand and pressed a kiss to it. "We will speak again at dinner, Lyudmila Dmitrievna. Han Aleksandrovich." He extended his left hand and shook Han's. "Thank you for returning, and for bringing your wife. I look forward to seeing you again soon."

Han

Baron Ilya led us out of the tunnels, directly into his castle, where a tall manservant in simple gray livery waited. "Our guests," he told the servant, who didn't blink at the strangers appearing from underground with his master. "Please see that they're well taken care of." To us, he added, "I ask that you remain in this wing for the duration of your stay. For your own safety, and for the tsar's."

"We will, my lord."

As the manservant left us alone in the guest suite, a large sitting room opening into a comfortable bedroom, I watched Mila. Her posture was tense, not inviting conversation. A bookshelf stretched along one wall; she went to it and selected a large book titled *Made of Stone: How the existence of the Drakra race reveals Otets' plan for humanity*. She took a seat by the window and began reading—or at least staring at the book. Her eyes didn't seem to be moving, and though I waited for several minutes, she didn't turn the page.

I wanted to go to her, to tear the book from her hands and insist she talk to me, but it wouldn't do any good. She'd walled herself off from me since the day we lost our son, and I didn't know how to bring us back together. She hid her pain from me, blanketing it in anger and aggression.

And now she wanted to help bring Borislav to the throne.

I didn't begrudge her the desire to support our tsar, but I couldn't bear to see her in danger again. Borislav's journey to the throne would be the death of hundreds, possibly thousands. It was worth it—of course it was worth it—but I couldn't let Mila face that.

"Why didn't you tell me?" I asked.

Her head jerked up from the book. "Tell you what?"

"Why didn't you tell me that you wanted to help?" I closed the distance between us, reaching for her hand. "Shouldn't I have had some say?" I didn't want to control her, just protect her.

Her eyes narrowed, but she didn't pull away. "What would you have said? That it's too dangerous? That I should stay home and wait for news like last time? I have as much a right as you to fight for what we lost."

"If you think I wouldn't do anything possible to change things, Mila—" I shook my head. "Revenge against the men who hurt you isn't going to bring our son back. I don't want to see you in danger."

She jerked her hand from mine. "I'm not looking for revenge. I'm looking for justice. And not just against the men who attacked me, but against the tsar who allowed it. Miroslav did this to me just as much as those soldiers did."

"Do you think—" I broke off. I didn't want to know the answer.

"What?"

I shouldn't have spoken. "Nothing. Nevermind."

"Tell me." Her face was carefully blank of emotion.

I let out a deep breath. "Do you think I'm not hurting as much as you? Do you think I don't mourn him enough?"

"What? No! Of course not."

She didn't quite meet my eyes as she said it, though. A vise tightened around my heart. "By the Blood, Mila. You do. Or," I paused. "Do you blame me for it?"

"Blame you?" Her voice grew shrill. "Did you attack me? Did you kill our son?"

I sank down onto the stool at her feet. "I didn't do it, but I didn't do anything to stop it, either. What if they were there because of the fight Yakov and I had in the city?"

"They weren't." She was firm. Whatever had happened, whatever horrors she still refused to tell me about, had been enough to convince her the two events were unrelated.

A knock at the door interrupted, and the manservant from earlier peeked in. "Dinner is ready, if you'll follow me."

I took a deep breath as I stood, trying to compose myself. I offered Mila my arm, but she walked past me. Whether she had missed my offer or deliberately ignored me, I didn't know. I brushed at an imaginary spot on my shirt and followed her, hoping it was the former.

The wing of the castle we were in was empty. The servant led us down a short hall and into a small dining room, simply furnished with only a table and chairs. The tsar and the baron were already seated.

"Please, be seated," the baron said as we bowed. "Thank you for joining us. I'm sure you understand the need for discretion—we don't want to draw attention to the tsar's presence—but I hope you will make free in your use of my private wing of the castle. Only my most trusted servants come here, and my wife, so there's no risk of discovery."

I bowed my head. "We're most grateful, my lord."

"It's I who am grateful." The baron's wrinkled white face was solemn. "Your service at Barbezht fills me with shame that I was not there to render similar service."

"We've discussed this many times, Ilya," the tsar cut in. "Otets designed your absence. If not for you, I would have been captured after the battle. And had you been able to openly support me in the beginning, you wouldn't be here today to pave the way for my victory."

"As you say, your majesty." Baron Ilya pinched his lips together as though he didn't agree, but the servants entered the room then. They carried fragrant trays of roast duck, stewed beets, and fresh-baked bread.

Once our plates were filled, the tsar lifted up his hands. "Pray with me, friends." He bowed his head. "Otets, great father who gives food alike to the wicked and the good, we ask that you would bless these gifts to our nourishment and grant us victory over the wicked who would seek to do us harm. Grant your blessings to your chosen Firstborn of the Sanctioned, and lead us to follow the mandates handed down to us by Witness, Steward, and Prophet. Let it be."

"Let it be," we echoed.

"Now, Han," Tsar Borislav said as we began eating, "the baron and I were speaking before your arrival this morning about you and your fellow survivors of Barbezht. The tsardom owes you a debt we can never repay, but I would like to try. Following my ascension to the throne, I intend to ennoble all the survivors of Barbezht in recompense for your losses and in return for your support in the coming conflict."

My mouth dropped open. Ennoble? He would make wounded soldiers, convicted traitors members of his court? "Your majesty, I—I don't know what to say."

"Say nothing, friend. It's no more than your due, and probably far less than that, by the time this is all finished."

I stared at the man sitting across from me, his eyes wide with sincerity. "I'm honored, but what possible benefit could a handful of cripples be to your cause?"

I heard the hiss of Mila's breath, but the tsar just smiled. "You underestimate yourself, Han. True, there are few of you, but who could be more important to me than those who have been my supporters since the beginning? And there could be no one more resourceful than the man who has lost a hand. Boris Stepanovich has made a living here in Tsebol. You and the young man you saved—I believe you said his name was Yakov?—have farmed the land the past five years. All three of you have shown great strength of character after Barbezht, and you will have learned things from the last uprising that I did not. You may not be able to wield a sword, but wars are not won primarily on the battlefield.

I looked down at my plate, my head swimming. "Your majesty is too kind."

"Not in the least." His smile turned rueful. "My motives are not all so pure as that. Grateful as I am for you and your fellow survivors and for your support, there are other reasons for my generosity."

I looked back up, an eyebrow raised in question.

"My brother alienated many of his supporters when he chose to maim unarmed men who had offered him their surrender. I don't wish to repeat his mistakes. By rewarding those who Miroslav punished, I can win the support of those he lost. True, most of them aren't of the noble class, but when I win the heart of the lower classes, I will have won the tsardom.

"I also wish to have a survivor of Barbezht present with me as a reminder not to repeat my brother's mistakes. I will have to be ruthless on the battlefield, and at times I will have to be ruthless off it, but I would not estrange myself from loyal supporters by administering cruel punishments to defeated enemies. Having one of my brother's victims constantly at hand, I hope, will keep me humble.

"So you see, Han, I am not the paragon of virtue you would paint me. A gift from a tsar is never truly generous; there's always a hidden agenda."

The tsar's motives sounded more noble with the explanation than without. "Your majesty, you are more worthy of the throne than I ever thought. Your motives do you credit. I would be honored to be a noble in your court, and as I vowed yesterday, you have my service, whatever you would ask of me."

Borislav listed his glass in recognition, then turned to Mila. "But Lyudmila Dmitrievna, you will think me remiss for my lack of attention. Don't think that because I ask for your husband's service that you've been forgotten."

"Not at all, your majesty." She smiled at him, the expression more sincere than any she'd worn in weeks. Was she pleased by his offer? She'd make a wonderful noblewoman. Marya Ivanovna would have been apoplectic with joy, I thought with a twinge of grief. "And please, call me Mila."

My lips twitched in an approximation of a smile. She hated her name. The only one who ever called her Lyudmila, rather than Mila, was her mother.

"Mila, then. Your husband tells me you were trained as a seamstress?"

She nodded, pushing her barely-touched plate back. "My mother wanted me to join her practice. I married Han instead, and she and my brother moved east."

"Ilya Sergeyevich and I have been working to place an informant in my brother's court, and an opportunity has arisen that you are perfectly suited for."

My chest tightened, and I gripped the edge of the table. He wanted to send Mila to court? She'd be in as much danger as if she were on a battlefield, if not more.

Mila's face showed surprise, rather than fear. "I'm honored, your majesty, but isn't there someone better suited for the position? Even my husband—" She broke off as Borislav shook his head, smiling.

"Han's missing hand makes him too conspicuous and marks him as one of my former supporters. My magic is strong, mistress, but even I cannot grow body parts where there are none. And the position requires certain talents your husband lacks."

"What would I be doing?"

She couldn't be considering this. I tried to catch her eyes, but she was fixated on the tsar, face screwed up in contemplation.

"There is an opening at court for a seamstress. Lady Heli, Lord Ilya's wife, was asked to make a recommendation. You would have a room and freedom to come and go throughout the city. A member of the lower classes at court has opportunities to hear things nobles cannot, and while Lord Ilya and Lady Heli have servants they trust, Miroslav is watching their household carefully. As a trade worker, you would not be a member of their household, and as such you would not be as strictly observed."

I could see by the expression on Mila's face that she wanted to accept the offer. She had no idea the danger she was putting herself in. If she was caught, Miroslav wouldn't spare her just because she was a woman. She'd be tortured, executed. I had to stop her. "Your majesty, while my wife has many gifts, she has no experience as a spy. How would she know what to do? What sort of information to listen for?"

She scowled at me, but the tsar nodded thoughtfully. "A reasonable question. She would have contacts at court—Lord Ilya's household, primarily—to help guide her. She would perform all the regular duties of a seamstress and to pass on anything learned in the course of those duties." He looked at Mila. "We have others in place who could do the more dangerous tasks of infiltrating heavily guarded areas or stealing sensitive documents. What we need from you is the appearance of neutrality, of being a trade worker with no particular loyalties, in order to overhear important news that might be passed through the women of court."

"How long would I be gone?"

My chest tightened. She couldn't leave. I placed my arm on her leg, but she ignored me as the baron answered.

"No more than a few months. I've been summoned to court. We leave in a week."

"We will, of course, extract you before marching on the city, should that become necessary," the tsar said.

The assurance wasn't comforting. If anything, I felt worse. Sending my wife into an enemy court, a court that might soon be the site of a battle for the kingdom? "But, your majesty, what would I tell people about her absence? Our servants would be concerned, to say nothing of our friends and neighbors."

"While I by no means wish to compound your personal tragedies, Han, if your wife consents to take this position, your journey to Tsebol this week provides a most convenient reason for her absence." Seeing our uncomprehending looks, he added, "Moon Fever. There's been a rash of cases in the city recently."

The horrid fever was named for the speed at which it killed. People woke healthy in the morning, and by the time the moon rose, they were dead. I stared at the tsar, struck dumb.

"To...pretend I died?"

Mila's expression matched my own, I was gratified to see. Maybe she would see sense after all.

"Not necessarily," the tsar said. "Han Aleksandrovich can spread the news that you contracted the fever during your visit to Tsebol, and once you survived the first night, your husband chose to have you sent east to recover fully." Survival of Moon Fever was rare, but if anyone survived the first night, they could make a full recovery, although their healing took months. "There's a hospital near the Spider Mountains where a team of Blood Bastards is studying the disease in hopes of finding a cure. You can explain to your friends that due to the nature of the hospital, she won't be able to receive visitors or communicate with anyone.

"Mila's absence would also provide a reasonable excuse for yours, Han." The tsar shared an inscrutable look with Lord Ilya. "With Ilya gone to court, I need someone to assist me. I've already told you of my desire to have a survivor of Barbezht with me. I can think of no one better to help me raise my army."

All thoughts left my mind. "Me?"

The tsar nodded.

"But what about Boris Stepanovich?"

"Boris Stepanovich prefers to work from the shadows. He'll remain here in Tsebol. But you, Han, you sought me out. Your story of life under my brother's rule, the trials you've faced, can inspire others to join me. I want you to help raise my army."

I swallowed. This was too much to process at once. "I'm honored, your majesty. May we have time to consider your offers?"

Mila cut in. "There's no need. We would be proud to assist your majesty in any way possible."

I caught her eye and held it. She was firm, mouth a tight line. I knew I would never be able to convince her otherwise.

"We are yours to command," she said.

The tsar raised his glass. "To my newest recruits: may Otets grant us swift success and expedient justice."

I raised my glass with the others, but my mind was in turmoil. I sat in silence, allowing the conversation to flow around me as talk turned to lighter subjects.

As we finished dining, the tsar turned to us again.

"Ilya Sergeyevich will leave for court on the first of the week. Mila, you will need to spend that time here preparing, of course. Han, in the morning you can journey home to ensure everything is taken care of during your absence. Tell whoever you must about the Fever and that you are going to stay near the hospital until your wife is well enough to return home. As soon as your business is finished, you can return here."

This was all happening too quickly. We had one night together. One last night, and then we would be separated for who knew how many months. My throat tightened.

The tsar rose. "Mila, if you would attend me in a short while, I would be most grateful. At your leisure, of course. I'm sure the two of you would like some time to talk."

11

A STRANGER'S BODY

Mila

I could sense disapproval radiating from Han as we walked back to our room in silence. As soon as he closed the door behind us, I rounded on him.

"What was that about?"

"What do you mean?" He tried to take my hand, but I shook him off.

"You weren't going to let me go." As though he had any right to *let* me do anything. As though he were my master, my lord.

"I never said that."

His voice was quiet, collected. By the Blood, couldn't he ever show his anger? He made me feel like a shrew. I crossed my arms and glared at him, unspeaking.

"You've barely recovered," he said. "This is no time for you to travel across the country."

"It's been nearly two months! I'm recovered. You can't keep treating me like I'm made of porcelain!"

"We're a family, Mila. That means we stay together." He sounded so sure of himself. So calm.

"We don't have a family!" He flinched back, but I didn't stop. "Miroslav took that away from us when he let his soldiers run rampant over the country. He deserves to pay for what he's done, and I have as much right as you to make him."

"I didn't swear loyalty to the tsar for a chance at revenge!" he shouted.

Good. I'd finally broken through that mask of calm. I stared him down, daring him to fight.

He took a deep breath and continued, quieter. "I did it because Borislav is the best leader for the country. Miroslav is a danger to the tsardom, and to our family." He nodded as I opened my mouth to speak. "Yes, Mila, we're a family. The two of us, even without a child. Killing Miroslav won't bring our son back, and getting yourself killed in some senseless attempt at revenge just gives him more opportunity to hurt us."

"This isn't about me!" I hissed. "The tsar believes I can best serve him at court. I agree with him."

He took a seat on the bed, rubbing his neck. "I don't want you to leave me, Milochka."

How dare he make me feel guilty? "You mean like during the last uprising, when you left me for months? And while you're following the tsar across the country, what am I supposed to do? Sit at home and pray? It's not like we have children for me to care for."

"I'm worried." He sighed. "I'd feel better if you were at home, where I know you're safe."

"You mean safe at home like I was when those men attacked me?"

He closed his eyes, a gasp of breath escaping his lips, and I felt a rush of regret. I'd lied to him about the attack so he didn't have to bear the blame for what had happened. It wasn't fair for me to throw it in his face like that.

I sighed and forced my voice to soften. "I'd feel better if you were at home, too. Will you stay?" He wouldn't. That wasn't who he was.

He gathered me into his arms and leaned in to kiss me, but when I tensed, he pulled back.

"I don't want to lose you."

"It's just a few months," I said, fighting the urge to roll my eyes. "You'll be so busy with the tsar that you won't have time to miss me."

"Just...be careful."

His task would be the more dangerous one, raising an army, fighting a war. Shouldn't I be the one worrying? I slipped out of his grasp. "The tsar's waiting." Before he could stop me, I left him alone.

The door to the tsar's room was open. He sat in an armchair at the window, facing away from me. I knocked on the doorframe, and he turned, smiling warmly.

"Mila! I didn't expect you so soon. Please, have a seat. May I offer you a drink?"

"No, thank you, your majesty." I took the chair opposite him and looked around the room. It was well furnished, but far from ornate. A writing desk, a table, and a few chairs and stools made up all the furniture. Through an open door on the far wall, I saw a simple four-poster bed. Not exactly a fitting dwelling for a tsar.

He followed my gaze. "You must be wondering why, in the baron's castle, I would be living such a simple life."

"I wouldn't dare to presume to ask."

He poured himself a drink. "Nevertheless, you were wondering."

I gave a small smile of assent.

"You know the events of Barbezht, of course. As my brother's reinforcements arrived, I was prepared to call a retreat. My commanders, however, predicted that even with a retreat, we would be followed and slaughtered by the overwhelming number of fresh troops at Miroslav's disposal. They sent a man to pull me from my horse and see me to safety, willing or no." His face darkened. "They were right. Once I was safely off the battlefield, they called for a retreat, but they were run down and killed almost to a man. None of my advisors survived. I escaped to Andinor, where Ilya Sergeyevich was serving as the Inzhrian ambassador.

"I waited there in hiding. Finally, Ilya was able to get news to me. My cause was defeated, all my men dead, and I was rumored to have fallen on the field." His gaze grew distant. "That was a dark time for me. The death of my father, followed so closely by estrangement from my mother and brother—not that we'd ever been close—and the destruction of all I held dear..." He shook his head. "I vowed to Otets that I wouldn't live a life of luxury while my people suffer under my brother's rule. I asked Him for a second chance to defeat my brother and give new glory to the Blood."

"And you will," I said softly, moved by his story. I could imagine how the tsar had felt, cut off from all his friends and family, trapped in a foreign land with no companions.

"Otets judges rightly. He's granted me the opportunity I sought. I spent the following years traveling from country to country, trying to raise support to return to Inzhria as word of my brother's misrule spread. No one would join me, and at last I realized that I would have to return without allies. As the true Heir of the Sanctioned, I had to trust that Otets would guide me, and so here I am, ready to take my rightful place. The people will rally to me; you yourself are proof of that. With your help, the help of my people, together we'll take what I am owed."

"Otets willing." I touched my forehead in a gesture of reverence.

"Otets willing." He set down his drink, still full. "And with that in mind, Ilya's wife, my cousin Heli, will prepare you for your time at court. Her intentions are good, so I'll ask you to forgive her aggressive exterior. She's merely trying to protect me." He smiled wryly, as one would at the mention of an overprotective sibling. "She'll teach you your role and anything you'll need to know in the capital."

The tsar stood and walked across the room, taking something from a small basket on the desk. He returned with a glass bottle and a small leather pouch. "You need two things from me. First," he held up the bottle, "this is for emergencies. I pray you have no need to use it, but I would be remiss not to send it with you." He looked earnestly into my eyes. "You must not allow yourself to be captured. I cannot over-represent the importance of this. You *must not* allow yourself to be captured. My brother will torture you and make you reveal all you know about me and my cause. This is a matter of life and death, not just for you, but for the entire tsardom."

I was glad I hadn't eaten much at dinner as my stomach did flips.

"It will cause instantaneous, painless death. If you believe someone has discovered you, you must find a way to get them to consume it. And if you are captured…"

"I'm to drink it myself." I swallowed nervously. I was willing to take the risk of going to court, but if Han found out the tsar had asked me to kill myself rather than risk capture, he would do anything to stop me. He'd probably lock me in the house until the war was over, with Anna and Yakov as jailers. "I understand."

"Only use it if there are no other options, but keep it with you at all times. You may wish to sew it into your clothing to keep it hidden."

I took the bottle and placed it in my apron pocket. The tsar picked up a long white staff from behind his chair and opened the leather pouch. He took out several long black hairs.

"Second," he said, "there is the matter of your appearance."

"My appearance?" I looked down at my clothes, and my hand went to my headscarf. Surely a change in wardrobe would be addressed by the baroness or someone less important. The tsar himself didn't need to concern himself with such trivial matters.

"While unlikely, we wouldn't want you to be recognized at court. Sofia Stepanova, your new identity, is from Tsebol. The baroness will ensure you can answer for your background—that is, Sofia's background—but you must have Sofia's appearance as well as her knowledge." He wrapped the hairs around the head of his staff. "You should remain seated. The effect can be slightly disconcerting, I'm told."

"Is..." My voice cracked. I swallowed and began again. "Is Sofia Stepanova a real woman?"

"She was. She died in the recent outbreak of Moon Fever." At my look of distress, he waved a hand. "Fear not. She was a private woman, with few connections. Taking her identity will harm no one and help many."

I bit my lip to quell the nerves and nodded. The tsar touched the staff to my forehead. A tingling sensation ran through my body, and I doubled over with nausea. My vision blackened.

After a moment, my eyes cleared, and the tingling stopped. The tsar stood before me, a cup in his hand. "Apologies. I should have given you more time to prepare. Drink this; it will help."

I took a large drink. It was medovukha, and the taste of honey and the burn of alcohol in my throat washed away the lingering nausea. Once I regained my bearings, the tsar handed me a small silver mirror.

I stared at the stranger looking back at me from inside the glass. Long eyelashes framed teardrop-shaped eyes, and my skin had darkened several shades. I nervously licked my new, full lips and ran a hand over my cheek.

How had the tsar done this? I knew he had magic—as descendants of Otets, all the Sanctioned had incredible powers—but I'd never imagined something like this.

What was Han going to say?

Most importantly... "Is this permanent?"

"In a sense." The tsar removed the hairs from the staff and placed them back in their pouch. "I can undo it, easily, upon your return. And of course, my death would undo any of my active spells, this included. But it requires no maintenance, so it is permanent until I remove the spell or I die."

I bit my lip. The old habit felt strange in my new mouth. "How...?"

"How is it done?" He gave me a crooked smile. "That's a question for the philosophers, Mila Dmitrievna. The simplest explanation is that by the powers of Otets' Blood, which flows in my veins, I can sense the essence of something, what makes it what it is. I use my conduit," he gestured with the staff, "to grasp that essence and manipulate it. When I touched you with my staff, I transferred that essence, drawn from Sofia's hairs, onto you."

"Oh." That explained precisely nothing, but it wasn't my place to question the tsar. I'd been too presumptuous already.

"You'll be eager to spend your final night with your husband, I'm sure. I'll have supper brought to your room this evening. I won't see you again until your return, so I wish you success. Go with Otets, and return safely and soon."

My head was still reeling as I bowed. "I will strive to do you honor."

Han

Mila had been gone for hours. At first, I had busied myself reading, trying not to dwell on our argument, but as the afternoon lengthened, I grew anxious. She couldn't have been with the tsar all afternoon.

It wasn't uncommon for her to ignore me after a fight. Normally I would wait until she was calm enough to approach me, but with so little time left together, I didn't want to wait to seek her out. Who knew how long it would be until she returned from court and me from traveling with the tsar?

I made my way through the empty halls of the baron's wing of the castle, hoping to see Mila or someone who might know where she was. I peered into an open door and saw a dark-skinned young woman reading a book. She looked up, and her eyes widened at the sight of me.

"Apologies. I didn't realize this room was occupied. I was looking for my wife."

She bit her lip, looking almost guilty. Had I seen her somewhere before? Maybe she'd been at the market last time I was in Tsebol.

I gave a small bow. "I'll leave you to your reading." I turned to go, but she called after me.

"Han."

Had we met before? I frowned at her. "I'm sorry...?"

"It's me." She stood, biting her lip again.

That expression. It was just like— "Mila?"

Words rushed out of her in a tumble. "I didn't know he was going to do it. I went to see him, and he said we needed to do something about my appearance, and then he pulled out these hairs and put them on his staff, and the next thing I knew I was a different person. He said he can change me back as soon as I return."

I leaned against the doorframe for support. Opening my mouth, I closed it again without speaking.

"It won't be permanent," the woman in front of me repeated.

"Mila?"

"I...think so." She raised a hand to the cloud of tight curls on her head, and I noticed Mila's headscarf on the chair where she'd been sitting. "Strictly speaking, I suppose I'm Sofia Stepanova now. At least, my body is." As I stumbled to a chair, she twisted her hands together "You could say something, you know."

"What do you want me to say?" I ran my hand over my face. "A little warning would have been nice."

"It's not like I knew it was coming," she snapped. Yes, that was definitely Mila. "If the tsar had told me he was going to do it, I would have told you."

"I'm sorry. It just surprised me, is all."

"Do you—do you like it, though?" She stepped back, watching my face.

I looked her up and down, but stopped short when I saw her pursed lips. "Of course," I said quickly.

"Hm." She sat down and picked up her book again, obviously disappointed with my reaction. "Well, you won't have to see me like this for long. The tsar will change me back when I return."

"No, really, Mila, I do. It's just..." I fumbled for the right word. "Different. I mean, of course I prefer you to this stranger. But I'll always love you, no matter whose body you wear." I grabbed her hand and pulled her to me for a kiss. It felt different, like kissing a stranger, but she didn't pull away.

"Will you come back to the room?" I asked as we broke apart.

She pressed a trembling hand to her lips, a gesture of uncertainty and desire that I hadn't seen from her in years. "Yes," she whispered.

I led her by the hand back to our room, racing from one emotion to the next. Anger at the tsar for changing her and at her for letting him. Pride that she would do what she felt was right no matter the consequences. Guilt that I couldn't protect her, and an aching need to be close to her.

We reached the suite, and she pulled me through the sitting room into the bedroom. She closed the door and locked it behind us, then threw her arms around me and kissed me fiercely.

I staggered at the weight of her embrace, wrapping my arms around her. What was happening? She hadn't let me touch her in weeks, had pulled away from even the most chaste of kisses. I pulled back, looking into her stranger's eyes.

"I'm sorry," she murmured. "If I'd known..."

"It's not your fault." Not her fault she'd changed. Not her fault those men had beat her so brutally that she couldn't stand to be touched. None of it was her fault.

She leaned in to kiss me again, and I pulled back. "Mila, what are you doing?"

She slid a hand underneath my shirt. "What does it look like I'm doing?"

I grabbed her hand, but she slid the other down my chest instead.

"This isn't you. You don't want this."

"Yes, I do." She looked up at me through heavy-lidded eyes.

Fuck, I wanted her. It had been so long, and that passionate look on her face, on that stranger's face, was so familiar, so like Mila.

I shook myself. No. It would be like being with a stranger. "You haven't let me touch you in weeks, Mila. You've hardly even let me kiss you. You can't expect everything to change just because you're..." I gestured to her new body.

She huffed and took a seat on the bed. "I just feel different, Han. In my body, as me, every touch reminded me of how they hurt me. But in this body, it's like all of that was erased. I feel like me again." Her voice, already deeper in the new body, turned husky. "And I want you."

The words sent a thrill of forbidden desire through me, followed by guilt and pain. My touch had hurt her, made her feel like those bastards were touching her all over again?

Something niggled at the back of my mind. It didn't make sense that a simple beating, however brutal, would make her respond like that. Did it?

What else could they have done? They couldn't have ra— I couldn't even finish the thought. She wouldn't have lied to me. They hadn't touched her like that.

She rose from her seat and wrapped her arms around my neck, twisting her fingers in my hair. "It could be months before we get to be with each other again. I don't want to leave things like they have been. Please."

I'd have to be a saint to resist her. With a groan, I let her pull the shirt over my head and run a hand down my muscled chest. Even her hands felt different, softer than Mila's garden-callused hands. She tugged my pants off, leaving me naked before her.

"Help me out of these clothes?"

I moved slowly, hesitatingly as I untied her apron and let it fall to the floor, followed by her skirt. Her shift clung tight to the new body, which was shorter and rounder than her own. I found myself looking away in discomfort.

She touched my cheek. "Look at me, Han." I did. "Please. Don't leave me like this."

I traced her new face. The eyes were different, but the expressions, the person behind them, were the same. "You'll come back to me, won't you?"

She pulled me down onto the bed next to her. "Give me something to come back to."

She kissed me again, then. Her plump lips tasted like honey. My hand roamed her body, reveling in the strange new sensations. Mila fit perfectly in my arms, but this stranger's body was soft, molding against me. Pleasure and shame warred within me. This wasn't my wife. How could I be finding enjoyment in a stranger's body? But it had been so long since we'd been together. She moaned as my fingers found a nipple.

I needed her. Desperately. I straddled her, deepening our kiss, pinning her to the bed.

She froze. Every muscle in her body went taut, and her breath came in short gasps.

I scrambled off the bed. Had I hurt her? Her eyes were wild and unfocused.

"Mila?"

She let out a whimper, but her gaze focused on me. She reached out, chin quivering.

Thank Otets. I'd expected her to push me away again. I gathered her onto my lap and pressed a gentle kiss to the small, textured curls on her head. "Did I hurt you?"

She shook her head, breaths still short but growing more even. "I'm sorry. I just need a minute."

"You're safe." I rubbed circles on her back. "You're safe."

We lay there for a few minutes in silence. Gradually, the tension in her body eased and her breathing became normal. I leaned down to brush my lips against hers.

The moment our mouths touched, she pulled me in closer, deepening the kiss. Her tongue flicked out, and she wrapped her arms around my neck.

"What are you doing?"

"Continuing where we left off." She trailed a finger down my chest. Lower.

I bit back a gasp as she palmed my length. "You just panicked. We can't keep going."

"Says who?"

I gingerly removed her hand. "Mila, no. I'm not doing this. You're not okay."

"I am." She knelt next to me and kissed a trail along my shoulder. I shivered as her breasts brushed my arm. "I need this."

"If you need this, why did you panic?" I forced myself to focus on the words, even as all the blood in my body rushed to my cock. I had to be firm. Hold onto my resolve. Someone had to protect her from herself.

"I'm fine." She pushed me onto my back, straddling my waist.

"Mila..." I groaned as she kissed down my body. "We can't do this."

"Han." She positioned herself over me. "I'm fine."

I needed her so badly it hurt, but I couldn't do this. I rolled her onto the bed next to me and reached for my pants. "You're not fine, and I'm not going to pretend you are. You can't even have sex with your husband without growing hysterical. How do you expect to survive at court like this?"

"I don't expect to be *having sex* at court," she hissed.

"No, just risking your life." I pulled my pants up and tied them. Feeling less vulnerable now that I was partially clothed, I turned back to her. "It's only been two months since you were hurt, and you can still hardly bear to be touched. What do you think it's going to be like, spending weeks, maybe even months in the court of that monster, constantly at risk of being exposed? The only thing you're going to achieve is getting yourself killed. I won't allow it."

"Won't allow it?" Her voice rose, and she stood, gathering her own clothes. "I wasn't asking your *permission*. The tsar has work for me, and I have every intention of doing it. Just because you think I'm not strong enough doesn't mean I'm not."

"It's not that I don't think you're strong enough, Milochka." I reached for her, but she stepped away. "You're the strongest woman I know. But you're not ready for this, and I can't risk letting you go. I can't risk losing you."

"You don't get to decide what I'm ready for. You don't get to decide where I can go or what I can do." She threw her clothing on, the movements stiff with anger. "It's my choice, and I choose to take the risk."

With that, she threw the door open and stormed out, leaving me alone in the bedroom with my heart in pieces.

12

BECOMING SOFIA

Mila

I didn't go back to Han that night. I was too angry, my emotions raw. How dare he treat me like a child? Why was it acceptable for him to join the war, but not for me to do the same? I had just as much right as him to defend my tsar. I was just as strong as he was.

An obliging servant found me another guest room I could use for the night, as far from Han as possible. I spent the rest of the day pacing and fuming. A little after sunset, I finally fell asleep, lying clothed on the bed atop the quilts

"Good morning, Sofia!"

A cheery voice woke me, and I bolted upright. A woman with pale white, almost grayish skin and coal-black hair stood smiling at me from the foot of the bed.

"Get up, sleepyhead." She tossed a bundle of clothes at me and winked. "Izolda Vasilievna. I work here in the castle. We've known each other since childhood."

I sat up, face burning. I was going to give myself away before I even got to court. Did she know who I was, or did she think I was the real Sofia Stepanova? "I'm sorry, Izolda—"

She cut me off. "You don't have to pretend that you know me. I was the closest thing Sofia Stepanova had to a friend, and one of only a few people who know she died." She grinned. "Don't worry. The baroness sent me. I'm to help you get comfortable in your new life. Get dressed."

I reached for the bundle of clothes. The long yellow sleeves of the shift were embroidered with red thread, and the thick fabric of the sarafan was a rich scarlet, embroidered with blue. A blue belt tumbled onto the bed as I unfolded the dress.

I slipped behind the privacy screen and changed quickly, coming out again fully dressed. Izolda hadn't given me a headscarf, and my hair puffed out around my head in a cloud of tiny curls.

"Do you have a headscarf?" I asked, twisting a curl around my finger. "I'm not sure how to braid this." The texture of Sofia's hair was thicker and coarser than my own, and I had a feeling my usual three-strand plait wouldn't keep all the tiny curls in place.

"No headscarf. Sofia isn't married." Izolda frowned. "I'll have to braid it for you. Lady Heli is expecting us. I'll teach you how to do it later." She dug in her pocket and drew out a comb, a small jar, and a povyazka. She handed me the povyazka; the thick headband was blue, embroidered with red and yellow flowers to match the sarafan.

"Sit," she commanded, pointing to a chair. I did, and she began attacking my new hair with the comb, separating it into sections. "It's a good thing I was prepared, or we would have had to spend all morning searching the castle for oil and a comb."

Unsure of how to respond, I remained silent.

Izolda laughed. "You'll do fine. You're as taciturn as the real Sofia was."

"Sorry," I said. "I'm a little nervous."

"Don't be. Fia was an accomplished seamstress, but she wasn't social. She was born here in Tsebol. Her mother died in childbirth, and her father apprenticed her to a seamstress. When the seamstress died, she took over the practice. Her father died at Sobralen in service to the tsar—Tsar Miroslav, that is. She had no siblings, and no particular attachments."

"How sad that she died with no one to miss her."

"You're too sweet," Izolda said. "I think she was happy enough, though. Her work was her life. She'd be glad to know that her legacy lives on after her."

"Even if it's being used to bring down Miroslav?"

"We didn't talk about politics, but I didn't get the idea she cared who sat on the throne. As I said, being a seamstress was her life. She wasn't interested in much beyond that."

The enormity of my actions struck me then. I'd taken on more than just a new body. This identity, this person I'd become, was a person. She'd had a life, opinions and desires of her own. Moon Fever killed her, but now I had her life. Her name, her face. I had to give her a legacy worth remembering.

"You don't need to worry about imitating her, though," Izolda went on, oblivious to my inner turmoil. "No one at court knew her, and she'd never been to the capital. You'll need to be more social than she was if you want to succeed at court. The more connections you have, the more likely you are to hear something important. Which, by the way, you'll pass on to me—or to the baroness, if need be. We have a connection in the city guard who can pass messages out, but it's best if you don't meet with him directly."

She took a deep breath before continuing. "Sofia's father fought for Miroslav in the rebellion, but before that he owned a smithy. She wasn't close to him, but he apprenticed her off when she was young—about four, I think—and she never really saw him after that. He sent money for her upkeep, but he was busy working in the smithy before the uprising, and then, of course, he was killed. Think you can remember all that?"

"I was born in Tsebol. My mother died in childbirth, and my father was a smith who died in the battle of Sobralen in service of Tsar Miroslav. I was apprenticed when I was four and took over the seamstress's practice when she died."

"Perfect!" Izolda sounded genuinely pleased.

Once the braid was finished, she took the povyazka and arranged it on my head. Observing her handiwork, she grinned. "You'll do. Come on, the baroness will be waiting."

I tried to look around inconspicuously as we walked through the warm, spacious hallways of the castle. The wing she led me to was much the same as the baron's private wing where I'd slept, though more populated. We reached a sitting room, and Izolda knocked on the frame of the open door and entered without waiting for an answer.

Next to the window sat an older woman in a silver kokoshnik. The high headdress resembled a halo over her serene figure as she remained focused on her writing. Izolda gave a small cough.

She glanced at us. Her eyes and mouth were wrinkled with laugh lines, but she wasn't smiling. "You're late."

"Apologies, my lady."

The baroness, Lady Heli, waved a hand. "No matter. Close the door. Come here, girl." She crooked a finger at me, and I took a cautious step forward. "From this moment on, you are Sofia Stepanova, my seamstress. I don't need to know who you were—unless and until your assignment is complete, whoever you were is dead. You will answer only to your new name. You will have no contact with anyone from your previous life. Do you understand?"

I nodded, though my chest tightened as the implications of my hasty decision hit me. No contact with anyone from my previous life. Months without word from Han, Anna, and Yakov.

"Good. You may sit."

I took a seat on a low stool across from her, and she gave me an appraising look.

"In case the tsar neglected to impress on you the gravity of your position, you must know the responsibility you hold." Her voice lowered. "By going to the capital, you are responsible for the safety of not only yourself, but also every other supporter of his majesty. A single misspoken word could reveal the rebellion. While you are at court, you are not to breathe a word about the tsar or his followers. If you betray us, whether intentionally or not, you had best pray to Otets that Miroslav finds you before I do, because what he will do to a spy is nothing to what I will do to a traitor. Do I make myself clear?"

My mouth was cottony. I swallowed hard. "Yes, my lady."

"Good." The baroness turned back to her writing. "Where are you from?"

"Tsebol, my lady."

"And your parents?"

"My mother died in childbirth, and my father died at Sobralen serving Tsar Miroslav."

"Where is your seamstress practice?"

"I—" I cast a nervous glance at Izolda. "Here in Tsebol."

The baroness's sharp eyes pierced me again. "Where *exactly?*" When I didn't answer, she huffed. "Izolda, did you teach her nothing?"

"We've only had a half hour, my lady. I'll have her ready."

"You will. Take her through the city. She should be as familiar with it as any local before we leave."

Izolda inclined her head. "Yes, Lady Heli."

The baroness turned back to me. "You will also examine my dresses to acquaint yourself with the styles of court and your work as a seamstress. I assume you are fully trained in the trade?"

I nodded, afraid to speak again.

"Good. You're dismissed."

I stood and gave a bow that the baroness ignored. As the door closed behind us, I let out a small sigh of relief. Izolda laughed.

"She's a little frightening, *da?* Don't worry about it. You'll do fine. Stay on her good side, and you won't find anyone more loyal."

I'd be sure to follow Izolda's advice. Lady Heli was a formidable woman despite her age. I prayed we'd never be enemies.

I didn't see Han as we left the castle, and I soon found myself too overwhelmed with information to think about him. Izolda led me through the busy streets and kept up a constant stream of chatter, interspersing stories about Sofia's childhood with explanations about the city.

"There's your father's old smithy," she said, pointing as we neared the market square. It was market day, and the square was full of people. Izolda stopped at a table full of hair ornaments to pick up a povyazka and a matching kosnik, a decoration for the end of a braid. Both were embellished with seed pearls. "Spider's Blood, isn't this gorgeous? I have to get it." She paid the woman behind the table, tucking the pieces into her pocket. "Mind you, I have no idea where I'll wear it. It's too formal for anything I go to with the baroness, but maybe I'll find an excuse to put it on at court somewhere." She led me deeper into the crowd. "Your shop's on the other side of the square, but you haven't eaten yet, have you?"

I shook my head.

"You like pryaniki?"

"They're my favorite!" The honey-sweet cookies, flavored with spices, sounded like the perfect breakfast.

We pushed through the teeming market crowd until we reached the baker's tent. A young woman was coming out; she saw us approach and smiled. "What can I get you?"

"Ulyana!" Had it only been a day since I'd seen her? It felt like ages.

She frowned in confusion. "I'm sorry, have we met?"

"Sofia Stepanova owns the seamstress shop on the other side of the market," Izolda broke in.

"Right," I said, my face heating. "We met at the market last week." I wasn't Mila right now. I was Sofia. I had to remember that.

Ulyana smiled again, embarrassment written on her face. "I'm sorry. I see so many people in the week, I don't remember everyone. Sofia Stepanova, is it? Well, it's a pleasure to meet you again. What can I get you?"

"Two orders of pryaniki," Izolda said.

"I'll be right back with them."

She disappeared into the tent, and I leaned closer to Izolda. "I...used to know her."

"Just be careful. You shouldn't come across too many people you know, right? We leave for court soon, anyway."

Once our purchase was made, we made our way back into the crowd. I nibbled on my cookies without tasting them, appetite gone. I couldn't do this. I was going to get us all killed.

Izolda stopped in front of a small storefront. "Here we are, Fia." She pushed open the door and gestured for me to enter. "Home."

The room we entered was dark and stuffy from being closed up. I stopped in the doorway, a sudden sense of foreboding locking my feet in place.

"Go on," Izolda said, not unkindly. "You'll be fine."

I took a deep breath and stepped inside.

Despite my first impression, the building was a fairly ordinary seamstress shop. Fabric lay draped over every surface, along with other tools of the trade.

Izolda gestured at a loft above us. "She slept upstairs. All her outstanding orders have been completed, and we told her regular customers she would be leaving the city, so she won't be missed."

I walked around the shop, letting my fingers trace the fabric. Was my own life so easily dismissed as well? A few small actions had been enough to erase Sofia's entire existence in this town. Would it be as easy for Han to erase mine? Or would everything go back to normal when I returned from court?

No, my life wouldn't go back to normal afterward. The tsar had promised to ennoble Han after the war—and Yakov, and every other survivor of Barbezht that supported him. We'd have to leave the farm behind and move to the new land the tsar gave us.

But unlike Sofia, I could come back to my friends and family, if not to my home. Help the tsar win the war. Make Miroslav and his men pay for what they took from me. Then I could go back. I could tell Anna, Yakov, and all the rest what I'd done and why I'd done it. My life wasn't the same as Sofia's at all.

I climbed the ladder into the loft. A wool-stuffed mattress lay on the floor next to a wooden chest. I knelt and opened the chest, ignoring the guilt that gnawed at my stomach. Sofia was dead. What was it the tsar had told me? *Taking her identity will harm no one and help many.*

I took a deep breath and rifled through the contents of the chest. It contained nothing personal, just some clothing and candles. No insight into who Sofia might have been.

Izolda's head peeked up from the ladder. "We'll have the chest brought to the castle, but you should pack up anything else you want." She cast an eye around the barren loft. "Not that there's much up here."

I nodded, closing the lid of the chest. "Let's go pack up my tools."

13

SETTING OUT

Mila

The next few days went by in a whirlwind. I spent my time refining my seamstress skills and learning about Sofia Stepanova. With the baroness's order not to contact anyone from my previous life, I did my best to stay away from Han, who had gone home for a single night before returning to the baron's castle in Tsebol. Avoiding him was easier said than done; his efforts to speak with me grew more frantic each time I rebuffed him. I hated leaving things the way they were between us, but we would both be safer if we didn't see each other until I returned.

The day before I was to leave for the capital, I was walking through the castle when someone grabbed my hand and pulled me into an alcove hidden behind a large tapestry.

"Han!" I breathed. "We can't be seen like this."

He pulled me close and pressed his lips to my forehead. "I was afraid I wouldn't get to see you at all before you left." Holding me at arm's length, he looked into my eyes. "You've been avoiding me."

"I had to." Footsteps approached, and I froze, hardly daring to breathe. After a moment, the footsteps receded. I glared at Han. "You'll give me away before I even reach the capital. It's not safe."

He drew my mouth to his, and despite my worries, I melted beneath his touch. Otets' Blood. I needed to stay away from him, for both our sakes, but the muscles of his chest beneath my hands, the feel of his tongue as it slipped into my mouth... A thrill ran through me, and everything left my mind. Every touch felt different now. Stronger, more intense.

No, that wasn't true. It didn't feel different; it felt like it had before I'd been attacked. I felt normal again in this stranger's body. Han's hand roamed my back, and I shivered with desire.

Too soon, he broke our embrace. "Don't go, Mila."

"Don't start." Why couldn't he let me do this? "You'll be the one waging a war."

"And you'll be the one in the viper's nest. What sort of man would I be, sitting at home while my wife goes into danger?"

"A sensible one. You can't even fight." He winced at the reminder of his uselessness on the battlefield. I instantly regretted my words, but I couldn't take them back.

"I won't be fighting. The tsar wants me to advise him, to raise support. I won't be anywhere near the battles." I could hear the longing in his voice, though. He was a soldier at heart. He wanted nothing more than to carry a sword for his tsar again. "I don't want to argue, Milochka. Just reconsider. Please. The tsar won't force you to go."

I took a step back. "Don't." A bell chimed somewhere in the distance, reminding me of the time. Shit. If Lady Heli found out about this... "I have to go."

I peered out of the alcove. The hall was clear, but before I could step out, Han swept me back up into a kiss.

"Don't forget who you are, Mila Dmitrievna," he said, touching his forehead to mine. "Come back to me."

The look on his face was pure desperation, and it tore at my heart. "I will." Before I could lose my resolve, I pulled from his arms and ran down the hall.

Just after dawn the next morning, the baron's household set out. Atop my borrowed horse, I scanned the crowd that waited to see us off. Where was he?

There, in the back of the courtyard. Han stood watching me from the shadows, his face melancholy. I nodded at him, trying to convey with my eyes what I couldn't say—that I loved him, that I'd be back soon, that I wouldn't forget him. That I was doing this for him, no matter how much he thought otherwise. He mouthed, "I love you," and I smiled back. I couldn't mouth the words back to him. Not with so many eyes around us.

I passed through the gate, and he was gone.

"Ugh." Izolda, riding next to me, groaned. "Two weeks on the road. I hope you packed warm, Fia. I don't know whose idea it was to travel just before the snow, but they must be out of their mind. Nights won't be so bad, since we'll stay at inns and such. But if we're going to get there before the season changes again, we'll have to push hard. And you'd best pray it doesn't rain at all."

She was right. The wind was already biting cold, and hours out riding in it were sure to be miserable. "Have you been before?"

"To court? Every year. My mother was Lady Heli's maidservant before me. She brought me along to help with small jobs as soon as I was old enough. She left the baroness's service when I was able to take over. My grandmother insisted she shouldn't be working for the humans at her age. It was 'undignified.'"

I frowned at Izolda. "Are you Drakra?" She had to be, at least in part, though she didn't look it. Why else would she call the baroness human?

She laughed. "A quarter. Why do you think I'm so colorless? My grandfather was taken prisoner in the second Spider War, where he met my grandmother. When he was released, he convinced her to come back west with him." She tossed her braid over her shoulder. "So my blood runs black—or at least a quarter black. Mind, it's a pain in my ass. Do you know how much rouge I have to wear every day to keep my cheeks pink?"

With the wind-chapped flush in Izolda's face, I never would have guessed at her inhuman heritage. Now that I looked close, though, I could see that her eyes were more yellow than brown, and while she wasn't unusually short for a human, her Drakra ancestry could account for her height, as well.

I was fascinated. "I've never met a Drakra before." My older brother, Sergey, lived near the East Mountains and traded with Drakra regularly, but I'd been too busy to visit since he'd moved east.

"I'm not really Drakra. Just a quarter. I grew up around humans. This is about the only interesting thing my black blood gave me." She held up a hand, and shadows wreathed it. "A touch of shadow-melding. Nothing like my mother can do."

My mouth dropped open. "You can control shadows?"

"A bit." She shrugged. "It's an entirely useless skill."

I could think of several uses, but my mind was spinning too much to contradict her. She glanced at the train of people ahead of us. "Come on," she said. "We're falling behind."

Han

Mila was gone. I tried not to dwell on it, but I was already packed for my own journey, and there was little else to do. I went to the stables, hoping the presence of the animals would soothe my troubled mind.

Why hadn't I tried harder to make her stay? I could have told the tsar she needed to be at home. He would have understood, at least. Anna and Yakov could have kept her there. She would have hated me, but at least she would have been safe. Or as safe as she could be with all these rabid soldiers roaming around.

It was too late now.

Our old mare looked up as I reached her stall. "Hello, old friend," I murmured, rubbing her nose. "How are you settling in?" The black beast nuzzled me, searching for a carrot or a lump of sugar. That was Mila's fault—she spoiled our horses. My heart clenched at the thought. "No treats today."

Once she'd determined I had nothing in my pockets to interest her, the horse turned away.

"There's no need to ignore me." I leaned against the door of the stall. "I suppose it's for the best that I can't take you with me. There's no treats on the road. You'd be miserable."

"On the road to where?" A familiar voice came from the stable doors behind me.

I turned slowly, heart pounding. "Yakov."

"You *absolute bastard.*" The younger man stepped forward and swung, his fist connecting with my nose. "How could you?"

I stepped out of his reach and pressed a hand to my stinging nose. Blood poured from it. "I'm sorry," I said, my eyes stinging.

"You're *sorry?* You disappear without a word, and we have to find out from your *steward* that Mila almost died of Moon Fever and we won't see either of you for months?" Yakov's arms hung at his sides, his fist still clenched. I took another step back in case he decided to hit me again. "I went to see Ulyana and her husband, hoping they could tell me where exactly you'd gone, and they didn't even know Mila was sick! They told me I might find news here at the castle, but I didn't expect to find you here."

This was why I'd left so quickly, why I hadn't told Yakov where I was going. I couldn't lie to my friend.

His shoulders drooped, and he sank onto a bale of straw. "What's going on, Han? Why are you here?"

"I—" I paused, rubbing my neck. I'd planned to write to Yakov, to tell him the truth once the army had gathered and it was safe to put word in writing, but he was here now. The tsar would want to meet him. "Come with me."

My nose, thankfully, had stopped bleeding. I wiped the blood from my face as I led him through the silent halls of the castle, into the baron's private wing, and stopped in the small dining hall. "Stay here."

"Where are you—" Yakov began, but I was already gone

An inconspicuous guard sat outside the tsar's door, a safety measure intended to draw as little attention as possible. He nodded in recognition as I knocked on the tsar's open door.

"Han!" Tsar Borislav said. "Come in. What can I do for you?"

"I told you about Yakov Aleksandrovich, another survivor of Barbezht and my dearest friend. He just arrived here at the castle. With your majesty's permission, I would like to present him to you. And..." I paused, unsure of how to continue.

"You wish to tell him the truth about your wife." Borislav folded his hands together, looking thoughtful.

"I can vouch for his loyalty and secrecy, your majesty. He's never accepted your brother's rule, and he would never do anything to endanger Mila or betray your cause. If he meets you, if he knows you're alive, he'll know I lied about Mila, that she's involved in this all somehow. He—"

The tsar held up a hand, forestalling the flow of my words. "I trust your judgment. If you feel it necessary to tell him the truth, I will allow it. I ask that it go no further." He gave a warm smile. "And I would be honored to meet Yakov Aleksandrovich."

"Thank you, your majesty." Heart thundering with excitement, I hurried back to fetch my friend.

"What in the name of the Blood are you doing?" Yakov asked as I gestured for him to follow.

"There's someone I want you to meet." With a grin, I led Yakov past the silent guard into the tsar's quarters. "Yakov Aleksandrovich, may I present his majesty, Tsar Borislav Vyacheslavovich of the Blood, Heir of the Sanctioned and rightful ruler of Inzhria."

Yakov's face turned white, and he dropped to one knee.

"Rise, Yakov Aleksandrovich." The tsar's face was solemn, but his eyes were bright with amusement.

He stood, looking between me and the tsar with a wide-eyed stare.

"Han has told me much about you. I thank you for your service, sir." The tsar inclined his head.

Yakov opened his mouth to respond, then closed it again.

"Please, sit." Borislav smiled. "I fear you'll collapse if you remain standing much longer."

Slowly, Yakov sank into the offered seat. Too animated to sit, I clapped my friend on the back. "It's real, Yakov! He's alive."

When Yakov remained silent, mouth opening and closing like a fish, the tsar smiled at me. "Han, I believe you've brought me a mute. Did my brother take your tongue on the battlefield as well as your hand, Yakov Aleksandrovich?"

Yakov shook himself. "Your majesty, I don't know what to say. I am your man." He placed his wrist over his heart.

The tsar inclined his head. "I thank you for your allegiance."

"And there's something else." I paused, looking to Tsar Borislav for confirmation. He nodded for me to go on. "This can't leave this room. Not even your mother can know."

He furrowed his brow. "Whatever you need."

"The tsar offered both of us—me and Mila, I mean—positions serving him. I'm going to travel with him to help him raise his army, and Mila...Mila went to court." I watched for a reaction, but Yakov's face remained blank.

"Mila Dmitrievna has taken on an alternate identity and is traveling to court with Lord Ilya and Lady Heli," the tsar explained. "She's graciously agreed to do so in order to pass information to me about my brother. I regret that you were deceived, but it was necessary that no one question her absence and discover where she had gone."

"I understand." He didn't appear to, but I knew he wouldn't say so to the tsar. When we were alone again, I would have a lot to answer for.

I wondered briefly if I should find some sort of shield, given Yakov's tendency to think with his fist.

"Enough about that," the tsar said. "Let us have a drink, and you must tell me all about yourself." He took from his desk a bottle and three mugs. "Han tells me you helped each other home after Barbezht. You must have been very young. What brought someone of your age to the battlefield?"

Yakov accepted a mug. "My father died fighting for you, your majesty. Early days, at Zavusy." He took a swallow of his drink. "I wanted to take his place, so I found a unit that would take me. Had to tell them I was older than I was, but they didn't look too close. They'd lost a lot of men, needed anyone they could get."

I accepted my own mug and took a drink, watching the two men. The taste of mint and rye filled my mouth—mint kvass. Mila had started some before we left; it would probably be finished by now.

I dragged my thoughts from my absent wife and refocused on the conversation.

"I'm sorry that any of my commanders would have accepted children." A steely glint came into the tsar's dark eyes. "That will not happen again. I will not have our country's future maimed and killed on the battlefield."

"I don't regret it, your majesty," Yakov said. "I mean, obviously, if I had the choice, I'd take my hand back in an instant. But I'm glad I got to serve you, and I hope to again." He looked down at his arm, where his sword hand had once been. "If I can, I mean. I don't think I'd be much use on the battlefield, but I would like to help your majesty in any way I can."

"If I'm to win the throne, I will need all the support I can get. Han Antonovich will be traveling with me to raise troops, and I have others around the country doing the same. If you could call for men to join me and be ready to march when I send word, you would be rendering a service most necessary."

"I'd be honored to, your majesty."

I clapped my friend on the back. "Thank you for granting us this audience, your majesty. We'll leave you to your work."

"You'll be ready to leave at dawn?" Borislav asked me.

"Yes, your majesty. Until tomorrow." I bowed.

Yakov rose and bowed as well. We walked out of the castle and into the empty courtyard. I glanced sideways at him. "If you're going to hit me, you'll give me a warning, right?"

"Why would I hit you?"

"Why do you ever?" I rubbed my nose, which was still tender from his earlier punch. "I thought you'd be mad at me for keeping secrets. I did plan on telling you. I just thought it would be safer for everyone if we waited until the tsar was ready to declare himself openly."

"I'm glad you didn't wait. I would've had to hunt you down and kick your ass." Yakov gave me a crooked grin. "I should get home. I told Mama I'd be back tonight. I'll keep it to myself, but if you hear from Mila, tell her I'm praying, *da?*"

I hugged him. "I will. And tell Anna I'm sorry for leaving without saying goodbye. Mila can't write, but I'll write when I can. We'll be home in a few months."

Yakov elbowed me in the ribs. "I thought I told you not to hug me in public. You'll ruin my reputation."

"Shove off, *durachok.*" I grinned as I watched the younger man exit the same gates Mila had gone through just a couple hours earlier, my heart considerably lighter. We would all make it through this war.

14

RAISING SUPPORT

Han

I picked at the bean-filled glove strapped to my wrist, the disguise for my missing hand. I'd never become accustomed to wearing anything on that arm, no matter how often I'd had to do it, but I was too conspicuous without the glove. The Blood Brothers we traveled with had provided me and the tsar with their red-trimmed white robes, the mark of their order, and with Otets' blessing, we would reach our destination undetected by Miroslav.

The Brothers had taken a vow of poverty, so we journeyed on foot. I longed for my horse, if only to increase our speed. It would take us two days to reach the first town, and nearly a fortnight to reach Prince Radomir's dacha, his country home, where the tsar intended to petition his cousin for support in the upcoming war.

"Does it hurt?" the tsar, walking beside me, asked. I looked askance, and he nodded at the glove.

"Not much." I shrugged. "It'll chafe by tonight. I don't usually wear anything on it for this long, except during the harvest."

"I'm certain one of the brothers will have a salve for you."

"Mila makes salves for me and Yakov during the harvest." After spending the day in the hot sun, it was a relief to come home and let her spread her ointments on my aching muscles. She always smelled like whatever herbs she'd been working with—leckozht and comfrey, garlic and mint. I often teased her that she smelled like a roast dinner. I smiled at the memory.

"A woman of many talents," the tsar said. "Have no fear for your wife. Otets will protect her."

"Yes, your majesty." I believed that, truly, but faith didn't always translate to emotion.

"I believe we should avoid such formalities on the road, Han. First names only, and no bowing or deference. Out in the open as we are, any such behavior could get back to my brother."

"Of course." Many boys had been named for the princes; another Borislav traveling the countryside would not be questioned.

"I pray we are successful with Radomir. If we can persuade him to join us, we should have the numbers needed to campaign openly against my brother."

Prince Radomir, next in line after Borislav, commanded the loyalty of nearly a third of the country. Without him, this war was doomed before it even began.

Borislav sighed. "I must admit, it hurts my pride to depend so much on others to plead my case."

I skirted a puddle left by the overnight rain. "My father used to say a good leader knew when to let others take the lead."

"Your father was a wise man. And your mother, does she still live?"

"She died giving birth to me."

"Ah." The tsar's face crinkled with sympathy. "So you have no siblings?"

"My father had three daughters with his first wife, but we've never been close. My mother was the same age as my oldest sister, and they were all three married before I was born."

"And your wife? Does she have any family?"

This section of the road was heavily rutted, forcing me to watch where I stepped as I answered. "Her father and younger sister died of Moon Fever years ago. Her mother lives with Mila's older brother and his wife and children near the East Mountains." Another reason I shouldn't have let Mila go. Dobromila Nikolaevna hated me; if she found out I'd allowed her daughter to go to court as a spy against Tsar Miroslav, she'd probably arrange a gruesome death for me. I wouldn't put anything past her.

"A pity they live so far away," the tsar said. "It must cause her pain."

"Her mother is a...difficult woman. I think Mila would be more pained if they lived closer."

"Ah. I can understand the sentiment. My own mother is similarly difficult. Though I hope your wife's mother has never attempted to have her killed?" He raised a brow in question.

I choked on a laugh. "No, I can't say she has. Nor me, despite her dislike of me and disapproval of our marriage." I considered the tsar before looking ahead at the Blood Brothers talking amongst themselves. "Did your mother truly try to kill you? I thought that was a rumor." I'd heard the tsarina—now dowager tsarina—had attempted to have Borislav assassinated when she heard that her husband favored him for the succession. The throne typically passed to the eldest son, but given that Miroslav was only older by a few hours, the question had been raised by the tsar's advisors as to whether Borislav was better suited to the task.

"True, unfortunately." The tsar took out his water pouch and raised it. "To difficult mothers."

We reached our destination early afternoon on the second day. The Brothers had arranged housing for us in the temple, and a number of men from the town had been invited to the temple that evening, ostensibly to discuss a repair of the roof.

"The first test of your skills, Han," the tsar said when our host informed us of the meeting. "I will await your return."

Borislav wouldn't attend the meeting, for his protection. The Brothers were confident that the men they had invited would be open to joining the rebellion, but it wasn't worth the risk of betrayal. If I was captured, my life was in danger, but if Borislav was captured, the whole rebellion would be over before it began in earnest. If pressed, I was to indicate that the tsar was raising support in the east.

That evening, I sat in the corner of a small room in the temple as locals trickled in alone or in pairs. They were as widely varied as any town I'd seen. A bespectacled man with dark skin and short, coiled hair was, I assumed, a lawyer. He entered with a fair-skinned, yellow-haired man whose muscles and scars indicated he was the village smith. A small group with dirt on their clothes from a day's hard work came in laughing, followed by a harried-looking man whose fingers were stained with ink. The first few men gave me a curious look, but once the room began to fill up, they mostly ignored me, talking among themselves.

"Heard your wife's expecting again. What is this, number twelve?"

"Get that plow fixed?"

"Saw your oldest in the market last week. How long until the wedding?"

I tapped my foot impatiently. Why didn't we start already? Ages passed before the Blood Brother finally stood in front of the room.

"Welcome, brothers, in the name of Otets." The chatter died down as everyone turned their attention to the priest. "We are gathered here to honor our tsar."

A murmur of dissent ran through the assembled crowd. The Brother raised his hand.

"Yes, to honor our tsar, for that is his due as the Heir of the Sanctioned. A firstborn son, a father's heir, deserves the respect of his brothers, and we are all brothers of the tsar, children of our creator Otets."

A trickle of sweat ran down my back. Had Tsar Borislav been duped into taking a supporter of Miroslav into his circle? This man, this priest, was calling for loyalty to the man responsible for the loss of my hand, for the army that ran roughshod over the country, hurting and killing at will. He was calling for honor toward the monster responsible for the death of my son. I trembled with anger, watching as the Brother paced in front of the muttering crowd.

"Our tsar has done no great crime, done nothing to forfeit our honor. He has not sacrificed his position as Heir. After all, which of you would disinherit your firstborn for such minor infractions as our tsar has committed?" He stopped in front of a stout bald man. "Would you, Abram, disinherit Mikhail for the murder of his brothers? Or you, Nikolai," he gestured at another man, "would you disinherit Ivan for the mere offense of letting his friends make free with your daughters? Does an heir not have the right to treat other sons and daughters how he pleases?" He stared the men down, daring them to answer.

I leapt to my feet, unable to listen to another word. "No." All eyes turned to me, but my gaze, cloudy with rage, was fixed on the traitor Blood Brother standing at the front of the room. "No, he does not. And I won't stand here listening to you make excuses for that *bastard* who—"

"Just so." The Brother cut me off with a nod. "An heir's duty is to care for his brothers and sisters. When he becomes a danger to the other children, he no longer has claim to the rights and privileges of an heir. Brother, has our tsar not forfeited the title of Heir of the Sanctioned?"

The men shouted in unison. *"Da!"*

"Has our tsar not committed atrocities against the brothers and sisters Otets has charged him to protect?"

"Da!"

"I tell you now, until Miroslav repents and makes restitution for the crimes he has committed, he is no tsar of mine!"

A cheer went up, but the Blood Brother raised his hands for silence.

"We have a brother here who wishes to speak to you of Miroslav's crimes. Han Antonovich, may Otets bless your words." He took a seat in the crowd.

I walked to the front of the room, uncomfortably aware of the eyes on me. "My—" My voice broke. I cleared my throat and began again.

"My name is Han Antonovich. I come from Selyik, and Miroslav has cost me my brothers in arms, my reputation, my hand, and my child."

The room was silent. I took a deep breath to calm my racing heart.

"Most of the men in my town did not fight in the uprising. You know that with the baron out of the country, our region was not called to arms for either tsar. Some of the Selyik men chose to fight for Miroslav. I, along with my childhood friend Benedikt, fought for Borislav.

"You already know how the last uprising ended. After a few losses, Miroslav brought foreign mercenaries to Inzhria. He killed nearly every one of Borislav's soldiers. I narrowly survived, as did my friend. The survivors were rounded up and told to swear allegiance."

I saw tears in the eyes of some of the men. Who had they lost? Barbezht had touched everyone in the tsardom in some way. Some regions were more affected than others; those that had declared for Miroslav were almost completely unscathed, while others lost an entire generation of young men. Judging by the ages of the men before me, this town had suffered relatively few losses.

"Miroslav told us Tsar Borislav was dead. He promised us mercy if we would surrender to him. Benedikt, my friend, rejected the chance to surrender, and Miroslav turned the Gifts of the Sanctioned against him. He burned my friend to death." The scent of burning flesh came to me, and I clenched my fist, nails digging into my palms to bring me back to the present moment.

"With these options before us, we knelt, expecting the mercy promised to us. Instead, Miroslav ordered his men to cut off our sword hands." I lifted my maimed arm, no longer hidden by the glove, for them to see. "I bear a permanent reminder of Miroslav's *mercy*." I heard the bitterness in my own voice as I spat out the last word. None of the men moved, but I saw pity and disgust mingling on their faces.

"Most of the survivors died of their wounds. Only a handful of us made it home. I thought that having survived the war, I had made it through the worst of it. I mourned the death of Tsar Borislav. I recovered from my injuries. I found a way to live without my hand. As a survivor of Barbezht, I was branded a traitor, but I pressed on. I married a strong, beautiful woman who refused to let me give in to despair. We built a life together. For a short time, we were happy.

"But Miroslav wasn't content with defeating his brother. Inzhria wasn't enough for him. He wants an empire, and to build it, he's formed an army." A few of the men nodded their agreement. "He took idle, cruel men and gave them authority to do whatever they wanted.

"In my small town with my newly pregnant wife, I assumed we were safe from Miroslav's standing army. We heard news of crimes committed by the soldiers, but they were far enough from us, I thought we would remain untouched. They would leave the region soon, I was sure, to build the tsar's new empire. But they didn't leave.

"While I was away from home one day, a few deserters, some of the violent men Miroslav couldn't keep control over, came to my house. My wife was at home with our housekeeper." The room was deadly silent, as though no one dared to breathe. I was barely breathing myself. "They killed our housekeeper and beat my wife nearly to death. They murdered our unborn son."

My eyes filled with tears, and I struggled to force the words out. "Because of Miroslav, I lost everything. I could have surrendered to despair. I wanted to, but Otets guided me. He showed me His plan for the tsardom. He led me to Borislav."

A wave of whispered confusion swept through the room. One man in the back spoke up over the murmurs. "Borislav is dead, sir."

"I thought so, too, but he is not. Through a miracle, he survived Barbezht, and he's returned to take his rightful place as Heir of the Sanctioned."

A clamor of voices broke out as everyone vied to speak at once.

"Brothers!" The priest stood, shouting over everyone. "Let Han Antonovich finish speaking."

The room quieted. I looked around, meeting a few suspicious gazes. "I understand this is hard to believe. I didn't believe it myself until I met the tsar. But I assure you, he is alive, and he will guide the country back onto the path Otets revealed for Inzhria through the Prophet. I ask you, brothers, to join us. Gather your weapons, be prepared, and in a few weeks the tsar will call for you. He will gather his army, and you can see him for yourselves. We will take back the tsardom from Miroslav." I paused, letting my words sink in. "Will you join us?"

There was silence for a moment. A sallow-skinned man stood. "I will, sir."

Another man followed him, his long black coils of hair swaying with the movement. "As will I."

In a moment, everyone was on their feet. My chest swelled as their declarations of allegiance rang through the room.

15

IDESK

Mila

The white towers of the city wall loomed against the cloudless blue sky. I gaped at the giant gate, twice as tall as the gate to Tsebol. As we rode into the shadow of the wall, I felt a chill that had nothing to do with the frigid air.

"Your mouth is hanging open, Fia."

I grinned sheepishly at Izolda. In the two weeks we'd been traveling, I'd grown used to my new identity, including the nickname she insisted on using. "Sorry. It's just so big."

"Wait until you see the palace. It's always been beautiful, but Tsar Miroslav completely renovated it. Huge marble balconies over the ocean, formed by magic—he had all the Sanctioned come to the capital to work on it—and a throne room so ridiculously pretty I can't even begin to describe it."

"It sounds amazing."

She winked. "Once Lady Heli is settled in, I'll give you a tour."

The retinue passed through the gates, and the city rose up before us, narrow streets bustling with people. Vendors hawked their wares, brightly colored Drakra-woven tapestries or fragrant fish pirozhki.

Rather than going down that road, we turned sharply left, onto a wide but comparatively empty road that followed the path of the city wall.

"Where are we going?" I asked Izolda, turning to look back at the busy streets.

"The roads are too narrow for us to get through that way. Big enough to ride if you have to, but only single file. This is the only road to the palace that fits wagons. Guess what they call it?" She grinned. *"Telezhnaya Doroga.* Wagon Road. Original, right?"

I laughed. "But how does everyone get around? I mean, how do they move things to market and such?"

"Hand carts, mostly. The nobles all ride sedan chairs, if you can believe it." She rolled her eyes. "Thankfully, the baroness doesn't usually leave the palace while we're at court. Sedans are such a pain."

We rounded a corner, and I gasped. The palace ahead of us dwarfed the city below it. The onion-shaped domes of the towers were striped in brilliant blue and red, topped with gold points that glinted in the sun. Two domes reached above the rest, opposite each other and fully gilded. They looked like something from the stories my father used to tell me, like at any moment a bird made of fire might swoop down and perch on top of one of those golden domes, or a sorcerer might come to a window and call down thunder from the sky, turning the brilliant day into darkest night.

"What did I tell you?" Izolda said.

"Prophet's Balls!" I looked at her smug, bloodless face, my eyes wide. "I see what you mean."

A second wall separated the palace from the rest of the city. We rode through the gate into an opulent courtyard of white marble. In the center stood a statue of the Prophet, staff raised high in blessing over Tsar Fima, the founder of the country and ancestor of Miroslav and Borislav. Blood poured from the staff onto the legendary tsar, forming a pool around the feet of the statues. I recoiled.

"It's not real blood," Izolda said, low enough that only I could hear. "Just an enchantment that Miroslav did to the water. Gross, huh?"

Before I could respond, she climbed off her horse to attend to the baroness, who was descending from her carriage. I looked back at the fountain, my skin crawling. Real blood or not, it was disgusting. So much for first impressions.

"Sofia!" The baroness's voice drew my attention from the gruesome image. I hurried to her. "The new seamstress," Lady Heli said to a nearby servant, waving a hand at me.

"If you'll follow me, miss, I'll show you to your quarters. Your luggage will be brought later." The man turned on his heel and walked off.

I grabbed my saddle pack and rushed after him. He didn't wait to see if I followed, and I didn't have time to take in the sights as we made our way through the palace grounds. I had a vague impression of colorful buildings, a large glass structure that might have been a greenhouse, and a lush green courtyard before we reached the much humbler building that housed the trade workers, those who worked in the palace but weren't assigned to any particular noble. He led me into the building and down a dimly lit hall, stopping at the end.

"This will be your room, miss. If you need anything, the trade steward's quarters are down the hall and to your left." He gave a curt bow and left me alone.

The room I'd been assigned was comfortably large. Long tables lined the walls, and a wide window let in plenty of natural light. All that light would be good for work, I noted, but it would come with the consequence of making a frigid workspace through the winter. The room was already cold, thought not unbearably so, but the weather was far from its coldest of the season, and winter was still a couple weeks away. I glanced at the small fireplace. I would have to see what the daily firewood allowance was. Likely not enough to heat the room all day.

The fireplace was unlit, and I could see through it to another room. I went through the door and found a small bedroom with no windows. It was sparsely furnished, with a simple bed and a desk, but there were posts to hang curtains around the bed. This room, at least, would be warmer than the other.

"Fia? You here?" Izolda's voice came from the workroom.

"In here."

She poked her head in and whistled. "Nice rooms."

"You're done early." I cocked my head. "The baroness didn't need you?"

"Nah. She wanted to rest, and since no one's brought up our luggage yet, there wasn't anything for me to do. Care for a tour?"

"Sure." I tossed my pack on the bed and followed Izolda out of the room.

She waved a hand around as we walked out of the building. "These are the gardens."

"How are they still so green?" It was too late in the year for the amount of fresh growth I saw as we passed.

"If you think they're green now, you ought to see them in the summer. As to how, it's all done by Blood Bastards. Miroslav has a whole team of them dedicated just to the upkeep of the grounds. His uncle, Tsar Vyacheslav's illegitimate half-brother, leads them up. They make potions to extend the growing season in the gardens, prevent the stones around the palace from weathering—they even invented a new type of golden paint, one that glints even when the sun isn't out. That's what's covering the towers." She jerked her chin toward the gilded towers above us. "But this is nothing. What I really want to show you is the throne room."

We entered the main palace through a side door and turned down a bright hallway. Windows lined one wall, giving a view of the courtyard I'd seen when we first arrived. I caught a glimpse of the bloody fountain and shuddered, turning away from the windows. The other walls were covered with rich tapestries, depicting religious and secular scenes.

"Most of the nobles are housed on this side of the palace." Izolda stopped in front of a mirror and perused her reflection. "Lord Ilya and Lady Heli are upstairs, third floor. The higher the status, the lower the rooms, and the closeness to the tsar's tower indicates favor, too. The baron and baroness haven't been closer than halfway down the hall since Tsar Vyacheslav died."

Standing behind her, I caught sight of my own reflection. Izolda had spent the journey teaching me how to care for my new, more textured hair, and her lessons seemed to have paid off. The tight rows of braids I'd put in the previous day were still intact, coming together to form a two long braids down my back. I felt a sense of pride in my appearance; even though it wasn't really my body, I felt beautiful living as Sofia.

Izolda finished checking her appearance and walked down the hall, toward two guards standing on either side of an enormous wooden door. As we passed them and rounded the corner, she took my arm. "That's the tsar's tower. You won't have any reason to go in there, but on the opposite side of the palace is the tsarina's tower. You should try to get a commission from the tsarina or the dowager tsarina. It would be a great achievement for your career."

I heard the undertone in her words. She wasn't speaking of my career as a seamstress, fighting for notice among the half-dozen other seamstresses at court, but of my work for Tsar Borislav.

She led me down a servants' corridor and stopped outside a nondescript door. "This, though... This is the best part of the whole palace." She swung the door open with a dramatic flair.

My breath caught in my throat as we stepped inside. Enormous white pillars lined the room, and on the far end of the hall to my left was an alcove covered with stained glass windows. The vaulted ceiling was the color of the night sky, and its golden stars twinkled in the light from the windows. The throne, on a raised dais at the end of the hall, was made of pure gold and cushioned with blue velvet.

"They say Tsar Fima himself built that throne," Izolda whispered reverently. "He cast a spell so only the rightful Heir of the Sanctioned could be seated on it."

"Do you believe that?" I matched her whisper, unwilling to break the spell the room had cast.

As she shook her head, grinning, the main doors to the hall opened, and a man stepped in. I froze as he caught sight of us. I would have recognized him anywhere, the orange hair and beard, the narrow eyes in his large red face.

The lord of Arick. The man who killed my son.

"What are you doing in here?" he demanded, his voice low and sharp.

"I beg your pardon, my lord." Izolda bobbed a bow. "This is the new seamstress. I was showing her around the palace."

He scowled. "The throne room is not for gawking. Be on your way."

"Yes, my lord." She stepped back toward the servants' entrance, but I remained rooted to the spot, my chest so tight I couldn't breathe. Murderer. *Murderer.*

The nobleman walked toward us. "I said, 'be on your way,'" he growled.

"Fia!" Izolda grabbed my hand.

I flinched at the touch. My breath came back to me all at once. "Apologies, my lord." I ducked my head in imitation of a bow. "I don't know what came over me." I moved to follow my friend, but he blocked my way.

"Have we met?" he asked, stepping too close.

He couldn't recognize me. I wasn't me. I was Sofia Stepanova, a seamstress who had never met him before. "I don't believe so, my lord." I backed away, trying not to smell his rancid breath. I'd smelled that before. Fuck, I was going to vomit. The room spun around me.

"Hm." He peered at me, then took a step back. "Go. And be more cautious about where you find yourself in the future. Others are less forgiving than I am."

"Yes, my lord. Thank you, my lord." Izolda grabbed my hand and dragged me from the room.

Once we reached the end of the servants' corridor, we stopped. I backed against the wall, eyes closed, drawing shaky breaths.

"What was that about?" she demanded.

I shook my head, not opening my eyes. "Nothing."

"Nothing? 'Nothing' doesn't make you cry."

I opened my eyes a crack and realized they were filled with tears. I wiped furiously at them and took a deep breath. "He...reminded me of someone."

Izolda looked up and down the hall, and seeing it was clear, stepped closer. "You could have given yourself away back there. If your past is going to be an issue, I need to know. Now."

"I'm fine." I stood up straight, dabbing at my eyes with the long sleeve of my sarafan. "It won't happen again."

"I hope it won't." The words didn't sound like a reprimand.

She looked away, giving me a moment to compose myself. I brushed the wrinkles from my dress. I should have expected to see him. If the tsar had summoned most of the nobles, it stood to reason that the lord of Arick would be at court as well. The shock of seeing him was what had affected me, more than any lingering fear. I wasn't afraid of him. What else could he do to me that he hadn't already done?

When my heart finally stopped beating like a douli drum, I asked what I hoped was a casual voice, "Who was that, anyway?"

"Kazimir Vladimirovich, childhood friend of Tsar Miroslav." She wrinkled her nose. "Now the baron of Arick, by no merit of his own."

Kazimir Vladimirovich. The man who had murdered my child. And he was a friend of the tyrant. I felt a spark of something that resembled satisfaction. It hadn't been the right time to tell Tsar Borislav what had been done to me, but perhaps I didn't need the tsar to make justice for me. I could make it myself.

My body still trembled, but my mind raced with anticipation. I could make him pay for what he'd done and serve my tsar all at once.

16

RADOMIR, PRINCE OF THE BLOOD

Han

After the first time, I found it easier to tell my story. Every day or two, the tsar and I reached a new town, where the local Blood Brothers had arranged for a meeting with anyone who might be sympathetic to the cause. Sometimes one of the priests made a speech beforehand; other times they simply introduced me. We met in temples, in taverns, in houses. In some towns, dozens came; in others, only a few. The response, no matter the number, was overwhelmingly positive. In every town, I heard new stories of people who had suffered under Miroslav's reign. Some families had been unable to pay the new taxes to support Miroslav's army. Others were still angry over the loss of loved ones in the last uprising. In one town, soldiers had come through and taken over half of their crops, leaving them with little to survive the long, harsh Inzhrian winter. Borislav, having heard of this on our arrival, wrote in code to Lord Ilya's castle, asking for emergency supplies to sustain the town. When I told the men of that town what the tsar had done for them, every man in the room had been on his feet, declaring for Borislav, before I had finished speaking.

"Eight towns visited, and every man you spoke to agreed to join us. Han, you must be the Prophet reborn," Borislav said when I returned to our small room in the temple after the latest meeting.

I flushed at the slightly blasphemous praise, taking a seat on the simple bed across from him. "I'm just telling my story. They're rising up for you."

"Be that as it may, your words are what brought them to me. I could have chosen no one better to accompany me on this journey." He rose, looking out the window at the night sky. Nearby, the bells chimed for polnoch, the midnight service. "We'll be at my cousin's estate tomorrow. I had thought to approach him myself, but knowing Radomir, I can't be sure he wouldn't send me to my brother on first sight." He turned back to me. "I must, once again, rely on you to speak for me."

"I am yours to command."

He took a ring off his pinky. It was gold with a small ruby. "I will go with you as far as I can tomorrow. Two of the Brothers will accompany you to my cousin's dacha, where you will ask him for a private audience. When he grants it—and he will grant it. Radomir denies the Blood Brothers nothing—give him this and ask him to grant me a safe reception, to hear my tale from my own mouth. Have him swear on the Gifts of the Blood; he's a pious man and would never forswear himself. Once he has sworn, send the Brothers back for me, and I will join you promptly."

I took the ring. "I will."

"You are a true and loyal friend, Han."

"Thank you." I pulled off my coat and belt, not bothering to remove my pants before lying down. I would need the extra warmth. The room was already cold and likely to grow colder overnight. I'd seen a fine layer of frost on the ground as I walked back to the temple this evening. "I'll bid you goodnight."

"Otets guard your sleep," the tsar said, blowing out the candle and looking back out the window.

Despite the cold and the stiff bed I lay on, the sound of temple bells and the smell of incense wafting from the nearby altar room lulled me to sleep.

I woke the next morning to the bells of utrenya, the dawn service. After a simple breakfast of unsweetened kasha with milk, the two Blood Brothers and I began the walk to Prince Radomir's dacha. Unlike the beginning of our journey, I wouldn't go to the prince in disguise. I wore my own clothes, setting me apart from the Blood Brothers who flanked me.

According to Tsar Borislav, his cousin would remain at his country estate until Prophet's Day, the holiest day, when we celebrated the Prophet first appearing to Tsar Fima. The prince, apparently, always remained home for the holiday, preferring to celebrate in his own way, rather than to join in the celebrations of the court. As he held the most power in the tsardom after the tsar himself, he was rarely denied.

I knew little about Prince Radomir. In Borislav's first rebellion, he had sided with Miroslav, though he was rumored to have distanced himself from Miroslav after the events of Barbezht. I said a silent prayer that his apparent break with Miroslav would bode well for our cause. With the number of men at his command, his support could ensure our victory, and his enmity could ensure our demise.

I scanned the estate as we trekked along the winding cobblestone road up to the dacha. The house sat in the middle of a sprawling, frost-covered field. Made of wood, the house wasn't fortified, but it didn't need to be. Dachas were made for peace-time. In times of war, the nobles would retreat behind the heavy stone walls of their cities and castles, as would any other citizens lucky enough to have access to such protection.

Though it wasn't fortified, the estate was set up much like a castle. To the left of the main house was a bathhouse, steam rising from the roof. To the right was a small chapel, the door painted red and a gilded hawk on the steeple. In the back, I could see a large set of stables. The walls of the main house were yellow, the roof a deep green, and delicate carvings surrounded the windows.

A servant let us into the house, his eyes lingering on me as though he wondered what business I, a travel-worn commoner, could have in the home of the highest prince of the land. Looking around at the clean, well-kept hall we had entered, I wondered the same. Who was I to ask a prince for anything, even as a messenger for the tsar?

"We seek an audience with his highness," one of the Brothers said.

The servant gave a reverent bow. "May I ask on what business, honored Brothers?"

The Brother's answer was curt. "Private."

He nodded and disappeared through a door on the opposite side of the room. He returned a few moments later and said, "Follow me."

He led us through the corridors and outside again, into the courtyard behind the house. My nerves were a stone in the bottom of my stomach as we stepped back into the cold morning air. In the middle of the courtyard stood two men and a large black stallion. The first man, a servant in the same livery as the man who had greeted us, held the horse's foreleg, rubbing its neck and murmuring. The second man was a noble, as evidenced by the fine make of his blue kaftan and black ushanka-hat. His gaze was fixed on the horse. In one hand, he held a wand; in the other, a small piece of iron. He closed his eyes, muttered something I couldn't hear, and tapped the horse's immobilized foreleg.

The stallion whinnied, tossing its head. The servant continued stroking its sleek neck, and after a moment, it calmed. The nobleman stepped back and tucked the wand and iron into his pocket. "Take him back to the stable. Let me know how that leg progresses. I'll be back to check on him later tonight."

"Yes, your highness." The servant released the horse's leg and took its lead rope.

The prince turned to us. "Forgive me for not greeting you inside. My stallion broke his leg this morning. A stablehand's foolish mistake, but my fault for allowing an untested boy to handle the creature. If I hadn't treated the injury immediately, the horse might have been permanently lamed."

He'd used his magic to heal a broken bone? Was there anything the Sanctioned couldn't do?

Even more pressing: what could possibly be done against them, if we had to face that power in battle?

The prince bowed his head. "Bless me, Brothers."

One of the Blood Brothers raised his hand in blessing. "May the wisdom of the Witness, the shrewdness of the Steward, and the courage of the Prophet be with you, Radomir, prince of the Blood."

He touched his forehead in reverence, then clapped his hands together. "What brings Otets' servants to my home?"

I stepped forward and bowed, heart in my throat. "Your highness, my name is Han Antonovich, and I am here at the request of your cousin, the rightful tsar. He asked me to give you this."

He took the ring I held and turned it over in his hands. "Borislav." He looked back at me, then to the Blood Brothers at my side. "Follow me."

He led us into the house and up a set of stairs. My blood thundered in my ears. When we stopped in a warm study, the prince took a seat behind the large desk and fixed small, suspicious eyes on me.

"You come bearing a token of Borislav Vyacheslavovich, a proclaimed traitor. By all rights, I should have you arrested for this. You have one minute to convince me otherwise."

I took a deep breath. If I spoke wrong here, it could mean the end of the entire rebellion. "Miroslav has long since forfeited his right to rule Inzhria, your highness. I think you know this." He didn't even blink. His gaze revealed nothing. "Borislav is the rightful Heir of the Sanctioned. He has the support of the people and of Otets himself." I gestured to the Blood Brothers, Otets' representatives. "He wishes to speak to you. Please, grant him safe passage to come here, to plead his case for himself. Once you hear what he has to say, I'm sure you will understand."

I held my breath, watching him. The prince sat back in his chair, fidgeting with the ring. For a long moment, he was silent. Then he nodded. "I will receive him."

"Thank you, your highness." I bowed. "These Brothers can bear witness to your vow for his safety and freedom, and then they will bring the tsar to you."

Prince Radomir scowled. "My word is not enough?"

One of the Brothers took a step forward. "The Heir's safety is too important to accept anything less than a vow on the Blood itself. It is not a mark on your honor, but rather an indication of the high value we place on the life of Borislav Vyacheslavovich."

The prince's lips pinched together, but he placed his hand over his heart. "I swear on the Blood of Otets, which runs through my veins, not to harm my cousin Borislav nor to turn him over to those who would harm him, so long as he is in my lands." He looked at me. "Are you satisfied, sir?"

I nodded, some of the tension in my chest easing. "Thank you, your highness." We would survive the day, so long as Borislav was right to believe the prince wouldn't forswear himself.

The two Brothers left, and the prince waved toward a chair opposite him at the desk. "Have a seat. Han, was it?" He squinted his eyes in suspicion. "That's not an Inzhrian name."

"No, it's not." I fought to remain still beneath the weight of his gaze. "My mother had a taste for the exotic, your highness. She named me after a famous Vasland warrior."

"I see." He rang a bell, and a few moments later a servant arrived. "Han Antonovich will be joining me for dinner, as will..." His gaze flicked to me. "Another guest."

"Yes, your highness."

The prince turned to the pile of paperwork on his desk as the servant left. Minutes ticked by, the only sound the low crackle of the fire in the grate. The glove I wore on the end of my right arm grew uncomfortable, and I tugged at the strap. Why was it so tight today? Another tug, and the glove fell onto the floor with a thud.

My heart skipped a beat, and I looked up to see the prince watching me. Comprehension dawned on his face. "Ah. You're a survivor of Barbezht."

"I am, your highness." I realized, belatedly, that his vow had made no mention of my own safety and freedom.

"I see why my cousin trusts you. You've already given up much for him." Seeing the cautious look on my face, he waved a hand. "Naturally, my vow extends to you as well. Safety for my cousin applies to his men. I would not break an oath to Otets on a mere technicality."

The tightness in my chest eased considerably. "Thank you, your highness."

The time dragged on. Finally, I heard footsteps in the hall, and a servant entered. "Your remaining guest has arrived, Prince Radomir. He awaits you in the dining hall."

As we entered the room, Borislav rose to meet his cousin. "Radomir. It's been too long."

"Would that I could say the same, cousin, but the last time we saw each other was on opposite sides of a battlefield. I can't pretend I'm glad to see you." He took a seat at the head of the long table and gestured for us to sit as well.

Borislav smiled sadly as he sat. "I'm sorry to hear that. I thought perhaps you had mourned my loss and were glad to hear that I was alive."

Radomir fixed him with a deadpan look. "You know as well as I that we knew you were alive. You can thank me for your survival. If it hadn't been for my council, Miroslav would have hunted you to the ends of the earth. I convinced him you had learned your place. It seems I was wrong."

"It's not I who has failed to learn my place, Radomir."

"I never discuss business on an empty stomach." The prince bowed his head and said a brief blessing over the food, hearty bowls of cabbage soup swimming with ham, black bread fresh from the oven, and large cups of dark kvass. He waved at the food. "Eat."

True to his word, the prince didn't let us speak until we had all eaten. At last, he pushed his plate back. "Very well, Borislav. Make your case."

Borislav cast a wary glance at the servants that were clearing food from the table.

"Speak, cousin. My servants are completely loyal to me. Nothing said in my house leaves these walls unless I wish it. Not even for Tsar Miroslav."

The tsar's mouth formed a line, but he nodded. "You're a pious man, Radomir. You've read our scriptures, the words of the Witness, Steward, and Prophet. What does Otets require of the Heir?"

"That he be just and merciful, a wise ruler, caring for all those he has charge of." He took a drink of his kvass. "What of it?"

Borislav leaned forward, his expression earnest, brow knit together. "Can you say, truthfully, that Miroslav meets all those requirements?"

"That would depend on how one perceives it, I suppose."

I gritted my teeth to keep from speaking. No one could pretend Miroslav cared for his people. Not for the common people, at least. Perhaps for the nobles, but not for me. Not for Mila. If this prince thought Miroslav was a fitting tsar, he was either a fool or wicked, but either way he would be no help to us.

"Do not mince words." The tsar's eyes narrowed. "My brother is neither just, merciful, nor wise. He cares for no one but himself. Don't the scriptures say that an Heir may be Disinherited if he fails to discharge his duties as Otets commanded? Miroslav *has* failed to do so. We *must* rise against him."

"The standards for a Disinheritance are high, Borislav. Are you certain they've all been met?"

I thrust my right arm forward. *"This* is Miroslav's 'mercy,'" I snarled. I was speaking out of turn, but I couldn't stop myself. "You know what he did to those of us who knelt after Barbezht. Most of my brothers in arms were killed when he ordered their hands removed."

Radomir looked dispassionately at me. "The Heir is required to uphold justice in the land, not just mercy. This was nothing more."

I clenched my fist. "There is no *justice* in maiming and killing a defeated enemy. Especially if that enemy has surrendered."

Before I could speak again, the tsar leaned forward. "Han Antonovich speaks the truth, Radomir. What my brother offers the people is neither justice nor mercy. This new army he has built is not a means of caring for the people, but for serving himself and bringing himself glory. Soldiers in this army are given freedom to do whatever they wish. They commit crimes with impunity. We passed through a town here on your lands just yesterday where the soldiers took half of their winter stores. Tell me, does that sound like Miroslav is caring for the people he has charge of?"

Biting my cheek to keep from speaking, I watched as the prince considered our words. "You have a point," he said. "But your last rebellion failed. What makes you think this one will be any different?"

Maybe he wasn't the fool I'd thought. Some of the tension in my body dissipated. I could respect a man who didn't rush into war, as long as he didn't claim that Miroslav was a good tsar. Still... "This uprising won't fail. The people are desperate for a change. Even if Tsar Borislav loses, if he dies, the people will continue to rise up. They'll make a Disinheritance themselves, and once they've removed one of the Sanctioned from the throne, they won't be eager to accept another."

The prince narrowed his small eyes at me. "Is that a threat, Han Antonovich? The Blood of Otets runs in my veins. I will not be frightened by the unSanctioned."

"No threat," Borislav said, leaning forward, "but a fact. Our ranks are already growing at an unprecedented rate. The people of Inzhria are going to end Miroslav's reign, and they are going to end whoever supports him, as well. The only reason Miroslav won at Barbezht was because he brought in a foreign army. Once they see the rebellion is still alive, no other country will be willing to lend him aid. This uprising will be Inzhrian and Inzhrian alone.

"Cousin." Borislav took the prince's hand, his voice going low and earnest. "You can ensure the safety of our people. You know I will care for them as Otets intended. Join me, make a Disinheritance of my brother, and we can ensure the tsardom comes through this war in one piece."

The two men stared at each other. Silence rang in my ears, unbearably loud. I clenched my fist, digging my nails into my palm. What would we do if he refused? How would we defeat Miroslav without Radomir's men?

At last, the prince nodded. "I will join you. But bear in mind, Borislav, this is not for your glory. This is for the faith and the good of the realm. Were you found to be as undeserving an Heir as your brother, I would not hesitate to make a Disinheritance of you as well."

"I would expect nothing less," Borislav answered.

17

MIROSLAV'S COURT

Mila

The clatter of plates and the sound of raucous laughter filled my ears as I entered the dining hall, searching for a familiar face. The entire court—royalty, nobles, trade workers, and servants—had been invited to a feast to celebrate the annual gathering of the nobles. It was the first of many celebrations, Izolda had told me, balls and pageants and banquets that would last until Prophet's Day.

The main dining hall wasn't large enough to accommodate everyone, so most of the servants and trade workers had been relegated to a simpler hall on the lower level. I caught sight of Izolda near the door and let out a sigh of relief. I wouldn't be alone, at least.

"Finding your way around alright?" she asked as I took a seat.

"It's a little overwhelming." I looked around the stone room at the hundreds of people seated along the long tables. I'd never seen so many people in one place before. "Is it always like this?"

She shook her head, spooning a generous helping of pickled cabbage onto my plate. "Only at feasts and such. Most everyone eats in their own quarters, unless the tsar is going to make an appearance. Which he's supposed to do tonight, obviously."

I cast a sharp glance around the room, and Izolda laughed. "He's not here yet. Trust me, when he comes, you'll know. He won't stay long. Just long enough to allow his adoring subjects to express their admiration," she added dryly.

A trumpet blast rendered the hall silent, and the large doors opposite us opened. A page stepped through. "His majesty, Tsar Miroslav of the Blood, Heir of the Sanctioned and rightful ruler of Inzhria. Her majesty, Tsarina Desislava. Their royal highnesses, Grand Duchess Yevgeniya and Grand Duchess Yevpraksiya."

Benches scraped, and I realized belatedly that everyone was standing. I rose to my feet in time to see a round-bellied man bedecked in jewels and fur step up onto a small dais at the front of the room. My stomach clenched. So this was the man who had taken everything from me. I barely noticed the tsarina and grand duchesses standing next to him.

"My people!" Miroslav said in a high voice. "I thank you for your attendance, and I welcome you to my palace. Please, be seated. Enjoy the fruits of our union and the gifts of my court."

No one sat, but the hall broke out into thunderous applause. I clapped as well, not wanting to draw attention to myself, though my throat was tight with disgust. How could they cheer for him? Didn't they know what he was, what he had done? Did no one remember Barbezht and the hundreds of men his soldiers had slaughtered?

For a few moments, he stood smiling, hands raised in acceptance of the praise. At last he turned and strode out of the room, the black fur of his kaftan swaying in his wake. His wife and daughters trailed after him.

The chatter in the hall resumed as everyone took their seats again. Izolda rolled her eyes. "'Gifts,' my ass," she said, just loud enough for me to hear. "He charges every noble for their room and board, and for that of their retinue."

A deep voice came from behind us. "If it isn't the lovely Izolda Vasilievna. Welcome back to court."

The speaker was a tall, dark-skinned man with high cheekbones. His eyes held a mischievous twinkle as he smiled down at Izolda.

"Alexey!" she said. "I didn't know you were in the capital. Last I heard you were up north." She slid away from me, making space on the bench between us.

"I recently accepted a position with the baron of Arick." He turned to me. "I don't believe I've had the pleasure."

"This is Sofia Stepanova, a new court seamstress. Fia, this is Alexey Grigorovich."

"It's a pleasure." He took my hand and kissed it softly, never removing his eyes from my face.

I pulled my hand from his grasp and nodded politely. His steady gaze unsettled me.

"Lord Kazimir, huh?" Izolda asked as he took a seat between us. "How has that been? He's got quite the reputation."

"It's not been terrible. He's demanding, but no more so than other nobles. And he has the tsar's favor, so it's an opportunity to improve my position." He turned back to me as he scooped onto his plate several pelmeni, fragrant dumplings filled with meat and onions. "You're from Tsebol? And what do you think of our fair capital?"

"It's beautiful," I said honestly. "What I've seen of it, at least. I only arrived yesterday. It's larger than I expected."

He let out a booming laugh. "I've seen many cities, and none of them were as large as Idesk. The capital makes for an unfair comparison for any city."

"I wouldn't know. I've never been far from Tsebol." It wasn't a lie. Selyik wasn't far from Tsebol. Izolda had told me to keep to the truth as much as possible when telling others about myself. The truth was easier to remember. "I'm looking forward to seeing more of the city."

"We shall have to give you the grand tour." Our eyes met, his gaze intent. I looked away, and Izolda cleared her throat.

"Do you expect to be at court all winter, Izolda?"

She sniffed and tossed her head. "No need to acknowledge me. You were getting along quite well before."

He threw me a wink over his shoulder as he took Izolda's hand. "Hold not your favor from me, fair one! Though I bask in the sunny countenance of Sofia Stepanova, I do not forget the glorious moonlight that radiates from Izolda Vasilievna's face."

Izolda laughed as I shook my head. He was ridiculous. He reminded me a little of Yakov, if Yakov had been more eloquent. An insincere flirt with every woman he met. The sort of person who might have made me laugh, if there hadn't been something almost too earnest in his eyes. He seemed to see through me and straight into my soul.

"I suppose it makes sense that I'm overlooked, then," Izolda said, "if I'm only the moon, and Fia's the sun."

"The sun warms the earth, and the moon pulls the tides." His voice was intense but hinted at a smile as he looked between us. "Both necessary, and both beautiful."

"Flatterer," she accused.

He raised his hands in surrender. "The moon has a harsher burn than the sun. I shall flee the night in favor of the day." He turned his back on her. "There's a dance planned tonight in the greenhouse, Sofia Stepanova. For the servants and trade workers. I hope you'll come?"

Izolda answered for me. "She'll be there."

"I don't know," I said. "It's been a long day, and I'm a bit tired." I'd spent the day unpacking and organizing my workshop. A dance sounded like the last thing I wanted to do.

She gave me a meaningful look around Alexey. "It's the perfect way to get settled in. You can get to know some people, start building a reputation. The best way to get any orders is to get to know the servants. You won't get anywhere at court if Lady Heli's your only client."

I bit my lip. "I suppose it wouldn't hurt, for a little bit."

"Wonderful!" Alexey clapped his hands together. "If you'll excuse me, I see someone I must speak with." He stood and gathered his plate. "I'll see you both tonight."

As he left, Izolda turned a mischievous grin on me.

"What?"

"I think he likes you."

"Hm." I mopped the juices on my plate with a piece of black bread. "He seemed like a flirt."

She laughed. "I've known Alexey for years. He's sweet. A bit dramatic, but he's loyal and kind." She paused. "And good-looking, too."

I rolled my eyes. "Sweet or not, I'm not interested. I'm here to work."

"Building contacts is excellent for your work, as I said. And I have a feeling Alexey would be more than willing to...'build contacts' with you."

I flushed. Alexey Grigorovich was attractive, yes, but I was married. Not that Izolda knew that.

Mila was married. Sofia wasn't.

Before I could organize my thoughts enough to answer, someone approached and whispered in Izolda's ear. She pushed her plate back and stood. "Lady Heli just left. Give me a bit to get her settled for the night, and I'll meet you at your room. We can get ready together."

It took two hours of preparation before Izolda pronounced me ready. My sarafan, a warm yellow that complemented my dark skin beautifully, had a belt of red to match the long-sleeved red shirt that showed beneath the dress. A matching povyazka decorated my hair, and my tightly coiled braids had been woven together into a rope down my back.

We walked through the frigid night air into the greenhouse, where we were ushered inside. A band played in the corner, and dozens of people danced among beds of fragrant and exotic flowers I'd never seen before.

"Come on!" Izolda pulled me toward the dancers.

Before I could protest, we were swept up into the dance. It was familiar, a fast-paced tune called a kazachok that I'd danced many times before. A young man about Yakov's age partnered me, his brown face lit up with a smile. I laughed as we spun around, breathless from the exertion.

Too soon, the song ended, the band transitioning seamlessly into a much slower tune. My smiling partner melted back into the crowd of dancers. Izolda had disappeared, but I wasn't left alone for long.

"If it isn't the fair sun, Sofia Stepanova," Alexey Grigorovich said, taking my hand and pulling me into the new dance.

"Izolda insisted I come." I half-shrugged as he led me in a wide circle, following the other dancers.

"I'm glad she did. It would be a tragedy to deprive everyone of seeing the most beautiful woman at court."

I laughed despite myself. "I believe Izolda was right, sir. You are a flatterer."

"You wound me, madam." He didn't look wounded, with his wide grin showing all his white teeth. "I speak nothing but the truth."

I raised my eyebrows in doubt but elected not to answer. The movements of the dance drew us apart.

"How long have you worked for Lady Heli?" he asked when we came back together.

The first chance to test my knowledge of Sofia's history. "Just a few years. I apprenticed with her previous seamstress."

"You've come a long way in a short time."

He had no idea how true that was. Unsure of how to respond, I focused on the movements of the dance.

"Do you have any family?"

"No. My mother died when I was young, and my father died in service to Tsar Miroslav."

"I'm sorry to hear that." His smile disappeared, sympathy filling his face. "You have no other family?" When I shook my head, he added, "And suitors?"

"I—" I hesitated, caught off guard by the question. "No."

The music ended, and he let go of my hand. "I hope I may have the opportunity to change that." He bowed.

The room was stifling. A churning sensation developed in my stomach. He was near, far too near, and the earnestness on his face... Filled with a sudden need for fresh air, I muttered, "I have to go." I turned and fled.

Once outside, it was easier to breathe. I stood with my back to the greenhouse, relishing the cold air on my heated skin.

No one had mentioned what to do if I found myself romantically pursued at court. I was married, but Sofia Stepanova wasn't. There was no reason for Sofia to reject the advances of an attractive, eligible suitor. And whatever else he was, Alexey Grigorovich was an attractive man.

Otets' Blood. I'd been at court less than two days and already found myself in a mess.

Not wanting to go back to the dance and risk seeing him again, I walked slowly back to my quarters. Izolda would discover I'd left soon enough. For now, I needed to be alone.

Back in my bedroom, I built up the fire and took a seat on the nearby bed. I could guess what Han would say about Alexey Grigorovich's not-so-subtle advance. Han wasn't as hot-headed as Yakov, but if he thought someone was pursuing his wife, he wouldn't hesitate to call the man out.

Still, Alexey Grigorovich served Lord Kazimir. I shuddered, rubbing my hands together for warmth. Getting close to him might give me an opportunity to exact vengeance on the man who killed my son. And Kazimir held Miroslav's favor. Ingratiating myself with the manservant might lead to more information for the tsar, as well. Flirtation wasn't infidelity. I could encourage his attentions, use the dalliance to my advantage, and still remain true to Han.

I sighed. I didn't need to worry about Han. The distraction could put us both in danger. What I needed was to focus on the task at hand. I owed it to everyone we had lost. I owed it to Han.

I stood and stretched, my mind made up. I could use Alexey Grigorovich to my own ends, could find a way to use his interest to my advantage and help end this war. Whatever I had to do to bring down Miroslav would be worth it.

18

BETRAYED

Mila

After a week at court, I had finally settled in. The palace itself was easy to navigate, the layout deceptively simple, but it was difficult to remember where, exactly, each noble was housed within the ornate halls.

I looked up and down the long corridor, frowning. Where were Princess Alisa's quarters? I was supposed to meet with her to discuss a new commission, but all the rooms looked similar.

As I considered, the door in front of me opened. A tall young noblewoman, her skin a warm, dark brown but speckled with white, stepped into the hall, followed by her maidservant.

I'd heard of people with skin like this, but I'd never actually seen it. It was a skin condition that caused the skin to lose its color, and according to research by Blood Bastards, it wasn't contagious or harmful. I'd never heard of a noble with the disease; it lent the woman an air of exotic beauty.

"Can I help you?" she asked.

I bowed. "Apologies, my lady. I'm looking for Princess Alisa's quarters."

"You're a few doors too soon. I'm headed that direction already. I'll show you the princess's rooms." She turned and glided down the hall, the maidservant and I trailing after her.

The lady looked back. "What is your trade?"

"I'm a seamstress, my lady. Sofia Stepanova."

"Are you? I'll have to call on you when I need a new dress. Princess Alisa always wears the finest fashions. Anyone she commissions must be talented indeed." She stopped. "Here we are, Sofia Stepanova."

"Thank you, Lady…"

"Yelena Kyrilovna. Baroness of Arick."

Baroness of Arick. The wife of Kazimir Vladimirovich. I bowed, my shoulders tight. "Thank you, Lady Yelena."

The baroness and her servant continued down the hall, and I took a moment to compose myself. Lord Kazimir, the monster who'd attacked me, was married to that gentle young woman. I couldn't believe it.

Shaking myself, I knocked on the door. A servant ushered me into the sitting room, where the princess was already waiting. Sister to Prince Radomir, the highest-ranking Sanctioned in the land after the tsar, Princess Alisa was a widow who spent most of her time at court. She was a large woman with light skin and small eyes that stayed fixed on me as I came up from my bow.

"Sofia Stepanova," she sniffed. "My cousin says you are an accomplished seamstress. As Heli's fashion sense has never been particularly strong, that remains to be seen. I trust you're familiar with the most recent Andinorian styles?"

"Yes, your highness. If you'd like to see some sketches, I have them right here." I reached for the papers, but the princess waved a hand.

"No need. I already know what I want. Just show me your fabric samples."

She chose a gold brocade for her new gown. The style was wide-bodied with a bell-shaped skirt called a farthingale. It was designed for the warmer seasons of Andinor and not likely to be comfortable throughout the long Inzhrian winter, but she had made a single concession to the weather: the collar would be lined with fur, providing a modicum of modesty and warmth.

"And I want the sable for the color," she said as I began taking her measurements.

"Yes, your highness." I didn't bother to remind her that she'd made the same request twice already.

A loud noise from the outer hall made me jump. The princess's head jerked up. A bout of shouting rang out, and a moment later a maidservant rushed into the sitting room, her eyes full of tears. "His majesty Tsar Miroslav is here to see you, princess."

The tsar charged past the girl. "Traitors!" he thundered.

"Your majesty." The princess sank into a stiff bow. "I apologize for my state. I was unaware of the honor."

Having bowed as well, I stepped back, trying not to draw attention to myself. My heart raced. Miroslav, the monster responsible for Han's missing hand and for so many other hardships, was mere steps away from me.

"'Unaware of the honor.'" He sneered at her. "As if you don't know exactly why I'm here. Traitors! Traitors to the Blood, all of you!"

Princess Alisa's small eyes widened. "Your majesty, I must protest. I and my household live only to serve you."

"You lie!" He thrust a paper under her nose. She took it and skimmed the contents, the blood draining from her face as she read.

Her voice trembled. "He is no brother of mine!"

Her brother. Radomir, possibly the most powerful Sanctioned in the tsardom. Had he joined Borislav? I couldn't imagine another reason for Miroslav's fury.

"You will swear to it you had no knowledge of this treachery?" Miroslav's skin was flushed with anger, a stark contrast to his cousin's ashy countenance.

"By Otets and the Blood."

"I will hunt him down." The tsar paced the room. "My brother's foolish rebellion was enough to bear, but I crushed that. Radomir was the leader of my forces! No one had more of my trust." He stopped in front of a large tapestry depicting Otets' Bloodline. "I was content to let Borislav spend the rest of his days in exile. I was not vengeful. The tsardom believed him dead. His cause was vanquished, and so I didn't hunt him down. See what that munificence brought me? He's taken my greatest ally, and they're raising an army." He spit on the tapestry, and a glob of saliva landed on Borislav's name. "I'll see them both hanged."

The princess opened her mouth and closed it again.

"Call your sons to court," he said, turning to leave. "I'll not give that traitor my throne nor my men. The court will travel to meet my army, and everyone can see what I do to traitors."

Princess Alisa and I both bowed as he swept out of the room without a backward glance.

As soon as we heard the door close, the princess called for her clerk. Noticing me, she said, "You may go. Come back tomorrow at the same time."

"Yes, your highness." I gathered my supplies, packing them up slowly and carefully.

The clerk appeared with the instruments of his trade. "We must write to my sons," the princess told him. "My cousin, the traitor Borislav, has returned to Inzhria, and my brother has joined his rebellion. Both of my sons are ordered to court immediately, and they must denounce Radomir and Borislav most vehemently to anyone they meet. I won't have the stench of treason attached to our name." Noticing me still in the room, she snapped her fingers. "Out, girl! You're not needed."

I went directly to Lord Ilya and Lady Heli's quarters. "Is the baroness available?" I asked the footman that answered the door.

He gestured for me to wait in the small entrance hall and went to announce me. He returned a moment later. "My lady asks you to attend her in the drawing room."

The baroness didn't look up as I entered the room. "I hope you're not here to change the fabric on my order, Sofia Stepanova. I must tell you, I'm quite settled on that color."

"Not at all, my lady. I had some new trim arrive this morning, and I wanted to show you."

Lady Heli glanced at me. "Close the door, child. There's a draft, and these old bones don't tolerate the cold."

As I did, the baroness set aside the book she was reading and beckoned me closer. "Do you have news?"

"Yes, my lady. I would have waited to tell Izolda, but I was nearby, and I do have some new trim with me."

"So long as you don't make a habit of coming to my quarters. What news?"

I took out the trim and handed it to her as I relayed what had happened in Princess Alisa's quarters.

The baroness ran her fingers over the sample of fabric. "Good. It's good that we're the first to hear of this. His majesty will be glad to know how quickly news reaches court. Well done, Sofia." She offered a rare smile.

I smiled back, grateful for the compliment. Perhaps I wouldn't be a complete waste here at court.

A moment later, the baroness was back to her usual business-like self. "You should build contacts within Alisa's household. She's close to the tsar and highly ambitious. News always reaches her first. The tsarina and dowager tsarina are more sequestered than the rest of the court, but an ally or two in the Tsarina's Tower wouldn't go amiss, either."

Being with the princess when the tsar stormed in was lucky, but Lady Heli was right. I couldn't expect to be so fortunate all the time. Most of the information I would gather would come from allies and contacts, friends I made at court. I needed to extend my social circle. "I met the baroness of Arick today, and her husband's manservant last week. Those connections would be worth developing as well, yes?"

"Kazimir Vladimirovich. Pah." The baroness scowled. "Common trash marrying his way into nobility. He sullies the tsardom. But you're correct. He has Miroslav's favor, and having eyes on him could be beneficial. "You have good instincts, girl."

"Thank you, my lady."

"Remember, in future, send your news through Izolda. If you're seen coming and going from my quarters too often, we'll both draw unnecessary attention." She handed me back the trim sample and waved a hand in dismissal.

I bowed. "Yes, my lady."

As I left, the baroness called after me. "Close the door, child! The draft!"

19
GATHERING AN ARMY
Han

Things moved quickly once Prince Radomir joined our cause. The tsar sent messengers around the country, calling men to meet us at the prince's fortified castle, a day's ride from his dacha. We moved into the castle before the first snow, and the recruits began arriving just as a thin sheet of white spread over the ground.

Upon their arrival, Tsar Borislav and the prince locked themselves in a room and began drawing up campaign plans, leaving me with the overwhelming task of organizing the men into units.

I sat in a small room inside the front gate. Outside the door, an endless line of men stretched down the road. My chest swelled with pride. So many. So many had come.

"Full name and town of origin," I said to the next arrival, a slight man with a crooked nose.

"Nikolai Igorovich of Sobralen, your highness."

I fought back a laugh. "I'm not the prince, sir. I'm Han Antonovich. Soldier. Former soldier," I corrected, seeing the man's eyes snag on my arm. "Any combat experience?"

"No, sir."

"Not a problem. We'll train you." The prince's clerk was assisting me. I pointed to a spot on his paper. "Put him here. Nikolai Igorovich, you'll be reporting to Captain Matvey Il'ich. Last I saw him, he was in the smithy. He'll get you settled in."

The next few hours passed similarly, men stating names and locations until their faces all began to bleed together. I rubbed my hand over my face as another recruit opened the door.

"Name?" I asked, not opening my eyes.

"Yakov Aleksandrovich of Selyik."

"Yakov!" I looked into the grinning face of my friend. "I didn't expect you so soon." Behind him was a crowd of men from Selyik, my tenants Pyotr and Yegor at the front.

"Think I'd miss the fight? Soon as we got word where to meet, we left."

"Thank you," I said earnestly. "All of you." I raised a brow at Yegor Miloshovich. The older man had always made his opinion of Tsar Borislav clear. He believed Miroslav was the rightful ruler by birth, and any rebellion was indefensible.

Yegor shrugged in response to my unasked question. "Birthright or no, any tsar that can't keep his army under control is no tsar of mine. If you're looking for justice for Marya Ivanovna and your wife, I'll follow you."

Pyotr took off his ushanka, holding the fur hat to his chest. "I hope you know how sorry we are, Han, to hear about Mila Dmitrievna's illness. I pray she'll recover quickly."

I swallowed a lump in my throat. It grated on me, lying to my men, and I still hadn't forgiven Mila for leaving. How dare she put herself in danger like that? It was my responsibility to protect her, not the other way around. She should be safe at home, not in the middle of Miroslav's court, risking her life.

I tamped down my emotions. "Thank you, friends." To the clerk, I said, "Yakov Aleksandrovich served with me at Barbezht. He'll be quartered with me until the tsar decides what to do with him."

Thirty men had come from Selyik, all men I knew in some way or another. I spread them out as much as possible. If a unit took a large number of casualties, I wanted to be sure the losses didn't disproportionately affect any town or region.

Once the men from Selyik were assigned, there was a lull in the arrivals. I clapped the clerk on the back. "Take a break, but don't go far. I want to see my men settled. If anyone else comes while I'm gone, send someone for me."

I directed the men to their assigned places. I'd placed both Pyotr and Yegor under Captain Fyodor Yakovlevich, and I wanted to personally introduce them.

Fyodor Yakovlevich was the young commander of the prince's guard, a light-skinned man with a stern face and a short, dark beard. We found him in the stables, talking to a young woman. The captain looked up at our approach.

"Han Antonovich. Bringing me new recruits?"

"Yegor Miloshovich and Pyotr Vasilievich, captain. They were my father's tenants before me, and you won't find more loyal men anywhere."

He studied them for a moment. "Combat experience?"

"Spider Wars, sir. All three. We served together driving the Drakra east," Yegor said.

"Good. You can help me turn these boys into soldiers. I'll show you to your barracks." He nodded at me, Yakov, and the young woman. "Afternoon."

As they left, the woman looked me up and down with deep-set eyes. "You must be the man who talked my father into a rebellion. He doesn't often change his mind. I imagine you're quite persuasive."

I bowed. "My apologies, princess. I didn't realize his highness had family in the castle."

She laughed heartily, her long black braid swaying as she tipped her head back. "I'm no princess, sir. Blood Bastard Lada Radomirovna."

I'd never met a Blood Bastard, a magic-wielding illegitimate child of the Sanctioned. This woman didn't look dangerous, but appearances meant little when it came to magic. I'd seen the power of the Blood already. I bowed again, wary of offending her.

She turned to Yakov, a smile playing on her full lips. "But you haven't introduced your friend."

"May I introduce Yakov Aleksandrovich, another survivor of Barbezht?" Yakov was staring at her, transfixed. I elbowed him.

He flinched. "A pleasure to meet you, Lada Radomirovna."

They stared at each other. After a moment, I cleared my throat. "If you'll excuse us, Lada Radomirovna, I need to see Yakov settled in." I bowed once more and grabbed Yakov's arm, pulling him away.

As we stepped out into the frozen courtyard, I let go of him. "Your tongue almost hit the floor, your mouth was so wide."

He glanced back over his shoulder. "Fuck. I've never seen anyone so…" He shook his head, at a loss for words.

I rolled my eyes. She was beautiful, with full curves, red-brown skin, and a braid that reached her waist. And he was out of his depth with her. "You should keep your distance. Her father's a prince. Even if she's not legitimate, I doubt he'd let just anyone court her."

"I was just looking." He glowered at me.

"Anyway, she's a Blood Bastard. If her father doesn't kill you for the impertinence, she could." Not that she'd been opposed to the attention. In fact, she'd seemed inclined to encourage him.

He waggled his eyebrows. "I'd die happy."

We'd reached my quarters. I pushed open the door. "I need to get back to the gate. I'll leave you to get settled in. And stay away from the Blood Bastard, *durachok*," I teased.

"No promises."

I wound through the castle grounds, dodging men as they moved from tent to tent. The sharp tang of snow mingled with the smoky smell of cooking fires. My stomach rumbled, but supper would have to wait until the meeting with the tsar was over. I pulled open one of the enormous castle doors and cast a longing glance back at the men on their way to supper. Hopefully the meeting wouldn't take long.

Yakov caught up to me as I strode down the hall. "What's going on?"

"I know as much as you." I brushed snow from my sleeves and nodded a greeting at Fyodor Yakovlevich, who reached the war room as we did. "Any idea what this is about, captain?"

"Not an inkling. The scouts have been quiet, as far as I know." He opened the door to let us pass.

We were the last to arrive, save for the tsar and the prince. The other men waited around a table covered with maps. As I took my seat, the opposite door opened, and the tsar entered, followed closely by Prince Radomir. Everyone stood.

"Be seated, friends." The tsar sat and waited for the scraping chairs to fall silent. "I've received word from the capital. My brother is aware that I'm in the country and raising an army. He's been informed of our location and will be bringing not just the army, but the entire court with him for battle."

My heart leapt to my throat. Was Mila the source of this news? Was she in danger? I shook myself. Surely I would have been told if something happened to her.

He looked around the table, meeting the eyes of each man. "We must prepare for an attack. Radomir and I have been deliberating, but we look to you for counsel."

"With the time until Miroslav arrives," Radomir said, "We can choose where to make our stand and fortify it."

Matvey Il'ich spoke. "Respectfully, your highness, the castle already makes a strong defense. Wouldn't it be better to use the time to prepare the men, instead of taking them from their training to fortify a second position?"

The prince gave him a withering look. "The tsar and I can fortify the battlefield without taking the soldiers from their training. We must have a place to retreat if the battle goes against us."

"That was my mistake—one of them—at Barbezht," Borislav said. "We had nowhere to retreat when the tide of battle turned."

Fyodor Yakovlevich pointed to a spot on one of the maps. "These hills would be defensible. If we camped here, we'd have the sun to our backs in the morning."

"Why wait for morning to attack?" asked a commander whose name I couldn't remember. "We can attack as soon as they arrive, take advantage of their exhaustion from the march."

"No!" the tsar said sharply. The room fell silent. "No, I will not host a surprise attack, not when he brings my court with him. I have allies at court whose safety I will not risk. We will wage open battle, honorably, on a field of our choosing."

The prince folded his hands on the table. "As the Prophet tells us, 'He who wages war on the innocent has no place in Otets' inheritance.'"

"But we are agreed?" Borislav asked. "We leave the castle before my brother arrives?"

A murmur of assent went through the room.

"Good." The tsar leaned forward. "Yakovlevich, I'd like your men to take the vanguard, and I can lead the next wave. Then—"

Prince Radomir cleared his throat. "Your majesty, with all due respect, you will not be leading anyone on the field."

"I beg your pardon?" Only the tightening of the tsar's eyes betrayed any emotion. His voice was deathly calm. "You do not lead this army, cousin. Sanctioned you may be, but you are not the Heir."

"Nor are you, Borislav," the prince said, unperturbed. My breath caught at his audacity. "Not yet. And if you lose your life on the battlefield, our Disinheritance ends where it began. Your place is in the camp. 'Let the Heir not abandon his brothers in foolish enterprise,' as the Prophet wrote."

Their eyes locked for a moment, the room thick with tension. The tsar sighed. "You are right." He looked around the table. "I would not ask you to fight for a cause that I myself would not willingly die for, but if I fall, this was all for naught. I must trust you to fight for me."

The talk turned back to organization of the battle lines, and my mind wandered to Mila. Had she been the one to discover Miroslav's plans? If she had, how? I pictured her crouching in a shadowy corner, hidden behind a curtain, listening as Miroslav plotted with a room full of faceless advisors. The corner of my mouth twitched upward at the thought. No, the reality was likely much more mundane, if no less dangerous. Perhaps she'd made a friend at court who worked directly for Miroslav, or maybe she'd overheard something while working for the tsarina.

However she'd heard the news, if she was the tsar's informant, she'd undoubtedly risked her life to pass it along to us. I clenched my fist, focusing on the feel of my nails digging into my palm. I shouldn't be thinking about it. She would be fine. Even considering otherwise felt like ill-wishing.

I forced my attention back to the tsar, who was speaking. "Tomorrow morning, Radomir and I will begin preparations on the battlefield. Matvey, could you prepare a sufficient guard to accompany us? Han and Fyodor, I'd appreciate your insight on the field, if you would join us as well."

I shivered, wrapping my warm shuba tighter around me. Why the tsar thought we needed to be out so early, I didn't know. Not that I had difficulty waking, but a hot breakfast would have been nice.

But if we'd waited, we would have missed seeing the sun rise over our chosen battlefield. Yakovlevich had been right; we would have the sun at our backs, putting Miroslav's army with the disadvantage of fighting with the sun in their eyes. I scanned the region. The hills wouldn't be the most convenient place to camp, steep as they were, but the field they overlooked would be ideal for battle.

The tsar, sitting atop his horse, came up next to me. "What are your thoughts, Han?"

"It will serve, your majesty." I frowned. "Though I wish it wasn't quite so open."

Fyodor Yakovlevich, on my other side, nodded. "A wall to the south, or at least another hill or two, would keep us from being flanked without leaving us trapped."

"I agree." Borislav looked to his cousin. "Radomir?"

The prince dismounted and handed his horse's reins to a guard. From inside his fur coat, he took his wand. "Stone or ice?"

"Ice, I think. No need to upset the local geography more than we have to." The tsar dismounted as well, long white staff in hand.

The tsar raised his staff. "You might want to stay back."

Radomir raised his wand. The hairs on my arms stood on end as I heard a faint crackling sound, like tiny icicles breaking. I looked over at Fyodor, but he was unperturbed. The tsar and the prince stared intently at a point on the field below us, and I followed their gaze as the crackling grew.

A wall of ice rose out of the snow. Thin at the foot of the hills, it thickened as it stretched along the edge of the field. As it grew, so did the sound of cracking ice. The wall was nearly ten feet tall before the tsar shouted over the now-thunderous cracking, "That's enough!"

Silence fell. My ears ringing, I stared at the tsar as he surveyed their handiwork.

I'd known the Sanctioned were descended from Otets, but they were human like me, I'd always thought. Even the small healing spell I'd seen Prince Radomir do to his horse had been nothing compared to this. But the powers the two Sanctioned had just shown—those were godlike. Beyond anything I'd ever expected.

"That should be sufficient, don't you think?" Borislav asked his cousin. The prince had already walked away with Fyodor Yakovlevich, gazing down at the field in contemplation. The tsar turned to me instead. "I believe that should suit what you had in mind."

I blinked, staring open mouthed at the newly formed wall of ice. "Yes. I—Yes. Your majesty, I had no idea you were capable of this."

The tsar smiled slightly. "Yes, I suppose it can be a little overwhelming if you've never seen it done."

I looked at our companions, all men from Radomir's personal guard. They scanned the horizon for threats, no sign of shock or awe at the scene they'd witnessed. Even my horse, borrowed from the prince's stables, hadn't spooked at the sound. Perhaps such wonders were commonplace when one worked for a Sanctioned. "It's unbelievable, your majesty. Truly, with the two of you, I don't see how we can lose."

His smile disappeared. "That might be true, were we able to use our Gifts in battle. As it is, we can only prepare the field."

"As it should be." Radomir turned from his observation to join the discussion. "The Prophet's mandates were clear. The Gifts of the Blood should never be used against the unSanctioned, even in battle."

"Even so," I said, "this is incredible. With the nature of the terrain and your Gifts to enhance it, we have a strong advantage." I wasn't foolish enough to assume that meant we'd win, but with two of Inzhria's most powerful Sanctioned on our side, I had hope.

The tsar nodded, looking out over the field again. "I hope so, Han. I hope so."

20

COMPLICATIONS

Mila

"Fuck," I muttered as I pricked my finger. I threw the needle and fabric down and sucked at the tiny wound. I hadn't bled on the fabric, thank Otets. Princess Alisa was sure to notice if I did. I reached for the needle again, but it had fallen when I threw down my fabric. I knelt down, searching the floor. There—a slight sparkle next to the table leg. Object in hand, I stood, only to smack my head on the table.

"Witness, Prophet, and Steward," I swore, rubbing the spot I'd hit. The day kept getting worse and worse.

It wasn't as though I had any pressing work. My only orders were from Lady Heli and Princess Alisa, and they were leaving with the court in the morning. I tucked the needle safely into its pouch and stretched. Maybe getting out of the room would improve my mood.

Bundled up in my fur-lined overcoat, I headed outside with no particular destination in mind. Snow crunched beneath my feet. It was a bad time of year for travel, let alone for battle. A snowstorm could strand the whole army on the road. Then again, the good season was short. The winter snows lasted nearly half the year, and the spring and fall rains could be as bad as the snow, if not worse.

If Miroslav hoped to ambush his brother's army with this sudden attack, he was mistaken. Otets willing, Lady Heli had gotten word to Tsar Borislav, and he was preparing a defense even as Miroslav readied to leave.

A defense, I hoped, that Han would be far from. I said a silent prayer that the tsar wouldn't expect Han to be on the battlefield. He'd practiced swordplay with Yakov, I knew, but he would never be a skilled fighter without his sword hand. He couldn't even write well, despite constant practice; he dictated most of his letters to me or to Kyril Kyrilovich. If he fought, he'd never survive.

No, I couldn't think like that. The tsar wasn't stupid. He knew where Han's skills lay, and they weren't on the battlefield. He'd keep Han away from the fighting.

"Ah, if it isn't the fair sun Sofia!"

Lost in thought, I hadn't noticed Alexey Grigorovich walking across the courtyard toward me. He reached me and bowed. "Whose day are you off to brighten today?"

"Good afternoon," I said tersely. I was in no mood to banter.

"Do clouds darken the sun's countenance?" He fell into step beside me. "Would that I could remove those clouds."

"Aren't you preparing for a battle?" I snapped.

"I was on my way to the stables." He took my arm and pulled me off the path, stopping under the shade of an evergreen tree. I tensed at the touch, but he let his hand drop. He took a step back, giving me space as I folded my arms across my chest. "I apologize if I've offended you, Sofia Stepanova. I meant no disrespect."

I took a deep breath, uncrossing my arms to shove my hands in my pockets. The man was harmless, if a flirt. "I'm a little on edge," I said by way of apology.

"Is it because of the battle?"

I nodded, not meeting his eye.

"You won't be traveling with the court, will you?"

"No, I just..." I scanned my mind for a reason that wouldn't arouse suspicion. "My father died in the last uprising," I said finally, looking up at him. "The talk of battle brings back memories, I suppose."

"I'm sorry to hear that."

I waved a hand, dismissing his concern. "It was a long time ago. I shouldn't let it bother me."

"It's my experience that pain is no respecter of time. But I'll do my best to end this uprising, so no talk of battle can cloud the sun's countenance." He winked.

I rolled my eyes, my lips tugging upward in spite of my sour mood. "Alexey Grigorovich, I believe you have an inflated sense of self-importance."

He flashed a grin. "If increasing my importance is what it takes to set your mind at ease, I'll do it gladly."

I shook my head. The man was shameless, but at least his ridiculous conversation was a distraction from my worries. "I should let you get back to work. I'm keeping you from the baron, and I was going to see Izolda." Since she would be leaving with the court, I doubted she would have time to spend with me, but it wouldn't hurt to find out.

"I'll escort you." He offered me his arm.

I hesitated. "I wouldn't want to make you late."

"Nonsense." He took my arm and tucked it in his. "Lord Kazimir has enough to think about. He'll hardly notice my absence. Lord Ilya's quarters are on my way, besides."

I let him guide me into the castle. He kept up a steady stream of cheerful conversation as we walked down the servants' corridor, pointing out doors and telling me about the nobles who lived behind them. He seemed to sense I wasn't in the mood to talk, because he didn't pause for any responses beyond the occasional "oh?"

"And here, of course, we have the quarters of Lord Ilya, baron of Tsebol," he said as we reached the door. "I trust you can find your—ah, here is the moon!"

The door in question had opened to reveal Izolda, her arms full of linens. Catching sight of us, she arched a brow, looking amused. I yanked my arm from Alexey's, guilty heat suffusing my body, and she smothered a laugh.

"Alexey." She nodded a greeting. "If I'm the moon, and Fia's the sun, what does that make you?"

"Blessed by Otets." He bowed, a self-satisfied grin on his face. "My master awaits, but I hope to see both of you soon." He strode off down the hallway.

As soon as he was out of earshot, Izolda turned to me, smirking.

"What?"

"Nothing." She started down the hall. "I'm taking these to the laundry. Come with?"

I fell into step "It's a bit late to be doing laundry, isn't it? They won't be dry by morning."

"It's just bed sheets. Everything we're taking is already packed." She glanced sideways at me. "So what was that about?"

"Alexey? Nothing. He caught me outside, and I couldn't think how to get rid of him without being rude."

"I see." Her tone was skeptical, and I scowled. "And I suppose you won't give him a favor to take into battle?" She tutted. "To think, you could send a man off to his death without a warm thought to comfort him."

My chest tightened. No, we weren't talking about Han. Izolda didn't even know Han existed. He wouldn't be in the battle. I took a deep breath, fighting to get air in my lungs.

"Fia?" Izolda realized I had stopped walking. She turned around. "You okay? You've got an odd look."

"I'm fine." I took another breath and started walking again.

"Hey." She stepped into an alcove, jerking her head in indication that I should follow. She peered down the hallway, then dumped the linens on the floor and crossed her arms. "There's no one to hear. Talk to me."

The shadowy alcove darkened—Izolda's doing, I realized, with the minor shadow-melding abilities she'd inherited from her grandmother. The effect was disconcerting, the darkness unnatural, but no one passing by would see us unless they were looking for us.

Still, I didn't want to talk. "It's nothing."

"And I'm the grand duchess." Through the shadows, I saw her lean against the wall. "You can trust me, you know. I may not know who you were before all this, but you're not my friend because I knew the real Sofia. I respect you. I like you. If there's something wrong, I'd like to help."

I sighed. "It's not something you can help with. It's this battle. This," I gestured vaguely, "everything."

"Was it what I said about Alexey?"

"No! Well, not exactly." I bit my lip. How much should I reveal? I could trust Izolda—she had as much to lose as me, if I was discovered as a spy—but should I tell her about Han?

I had to. She was my friend. And Otets knew I needed a friend. Someone to confide in. "There's...someone else."

"You have a suitor?"

I smiled ruefully. "Not exactly." I glanced down the hall. Still empty, but I lowered my voice. "I'm married."

"Huh."

Not quite the overwhelming reaction I'd expected. "He's—"

"The scarred stud who was staying in the baron's wing at the castle in Tsebol?"

I froze, and Izolda laughed.

"There aren't many people who get to stay in the baron's wing. You were both there at the same time, so I assumed he was related to you somehow."

"Why didn't you say anything?"

She shrugged. "You didn't trust me yet. You didn't even know me. I didn't want to push it."

"Oh." I stared unseeing at the wall, mind reeling.

"You think he's going to be in the battle?" she asked after a moment.

"I don't know. I hope not."

"I see."

I sighed. "And Alexey..."

"Complicates things."

"Exactly." Even though there was nothing real between me and Alexey Grigorovich, I couldn't help feeling like I was being unfaithful to Han.

The shadows around us lightened. "Well, no sense dwelling on things we can't change. Stay busy, and try not to think about it. Take one step at a time."

"Thank you, Izolda." It was a relief to have someone else to confide my worries in.

"No problem." She grinned. "C'mon. I need to get these to the laundress before the baroness starts missing me."

21
BATTLE JOINED
Han

Looking down from the entrance of my tent, I could see Miroslav's camp, the multicolored tents a stark contrast to the snowy horizon they sat upon. Many of the tents, I knew, housed the nobles of the court, but they gave the appearance of a much larger army than had been reported. In comparison, Tsar Borislav's army was miniscule.

The battle lines were forming on the field, but off to the side, opposite the ice wall, was a hastily-erected platform where the nobles were gathering with their retinues. The platform was positioned far enough from the armies to prevent collateral damage, but close enough that the occupants would be able to see the outcome of the battle as it happened. As though war was a jousting tournament, to be enjoyed while drinking spiced wine.

In Miroslav's camp, a few figures moved about. I peered down at them from my spot in the doorway of my own tent, squinting to see better.

"She's not there, you know," Yakov said from his cot inside the tent.

"I wasn't looking for her," I lied. Objectively, I knew Mila wouldn't have traveled with the court—as a trade worker, there was no reason for her to leave the palace—but I couldn't help hoping for a glimpse of her.

"Sure, you weren't." Groaning, he stood and stretched. "Prophet's balls, why do battles always have to be so *early?*"

"You could always go back to sleep after the tsar dismisses us." Borislav and his brother had agreed to talk terms before the battle. A meaningless gesture, everyone knew, but one that must be made. The tsar had requested Yakov and I join him for that meeting.

He snorted. *"Da,* with cannons going off halfway down the hill. That'll be easy."

"Get dressed, *durachok.* The tsar's waiting."

A short while later, we rode from camp with the tsar, Prince Radomir, and several of the tsar's advisors. Passing through the shadow of a plateau formed by the tsar's magic, I glanced up. At the top of the structure, I knew, was a cannon and the team of men to operate it. In front of the platforms, soldiers stood silent in formation. An ice abatis jutted out of the ground, angled toward the enemy. I shivered at the sight, picturing the bodies that would soon be broken on the frozen spikes.

Miroslav's retinue reached the center of the battlefield at the same time we did. Revulsion turned my stomach as I saw the tsar's brother for the first time since Barbezht. This was the man who had taken my hand, who had slaughtered and caused suffering for so many.

I looked sideways at Yakov, knowing his mind was in the same place. His teeth were clenched, knuckles white on his horse's reins. His gaze bored into Miroslav, who wore a scowl beneath his shining black fur hat.

Miroslav's party was no bigger than Borislav's, but while Tsar Borislav's advisors were simply dressed, Miroslav's were dressed too finely to be anything but nobles. I didn't recognize any of the noblemen, but that wasn't surprising. Aside from the first uprising, I'd never traveled beyond Tsebol.

Behind the small group of nobles was an enclosed sleigh. It was simple, almost rustic, and the windows were covered so no one could see the occupants. As the black-hooded driver halted the horses, a sense of dread crawled up my spine.

Tsar Borislav nodded in greeting as the two parties drew to a stop. "Brother."

Miroslav's scowl deepened. "Borislav. Are you ready to submit?"

The tsar's voice was quiet. "You know I can't do that. You've forfeited your rights as Heir of the Sanctioned, Miroslav."

"*I* am the Heir," Miroslav hissed. "You can't take that from me."

Radomir cleared his throat. "The Prophet said, 'If the Heir burdens his brothers and does not follow the precepts of Otets, his brothers are to make a Disinheritance of him.'"

The nobleman nearest to Miroslav spat on the ground. "Superstitious drivel used to excuse treason. The tsar rules by birthright, not by some divine nonsense."

Something about the spitting nobleman left a bad taste in my mouth. His face was red, his hair and beard a dusty orange. The expression he wore was one of pure contempt. He looked at me, eyes snagging on my missing hand, and a wicked grin crept across his face. I clenched my fist and turned back to my tsar.

"You've surrounded yourself with unbelievers, Miroslav." Borislav spoke calmly, as if addressing a child. "You've used the Gifts of the Blood against those you were charged to rule, and you've overburdened the people with taxes to support an army in times of peace. Otets—"

"Times of peace? Is that what you call this, when you raise an army against me?"

"Otets has charged us to make a Disinheritance," Borislav went on, as if his brother hadn't spoken. "If you surrender now, you won't be punished. Accept your Disinheritance, and all your needs will be met. But you must allow me to rule. For the good of the realm."

"Do you honestly believe your self-righteous drivel? You want the throne for your own glory. You think that because our father favored you, you deserve to be tsar. The birthright is *mine!*" His voice became louder, more shrill with every word. "You won't win this, Borislav. I defeated you before, and I will again. Or have you forgotten Barbezht?"

The tsar beckoned me and Yakov forward. "I haven't forgotten, brother. Have you?"

Miroslav stared collectedly at us. "I wondered where they had gone. No matter. I found the rest." Turning his horse, he nodded to the hooded driver, who climbed down from his seat at the front of the sleigh and opened the door. A guard came out, followed by a group of men changed together by their ankles. Another guard followed them.

The prisoners' hands weren't chained. As I watched them approach, I realized with a sinking feeling that each of the men was missing his right hand. One man was familiar; his deep-set eyes held an expression of resignation, contrasted with the terror on his companions' faces.

"Boris Stepanovich," I breathed. Yakov and I shared a look of horror.

The remaining survivors of Barbezht. So few. I'd known only a handful of men had survived, but was it really so few? Eleven men, plus me and Yakov. Only thirteen survivors, of the hundreds of men who had taken the field for Tsar Borislav.

Borislav had recognized the men as well. He sat straighter on his horse, meeting each man's eyes in turn. "My friends, I'm so sorry for the indignities you've been forced to suffer in the wars between my brother and me."

"You can end this," Miroslav said. "Their lives are in your hands. Surrender, and I'll release them. They knelt to me at Barbezht; I won't hold your latest treason against them."

He would never let them go. Borislav had to know that. I gritted my teeth, wishing I could drive a sword between the monster's ribs.

My tsar closed his eyes and took a deep breath as if to steady himself. He looked at his brother. "No, Miroslav. Their lives are in your hands. I cannot and will not surrender."

Miroslav nodded over his shoulder, and the guards drew long daggers from their belts. "This is your last chance. Surrender, or they die."

Borislav turned to the prisoners. "I am sorry. May Otets receive you." He raised a hand in blessing.

"See what cowardice," Miroslav sneered. "He would rather sacrifice thousands in war than die himself." He waved a hand at the guards. "Kill them."

The prisoners erupted in cries for mercy that pierced my heart. What if I hadn't gone to Tsebol in search of the tsar? Would I have been kneeling there, begging for my life? I forced myself to watch as the guards stepped behind the first two men and sliced their throats. Their bodies thudded onto the ground, twitching as blood stained the snow crimson. Man by man they went down, until only Boris Stepanovich remained. His eyes remained fixed on our tsar, and Borislav met his gaze, unflinching. He didn't fight as the guard grabbed him by the hair and forced his head back. The knife tore through his throat, and his body dropped to the snow.

Miroslav turned back to his brother. "After I defeat you, you'll suffer the same fate, and your head will hang above the gates of Idesk."

Borislav didn't respond. I couldn't look away from the blood freezing in pools, the limp bodies of my brothers-in-arms. Anger roared in my ears, and my fist was so tight around the reins that my nails split the skin of my palm. Miroslav was a monster. A beast. He deserved to burn.

Over the thunder of rage in my head, I heard Radomir say, "This is why we're making a Disinheritance, cousin. You've abandoned Otets' precepts, and so He has abandoned you."

The tsar, still silent, turned his horse and rode back to the army. Tearing my gaze from the scene of the massacre, I joined the rest of Borislav's men, following him back to our line.

When we reached the assembled men, Radomir stopped. "Soldiers!" he began, but the tsar stopped him.

Borislav touched the tip of his staff to his throat. "My friends." His voice, magically amplified, made me flinch. "My friends, today my brother has yet again committed an atrocity against the subjects entrusted to him by Otets. Rather than face his Disinheritance with honor, he brought prisoners, innocents, hoping to force me to surrender by threatening their lives. Thirteen men survived the battle of Barbezht. Moments ago, while they knelt before him, Miroslav killed eleven of them."

He paused, looking up and down the lines with fire in his eyes. I saw soldiers glance at me and Yakov, and guilt and rage twisted in my gut. Guilt for surviving, and rage at Miroslav for making it so. All those hundreds of men that had gone onto the field at Barbezht, and only Yakov and I remained.

"I am filled with a righteous fury," the tsar went on, face contorted with the depth of his emotion. "My brother and all who condone such actions deserve to pay for what has been done today. I would ride at your head, bringing Otets' justice to the army opposite us!" As a cheer went up, he raised his staff, turning his eyes to the sky. Radomir scowled, his eyes narrowed in warning.

Borislav lowered his staff, and the army quieted. "But I heed the counsel of my advisors. They temper my anger, urging me not to risk our cause by placing myself in danger. So, reluctant though I am, I leave this battle in the capable hands of each one of you. I have done all I can; the rest is up to you.

"Know this, my friends: Prince Radomir will lead you well, Otets will guard you well, and you will acquit yourselves well. And when this war is over, you will know that it was won not because you had a Sanctioned at your head, but because each and every one of you fought for justice, for mercy, and for Inzhria!"

"For Inzhria!" the men echoed. For our homeland. The cry repeated as we rode through the troops back to the camp. I kept my eyes trained on the ground. I couldn't face the anger and blame in the soldiers' faces. Why should I, of all those who fought at Barbezht, be alive? I couldn't even fight this battle.

Among the cries of "For Inzhria," I heard another phrase. "For Barbezht!" My head jerked up, and I looked around for the source of the cry. The men nearby were watching me, their eyes blazing with anger, though not at me. Each man whose eyes I met nodded or saluted. Their rage was targeted toward Miroslav, toward the enemy. The kind of fury that would keep them alive through the battle. A righteous anger, a fire that would burn through all that stood against it. They weren't angry at me, they were angry *for* me.

I sat up straighter in the saddle, returning the salutes of the men I passed. I couldn't fight this battle, but they could. They would fight for me.

22

MIROSLAV'S RETURN

Mila

Two weeks. Two weeks since the court had left to follow the army, and the palace was as silent as a tomb. Even most of the trade workers had gone home when the court left. Without a tsar and a court, there was little reason to keep the palace fully staffed.

Sitting in my room, I cast my eyes around for something to do. I'd already managed to finish Princess Alisa's ornate dress. Hopefully, the princess would be pleased, though knowing the woman's temperament, I doubted it. Hateful woman. With any luck, she would freeze to death watching the battle and put everyone else out of her misery.

I sighed, two weeks of silence, with nothing but my own thoughts for company, save for the rare times when I saw one of the skeleton crew of servants left to keep the palace in order. What good was being a spy at court if I wasn't actually *with* the court? Miroslav could be slaughtering my tsar, my husband, and my friends, and there was nothing I could do about it.

Wan winter light pooled through the windows as the walls crept closer. What was happening out there, wherever Borislav's army had camped? Was the battle over? Had we won? Or was Miroslav on his way back to Idesk right now, with Han's head on a pike?

The room swam around me, bile rising in my throat. I couldn't stay in this room any longer. I needed a distraction. I stood, grabbed my coat, and fled the room.

Snow was falling, the air frozen, but I barely noticed the cold. I stalked across the palace grounds with no goal but to escape from my thoughts.

My footsteps led me toward the Frozen Boar. The inn was a long walk away, but at least it wouldn't be empty like the palace. I could lose myself in the bustle of people. My stomach growled, reminding me that I hadn't eaten since last night. Some beet soup or pirozhki might settle my nerves.

When I reached the palace gate, though, all thought of food vanished.

Miroslav was back.

He thundered into the courtyard atop his horse, his retinue close behind him. I drew back into the shadows with my heart in my throat. Were they fleeing a loss or hurrying back after a victory? They hadn't sent advance riders, and their horses were flecked with lather. They had obviously ridden hard, as though hurrying to escape Tsar Borislav. But surely the tsar wouldn't have pursued his brother all the way to the capital.

My eyes caught on one of Miroslav's retinue. Kazimir Vladimirovich. My chest tightened at the expression on his face. Fury, like the fury he'd shown on the day I first met him. The day he murdered my son.

I took deep breaths, in through my nose and out through my mouth. Control. I had to control my emotions. I couldn't afford to do otherwise.

If Kazimir Vladimirovich was angry, it had to be a good sign. Borislav must have won the battle. I closed my eyes and let my breaths wash away my tension. We would win this war. There was no other possibility.

After the fourth or fifth breath, I felt eyes on me. Alexey Grigorovich sat astride a horse near Lord Kazimir, and he frowned at me, his gaze intense.

I dropped him a bow. He dismounted and handed off his reins to a stableboy. The tsar and noblemen were already walking into the palace, but he didn't follow them. He dusted off his coat and strode toward me.

"Sofia Stepanova." He bowed.

"Welcome back," I said. "I trust our tsar successfully defeated the rebels?"

He scanned my face, an unreadable look on his own. His full lips tightened, and he shook his head. "Unfortunately not. They were better prepared than we expected, and I fear the tsar's—" He cut himself off. "We were defeated soundly. The tsar and his advisors rode ahead of the court."

I nodded, not trusting my voice to hide the relief coursing through me.

"You are well?" he asked, that unreadable look back in his eyes.

"Yes, thank you." We'd won the battle. Han would be safe. "Were there many casualties?" I hoped the tremor in my voice would be attributed to feminine weakness.

"No more than expected. Although..." He trailed off, dark eyes fixed somewhere in the distance. He looked back at me, as if judging how much to share. "Tsar Miroslav had the surviving Barbezht traitors taken prisoner before the battle. All of them. A bargaining chip of sorts against the Grand Duke. When Borislav refused to surrender, the tsar had them killed."

No.

My stomach clenched and loosened. No. This couldn't be happening. Han was supposed to be with Borislav, supposed to be safe. How had Miroslav gotten him? The world swam around me, and my knees buckled.

Before I could fall, strong arms caught me and guided me to a nearby seat.

"I'm sorry." His voice was distant and muffled. "I shouldn't have shared such gruesome news."

I gasped for air. My coat was suffocating me, but I couldn't get it off. I clawed at the clasp, unable to make my stiff fingers move properly.

He pulled my hands away, and then I was free of the coat. I still couldn't breathe. I curled in on myself, gasping for air.

Gone. Just like that, Han was gone. He'd wanted me to stay, practically begged me, but I'd left him anyway, and now he was gone. And Yakov, young, cheerful Yakov was gone, too. Did Anna know? The loss of her only son would break her.

After a few eternal minutes, I realized Alexey was still watching me. I struggled for a breath. "What—" I gasped for air. "What happened?"

"I don't want to disturb you with details." His voice was soft, pitying.

"What happened?" I clenched my fists in the skirt of my sarafan. I had to know. "Please," I choked out.

He studied me silently, his dark face full of concern. Then he took a seat next to me on the bench, not touching me but close enough I could feel his body heat. His eyes were fixed on mine. "The tsar rounded up the survivors of Barbezht. There weren't many—only about a dozen. Some of them had already declared for Borislav and were working for him in secret. On the morning of the battle, he brought the survivors onto the field and ordered Grand Duke Borislav to surrender. Borislav refused, so Tsar Miroslav had...had them killed."

Dead. Han and Yakov. Dead. The words echoed in my head.

I shivered, and Alexey wrapped my coat around my shoulders again.

"You shouldn't be out here in the cold, Sofia." He stood and held out a hand. "Can I escort you back to your quarters? Or is there someone else I can take you to?"

I shook my head and let him pull me to my feet. It didn't matter where he took me. A yawning abyss had opened inside my chest, and it would follow me wherever I went.

He took my arm and guided me across the palace grounds. The walk took a lifetime, each step an effort. I leaned on him, pitifully grateful for the support.

In my quarters, he guided me to a chair by the fireplace. He placed another log on the fire, removed my coat, and brought a blanket from the bed to tuck around me.

"Lord Kazimir will be expecting me," he said quietly. "But I'll return this evening to check on you. Will you be alright until then?"

I nodded, staring blankly at the fire. I wouldn't be alright, but his presence wouldn't change that.

He placed a hand on my shoulder. "I'll be back as soon as I can."

The door closed behind him, and I sank to the floor.

Dead. Han and Yakov were dead. Miroslav had captured them and slaughtered them, not even giving the mercy of an honorable death in battle. Han was supposed to be safe with Borislav. He was supposed to be leading the war effort, not becoming a casualty of it. How had this happened?

I'd thought Miroslav had taken everything from me before, but I'd been wrong. Through it all, despite everything I'd lost, I'd still had Han.

Not anymore. Now Miroslav had well and truly taken it all.

Darkness crept through the room. I'd lain on the floor for hours, unmoving, unable to even conjure tears. My stomach rumbled. I didn't feel hungry—didn't feel anything—but my body hadn't caught up with my mind.

I dragged myself off the floor.

Han was dead, but I wasn't. I owed it to him, to everyone I'd lost, to see this through. I couldn't give up. Not now.

I had nothing left to lose. Nothing to hold me back from seeing everyone who'd hurt me punished.

I glanced at my small mirror as I stepped into the bedroom. My eyes were dark and hollow. Empty.

I'd use that emptiness. I'd do everything I could to see Tsar Borislav on the throne. Whatever it took to see the monster punished for what he'd taken from me. I'd listen for every scrap of news, every bit of knowledge I could pass on to the rebellion, and I'd use it to ensure Borislav defeated his brother.

For Han.

For Yakov.

For my son.

For all those I'd lost, and for all the others who'd suffered similar losses. I'd do this.

I splashed some cold water onto my face and changed into a clean blue sarafan. Alexey Grigorovich had said he would return, and I wanted to be ready when he did it. He would be my first step toward seeing the monster dethroned.

23

A MISSION

Han

My bones ached. After a whole day riding in the cold, my hand was practically frozen to the reins. I slid down from the horse, pain radiating with every move, and looked around. The camp was well chosen, with a river to the east preventing attack. A thin sheet of ice lined the riverbanks, but the bulk of the water still flowed.

Tsar Borislav had set his sights on Sevken, his rightful seat as Grand Duke, for our winter base. One of Miroslav's loyalists held the castle—another Sanctioned, although not a particularly powerful one—and Borislav was ready to take it back. The tsar was confident that the majority of the castle residents remained loyal to him, but if

Miroslav had sent a troop of soldiers to defend the castle, who knew how long the siege would take? In addition to the two months of travel, between the slow pace of the army and the poor weather that would slow our progress.

I made my way through the camp, looking for the tent I shared with Yakov. The tsar always sent forerunners ahead to scout out a location and set up camp before the bulk of the army arrived, for which I was grateful. After a day on horseback, it was a relief to get out of the wind and rest.

Yakov was already lying on his cot, tossing a ball up in the air, when I walked in. "Wondered when you'd get here."

I shucked off my coat. "You can't have been here long. I saw you a quarter hour ago, mooning over the Blood Bastard." Wherever Blood Bastard Lada went, it was safe to assume Yakov would be nearby. He was her constant shadow, no matter how many times I warned him away from her. Luckily, the woman herself didn't seem opposed to the attention. Yet.

"I don't know what you think you saw, but I've been here an hour, at least." He chucked the ball at my head.

I ducked and sat down on the bed to remove my boots, but before I could, a servant knocked on the tent pole and poked his head inside. "Han Antonovich? The tsar requests your presence in his tent as soon as convenient."

I sighed, casting a longing glance at the cot. I'd planned to go straight to sleep, but obviously the tsar had other plans. "I'll be right there."

"Shame to be important," Yakov said as the servant left. "I'll just be here, sleeping unimportantly in my unimportant cot, in my unimportant tent."

I rolled my eyes. "I'll make sure the tsar finds something to keep you busy, if you're feeling useless, *durachok*. Brushing the horses, maybe, or digging latrines." I grabbed my hat and coat, shaking off the excess water, and stepped out into the snow again.

What could the Borislav want now? I saw Matvey Il'ich walking in the opposite direction; apparently not all the advisors had been summoned. Had the tsar heard from Mila? I quickened my pace, fear and anticipation urging me onward.

As I approached the tsar's tent, I could hear Prince Radomir's voice raised in anger.

"—little more than beasts," the prince was saying. "Otets needs no pagans to carry out his plans."

"I've made my decision," Tsar Borislav responded calmly as I entered the tent. "I can't risk my brother getting to them first." He turned to me.

"You asked for me, your majesty?"

"Yes." The tsar sank into a chair and gestured for me and the prince to do the same. "To put it simply, Han, we need allies."

Radomir snorted, but the tsar shot him a look. He fell back into silence.

"You know I spent the better part of the last five years in Andinor. While there, I sought allies to support me in my brother's Disinheritance. All the dignitaries I met with refused me. We can expect no foreign assistance, and I fear our army will be insufficient to face my brother."

He was right. The last battle had been a solid victory. We'd been lucky, but we couldn't grow complacent. "I've been worried about that as well, your majesty."

"What do you know of the Drakra?"

I frowned. "A little. My wife's mother and brother live near the East Mountains." I thought back to what Sergey's letters had told us. The Drakra were a matriarchal race of ferocious warriors. They worshiped a spider goddess, and most Inzhrians were either terrified of them or hated them. The last tsar had led three wars—commonly called the Spider Wars—against the Drakra, driving them east into the mountains. "Her brother says they're not as bad as their reputation. He trades with them on occasion."

"Good." The tsar nodded his approval. "I need someone who's able to approach this situation without bias." He gave the prince a pointed look. "I want you to go to Yixa na Chekke, high priestess of the Drakra, and treat with them on my behalf. Convince them to fight for me against my brother. Once I take the throne, I will recognize them as an independent nation. We can return some of the land my father took in the wars, and they can send an ambassador to my court, with all the rights and privileges of a human ambassador from a foreign court."

He was trusting me to negotiate an alliance for him? This was a far cry from asking farmers and smiths to join an army. Treating with the Drakra was a task for a politician, an ambassador. Not for a one-handed soldier.

"You would make them equal to the people of the Blood." Prince Radomir's lip curled in disgust. "This is a mistake."

He ignored his cousin. "I give you leave to choose your own traveling companions, but your group should remain small. No more than two or three others. I can't spare the men, and I don't wish you to draw attention to yourself. You saw what my brother did to your fellow survivors of Barbezht." His face darkened. "He would do the same to you, or worse, were you to be captured."

And to Mila, if Miroslav found out who she was. I tamped down a spark of resentment toward Borislav for sending her away. It had been her choice. If I had to be angry with anyone, it should be with her, for leaving me.

I forced the thoughts of my wife away. "I'm honored you would choose me for this, your majesty, but is there not someone more qualified?"

"I don't wish to honor you. I wish for you to negotiate my way out of this war." He gave me a wry smile. "If I had a full court, I would have other ambassadors to send with you, but we are at war. You are the most qualified man I can spare at the moment."

Most qualified, or most disposable? I immediately hated myself for the thought. Tsar Borislav trusted me. "I will strive to do you justice, your majesty."

"Who would you have as your companions?"

I went through the list of men in my mind. I couldn't ask the tsar to part with any of the commanders in the middle of the campaign. "With your permission, I'd like to take Yakov Aleksandrovich. I know he's young, but he's loyal. You won't find anyone more devoted to your cause." My friend was impulsive, but when he used his mind rather than his fist, he was smart. There was no one I'd rather have with me for something like this.

"Of course. Who else?"

I thought for a moment. "They might be offended if you send a party of all men. Given their matriarchal culture."

"Pagan nonsense," Radomir muttered.

"I had thought of that," the tsar said. "They value strength, especially mental strength. Loath as I am to part with a healer in the middle of a war, I believe Radomir's daughter may be the best choice."

The Blood Bastard. The prince didn't seem surprised by Borislav's suggestion. Perhaps that had been the cause of their earlier argument.

He stood, shaking his head. "This war is changing you, cousin." He strode out of the tent without waiting for a dismissal.

Borislav turned back to me. "I had hoped he would come to see reason." He sighed. "Perhaps he will before your return. So, the Blood Bastard and the Barbezht survivors. Do you need anyone else?"

"No, your majesty." Yakov would be glad to have a purpose and ecstatic once he found out who was joining us. *Otets help me.* He was going to be insufferable for the next few weeks, alone with just me and the Blood Bastard. It could be a long journey.

"Good. I'll have what you need brought to your tent. Inform your companions that you'll leave at dawn."

I stood, but the tsar motioned for me to sit back down. "There's one more thing."

It was still dark when we left the next morning, though the snow, thankfully, had stopped. The tsar had provided us with a sleigh and horses, as well as a few small but expensive gifts for the Drakra and the necessary papers and supplies for the journey.

I sat in the driver's seat, but my mind was back in the tsar's tent. What he'd asked me to do...I didn't know if I could do it. It went against every moral, every standard I'd ever held dear.

It was a last resort, I reminded myself. With a little luck and hard work, things wouldn't come to that. We could persuade the Drakra to join us without employing such drastic measures.

I looked over my shoulder, trying to put my worries away. Yakov was half-asleep, buried beneath the furs, though carefully not touching the Blood Bastard sitting next to him. Lada appeared more awake, watching the snow-covered countryside pass by, but I could tell by the stiff set of her body that she was every bit as aware of Yakov's presence as he was of hers.

This was going to be a long journey.

I broke the silence. "Thank you for joining us, Lada Radomirovna."

"Call me Lada."

I turned my attention back to guiding the horses. "If you'll call me Han," I said. "And once *durachok* back there wakes up, you can call him Yakov. Or *durachok*. Whichever you prefer."

Lada laughed.

"I don't know why we had to leave so early," Yakov grumbled. "The sun's not even up yet."

The sky was, in fact, beginning to lighten in the east, though it remained gray. A cold wind blew, but without the oppressive feeling of impending snow. We wouldn't be soaked to the skin by the time we stopped for the night.

"I'll tell you what, Yakov." I glanced back at my friend. "The next time the tsar tells us to do something, you can let him know it's too early. Let me know how that goes."

"I don't believe this was the tsar's idea. It was all you and your unholy thoughts of what morning is."

I shrugged. "As I said, you can talk to the tsar if you've got an issue. But it's too late now, anyway." To Lada, I said, "Yakov thinks doing anything before midday is a sin against Otets and a personal attack."

"I can relate, when it's this cold," she replied. "We won't be camping in this weather, will we?"

"Not unless there's no other choice. We'll stay at inns if we can find them, or Blood Temples if we can't. If anyone asks where we're going, we're on our way to see my wife's family while she recovers from Moon Fever in a hospital near the mountains."

"Does your wife's family actually live near the East Mountains?"

"Yes. Her brother, Sergey, trades with the Drakra." I couldn't rely on their introduction, though. Mila's mother was a staunch supporter of Miroslav, and my relationship with Sergey was tenuous at best.

"And your wife? Is she actually recovering from Moon Fever?"

I tensed. I hadn't had to lie about Mila since the army had gathered. Still, if it kept her safe... "That part is true," I said, my grip tightening on the reins. I shouldn't have to be lying to protect my wife. She shouldn't be in a place where she *needed* protection. I gritted my teeth, fighting against my growing resentment.

"I'm sorry." Lada must have sensed the shift in my mood, because she didn't question me further. "How long have you known Han?" she asked Yakov.

Whether from the cold or the conversation, he was finally alert. "Since Barbezht. He saved my life. Him and Mila, I mean. His wife."

"How did you end up at Barbezht in the first place? You can't be older than me, and I was only fifteen when it happened."

"I was thirteen," he said. "My father fought for Tsar Borislav. When he was killed in battle, I wanted to take his place. Mama nearly murdered me for running off. If I hadn't come back missing a piece, she probably would have. Still better than Han, though," he added cheerfully. "Mila almost castrated him."

"For leaving?"

"No. When he came back, he tried to break their engagement." I could hear the mischievous grin in his words. "She'd spent long enough fighting her mother over the wedding, she wasn't going to let a little thing like an unwilling groom stop her."

"That's not what happened," I protested.

"You came back and said you wouldn't marry her, she called you a bastard and an ass, and the next day you got married. What part did I miss?"

Lada laughed. "I hope I can meet her someday. I think we'll get on wonderfully."

I rolled my eyes. "He makes it seem like I didn't want to marry her. I was trying to protect her."

"From what? Being stuck with an old grouch for the rest of her life?"

"Is the whole trip going to be like this?" Lada asked. "Or do you two ever stop fighting?"

I grinned. "No, this is pretty much it."

She sighed with feigned long-suffering. "Well, at least you'll be comfortable among the savages."

I chuckled. "What about you, Lada? How did you become a Blood Bastard?"

"Well, I'm a bastard, and my father is third—or rather, second—in line for the Blood, so "

I glanced back at her, frowning. Was she serious? I'd thought being a Blood Bastard required extensive training. Inzhria was filled with illegitimate descendants of the Sanctioned, but only a small fraction of them became Blood Bastards.

"That's really all there is to it," she said. "My father doesn't have any other children. Miroslav wouldn't let him marry, probably because he feels threatened by my father's power. As a servant's daughter, I didn't have many options, but as a child of the Blood, even a natural one, there were more opportunities. And Father's never been inclined to deny me what I asked for. When I was ten, a traveling Blood Bastard came to visit. I asked to train with him. When my training was done, I came back home, and I've been the resident Blood Bastard ever since."

"I've never met a Blood Bastard before," Yakov said, his voice full of admiration.

"That's probably a good thing," she replied. "Most of us are asses."

I coughed to hide my laugh.

It was late evening before we reached an inn. After a brief stop during which we rested the horses and ate a cold midday dinner, Yakov had taken over driving, but even so, I was exhausted. I pulled my fur cap down over my brow, covering my scar, and tightened the strap on my bean-filled glove as I climbed down from the sleigh.

The inn was empty but for the owner, and I didn't know if I should be glad or worried. The fewer people we saw, the lower our chances of being recognized, but there was something to be said for the anonymity of a crowd. Inside, a fire burned low in the corner, its heat not quite reaching the entire room.

The innkeeper approached, his ruddy face bright with a welcoming smile. "Looking for a room?"

"Two, if you have a spare," I said. "And a hot meal."

"I do. Have yourselves a seat, and I'll bring out some nice hot bowls of shchi with this morning's bread."

As he left the room, we seated ourselves at the table nearest to the fire. Lada and Yakov removed their hats and coats, but my only concession to the warmth was unbuttoning my coat.

The innkeeper returned soon with our food. "Where are you heading?"

"We're on our way to visit my wife's family," I said, swallowing a large spoonful of the cabbage soup. I would have preferred not to answer any questions, but that wasn't likely. I'd never met an innkeeper that didn't like to talk.

"Ah, that's nice." He pulled up a chair and took a seat next to Yakov. "It's good to be near family. My children all live nearby, so I don't have to travel to see them. My eldest daughter lives here with me, actually. Helps me run the place. She's in town tonight, though, helping at her sister's childbirth. My sixth grandchild, you know."

"Congratulations," Lada said. "You must be very proud."

"I am, I am." He looked at me. "You have children?"

I shook my head, my jaw clenched tight at the sudden reminder of the loss of my son. I hid it well, most days, but the grief still haunted me. "No, we haven't been so blessed."

"You ought to get on that, son." The innkeeper guffawed and winked at Lada.

Of course, he'd thought Lada was my wife. Why would I be traveling to visit my wife's family without my wife, after all? Yakov's pale, freckled face reddened with anger. I opened my mouth to change the subject, but the oblivious innkeeper beat me to it.

"Quite a year it's been, *da?*" He leaned back in his chair and stretched. "The Grand Duke's alive and fighting against the tsar again. I never would have guessed it. Some of the tsar's army passed through here right after the battle. Such a shame they lost, but I'm sure they'll get him next time."

"Yeah, a shame." Yakov's voice dripped with irony. Lada shot him a warning look as I kicked him under the table.

"But you've been on the road," the man said. "Did you see either of the armies? Gossip is my business, you know. People come in here for news as much as they do for food and lodging."

Lada shook her head. "We must have missed them. Our travels have been quiet."

"Ah, too bad. I heard the tsar killed all the traitors of Barbezht, too—or almost all of them. It seems Borislav has a couple working for him, but I'm sure they'll be executed as well, once the Grand Duke is defeated."

Yakov jerked his chair back as if to stand, but Lada laid a hand on his arm. "One can only hope," she said.

"Keep an eye out. There's a reward for anyone with information on Borislav's followers. Come to think of it, when the army passed through, they left some sketches of the traitors. Let me fetch those. Maybe you'll see someone on the road."

He stood and left the room, and I turned to my companions, heart in my throat.

Yakov lowered his voice. "You don't think any of us will be in those sketches, do you?"

"I doubt that I will," Lada said. "I'm a woman and a healer. Miroslav doesn't see me as a threat. But he wants the two of you dead, for sure."

"What do we do?"

I took a deep breath, trying to calm myself enough to think logically. "We stay calm. He's not suspicious yet, but if we panic, he'll know something's wrong. Maybe he won't recognize us."

The door across the room opened again, and the innkeeper came back with a stack of papers. "Here we are. Of course, you won't be likely to come across the Grand Duke or Prince Radomir, but here's their sheets if you do." He put the two papers on the table and flipped through the rest. "A couple of the Grand Duke's advisors and commanders...oh, and here's the survivors of Barbezht!" He pulled out the last sheet and looked closely at it. "They're both young. Obviously missing their right hands. One of them has a scar across his brow." He peered at the sketch and looked up at Yakov. "This one looks almost like you." He grinned, but Yakov didn't return the gesture.

Lada glanced at the paper and snorted. "I don't know. I think he's better looking than the traitor." Her tone was light, dismissive.

The innkeeper looked between Yakov and the page, silent. His eyes fell on Yakov's bean-filled glove, still attached to his arm and resting on the table. "Awful warm in here, isn't it? Feel free to take off your hats and gloves."

Yakov moved his arm under the table. "Still chilled," he muttered.

My hand went to the dagger on my belt as my heart pounded out a deafening rhythm in my ears. "Actually, I don't think we'll stay tonight. I'd like to be with family as soon as possible, and it's a bright night. Now that we've warmed up and rested a bit, we can make it to the next town."

"Nonsense," the innkeeper said, smiling too brightly. "Your horses must be exhausted. You wouldn't want to push them too hard. You'll stay the night. Let me see you to your rooms."

Not knowing what else to do, we followed him upstairs in silence. "Here we are. Get some sleep, and you can leave at first light." He gave a small bow and left us alone.

As his footsteps receded, Lada turned to us. "We have to leave. Now."

I nodded, my fist tight around my dagger. "What if he sends someone after us?"

She rummaged through her bag and pulled out a small clay vial. "Let me worry about that. Go get the sleigh ready."

We crept quietly down the stairs, alert for any noise or movement. The innkeeper wasn't in the main room. Lada stopped and peered through the door into the kitchen. "Not there," she whispered.

"What if he left?" Yakov whispered back.

"We'll catch up to him."

Outside, a light shone through the open door to the stables. As we entered, I saw the innkeeper saddling his horse.

"Oh!" He started when he saw us. "I hope I didn't disturb you. I received word from my daughter that I'm needed at the birth. I'll be back soon."

"Prophet's balls," Yakov swore. "Drop the act."

"I—I don't know what you mean."

I stepped forward, taking off my hat to reveal the scar on my brow. "We know you recognized us, sir. We mean you no harm. We're on a mission for the tsar—the true tsar, Borislav. All we ask is that you let us go on our way and tell no one you saw us."

He straightened himself up to his full height. "I am no traitor, nor will I cover for traitors. Borislav is no tsar of mine."

"We mean you no harm," I said again, stepping toward him. I had to solve this, had to stop him before someone got hurt. Got killed. "This doesn't have to come to a fight."

"Han..." Lada's voice was low, full of warning.

The man drew a dagger from his belt. "Stay back, traitor!" Keeping us in view, he scrambled onto his horse.

We stood between him and the door. "We can't let you leave," Lada said.

Anger and contempt filled his face. "I'll run you down."

We stood facing each other for an endless moment. Then the innkeeper kicked his horse.

"Don't breathe!" Lada shouted as she threw the clay vial at him.

It burst beneath the horse's hooves, letting out a cloud of smoke that filled the stables. The innkeeper let out a strangled cough which cut off suddenly. Lada grabbed me and Yakov by the arms and dragged us backward, out into fresh air.

Yakov gasped for breath. "What was that?"

"A strangler potion. Efficient and deadly—to humans, at least. Our horses will be fine. I had some things on hand in case we ran into trouble."

I looked back at the stable, my eyes wide with horror. "He's dead?"

"If he's not yet, he will be in a moment." She shuddered. "Let's go back inside. It'll take a while for the smoke to clear out. We might as well stay warm while we wait."

She and Yakov walked back toward the inn, but I stared at the stables. I'd killed men before, in battle. This was different. The innkeeper's daughter would be back, probably in the morning, ready to tell him about his newest grandchild. What would she think when she found him dead?

"Han?" Yakov's voice broke through my dark thoughts.

I turned, clearing the emotion from my face. "I thought you were going inside."

"She had to do it. He would have gotten us killed."

"I know." He was right. We hadn't had a choice. The tsar was depending on us. "He was a father. A grandfather."

"Everyone we face has someone who cares about them. It's war," Yakov said. "Death happens."

"I know," I said again. But where did we draw the line? Murdering old men in their homes? Children in their cradles? Selling our own to the highest bidder? This war was fracturing my soul. I turned back to the inn. "But I don't have to like it."

24

TRAINING

Mila

I stepped into the stables, out of the breathtakingly cold air. The silence in my rooms had been driving me mad. I hadn't been able to stop thinking about Han. How he'd been captured, what his last moments had been like. Remembering the look of devastation on his face in that last week before I'd left for court, when I'd told him we didn't have a family. Regretting that I'd wasted our last days together avoiding him out of a misplaced desire to protect him.

I couldn't protect him now. I could only hope to avenge him.

A stablehand shoveled muck in the farthest stall, but other than that, the stables were empty of people. Nearly empty of horses, as well.

The full court wouldn't return for another day or two, bringing the rest of the stable's occupants with them.

I wandered through the quiet building, stopping to rub the nose of a friendly mare who nuzzled me in search of treats.

"None today," I murmured. I'd have to bring some carrots the next time I came.

A clanging sound drew my attention. I gave the horse one last pat and followed the noise to a door on the other side of the building.

The door was open, and I peered inside. A large room held wooden swords and blunted weapons, stuffed dummies and large unlabeled sacks. A training room. In the middle, shirtless, with sweat dripping down his back, was Alexey, a blunted sword in his hand. He faced away from me, executing a series of positions. The muscles in his back rippled as he moved.

Such grace, and yet such power as well. I didn't need to see him face an opponent to know he was deadly. What would it be like to have that power? To know that no one could hurt me? If I'd had a weapon and the skill to wield it, how different would my life be? I could have saved my son and Marya Ivanovna. Saved myself.

Possibly even stayed with Han and saved him when Miroslav had come to take him.

Alexey turned, following the motion of his sword, and froze as his eyes met mine.

"Sofia!"

My cheeks heated, and I bit my lip. "I didn't mean to interrupt. I heard a noise, and—" I broke off, looking away. There was nothing I could say to explain why I'd been staring at him. Nothing that wouldn't sound ridiculous.

He strode to the wall and set his sword down, picking up a crumpled shirt and pulling it over his head. "I apologize for my appearance. I didn't realize anyone else was here."

I should apologize and leave him to his training, but I had to ask. "Where did you learn that?"

"The drills?" When I nodded, he shrugged. "I've been studying swordplay since I was a child. My father worked here in the stables, and when I wasn't working with him, I'd come in here to watch the men train."

No wonder he was so skilled. He'd been training his whole life. "It's incredible. I wish I'd learned swordplay as a child."

The words had slipped out before I could stop them. Alexey frowned, looking me over. Would my mouth never stop? He probably thought it was inappropriate for a woman to want to learn such a masculine pursuit. "I mean—"

He cut me off. "You'd be better suited to a dagger, if you're looking for something to defend yourself."

I blinked, staring at him, as he walked to a large chest and opened it.

"Here." He pulled out a wooden dagger and tossed it to me.

It slipped through my fingers and landed on the ground at my feet. My face was in flames as I bent to pick it up. Thank Otets for Sofia's dark skin; as Mila, my embarrassment would be visible to everyone, but as Sofia, my tendency to blush was less apparent.

"Something that size would work better, and you could keep it on you." He walked toward me, stopping an arms-length away. "If it would help you feel more at ease, I could teach you to use one."

He was offering to teach me? I'd never considered it as an actual possibility. Fighting was for the men. Even my father, who'd taken me to inns and sang bawdy songs with me—much to my mother's chagrin—had never given me a weapon, never taught me to defend myself.

After a moment of silence, he pulled his hand back, glancing away. "I'm sorry. I was being presumptuous."

"Yes."

He looked into my eyes. "Yes?"

"Yes. I want to learn." Anything to give me a way to protect myself from men like Kazimir Vladimirovich.

Alexey gave me a wide grin. "Well, then." He took my hand, the one holding the dagger, and held it up. "The first thing is knowing how to grip it. How you're holding it now will only work if you're coming down from above. Since you're small, you'd usually be attacking from below." He took the dagger from me, flipped it over, and placed it back in my hand, wrapping my fingers around it. "Make sure to keep all your fingers below the blade, or you'll injure yourself as much as your opponent."

"Like this?"

"Exactly. There are three spots you should strike for maximum damage. Here," —he held my hand with the dagger to his neck— "here," —he moved it lower, to his gut— "and here." He stopped with my hand below his waist, the tip of the wooden dagger pressed against his inner thigh.

My breathing hitched at the intimacy of the position, but he released my hand and stepped back.

I stared at the dagger, wishing my heart didn't race with terror whenever someone stepped too close. "Shouldn't I aim for the heart?" I asked, more to distract myself than out of a desire for an actual answer.

"Not if you want to keep your weapon. It's hard to slip it between the ribs. If you hit bone, you could lose your dagger."

"The neck, the gut, and the inner thigh." I forced myself to meet his gaze. "Got it."

"Let's go through some exercises to get you used to it." He took a few steps back and stopped, leaning toward me with his legs spread wide. "I'll come at you, and you aim for my stomach."

I nodded, took a deep breath, and held the wooden weapon out before me.

He lunged, sending my heart back into a panicky rhythm, but I ducked under his outstretched arms and shoved the dagger into his stomach, hard. He jerked back, holding a hand to the spot where I'd hit.

"Otets' Blood!" I swore. "I'm so sorry. Did I do it wrong?"

He covered his face with a large hand, and his whole body shook.

"Fuck." Was he having some sort of shaking fit? Had I hurt him? "Should I get someone?"

He dropped his hand, and I let out a sigh of relief at the laughter filling his face. Not hurt. Laughing at me, but not hurt. "I'm fine. It was my fault." He lifted his shirt to examine the spot I'd hit. A bruise was already forming, a deep red on his dark skin. "You're stronger than you look. I should have put on a vest before we started."

"So I didn't do it wrong?"

He shook his head as he strode back over to the chest and pulled out a large leather vest. "Not at all. You did wonderfully." He shrugged into the vest and gave me a crooked grin as he tied the laces. "Now, let's try that again."

An hour later, I was sweating through my sarafan.

"I think that's enough for today." Alexey picked up a towel and offered it to me, taking the wooden dagger in exchange. "Lord Kazimir is expecting me, and I'm sure you didn't plan to spend the whole day here."

I wiped my face as I leaned against the wall, breathing heavily. "I didn't mean to keep you from your work."

His eyes twinkled. "This has been the most pleasant training session I've ever had. You've kept me from nothing."

I flushed at the blatant flirtation, even if he wasn't being sincere. "Well, I thank you for it. I've learned a lot." Not enough to fight a battle, but at least enough that I wouldn't feel completely unsafe when alone anymore. Tomorrow, I could go into the city market and buy myself a dagger.

He frowned at me. "I hope you don't think you're finished learning."

"I...yes?" I tugged at my braid, twisting the coiled curls at the end of it. "I didn't expect you to teach me everything. Or to teach me at all, honestly."

He stepped closer. I could smell sweat and leather, and my heart, which had started to calm, began racing again. From fear at his proximity. That was all it was.

"And you think you can defend yourself now?" he asked.

I opened my mouth and closed it again, shaking my head slowly.

"Then I suppose you'll have to continue learning." He gave me a cocky half-grin. "And who better to continue to teach you?"

I bit my lip. Did he really want to teach me, or was he being kind, in his own vain, flirtatious way. "I don't want to keep you from your duties or take up your leisure time."

He leaned in, one arm on the wall next to me, and said in a low voice, "You can take up as much of my leisure time as you wish."

Shiver ran down my back. I stepped sideways, putting distance between us, and swallowed. "It's a generous offer, Alexey."

He stood upright. "Then I'll see you here tomorrow before supper. Say six o'clock?"

He wasn't giving me many options. Not that I wanted them. If he was willing to teach me, I was willing to learn. I nodded.

He bowed. "Have a pleasant day, Sofia."

I walked slowly back to my quarters, relishing the feel of the cold air against my heated skin. I'd misjudged Alexey Grigorovich. I'd thought he was nothing but an insincere flirt, but he'd been sincere today, focused. Not until he'd pronounced the lesson complete had he returned to the teasing banter I'd come to associate with him.

I'd enjoyed the lesson. The exertion had been a welcome distraction, and I felt safer than I had in a long time. Brazen and vain as he was, it seemed Alexey was just the friend I needed here at court.

A few days later, I walked across the dining room of the Frozen Board, heading to where Izolda sat at our usual table.

She looked me over. "You look awful."

I glared at her as I took off my coat and sat down across from her. "Thank you, Izolda."

"No, I mean it. Were you mauled by a bear?" She leaned back in her seat and waved over the barmaid. "Your hair is frizzed out of your braid, and—ugh!" She sniffed. "You stink of sweat."

Training with Alexey had taken longer than expected tonight, and I'd barely had time to change dresses before meeting Izolda. "I missed you, too. I'm glad you're back safely. You look lovely today, as well," I said, irony coating each word. I gave my order to the barmaid and turned back to my friend. "If you must know, it's been a terrible week." As if *terrible* could encompass learning that my husband and my best friend had both been killed by that monster Miroslav.

She frowned. "Why?"

I swallowed, staring down at the table. I hadn't told anyone about Han yet. Hadn't had anyone *to* tell. I'd done my best to put it out of my mind, sinking into my new identity as Sofia during the day. At night, nightmares plagued me, so I slept as little as possible, sitting up late by the fire drawing designs for new gowns and dresses.

But Izolda was a good friend. I could trust her, if no one else, with the truth about what had happened. Maybe telling someone would help stop the nightmares.

The dining room was loud enough that we wouldn't be overheard, but I lowered my voice anyway. "I heard what happened before the battle."

"Ah." Her face fell. "Yes."

"And H—" I choked on his name. He was dead. Even if someone overheard, they couldn't hurt him, but I couldn't say it. Couldn't bring myself to actually speak the words out loud.

Her brows knit together. "Your scarred stud?"

I nodded. Tears pricked my eyes.

"Oh, Fia." She reached out and squeezed my hand. "I'm so sorry."

Her sympathy felt worse than keeping it all trapped down inside. I pulled my hand from her grasp. I needed distraction, not pity. Distraction like my work. My vengeance. My training.

"I'm fine." I blinked the tears away. "Keeping busy." I gestured at my frazzled appearance. "I came from the training room."

Thankfully, she allowed the subject change. "Training room? What, are you learning to swordfight? Going to join the army?"

"Dagger, actually, and no." I nodded my thanks as the barmaid set a bowl of pelmeni and a mug of kvass on the table before me. "Alexey offered to teach me."

Izolda thumped her drink back on the table. "He *what?*"

Well, that reaction was disproportionate. "I came across him training and mentioned that I'd like to learn to defend myself. He offered to teach me the basics."

"I don't believe it." She stared at me. "Alexey's never even let me watch him train, let alone offered to teach me anything. And I've known him for years!"

"I'm sure he's just being friendly." I took a bite of the dumplings, savoring the taste of mushroom and onions. I was half-starved after training, which was another benefit; not only did it keep me distracted enough to keep my thoughts from dwelling on Han, I also didn't forget to eat. "Or maybe he wants the extra challenge."

"That's not 'friendly.' He takes his training seriously. If he's giving up training time to teach you, especially in the middle of a war…" She shook her head. "He's got it bad for you."

"No, he doesn't." During our daily sessions over the past week, Alexey had been practical, to-the-point. He hadn't acted like someone with ulterior motives. He flirted with me afterwards, yes, but he flirted with Izolda, too. Otets, he probably flirted with everyone.

"Fia, I've never seen Alexey give up training time. For *anything*. Trust me on this. If he's even letting you *watch* his training, he wants more from you than friendship." She took a large swallow from her cup and shook her head. "He's dedicated, too. If he wants something, he goes after it with everything he has."

I picked at my food. What if Izolda was right? She had known him most of her life, so she would know his character better than I would. Flirting with the man was one thing, but if he wanted more…

She seemed to be thinking the same thing. "Talk about complications, huh?"

"I need a distraction. He's available." I shrugged, taking another bite. "I'm sure there are benefits to a relationship." I gave her a suggestive grin, but I wasn't referring to physical benefits. His position allowed him to hear things I couldn't, and if he wanted a relationship, I'd be able to glean more information from him. It wasn't as though I had anyone waiting at home for me.

I pushed that thought away. I wasn't Mila. Mila had died with Han. No, I was Sofia, and I would employ every strategy possible to make sure I got revenge against the monster who'd killed me.

Even if some small part of me rebelled at the thought of lying to Alexey Grigorovich.

25
DRAKRA
Han

The mountains loomed over us, and a sense of dread settled in my stomach. Since that first stop, we had traveled without incident, but now we were nearing Drakra territory. Here, the danger we faced wasn't human.

We stopped in a small village for directions to the high priestess's temple, and we exchanged our horses for a set of large mountain goats, which were better suited to pulling the sleigh along the rocky roads. We would return the goats when—or rather, if—we returned. If the Drakra didn't hand us over to Miroslav, or worse.

The air grew colder, and the roads narrowed the higher we went up the mountain. I made the mistake of glancing down once and immediately wished I hadn't. A chunk of ice, knocked loose by the goats' feet, tumbled down the sheer cliff edge, echoing as it fell. I pulled my fur coat tighter around me, praying the goats remained sure-footed. No one would survive that drop.

I breathed a quiet sigh of relief when the road widened slightly and a town appeared. Stone houses rose up on each side of the road, some carved directly into the mountainside. The stones were smooth from centuries of weathering.

"I thought it would be bigger," Lada muttered. I grunted in agreement.

We passed a number of abandoned houses on the outskirts of the town. Doors hung lopsided from their hinges, and no smoke rose from the chimneys. The Drakra had lost a significant portion of their population in the Spider Wars, I knew, but I hadn't realized how poorly they had fared. This was no thriving settlement. It was a ghost town.

Short, gray-skinned Drakra, both male and female, ignored us as we passed. They were obviously used to seeing humans; even the children paid us no heed. I, on the other hand, had to remind myself not to stare. Their rough, callused skin looked as though all color had been leached from it. Most wore furs to guard against the biting wind, and the gray furs of rabbits and wolves matched the Drakras' colorless skin, making it difficult to tell from a distance where the furs ended and their skin began. A time or two, we passed a corner that seemed darker than it should have been. The hairs on my neck rose. The Drakra could shadow-meld—were those shadows Drakra watching us?

We climbed through the town until we reached the highest point. A set of stairs, carved into the mountainside, led to a temple. At the top of the stairs, two Drakra men, no more than five feet tall, guarded the door. They held their spears erect, unmoving as my companions and I climbed down from the sleigh and tied the goats to a post.

Wind swirled around us, making me shiver, but despite the guards' bare arms, they didn't react to the cold. Their skin appeared thick, coarse, as if carved from stone, and I wondered if their thicker skin kept them warm.

"We come on a diplomatic mission," I said to the guards. "We wish to treat with Yixa na Chekke." We hadn't been able to send word ahead of our arrival, for fear that Miroslav's men might intercept it. I said a silent prayer to Otets that the high priestess of the Drakra wouldn't send us away.

One of the guards beat the butt of his spear against the ground, and the other opened the door for us.

I glanced at Yakov and Lada before stepping into the darkness of the temple.

Once inside, my eyes took a moment to adjust. We were in a high-ceilinged hall. Seven doors led from the hall—eight, if I included the door we'd entered through. The spicy, intoxicating scent of burning leckozht needles filled the air. In the center of the room was a table atop a dais. Next to the table stood a Drakra woman, her skin the color of charcoal. Her long hair was black, striped with red, and she held a bowl full of something smoking. Burning leckozht, I assumed.

The priestess placed the bowl on the table and bowed her head. Then she turned, staring down her long nose at us.

"What brings three humans to speak with Yixa na Chekke, voice of the goddess Xyxra?"

Out of respect for the Drakras' matriarchal culture, we had chosen Lada to speak for us. The Blood Bastard stepped forward and bowed before introducing us. "We come to you on behalf of Borislav of the

Blood, rightful Heir of the Sanctioned and Tsar of Inzhria, who has charged us to form an alliance with our respected friends, the noble race of Drakra. We have letters and gifts from his majesty." She opened her pack and brought out a set of glass bottles. "A gift made by the Blood. These potions will cure minor illnesses swifter than any natural remedy. They were specially created to be used by Drakra." She placed them in front of the dais, at the priestess's feet.

The priestess's face was unreadable, like the stone it seemed to be carved from. I nodded at Yakov to offer his gift.

He brought out a block of salt. "A gift made by the sea. Sea salt, from the western coast of Inzhria." He set the block next to the potions.

"And a gift made by the land." I stepped forward with the potted spruce sapling I held. "This tree was enchanted by the tsar to thrive as long as the friendship between his people and yours thrives." I placed the final gift next to the others, along with the ambassadorial letters. "His majesty Tsar Borislav also sends his regards in these letters and authorizes us to speak in his stead."

The priestess watched us for a moment, unspeaking. She rang a bell, and a young Drakra woman came from the room behind her. "They will be staying with us for a few days," the priestess told her. "See to their comfort."

That was promising, at least. She didn't insist we leave or call guards to throw us in a cell.

The young woman led us to a small house near the town center. "The priestess will summon you soon."

Lada bowed. "Thank you."

As the woman left, I looked around. The house was one room, with low tables on each end. A pile of unlit firewood filled the pit in the center of the room, beneath a hole in the ceiling that couldn't quite be called a chimney. Furs covered the ground, but there were no chairs. I wondered if the lack of chairs was calculated, meant to discomfit us, or if the Drakra simply didn't use them. Given the warm, comfortable appearance of the house, I was inclined to believe the latter. I hadn't noticed any in our drive through the town, at least.

Yakov took seat by the fire pit while Lada started a fire. "Well, that went well," he said drily.

"I expected her to say more," Lada said. "But she didn't have us killed, at least."

Yakov fished in his pack and pulled out a strip of dried meat. "Still, she could have said a little more."

Lada swiped the food from his hand, and Yakov reached into the pack again.

I shook my head at their childish behavior. "She's giving herself some time to consider before listening to what we have to say. It'll probably be a while before someone comes to get us."

"Probably," Lada agreed. She pulled a dice bag from her own pack. "Might as well settle in for a bit. Anyone want to play?"

I shook my head and seated myself a ways back from the fire. I wasn't in the mood for dice, but I watched as the other two began their game. They were both careful to avoid touching each other, as I'd noticed during the journey. I'd warned Yakov to stay away from her, but I no longer believed Lada posed a threat to him. She clearly felt the same for him as he did for her, and he'd never been one to let my interference prevent him from going after something he wanted. Was it fear of her father that was stopping them, or something else?

It wasn't any of my business, I reminded myself. Mila would call me an interfering busybody for getting involved. Though she'd secretly be watching them as well. She was worse than an old woman when it came to matchmaking.

As I'd expected, it was a couple hours before someone came to meet us. The woman who came to the door was tall for a Drakra, and her skin was slightly softer and pinker than the rock-like Drakra skin. Her eyes were more brown than yellow. "I am Xhela na Zanik, Mandible to the high priestess."

"You're human," Yakov blurted as we stood to greet her.

The woman stiffened, and I shot him a glare. The Mandible was second only to the high priestess herself among the Drakra. If Yakov couldn't control his mouth, we could end up as sacrifices to their Spider Goddess, or worse.

"Half," she said.

"My apologies, Xhela na Zanik." Lada bowed. "We meant no offense." She scowled at him, and he mumbled an apology.

Xhela nodded in acknowledgment. "Yixa na Chekke, voice of Xyxra, wishes you to attend her at dinner."

"We would be honored," Lada said.

Xhela led us back to the temple, but rather than stopping in the main hall, we went through one of the doorways I had seen earlier. Inside, brightly colored woven tapestries decorated the walls of the warm room. The tapestries didn't depict any particular imagery, just geometric designs, but they were still beautiful. My eyes caught on one in particular, a blue- and red-striped piece that reminded me of the quilt Mila had made in the first year of our marriage. I felt a twinge of homesickness. Did she miss home as much as I did?

Thinking of Mila fueled that ever-present spark of resentment at her for leaving. I looked away from the tapestry and put her out of my mind.

The high priestess, Yixa na Chekke, sat on the floor at the head of a low table laden with food. A short-haired Drakra man sat next to her, and across from him, two small children squirmed in their seats.

I had expected something more formal. This was less an ambassadorial dinner than a family one, and it felt as though we were intruding.

"Please, sit," the priestess told us. "Be welcome. Meet my husband, Xolok, and our sons."

"It's an honor to meet you," Lada said. Yakov and I echoed her as we, along with Xhela na Zanik, took our seats on the furs around the table.

Yixa na Chekke served us herself. The food was simple, similar to what I ate at home, and the familiar fare filled me with a comfortable, homey feeling. There were clay-baked birds—something like a quail, I thought—and currant jelly, with a flat type of bread I didn't recognize.

Once everyone had been served, the priestess turned to Lada. "You are the daughter of Radomir, prince of the Blood, are you not, Blood Bastard?"

She was well-informed, even if we had taken her by surprise. Lada dipped her head. "I am, Lady."

The priestess raised one dark eyebrow. "Your father fought against Borislav in the first rebellion. How do you find yourself speaking on behalf of Borislav now?"

"My father is a religious man." Lada gave a small smile. "In order to make a Disinheritance, certain standards must be met. My father didn't feel that those standards had been met at the time of the last rebellion."

"But he has changed his mind, now," Xhela na Zanik, the Mandible, said.

"He has, yes. Thanks to Han Antonovich." Lada gestured at me.

Xhela, the priestess's husband, was silent throughout this exchange. The smaller of the two sons had left his seat at the table to climb into his father's lap and whisper something. Xolok sighed.

"Yes. But don't expect to get anything else later!" he added as the child ran out of the room.

The older boy, who had been picking at his food, looked at his father expectantly. As soon as Xolok nodded, he was on his feet and out the door. Xolok sighed heavily and stood. "Excuse me," he said, following the boys from the room.

I chuckled. "Your children are beautiful, Yixa na Chekke."

"Do you have children, Han Antonovich?" the priestess asked.

"No." I caught Yakov's eye, the memory of my unborn son heavy on my heart. "Not anymore, no."

"I'm sorry to hear that."

Conversation stalled as we finished eating. Finally, Yixa na Chekke folded her arms on the table. "You say Miroslav has earned a Disinheritance, and you wish for the Drakra to join you in making it. Tell me, what has Miroslav Vyacheslavovich done to disqualify him from ruling?"

Lada met her yellow-eyed stare. "In addition to creating an army in peacetime and mutilating prisoners of war," she inclined her head toward me and Yakov, "he's committed the most grievous of sins a Sanctioned can. He turned the Gifts of the Blood on his unSanctioned subjects."

"Miroslav is a brute," Yakov said. "Did you know, Lady, that only thirteen of us survived the battle of Barbezht? And only two of us are alive today, because Miroslav slaughtered the other eleven to make a point to his brother."

"A monster he might be," the Mandible said, "but why would we risk our already depleted people to support a man who already lost one rebellion? If Miroslav won before, why should we not ally with him? Or perhaps we should remain neutral, to mitigate our risk."

"He won't stop," I said quietly. They looked at me, and I cleared my throat. "Miroslav has left you alone so far. He's been busy solidifying his power, building his army. But once he's dealt with the other threats to his throne, he'll turn his gaze east. His father drove your people into the mountains, slaughtering you, but Miroslav is ten times worse than his father. He won't stop until the Drakra are wiped out and he has complete control over the entire territory, all through the mountains."

The priestess's mouth pinched together. "Is Borislav any different? They come from the same womb. Who's to say one is any better than the other?"

"Tsar Borislav is prepared to make assurances to you," I said. "He sent us as a gesture of goodwill. We can negotiate some of the lands you lost in the Spider Wars, as well as establishing trade and ambassadorial relations between our two peoples." I prayed that was all it would take to establish the alliance. I didn't know if I could stomach carrying out the tsar's other order.

Yixa na Chekke stared at me, contemplating. "This is quite sudden. I must consult our goddess and speak with my advisors. We will meet again tomorrow."

26

A NIGHT OFF

Mila

Shouts of anger echoed through the hall. As I reached the quarters belonging to the baron and baroness of Arick, the door swung open, and Lord Kazimir came out, his face contorted with fury. I cringed, but he didn't spare me a glance as he stormed past. Alexey, following the baron, wore a grim expression. He caught sight of me and stopped.

"Is something wrong?" I murmured.

He grimaced. "Lady Yelena was sick in front of the baron. It dirtied his shoes, and..." He shook his head.

"Grigorovich!" Lord Kazimir yelled from down the hall. "I don't pay you to stand around gossipping with the help!"

"Coming, my lord!" he called back. He turned back to me. "Your training is coming along nicely. I thought we could take the night off, *da*? We could have supper, maybe take a walk through the city."

"I'd like that." After almost a month of daily training sessions, I deserved a break. And Alexey wasn't inclined to conversation while sparring, so maybe an evening of leisure would loosen his tongue.

"I'll come to your quarters when he's finished with me." He pressed his lips together and inclined his head toward me before following the baron.

Lady Yelena was reclining on a low divan in the sitting room. "Sofia Stepanova." She smiled at me, then winced and pressed a hand to her piebald face. "Apologies. I fell this morning, and I believe I have a bruise forming."

The white patch of skin around her left eye was swollen and red. My stomach clenched as I pasted on a smile. The bastard had hit his wife for nothing more than being ill? I knew how brutal he could be—I'd been on the receiving end of that brutality, after all—but I would have expected him to be kinder to the woman he married.

"Not at all, my lady," I said. "What can I do for you?"

"I'm afraid I may be too late, but I wondered if you might be able to make me something to wear for Prophet's Day? My lord is to be granted a new title during the celebration, and he wishes me to be dressed as befits his station."

"Not too late at all," I assured her. The baroness was my social superior, but she was so polite, almost deferential. It was a welcome contrast to the demanding noblewomen I'd come to expect. "I have some designs here, if you'd like to look at them." I drew the papers out of my pack and set them on the table in front of her.

Lady Yelena picked up the papers and rifled through them. "I do hope I'm not ill on Prophet's Day." She glanced up at me with a wry smile. "I haven't been able to keep any food down this week. It seems capital food doesn't agree with me."

I nodded sympathetically. "I know what you mean. The food here is quite rich."

She held out a page. "This one would be perfect."

It was a simple sarafan, wide-skirted, with a sleeveless dushegreya vest lined in fur. I'd made similar styles for myself dozens of times; it would take next to no time to make. "I'll just need to take your measurements, and then you can choose your fabrics."

She stood, and her maidservant, who had been hovering unobtrusively in the shadows, stepped forward to help her up onto a stool. I took out my measuring line and looked up as the baroness blanched.

"My lady!" The maidservant caught her arm before she fell.

"Are you alright?" I asked, taking her other arm and helping her to the divan.

"I'm fine. Just a tad dizzy. As I said, I haven't been eating well lately."

"Let me get you a drink." On a shelf across the room was a crystal bottle filled with amber liquid—medovukha, I assumed—with matching glasses next to it. I picked it up.

"Oh, no, not that!" Lady Yelena exclaimed. "That's my lord's. He never allows me to drink from it. There's a pitcher of water to your left."

"I apologize, my lady." I poured her a glass of water and handed it to her.

She took a sip. "Thank you. Truly, I haven't felt myself this week. There must be something in the air." She smiled weakly, setting down her glass.

Dizziness, nausea, an inability to eat...I'd had similar symptoms during the first weeks of my pregnancy. A wave of grief hit me hard, and I blinked away the stinging sensation in my eyes. Was it possible the baroness was pregnant? It seemed unlikely that she hadn't already made that assumption, but she was young, no older than twenty, and from what I understood, she'd been orphaned as a child. Maybe she hadn't received the proper education about childbearing.

"My lady," I began, then cut myself off. It wasn't my place to educate a noblewoman.

"Yes?"

"Nevermind." I caught the maid's eye and saw a similar understanding in her face. "I spoke out of turn."

The baroness looked between me and her maid, frowning. "If there's something you've noticed, speak plainly."

I hesitated. "Is it possible that it's not the capital air causing your illness?"

"What do you mean?"

"I hadn't said anything because I thought you knew," the maid said. "My lady, it's been almost eight weeks since you last bled."

A look of comprehension dawned on the noblewoman's brown and white face. "You think I'm...with child?"

Her maid nodded. "I'm sure of it."

"Oh, thank Otets!" she gasped. "Thank Otets."

"I offer my congratulations," I said. "What a blessing." Even if the child belonged to Kazimir Vladimirovich.

"Yes, my lord will be pleased." She placed a hand over her stomach and mumbled absently, "Thank Otets."

"A second sunrise in one day," Alexey said as I opened the door. "Truly, this day is blessed." His expression was serious, but his dark eyes twinkled mischievously.

"Good evening, Alexey." I rolled my eyes but smiled in spite of myself.

He stepped back from the doorway, arm swept out toward the exit. "Are you ready?"

I took my coat from the peg next to the door. "I am now."

As we left the trade quarters, he offered me his arm. I accepted, grateful for the warmth his proximity offered against the biting cold. The moon sparkled on the fallen snow, lending an enchanted air to the palace grounds.

"How was the baroness this afternoon?" I asked as we walked.

"Better than this morning." He glanced at me. "She had an announcement for the baron when he returned."

I put on a guileless expression. "Did she? What was that?"

Alexey narrowed his eyes. "Why do I get the feeling you already know?"

"I haven't the slightest idea." He frowned, and I couldn't suppress my grin. "Yes, fine. It may have come up in conversation."

He squeezed my arm. "I'm glad for her. If nothing else, this should give her some reprieve. Whatever else Lord Kazimir may be, I don't believe he'd risk hurting his heir."

I stopped, turning to him. "Why do you work for him? If he's so cruel, why stay?" I couldn't reconcile the kind, caring man I'd come to know with someone who would profess loyalty to such a villain as Kazimir.

He let out a sigh. "I thought it would be a good position for me. He had a reputation, yes, but he's close to the tsar. I'd like a permanent position at court eventually, as a guard for the tsar or something equally respectable. I thought working for him would grant me more opportunities."

"And now?"

"I wish I could leave, but who would be there to temper him?" He shrugged. "At least while I'm there, I can draw his attention away from the baroness. Keep him distracted."

"I see." I rested a hand on his arm, feeling the strong corded muscles through his coat. "You're a good man, Alexey."

He held my gaze, placing his hand over my own. "You don't know how much that means to me."

I swallowed and looked away, a hot flash of guilt going through me. I shouldn't be leading him on like this, letting him believe there was something between us. I was married.

No, not married. Not anymore. I had another purpose here, one that couldn't be pushed aside on account of something as trivial as guilt.

"Lord Kazimir must trust you a great deal," I said as we began to walk again. Flatter him. Gain his trust. Find the knowledge he had access to, and use it to bring Miroslav and Kazimir down.

"I suppose so. I strive to be trustworthy, no matter what I think of him personally."

"And the tsar?" I glanced up at him, seeing the moonlight silhouette his sharp face. "Has he noticed you at all?"

He shook his head. "Tsar Miroslav is too busy fighting a war to notice me. And it's not really his attention I need. He doesn't oversee the hiring of his household himself. I'd do better to earn the regard of his advisors."

"I can't imagine who could be more deserving of his attention than the man who promised me he would single-handedly end the rebellion." I nudged him with my elbow, giving him a flirtatious smile. "Surely honoring you should be his highest priority."

He inclined his head toward me, a smile playing on his face. "Much as I appreciate your esteem, fair sun, the rising tensions with Vasland and the Grand Duke's rebellion take priority over even me."

Rising tensions with Vasland? Our northern neighbors had allied with Miroslav during the previous uprising. I hadn't heard about any conflict between them and Inzhria since. "I thought Vasland was our ally." I injected a tremor into my voice. "They won't back Borislav, will they?"

He patted my arm. "No, they won't join Borislav. They're angry that Tsar Miroslav hasn't paid them for their aid at Barbezht, but they won't want to risk allying against him and going unpaid. They're more likely to try to take the country for themselves."

And if Vasland attacked while Miroslav was still on the throne, they wouldn't be likely to stop their attack once Borislav took the country. I frowned.

"There's no need to worry," he said. "I'm sure Tsar Miroslav will resolve things before it comes to that."

"I hope so."

We'd reached the Frozen Boar, the inn near the palace. It was busy, the court's return having brought life back to the capital. Alexey led me to a table in the corner and ordered our supper.

"So, what happens next?" I asked as the barmaid left. "Against the rebellion, I mean. It's been over a month since the last battle." A minor battle had been fought somewhere in the midlands, concluding in another victory for Borislav. "Will you be leaving to join the army again?"

"I don't know. The Grand Duke's army is still traveling, so Tsar Miroslav may send Lord Kazimir to oversee an ambush soon, or he may choose to keep him here as an advisor."

"Where?" I asked, then realized my mistake. If my questions were too eager, he might grow suspicious. "I'm sorry. I only mean—they won't be near Tsebol, will they?"

"Not at all. They're heading toward Sevken. Their path shouldn't take them anywhere near your home."

I filed that bit of information away for later. "So you'll be heading toward Sevken, too, if the baron goes."

"Much as it pains me to be from your sunny countenance..." He grinned as I pursed my lips. "Yes, if Lord Kazimir is sent away, I'll go with him. Wherever he's sent."

And if the baron chose to attack another defenseless woman?

The thought came from nowhere. Alexey hadn't been with the baron when I was attacked. He would have stopped it. Not like the soldiers who'd been there. I would never forget their faces, the bloodlust in their eyes. How they did nothing as Lord Kazimir murdered my housekeeper and beat me. How they'd held me down for him, helped him violate me and murder my son...

"Sofia?"

I flinched. My nails dug into my palms where I'd clenched them, and bowls of solyanka sat on the table between us. When had the barmaid returned? I forced my muscles to relax, inhaling a deep breath of the salty, vinegary steam rising from the soup before me. "Sorry. I was lost in thought."

He reached out and took my hand. "Is something wrong?"

I smiled brightly at him—possibly too bright, given the curious look he gave me. "I'm fine. How long have you been working for Lord Kazimir, anyway?"

"Four months now."

Just after the attack. Had he been nearby? In Tsebol, or possibly even closer? No, he'd told me at one point that he'd never been to Tsebol. I scooped a spoonful of sour cream into my soup and took a bite.

While we ate, he kept the conversation light, entertaining me with stories of his childhood in the capital. When we finished eating, he stood and held out a hand. "Come. I want to show you the best view in the city."

He led me back outside and toward the city proper. The capital wasn't silent—it never was, even when the court was absent—but we walked down side roads, away from the noise of the busier streets.

As we walked further from the city center, the sound of crashing waves grew. The air was thick and wet, and the smell of salt was stronger than at the palace. The temperature had dropped; I tugged my coat tighter around me.

"Close your eyes," he said.

I narrowed them suspiciously at him before doing as he asked. He guided me a few more steps, around a corner, and stopped.

He let go of my arm. "You can open them now."

We were on an ocean overlook. A stone wall marked the edge of the cliff, and down below, white-capped waves crashed onto the rocks. The full moon lit up the scene in brilliant light. I gasped. "It's beautiful."

"Yes, it is."

I turned to see Alexey staring, not at the scene in front of us, but at me. A laugh burst from my lips.

"That is the most ridiculous, trite thing you could have said," I told him, still laughing. "Did you honestly think I would fall for that?"

"Ridiculous, trite...and true." He brushed his thumb over my cheek, the corner of his lips tugging upward. "How could I look at the moon when I have the sun standing next to me?"

"I believe you are teasing me, sir." I tried to keep my tone light, but the earnestness of his gaze made my breath catch in my throat.

"Not at all." He stepped closer, and I took an involuntary step back. "Do you have any idea how beautiful you are?" He put a hand under my chin.

I should have stopped him, but I was transfixed. His dark eyes held a passion so intense it was almost frightening. His thumb brushed my bottom lip. "You are divine. Whenever you're near, I find it impossible to look away."

Warmth flooded my body. This wasn't supposed to be happening. I was using him. I wasn't supposed to *feel* anything. But I didn't pull back from his touch. He smiled that half-smile and leaned closer. I closed my eyes.

Then his lips were on mine. He wrapped his arms around me and pulled me close, his kiss both soft and demanding. I opened my mouth, letting him in.

He pushed me up against the stone wall, and I was trapped. His breath turned foul, his hands suddenly larger and more forceful. I shoved him off with all my strength.

He stepped back, holding his hands up. "I'm sorry. I shouldn't have—I'm sorry."

Alexey. It was Alexey in front of me. Not Kazimir Vladimirovich, not him and his vicious companions. "No." I shook my head, hands clenched in the folds of my sarafan. "Not you." I stared at the ground, counting pebbles as I took deep, gasping breaths, my whole body shuddering. "Wasn't you."

"Sofia."

Sofia. He wasn't Kazimir, and I wasn't Mila. I was going to give myself away. I forced my breathing into a regular rhythm and looked back up into his eyes.

"I'm sorry, Alexey. I just...everything is happening so fast."

He gave me an odd look and held out a hand. I took it, focusing on each breath as he led me to a bench and sat down next to me.

He pulled something from his pocket. "I'd meant to give this to you later, but..." He held it out.

It was a dagger in a leather sheath, simple but made with expert craftsmanship. I stared at it. "I can't take this."

He placed it in my hand. "You should feel safe." I opened my mouth, but he shook his head. "That—" He gestured at the stone wall. "That wasn't just fear of moving too fast. And you didn't agree to train with me for fun. Someone hurt you. I don't know who it was or how it happened, and I don't need to, but I do need you to know that I would never hurt you." He wrapped my fingers around the dagger's hand. "You're safe, and you will always be safe with me, my sun. But you can keep yourself safe, too."

What could I say to that? I looked at him with wide eyes. Han had never even considered that I could defend myself.

Han.

He'd not even been dead two months, and I was letting another man kiss me and give me gifts.

Tears blinded me. I blinked, and they spilled over. Then I was crying, every emotion I'd suppressed for months pouring in hot streams down my face. Alexey pulled me to him, and I sobbed into my shoulder.

I hated myself.

27

ETHICS OF WAR

Han

The next morning dawned bright and cold. We were all awake by the time the Mandible knocked at the door.

"The high priestess asked me to accompany you this morning after you've broken your fast," she said when I answered the door. "I have a meal prepared at my house, if you would be interested in joining me."

I bowed. "We would be honored, mistress."

She smiled, revealing long, sharp canine teeth. "We don't use honorifics, Han Antonovich—apart from the high priestess, who is called

'Lady' when not referred to by her title. You may call me Xhela in conversation, or 'the Mandible' in more formal settings."

I bowed again, wishing I'd had more time to study the culture before we came. Or that the tsar had sent someone with more experience. I was woefully unprepared for these negotiations. "We'll take your custom as our own during our time here." Hopefully that gesture would earn me a measure of goodwill.

Her home was on the same street as the guest house we were staying in. Carved into the mountain, it was a single room, but privacy screens made of leather separated it into sections. An iron grill hung over the fire in the center of the room, on which three large trout were nearly finished cooking. My stomach gurgled at the savory, smoky smell filling the air.

Xhela indicated the low table near the fire. "Please, sit."

We took our seats on the furs as she removed the fish from the grill. She served us each a generous helping, followed by an acorn cake. When she poured us our drinks, I sniffed mine. The scent was yeasty and familiar. I took a drink.

"Kvass?" I'd thought the drink was unique to Inzhrians.

She smiled again. "Most of my people don't drink it, but I've developed a taste."

"It's very good."

"Do you live here alone, Xhela?" Lada asked, taking a pat of what I assumed was goat butter and spreading it on her acorn cake.

"My mother lives with me, but she's visiting relatives for the time being."

I took a bite of my acorn cake. It was nutty and slightly sweet, though a bit dry. I spread butter on it as Yakov asked, "Are there many Drakra towns?"

"No more than a dozen, spread throughout the mountains." Xhela placed another serving of fish on Yakov's plate without asking.

"My father said there used to be Drakra settlements all over this side of the country," Lada said. "After the Spider Wars, the treaty restricted the Drakra to the mountains and claimed the towns for Inzhria." She looked to Xhela for confirmation.

I glanced at Lada, surprised, as the Mandible nodded. I'd known the Drakra had lost land during the wars, but I didn't remember their territory ever extending beyond the mountains.

"You're well educated on the topic," Xhela said. "You can't have been more than a baby at the time of the last war."

Lada smiled wryly. "My father insisted I have an understanding of the tsardom's most recent history, given my parentage."

"I see. I suppose you weren't born at the time of the wars, Yakov?"

"No," Yakov said. "My father fought in the last one, though." His eyes widened as he realized what he'd said, and he smacked his hand over his mouth. I tensed, watching the Drakra woman for her response. We would have enough difficulty making this alliance without insulting our hosts.

Xhela waved a hand, unbothered. "Don't worry. My parents met on the battlefield during the first war. He fought for the humans, and she for the Drakra. I don't hold a soldier's battles against him—or against his children."

I knew the Drakra took prisoners of war as slaves. Had her father been forced to sire children on a Drakra woman? The practice of slavery was monstrous, and I felt an accord with Prince Radomir, who had made his distaste for this alliance clear. The tsar couldn't allow such a practice to continue.

It wasn't my place to dictate what the tsar could or could not allow, I reminded myself. I was a soldier, a loyal servant of Borislav. I was here to serve, not to make demands.

When we finished eating, Xhela led us through the narrow streets. "This town has been home to our people since we emerged from Xyxra's eggs that formed these mountains." She gestured to the temple, several streets above us. "You've seen the temple, the high priestess's home. Each town has its own temple, though the priestess resides here."

"If she lives here, why build temples in the other towns?" Yakov asked, face screwed up in confusion.

"Does your tsar remain in only one castle?" she retorted. "The priestess lives here, yes, but she does travel to the other towns in her domain. A town would be dishonored if it didn't provide a dwelling place for the goddess and her chosen mouthpiece."

She pointed out sights as we walked—the home of a war hero who perished in the last Spider War, the place to buy the finest wool, the ancestral home of the former high priestess's family. I listened in fascination, grateful for her insight into the culture. Despite my initial impression, the town was not a ghost town. The Spider Wars had taken their toll, but the town was healing. The Drakra were a resilient people.

We turned onto the street below the temple, and a colorful scene came into view, a striking contrast to the rocky grays of the rest of the town. Tapestries hung outside the houses, lining the street with brilliant pieces of art. Each piece was detailed and unique, some depicting intricate scenes, while others were an abstract explosion of color. Along the street, weavers, both men and women, sat on low stools, working threads into designs.

"Weaving is sacred in our culture," Xhela explained as we walked. "The houses nearest to the temple are reserved for weavers and their families."

I stopped to watch a woman working on what appeared to be a shirt. Her hands moved almost too fast for me to see, weaving together strands of brilliant reds and browns.

"They're all handwoven," Xhela said. "You won't find any lazy human looms here in the mountains—meaning no offense," she added belatedly.

Lada stopped next to me. "None taken. The artistry is incredible."

Xhela practically preened at the compliment. "Drakra weavers are the finest in the world."

It was late morning by the time we reached the temple. The high priestess waited for us, not in the formal altar hall where we'd first met her, nor in the cozy room where we'd dined, but in a third room. I looked around as we entered. Furs covered the floor, as in the other places I'd seen, but the tables in this room were taller, surrounded by woven stools. Shelves, too many to hold the few books in the room, lined the walls.

The priestess, sitting on one of the low stools, gestured for us to be seated.

"I have consulted the goddess regarding Borislav's desire to form an alliance," she said without preamble.

My mouth was cottony. What would we do if she refused to negotiate? *Please, Otets, let her agree.*

"The webs tell me Miroslav's reign will end within the year. Borislav's future is harder to read." She peered at the table, as though seeing the omens of her goddess in it. "He has many paths he may take, and his web is tangled up with many others." She looked up at me, her yellow eyes narrowing. "Yours in particular."

Yakov and Lada looked at me, and I frowned, meeting the priestess's stare. "What does that mean?"

She leaned in, resting her chin on her knuckles, and considered me with furrowed brows. "Reading the webs takes skill. Many have misread them to their ruin. I do not know what this means, but your choices give Borislav the crown—or keep it from him."

I swallowed. That didn't sound promising. But hadn't I already had an influence on the war, just by telling his story? Maybe that was all her webs meant. If it wasn't all superstitious nonsense. The Drakra had magic, I knew, but that didn't mean they could see the future.

"If my decision can make Borislav tsar, he will be tsar," I said firmly. "But what is your decision, high priestess? The support of the Drakra could bring him to the throne sooner, saving countless lives."

Xhela, sitting next to the priestess, cut in. "Saving countless human lives, perhaps. Many of our people would still die."

She wasn't wrong. The Drakra were already depleted by the Spider Wars. I opened my mouth to respond, but Lada beat me to it.

"Many more of your people will die if Miroslav wins. Like his father, he believes these mountains should belong to Inzhria. Borislav would return some of the land their father took; Miroslav would take more."

The priestess tilted her head, considering us. She stood and took a sheaf of papers from a shelf. A stack of maps, I saw as she set the papers before us.

"Show me what you can offer."

Negotiations filled the next week. Occasionally, we were joined by other Drakra—most frequently, the priestess's husband Xolok—but for the most part, Yixa na Chekke and Xhela na Zanik met with us alone.

"What good will all this land do us if it lies fallow for generations?" Yixa na Chekke asked. "My people were slaughtered during the 'Spider Wars,' as you call them. We do not have enough people to work the territory your tsar promises us. I can't take this risk."

The talks were devolving quickly. If I didn't do something soon, the high priestess was going to refuse the alliance.

"Give us one more night to consider a solution, Lady," I said. "Please."

She pinched her mouth together and nodded once. "If we cannot reach an agreement by sunset tomorrow, I fear there may not be a reason to continue negotiations."

"Thank you for your patience." I stood and bowed, my body stiff from so many hours sitting at the table. "We'll have a solution for you in the morning." I just hoped it was one I could live with.

Back at the guest house, Yakov flopped down onto the furs. "She's going to refuse."

"We'll think of something," Lada said, taking a seat next to him. She put a hand on his knee. "It's in their best interest to join us, too. I wasn't lying when I said Miroslav would destroy them. He won't be satisfied until he rules the whole world."

My stomach was tight with nerves. I took a seat next to the fire pit and built the embers into a fire. "I think I know what we have to do." I couldn't look at them as I said it.

"What?"

"The tsar... The night before we left, he told me if they wouldn't agree to our terms—" I broke off, shaking my head. "He wants me to offer them the prisoners of war. As slaves."

Yakov swore. "You can't do it."

"Why not?" Lada crossed her arms. "We killed their people. It's only right we give them what they need to rebuild."

"People aren't wood and stone," he snapped.

I held up my hand. "It's not up to me. If negotiations look like they're going to fail, the tsar told me I have to make this offer. We've tried everything else. She's going to say no, and we can't afford to lose this alliance." I ran a hand over my face. "I don't want to do this, either, Yasha," I said, lapsing into his nickname. "But I need you on my side. Both of you."

"How long?" Lada asked. "They won't get to keep the prisoners for life, right? We'll place a limit on it?"

"Eight years. That's how long they traditionally kept their prisoners."

Yakov grimaced. "I can't. I can't agree to this. You're taking men from their homes, their families, for *eight years.* I don't care if the tsar ordered it. You can't do it."

Lada glared at him. "It's either taking Miroslav's men from their families for eight years, or getting all of our men killed." She turned to me. "If this is what we have to do, we'll do it."

I looked at Yakov. "I hate it, too, but do you see another way?"

Emotions battled for dominance on his face. Anger, frustration, reluctance. Finally, he sighed. "I'm with you."

The next morning, we sat around the negotiation table one last time. Xhela and Yixa watched me, their faces as unreadable as stone.

I took a deep breath. One last attempt before I made the tsar's proposal.

"Tsar Borislav will make a formal apology to you for the wrongs committed against your people," I said. "Perhaps you can allow the humans to remain on the land he has agreed to return to you. They can pay tribute until your population has grown enough to work the land yourselves."

She sniffed. "And take the chance that they may refuse to leave when my people are ready to take what was promised? I think not." Standing, she said, "I do not see anything you can offer that will make it worth the lives we would lose."

I had no other choice. I glanced at Yakov and Lada. Yakov gritted his teeth, but Lada gave me an encouraging nod.

I swallowed. "What about lives, Lady?"

She sat back down. "Go on."

"The Drakra's tradition is to keep prisoners of war as bondservants, yes?" She nodded, and I continued. "Tsar Borislav is willing to grant you the prisoners from this war to work the land he offers. He would keep any high-ranking officials and commanders, but the majority could return with you, according to your tradition. You may keep them for eight years, as you did in the past, at the end of which time they may return home."

"Or stay, if they so choose?" Xhela asked. "It's not unheard of for them to become one of us, to marry and settle among our people. My father was a bondservant who stayed here by choice. My husband, also, was a bondservant, though he served only a short time before he was freed by the treaty."

"I didn't realize you were married, Xhela." If her father and husband had both survived their service and agreed to marry their captors, perhaps it wasn't as cruel a fate as I'd thought.

Her expression softened slightly. "I followed him west after the war ended. He passed into the other realm, and our daughter is grown now, so I returned to my people."

"If your prisoners choose to remain after their service, the tsar will have no objection," I said. "As long as the decision is theirs alone."

The priestess considered me for a moment. "We will need time to discuss the issue." She stood and left the room without another word. Xhela followed behind her.

They were stalling, trying not to appear too eager, but I had seen the desperation in Yixa's eyes. They would return in a few minutes, ready to agree to all the terms offered. They needed the people too desperately to refuse.

All we had to do was live with ourselves.

28

A COMPROMISING POSITION

Mila

I sank into my bed with a sigh. It was late. I'd been working for hours past sunset, not unusual for the past few weeks. I kept myself busy to the point of exhaustion. Anything to forestall the thoughts and memories that haunted me as soon as I climbed into bed. I laid down and prayed for a dreamless sleep.

An urgent knock sounded at the door, and my eyes flew open. Who could be looking for me at this hour? Had I been discovered? Heart pounding, I wrapped a dressing gown around myself as I went to the door.

"Alexey!"

Not soldiers come to arrest me, thank Otets. Just Alexey. My heart slowed as I stared up at him.

He looked as surprised to see me as I was to see him. "I'm sorry to wake you," he said, looking anywhere but at my face.

"You didn't. Come in." I lit a candle. "What's wrong?"

"Nothing," he said quickly.

I turned to look at him, raising a brow. "You came to my quarters in the middle of the night to tell me nothing's wrong. Did you need something?"

"No." He blinked twice. "Yes. No."

This was so unlike him. Alexey was usually well-spoken, sure of himself. "You're acting odd. Are you feeling alright?"

He shook his head as if to clear it. "I'm fine. I wanted to see you before I leave."

I frowned, sinking into the chair next to the fire. "Where are you going?"

"We received word from one of our spies, a captain in Borislav's army." He took the chair across from me. "The Grand Duke was taking the army to Sevken, but he's sending a smaller host ahead to take it, hoping we'll be distracted by the bulk of his army. Tsar Miroslav is sending Lord Kazimir to cut them off before they get there."

"Ah." I looked into the fire, watching the flames dance with the shadows. He'd given me a wealth of information in such a few short sentences. One of Borislav's captains was a traitor. Was the traitor responsible for Han's death, the reason Miroslav had been able to get to him?

And Lord Kazimir was going to ambush the tsar's army before they could take Sevken. I needed to learn more.

"Will you be safe? Can you—can you tell me where you'll be? Will you be able to write?" My fear wasn't entirely faked. I'd come to care for him, and he was leaving for battle in the morning. I didn't want him to win the battle, but I didn't want him to be hurt, either.

Alexey reached out to take my hand in both of his. "I don't know if I'll be able to write, but I don't want you to worry. I'll be fine."

I nodded, biting my lip. He hadn't answered my question about where he'd be, and I couldn't ask again without drawing suspicion. But if I got word to the tsar, he'd be able to change his route and avoid the ambush—and hopefully discover the traitor, as well.

Izolda would already be in bed, but so long as I spoke with her the first thing in the morning, our message could reach Tsar Borislav before Kazimir did.

Silence filled the air, along with a strange tension. I glanced at Alexey and found him watching me.

I was wearing nothing but a long linen shirt and a dressing robe. Witness, Steward, and Prophet. No wonder he couldn't concentrate. My cheeks blazed.

"I should put on something more appropriate," I mumbled, but he grabbed my wrist as I stood.

"Don't," he said softly, pulling me onto his knee.

I let him. Otets help me, what was I doing? He smelled sweet and slightly musky, and his hands trailed up my arms, leaving goosebumps in their wake.

He stopped his ascent at my shoulders. He watched my lips but didn't move closer. He was giving me a chance to stop him.

Did I want him to stop? It had been so long, so long since I'd been touched like this. Since Han had touched me like this.

Han was dead. He'd never touch me like this again.

No, I didn't want him to stop. I needed to forget. Needed to lose myself in sensation.

I leaned forward, and our lips met. Lightly at first, barely brushing together, then deeper, hungrier. My robe slipped from my shoulders as his hands traveled down my back.

I shifted, and he grabbed my waist, moving so I straddled him. My shirt had bunched up above my waist, so there was nothing between us but what he wore. His hardness pressed into me, and an involuntary moan escaped my lips.

His hands roamed over my stomach and breasts, sending shivers of pleasure through me. "I want you." His voice was commanding, so full of desire it was almost a growl.

Otets, I wanted him, too. I reached down, fumbling with the ties on his pants, but he stood, picking me up with him. He carried me to the bedroom and laid me gently on the bed. He kissed me, deep enough to leave me gasping for air, and then kissed slowly down my body, over my shirt. He stopped to press a kiss to each breast, then down my stomach, stopping before he got to where I wanted him most. As he moved upward again, I whimpered. He kissed back up my body, far too slowly, and stopped at my lips. "I have wanted to do this since the moment I met you," he whispered against my mouth.

"I—" I started, but my words cut off when I felt his hand between my legs.

"I want to make you mine." His finger slid inside my drenched center, and I writhed beneath him. "I want to make you moan and see stars and climax with my name on your lips." I did moan, as his thumb traced circles where my thighs met. "And then," he said, fingers moving in rhythm, building the tension inside me, "I want to fill you and claim every part of you."

He touched me steadily, deliberately, until I couldn't see or feel anything else. He whispered something; I could hear his low voice, but I couldn't understand the words over the pounding of my heart.

My release crashed through me. He stroked me as I shuddered, coaxing every last wave. I lay there trembling, the stars he had promised fading behind my closed eyelids.

"I love you, Sofia."

Fuck. *Fuck.* My eyes flew open, and I jerked away from his touch.

"Sofia?" He didn't move closer, but worry filled his face.

I didn't answer him. By the *Blood,* what had I done? I tugged my shirt over my legs and grabbed for something, anything, to cover myself. My hands found a pillow, and I clutched it to my chest like a lifeline.

Alexey stepped away from the bed until he reached the wall. His hands were by his sides, palms toward me in what was obviously intended to be a non-threatening manner. I couldn't look at him. I couldn't *not* look at him. Why was the room so small? I couldn't breathe. What had I done?

"Sofia, look at me." It wasn't a command, but it wasn't a request, either. I swallowed hard and met his gaze. "I will never hurt you."

I let out a sound between a laugh and a sob.

"What can I do?" Desperation tinged his voice.

"I'm sorry," I choked out.

"No!" He moved toward me, but stopped when I flinched. "No," he said again, quieter. "It's not your fault, Sofia."

If only he knew. *That's not my name,* I wanted to tell him. *I'm using you. I'll never be yours. I can't be.* If he found out what I was, who I was, he'd hate me. I hated myself.

I'd used him for release, a way to forget my dead husband and the pain I felt. It wasn't fair. He deserved better.

"Do you want me to leave?"

I couldn't make my mouth form the words. I nodded, staring hard into the fire.

He turned to leave, but he stopped in the doorway. "Whatever I did…" He trailed off. "I don't know what's wrong, my sun, but I'm sorry. So sorry."

I woke the next morning no more rested than when I'd finally fallen asleep. My shirt was wrinkled, and not just from sleep. I yanked it off and dug in my trunk for a clean one.

Once I pulled my sarafan over my head and belted it, I felt marginally better. I rubbed some oil into the ends of my braids. The scent was familiar and comforting, a rose oil like I used to make from my garden at home. If I closed my eyes, I could almost believe I was back there.

But I wasn't. I couldn't stay in my room forever. I'd hired a new assistant to help with my growing stack of orders, and she would be arriving soon. I needed to go find Izolda. What had happened with Alexey…

I wasn't going to think about it. But before that, he had mentioned things that I couldn't ignore. A captain in Borislav's army was spying for Miroslav. Borislav was marching on Sevken, and Lord Kazimir was going to cut him off before they reached it. Time was of the essence, and no matter what mistakes I'd made during the night, I had things to do in the morning.

My assistant walked into the room as I stepped out of the bedroom. She stopped to pick something up from the ground.

"You have a letter here, Sofia Stepanova," the girl said.

"Thank you." I took it without looking and tucked it in my belt. Whatever it was, I'd read it on the way to see Izolda. I could use the distraction. "I have some things to do this morning, so I need you to pack up Lady Yelena's sarafan and finish cutting the green velvet for Countess Zoya's order. I'll be back by dinner."

"Yes, Sofia Stepanova."

As I walked outside, I took a deep breath. The weather was unexpectedly warm, and I opened my coat, soaking up the weak light of the sun.

I was halfway across the grounds before I remembered the letter in my belt. I pulled it out. It was unaddressed and unsealed. I frowned, curious, as I opened it.

My dear sun,

I folded it up and tucked it back into my belt. So much for a distraction. I wasn't ready to deal with that mess.

Lady Heli kept a predictable schedule. I found her in the gardens, taking her morning walk. Izolda, as usual, was with her, following some distance behind. This morning, the baroness was also accompanied by her husband. They made a courtly picture walking together, her arm on his. She caught sight of me but didn't stop.

"Izolda," the baroness called after a minute.

"Yes, my lady?"

"I believe I'll rest after my walk. I won't need you again until dinner; you may have the morning."

"Yes, my lady. Thank you." Izolda grinned as she walked toward me.

I tried to return my friend's smile, but I could tell by her reaction that the result was less than convincing.

She took my arm. "What's gotten under your skirt?"

I narrowed my eyes at her, trying to decide if that was a figure of speech.

"Oh!" Her face was triumphant. "Not a 'what' at all! A 'who!' Tell me everything."

I sighed. For a spy, I could be unbelievably bad at hiding my emotions. Now that Izolda had guessed, I'd never get out of it. I'd have to tell the whole story.

"Wait, let me guess. Was it a certain tall manservant we know? An incorrigible flirt who's been in love with you since he met you?"

I shot her a dark look. "He's not in love with me." He just thought he was, if his words from the night before were to be believed.

"What happened?"

I glanced around, ensuring no one was in earshot. "I have news. Alexey came to see me last night." I relayed the information he had let slip.

"Good." She nodded encouragingly. "We had suspicions that Miroslav had an informant. Anything else? Did he mention a name?"

"No. He was...distracted."

The grin was back. "And why might that be?"

"It was the middle of the night when he came to tell me he was leaving." I shrugged. "I wasn't dressed for company, and he'd come to say goodbye. One thing led to another..." I trailed off.

"Did you bed him?"

"Izolda!"

"Well, did you?"

I bit my lip. "Not...exactly."

Her eyes widened. "What do you mean, 'not exactly?' Either you did or you didn't."

"No. But we did…other things. Well, he did." I was sure she could see steam rising from my cheeks.

Her grin was positively wicked. "What sort of things?"

"I am *not* discussing this."

"You're no fun," she pouted.

I looked around again. We were alone. Still, I lowered my voice when I said, "My husband's not been dead three months. I shouldn't be *looking* at another man, let alone letting him into my bed."

Izolda squeezed my arm. "You're not a bad person for finding comfort after your husband died. It's only natural."

I stopped walking. "I should have stopped him. I don't know what I was thinking."

"I've seen Alexey. I know exactly what you were thinking." She laughed, ignoring my withering look. "You need the distraction. He's good-looking. And you have him exactly where you want him. You didn't even bed him, and look how much he told you. Imagine what he'd tell you if you did." Seeing me about to argue, she went on. "If you were going to get squeamish about things like this, the time for it is long past. War means compromise, Fia, and if you think the things they do on the battlefield are bad, the things we have to do to get them there are a hundred times worse. If you want to get us through this war, you have to play dirty." She let go of my arm. "I need to pass this to our contacts. If a rider leaves today, we can warn the tsar in time to avoid an ambush. I'll see you tonight for supper, right? The Frozen Boar, our usual time?"

"I'll be there."

As Izolda walked away, I pulled the letter from my belt. She was right. I couldn't afford to have scruples about using Alexey for information. Not if I wanted revenge on Miroslav and his men.

And it wasn't ass though I felt nothing for Alexey. He was a good man. I enjoyed spending time with him. If I'd met him in another time, another life, I might even have fallen for him.

I opened the letter and began to read.

My dear sun,

I did not wish to leave this morning on the terms we left last night, but I did not know if I would be welcome. I pray you will not see me as a coward for choosing to leave this letter rather than expressing my thoughts in person.

When you were in my arms last night, I was truly the happiest man alive. The taste of your lips is the sweetest memory, and I will wear your touch into battle with me like armor. Would that the thought is as sweet to you as to me, but I fear, given how last night ended, it is not.

I pray you know that my only desire was to give you pleasure. If anything I did caused you grief or pain, it was unconsciously done. Please, if you feel anything at all for me, grant me the opportunity, upon my return, to rectify the wrongs I have committed against you. If my advances were indeed unwelcome, I beg you not to spare me pain by silence, but to break my heart cleanly.

For now, I leave with hope, for my heart remains with you. I look forward to my return, when the sun shall once again light up my life, but until then, I remain,

Faithfully yours,
Alexey

29

TRAITORS

Han

Sevken.

I eyed the castle as it appeared on the horizon, dark against the snowy landscape. We'd received word that Borislav had taken it without bloodshed. How had he managed that? Were the servants still so loyal to him? Or had the steward Miroslav placed over it surrendered once he saw the army camped outside the walls?

The Drakra would join Borislav's army at Sevken once they had gathered their own troops. Yakov, Lada, and I had agreed to return ahead of them, to inform the tsar of the successful negotiations and to prepare for the arrival of the second army.

The sleigh skidded along the icy road, the castle drawing nearer by the second. Lada drove, giving me the freedom to observe the tsar's home.

Something hung above the castle gates. I frowned, trying to make out the details. They swayed lightly in the wind, too heavy to be banners.

Revulsion coursed through me as they came into focus. Bodies.

Yakov had noticed them, too. "Did Miroslav take back the castle?"

"No," Lada said. "Look." She pointed at the banners waving next to the figures. Borislav's standard, a white hawk on a field of red. Miroslav's hawk was black.

They hadn't been dead long. I recognized the bodies as we rode up. Six men. I'd assigned each of them to units myself.

Igorovich. The name clanged through my head. Nikolai Igorovich, the recruit who had mistaken me for the prince, now hung above the tsar's gate. By the Blood, what had happened?

Fyodor Yakovlevich met us in the courtyard. "I'm glad you're back." His expression was grave.

"What's happened?" I gestured behind us at the grim scene above the gate.

"Didn't the tsar send word?" The captain shook his head. "Miroslav sent an order through the country. He's demanding the slaughter of the families of anyone supporting Tsar Borislav. We've had a rash of desertions. Things are bad."

Yakov and I shared a horrified look. Was Anna safe? I had sisters, as well—we hadn't spoken in years, but that wasn't likely to bother Miroslav.

"What does that have to do with them?" I asked, jerking my head at the bodies.

"They were deserters."

Yakov swore. "They were killed for leaving after that?"

Fyodor nodded once. "Hanged, on the tsar's direct order."

"I need to see him," I said. Why would the tsar execute men who were trying to protect their families? That sort of cruelty was why we were fighting against Miroslav. Borislav had to be better. "Where is he?"

Fyodor's face grew stormier. "In the cells. He—" He broke off. "We received word from the capital that one of the captains was spying for Miroslav. There was an investigation, and Matvey Il'ich was caught with a letter detailing our plans. It was in his own hand, so there's no question about it. He's a traitor."

What? Matvey Il'ich was—had been—a loyal supporter of the tsar. He'd been in the first rebellion, as had a small number of the army, members of a unit that hadn't arrived in time to take the field at Barbezht. His counsel to the tsar, in the few months I had known him, had been good. How had he become a traitor?

"Is my father there as well?" Lada asked.

The captain nodded. "They've been with him all day, trying to determine how much information he fed to Miroslav."

"Take me to them, please," I said. I had to do something about all of this.

Fyodor cast a questioning look at Yakov and Lada. The latter shook her head.

"I'd like to get settled in. I'll find someone who can tell me where I'm staying. When my father's finished, I'll speak with him."

Yakov shoved his hand in his pocket, staring at the ground. "I'd like to get settled in, too, if you don't mind if I join you."

I gave them a distracted wave. "I'll see you two later."

Fyodor Yakovlevich led me to a small building near the back wall of the castle fortifications. He stopped at the door. "I'd rather not go in, if it's all the same to you."

They'd been close, I remembered. Yakovlevich and Il'ich. The betrayal had to feel personal. "Thank you, captain."

The air inside was musty and dank, and I heard the steady drip of water. At the end of the hall, torchlight flickered over Tsar Borislav and Prince Radomir, who stood together outside a closed cell door.

"Han." The tsar looked up at my approach. "Welcome back. Your journey was successful?"

I bowed. "They'll be here within the month, your majesty. Yakov Aleksandrovich and Lada Radamirovna can join me in making a full report."

The tsar waved a hand. "Later. We have more pressing matters."

"I assume you've been informed on the circumstances," the prince said, "since you found us here."

"Fyodor Yakovlevich told me." My mouth was dry, despite the damp. I swallowed. "Did he say why?"

Borislav's face held a mixture of fury and disgust. "No. Not that there's anything he could say to justify treason."

"May I speak with him?"

The tsar raised a brow. "If you wish. He's told us all I need to know. He'll be executed tomorrow. The guards aren't far—you probably saw them as you came in. Return the key to them when you're finished, and meet me in my quarters to make your report." Handing the key to me, he turned to Radomir. "I expect your daughter is waiting to see you, cousin."

The door creaked as I opened it. Outside, I heard the retreating footsteps of the tsar and the prince.

"Han Antonovich." Matvey's voice was hoarse, raspy. Chains held him to the wall. Surely the man wasn't such a danger as to merit chains. Who had given that order? And why had the tsar allowed it?

Then again, considering the rage I'd seen in the tsar's face, Il'ich was lucky only his hands were chained.

"Captain."

A brief expression of surprise flickered across his face, followed by sadness. "Not anymore, I'm afraid." A coughing fit overtook him. "You'll have to excuse me," he rasped. "Circumstances, you understand."

The cell held no drinking vessel, and even if it had, he wouldn't have been able to access it, chained as he was. I pulled out my waterskin and offered it.

He drank deeply. "My thanks." His skin was gray and pallid in the torchlight.

"How long have you been here?"

"A few days. Maybe a week," he said without emotion.

"Why did you do it?"

He looked up at me. "You know, they asked me that, but you're the first person I believe has had any real interest in my answer."

I remained silent, waiting.

"My sons," he said after a moment.

"I didn't know you had children."

"Two of them. They're young, just ten and twelve. Miroslav—" He choked on his words. "They were taken prisoner after I left to join the tsar."

He still called Borislav the tsar. His reasons weren't political, whatever else they might be.

"I received word of their arrest, along with a threat: report the tsar's movements to Miroslav, or they'd be tortured and killed." He coughed again.

"Why didn't you tell someone? We could have helped you."

He shook his head, the chains on his arms clinking slightly. "What could anyone do? The tsar wasn't going to waste men trying to rescue my sons. And they said they'd send my eldest to me bit by bit if I disobeyed a single order. Not the younger, of course," he said bitterly. "They needed to keep one alive to ensure my cooperation."

My gut rolled. I could imagine what I'd do if someone had threatened the same against Mila. Or Yakov, or Anna. Any of my family. "But after you were caught, why didn't you tell the tsar?"

He shrugged, the movement somewhat hampered by his shackles. "Who would care? I betrayed him. I put everyone's lives at risk." He looked at me, considering. "But I think you care. Thank you for that."

"I'll talk to the tsar." If I could convince Borislav, somehow, there had to be something we could do. The tsar could commute the sentence, release him, save the boys.

"I can't stop you, I know, but there's really no use. I'm to be drawn and quartered at dawn." His expression was nonchalant, but fear lay behind his eyes.

A chill ran through me. Beheading, I had expected. Hanging wouldn't have been a surprise. But the brutal death of drawing and quartering...

"I don't want you to interfere on my behalf, but if you could find it in yourself to help my sons—"

"I'll talk to the tsar," I said again. "Is there anything else I can do for you? Anything you need?" If I couldn't convince the tsar to stay the execution.

He shook his head. "My sons are all I have left. I don't know what Miroslav will do to them when I'm gone. I just need to know they'll be safe."

I knew better than to promise anything. "I'll do my best."

*****

I found the tsar's rooms with ease. Borislav, Prince Radomir, and Lada sat alone around the giant table.

"Lada was telling the details of our arrangement with the Drakra," the tsar said as I entered. "Well done, Han."

The prince scowled at his cousin. "The land was one thing. The trade, the economic compensation. But *slaves?* 'Men came from the loins of Otets himself, birthed into this world and bearing His Blood. Therefore over all the earth-dwellers men will have dominion.'"

"Sending traitors to serve the Drakra for eight years as punishment is not sacrificing the human dominion over the earth-dwellers, cousin. Traitors must be dealt with firmly and fiercely."

I tapped my fingers on my leg. I didn't disagree with the tsar, but Borislav's definition of treason was excessive. The executed deserters had joined of their own free will, out of a desire to see the rightful tsar on the throne, but they had deserted out of a desire to protect their families. Had they really deserved death for that, their bodies left exposed to the elements, food for the crows?

Were the thousands of men fighting for Miroslav traitors as well? They were fighting for what they believed in. They were willing to die for their cause. Did that mean that they deserved to be sold off as slaves for years? It was too late to change things now; the agreement had been made, but the thought of possibly hundreds of men being forced away from their homes and loved ones for the crime of fighting for their tsar... It curdled my stomach.

And Matvey Il'ich, was he a traitor? His actions were treasonous and merited punishment, no doubt, but his motives were pure. *Traitor* didn't seem to be the right word for him. Certainly he didn't merit the gruesome death the tsar had ordered for him.

Was Borislav's treatment of those who opposed him any better than Miroslav's?

"Something on your mind, Han?" the tsar asked.

I jolted from my reverie to find the other three occupants of the room looking at me. If I'd been hoping to speak with the tsar about my concerns, now would be the time.

"There is, in fact, your majesty. Matvey Il'ich."

His eyes narrowed. "As I said, traitors must be dealt with firmly and fiercely."

"He told me why he did it. It doesn't excuse his actions, of course, but I thought you would like to know his explanation."

His brow cocked, Borislav gestured for me to continue.

"His sons were taken prisoner by your brother's men, your majesty. They've been held hostage, threatened, to ensure his cooperation."

Lada made a sound of disgust in her throat.

"That's a truly despicable action by Miroslav," Radomir said. "If it's true."

"I believe him," I said. "He's prepared to die. I saw it in his eyes; this wasn't an attempt to avoid his fate. But if we could look into it, maybe find his sons for him. If he *is* telling the truth, doesn't he deserve mercy?"

The tsar opened his mouth, but Radomir spoke first. "He put thousands of lives at risk for the sake of a few. Regardless of his motives, his life is forfeit."

"I understand that he has to be punished—" I began.

"His life is forfeit." Borislav's voice was steel as he repeated his cousin's words.

Radomir stroked his beard. "Perhaps, cousin, we could reconsider commuting the sentence. Not from execution," he said at the flash of fury in Borislav's eyes, "but from being drawn and quartered to a milder death, provided his story proves true. Beheading or hanging. Something cleaner. Showing mercy would endear you to the men after the...difficulty following the desertions."

"I cannot afford the luxury of being seen as weak." Borislav's voice still bore steel. "Il'ich betrayed me, and he betrayed every man who serves me. He will receive the full sentence, and we'll send a message to anyone else contemplating treason."

My heart sank. "And his sons?"

"Once my brother realizes I have executed his spy, he'll have no need for them. He'll most likely free them, as their continued captivity would serve no purpose, but if they remain imprisoned, I will find and free them once the throne is indisputably mine. Assuming they exist at all."

His tone would brook no argument. In the ensuing silence, Lada cleared her throat. "What was the difficulty after the desertions?"

Borislav's nostrils flared, but it was Radomir who answered. "Some of the men felt the executions were unnecessary, or at least the display of the bodies. There was a small riot over it."

"The men involved were whipped," the tsar said, "but they should have been hanged."

Radomir sighed. "We can't execute the entire army. If you kill everyone who disagrees with you, you won't have anyone left."

This was clearly not the first time they'd had this discussion.

"If I executed everyone who disagrees with me, you wouldn't be here. I don't want to kill everyone, just those who stir up dissent among my subjects."

The prince shook his head. "That's a dangerous road, cousin. If you follow it all the way down, you'll end up alone."

I didn't disagree.

30

DISCONTENT

Han

A gnawing sense of dread filled my stomach. Yakov had woken without complaint—for possibly the first time in his life—to join me for breakfast, but I hadn't been able to make myself eat. Not with Matvey Il'ich's execution fast approaching. I wanted, needed, to be a friendly face at the man's death, having failed to convince the tsar to commute his sentence.

At least Yakov had agreed to go with me.

As we left the castle grounds, I saw a crowd had already gathered around the gallows that had been built outside the gates. I'd hoped Il'ich would be spared the cruel, jeering crowds that often attended executions. I'd never been to one, but I had heard execution spectators could be vicious.

The crowd was silent as still as the predawn sky, though. Il'ich wasn't there yet. He wouldn't be. The arrival of the condemned was a punishment in itself. I saw a few familiar faces, mostly men from Il'ich's unit. Fyodor Yakovlevich gave me a tight nod.

The sun had just peeked over the horizon when the tsar arrived, followed by Prince Radomir. Both of their faces were set. The tsar's held grim determination, while Radomir's held resignation.

From the castle gate came the steady clopping of hooves. The crowd turned as one toward the sound, and my stomach clenched.

Matvey Il'ich, wearing only a long, white linen shirt, was tied by the wrists to the saddle of a horse, stumbling behind it. Two guards followed it. As they exited the gate, the executioner, who held the horse's lead, dropped it and smacked the beast's flank. It broke into a trot. Il'ich raced after it. Stumbled. Fell.

The horse dragged him the rest of the distance to the gallows.

No sound came from the observing crowd when the guards lifted Il'ich to his feet. Scratches streaked his body, but he matched the crowd's silence. A guard released him from the horse, leaving his hands still bound together, and led him up to the gallows.

The executioner placed a noose around his neck, and the tsar spoke in a cold voice. "Do you have any final words, Matvey Il'ich?"

My chest tightened. Why hadn't I tried harder to convince the tsar? Surely there was something I could have done.

"I have betrayed my tsar, my country, and Otets." Il'ich's voice was clear, though thick with emotion. "I have betrayed the trust of the men who served under me, and I have risked countless lives. I deserve this punishment, and I hold no anger toward any of you." His gaze swept the crowd, resting momentarily on me. "I ask that you consider my debt to you paid with my death and forgive me. And for those of you that have that power, I beg you to have mercy on my sons."

Prince Radomir spoke. "The Witness reminds us that, 'In an abundance of care for His children, the Father ordained death for the evildoers. But though the Father is just, He is also merciful. If the condemned man be truly repentant, he will not be punished in the life to come.'"

The prince's words soothed some of the tension in Matvey Il'ich's face, and he closed his eyes. His lips moved in silent prayer. Then he looked at Borislav. "I rest my spirit in the hands of Otets. May He bless you, my tsar."

The tsar nodded at the executioner, and the trapdoor swung open. Il'ich dangled in the air, legs swinging wildly. By design, the distance hadn't been enough to snap his neck, and he clawed at the noose with his bound hands. The air left my own lungs as I watched. I could practically feel the noose about my neck, as though I hung next to him.

After what felt like an eternity, the executioner cut him loose. He fell to the ground, limp but still conscious—barely. The guards hauled him into a sitting position as the executioner approached, a large, curved knife in his hand. Il'ich opened his mouth in a silent plea, his eyes bulging

With the first slice, I looked away. I couldn't watch as they disemboweled him. Yakov hadn't moved, but as Il'ich's innards splattered, he leaned over and emptied the contents of his stomach onto the ground.

Trying to block out the sound of the slaughter, I watched the crowd. Several of them looked as nauseous as Yakov. The only unmoved observer was the tsar, who stood silent and expressionless, his hands by his side. Even Radomir looked slightly green beneath his dark beard.

I risked a glance at the gallows but immediately wished I hadn't. Il'ich's body—I assumed the man was dead by now, as he wasn't moving—lay prone on the snow, his stomach and groin like raw mincemeat, with entrails spilling out. The executioner had just begun the process of hacking the body into four pieces.

"How can you watch this?" Yakov muttered.

I glanced at my friend. His skin was pallid, covered in a thin sheen of sweat. Even his freckles had paled. "I'm not."

There was another squelching sound, and Yakov doubled over again, retching.

Finally, mercifully, the process was done. The tsar turned away as the guards tossed the disassembled body into a wheelbarrow. Still the crowd didn't move, as silent as the early moments of a Prophet's Day service. The tsar and his cousin walked back to the castle, but only once they had disappeared through the gate did the onlookers begin to disperse.

Yakov and I were the last to leave. He wiped his face with his sleeve as the body—what was left of it, at least—was carted away to be scattered for the crows.

"I thought Barbezht was bad," Yakov said as we, too, finally left. "This was so much worse than anything we saw there."

The smell of roasting flesh and the sound of Benedikt's screams filled my mind. I wasn't sure this had been worse, but it certainly wasn't better.

Borislav was supposed to be better.

Rather than returning to the castle, we headed for the camp surrounding it. I hadn't seen most of the men since our return, and I wanted to gauge the mood in the camp for myself. Between Miroslav's threat, the desertions, and the numerous executions, I didn't expect it to be good.

Despite the early hour, the camp was busy. Men, seated outside their tents, sharpened swords and axes and repaired leather armor. The clash of steel rang out somewhere out of sight as others honed their battle skills, and the smell of campfire smoke mingled with the scent of various breakfasts.

In front of one such campfire, we found Konstantin Anatolyevich, the baker from Tsebol, stirring a small iron pot. He offered a wide grin and waved us over.

"Han! How are you?"

I forced myself to return the smile. "Morning, Kostya. You remember Yakov?"

"Of course, of course. Won't you join me for breakfast?" He gestured for us to take a seat. "Nothing so nice as fresh-baked bread from my baker, but war has its consequences." He chuckled at his own joke.

I glanced at Yakov, whose face was still green. "No, thank you. We've eaten."

"What brings you to the camp so early?"

I grimaced. "We went to the execution."

Kostya's cheerful pink face turned grim. "Ah. Awful business, one of the tsar's commanders betraying him like that."

I nodded once. The reasons behind Il'ich's betrayal must not have circulated through camp yet. "I hear it's been a difficult few weeks."

"I think a lot of us are worried for our families, with Miroslav's latest edict. I told Ulyana to stay with her family while I'm gone. I hope Mila Dmitrievna is safe?"

"As safe as she can be." I didn't meet the baker's eyes. The ember of resentment toward my wife flared up in my chest again, but I forced it back down. This wasn't the time or the place to be thinking about her. "I hope your family remains out of danger. The tsar is doing everything he can to end this war soon, so you can return to them." I patted the big man on the shoulder. "Enjoy your breakfast, Kostya."

We walked on through the camp, stopping every so often to talk. The men were courteous, but I could tell they were worried. They executions weighed heavily on us, as did Miroslav's order. After our fifth stop, I turned to Yakov.

"I'm concerned about how restless they're becoming."

He stopped, leaning against a tent pole. "They're worried about their families. Can you blame them?"

I shook my head. "I'd already been going out of my mind thinking about Mila. And now I'm thinking about your mama, too. But with the rash of desertions, and now all these executions... I'm afraid if we stay here too long, we'll have more deserters. The tsar can't execute everyone."

The flap of the tent swung open, and we both jumped. Lada peered out at us, wiping her hands on her apron. "You do know these tents are made of cloth, *da?*" She rolled her eyes. "If you're going to gossip like old women, at least do it in here."

We followed her into the infirmary tent. Cots lined the walls, and tables in the middle held numerous bottles, some filled with potions, others empty. She pointed us each to a seat. "I assume you can work while you talk?" She didn't wait for us to answer before handing us both a large bunch of herbs. "Strip the leaves off and put them on the table over there." She picked up her pestle and began grinding something in the mortar.

Yakov and I shared a wide-eyed look and began doing as she commanded. "She's as bad as Mila," he muttered.

"So." She blew a loose strand of hair out of her face. "What were you saying about the desertions?"

"Just that I'm worried if we stay here too long, we'll have more."

She nodded. "My father says there's no plan in place for our next offensive. He's worried we'll lose the advantage if we don't leave soon." Her eyes flicked to Yakov. "You look pale. Something wrong? Or is the early hour making you sick?"

"Went to the execution," he grunted.

"Bit squeamish, are you? Here, this'll settle your stomach." She poured a cup of water and added a few drops of potion to it. He sniffed at it before taking a drink.

"Thanks."

Lada turned to me. "What about you? Did you lose your stomach like Matvey Il'ich did this morning?"

I shook my head, frowning at the poor joke.

"Oh, don't give me that look. You're as bad as my father." She turned back to her mortar and began grinding again. "The world's full of gruesome things. I've seen my fair share. If you don't laugh at it, you'll cry, and I'd rather not cry. So don't judge my gallows humor, Han."

The color in Yakov's cheeks was returning. "What's in this?" he asked, taking another drink of the potion.

She winked at him. "Blood Bastards' secret. If I share it with outsiders, I'll be executed myself."

He blinked, as if unsure if she was telling the truth. I wasn't sure, either.

"Of course, if you worked for me, I might be able to share some of my secrets. Not the sacred ones, but some of the skills I've learned."

Yakov looked to me and back to her, brows furrowed. "Work for you?" He waved his hand around the tent. "Here?"

"Why not? I know neither of you will be in any of the battles, so you might as well be useful somewhere. Han's busy with the tsar, but you don't have any other duties, do you?"

He frowned at her. "You mean helping in the infirmary? Fetching water, cutting linens for bandages, and such?" She nodded. "Isn't that women's work?"

I slowly edged back as she whirled on him. I'd seen that look often enough on Mila's face to know when to get out of the way.

"'Women's work?' Keeping your sorry asses alive is 'women's work?'" She glared at him, waving her pestle under his nose. "Sure, it is women's work, if by that you mean sewing off gangrenous limbs, setting bones, and sitting next to dying men so they're not alone when they say their last words." Her eyes narrowed. "I thought you might appreciate having something to do now that we're back with the army, but if you'd rather mope around waiting for a more manly task to come along, be my guest."

"I just remembered the tsar was expecting me," I lied. "I'll find you later, Yakov. Lada." Ignoring the glare he shot at me, I disappeared through the tent flap.

So much for spending the day at camp. I wanted to be far away from the impending storm between those two. I walked back to the castle. The tsar was walking across the entrance hall, and he waved me over.

"Ah, Han. I hoped we would have a chance to talk today. Will you walk with me?"

"Of course, your majesty."

Borislav led me through the doors I'd just entered and into the castle courtyard. "How was the adjustment for you?" At my questioning look, he nodded at my arm. "Going from two hands to one."

"Difficult," I admitted. "I never enjoyed writing, but learning to write again was awful. Mila made me learn, but most of my correspondence is—was—handled by my steward. I had to relearn how to handle an ax, a sickle, a spoon." I gave a wry grin. "For the first year, Yakov and I spent all day training with tools, and all night Mila harangued us about pens and spoons."

The tsar smiled. "Your wife is a treasure. But what about swords? I can't imagine a man like you accepting the fact that you'd never hold a sword again."

Was I so transparent? "We trained a bit, with sticks and the like. Yakov and I, I mean. But no one would sell us a sword after Barbezht, and it's hard to learn to swordfight without one."

We stopped outside the castle smithy. "And if you could fight again?" he asked.

I frowned, confused. "I made my vow to you, your majesty. If I could, of course I would fight for you. But I doubt I could learn to fight again with one hand. Not in time to be of any use."

Borislav pushed open the smithy door. A wave of heat and the smell of coal greeted us.

"Your majesty!" The blacksmith wiped his sooty hands on his apron and picked up a package. "I have it here."

"Ah, thank you." The tsar took the package and handed it to me. "You may not be able to fight again with one hand, but what about with two?"

I set the package on the blacksmith's bench and peeled back the paper. I stared at it, trying to process what I was seeing.

Before me on the bench was an iron hand.

"Your majesty, it's—" I couldn't finish the sentence. There were no words.

"It's a work of art," the tsar said, beaming. "Try it on!"

I fitted it to my wrist, fumbling with the straps. After a moment, the blacksmith reached over and showed me how to buckle it onto my arm.

"His majesty designed it," the blacksmith said, "and I worked with the saddlemaker in town to put it all together. You can adjust the gears here to move the fingers." He opened and closed the fingers, then had me try.

The tsar smiled. "You'll be able to hold a sword and a pen again. And while it might take some time before you're ready to be on the field again, I'd like you to be one of my commanders, Han."

The offer struck me dumb.

"I have an opening for a captain, and you have an eye for strategy, as well as a natural bent for leadership. The men trust you, and so do I. After recent events, we need someone we can trust. *I* need someone I can trust."

"I don't know what to say."

"Say yes."

"I—yes, of course!" I placed my hand—my new, iron hand—over my heart. "Your majesty, I told you before, I am your man to the end. I would be honored to command your soldiers."

"Good." The tsar nodded at me. "I believe you have some work to do. Go to the training rings and get yourself reacquainted with a sword. I'll see you at the meeting with the commanders after supper." He turned to the blacksmith and shook the man's hand, unbothered by the grime. "And thank you for such excellent work. You are a blessing to our war efforts."

I ran a finger over my new hand as Borislav left. What would Mila think of this?

It could be months before I would have the opportunity to show her. If we both lived long enough for her to see it. The resentment in my chest blazed up again, and I gritted my teeth. At least now, if—when—she returned, I could protect her. I could keep her safe, rather than allowing her to fight a war I couldn't.

Once she was home, I could make sure she'd never be in danger again.

31

SURRENDER

Mila

"Your roll." Izolda pushed the dice across the table. We were alone in the inn, our food long since finished, playing our third game. I was grateful for the distraction from my incessant fears about the war. Alexey hadn't written—not that I expected him to—and we'd had no news about their intended ambush of Borislav's troops. I prayed my message had gotten through in time. And, selfishly, I prayed Alexey was unhurt.

I shook the dice and tossed them on the table. Pushing my worries to the back of my mind, I tallied up the dots and grinned at Izolda. "I win."

She squinted at me. "I think you cheat."

"You're just jealous that I'm better than you." I gathered up the dice. "Play again?"

The door to the inn opened before she could answer. I glanced over to see Alexey stride in, and my heart leapt. His clothes were rumpled and dirty, like he'd been riding all day. When he saw us, he gave a half-smile, less cocky than usual.

"I've been blessed with an omen from Otets," he said as he approached. "The sun and the moon together, sent to bring me good favor."

Izolda grinned. "Flirt. Good news from the war effort?"

He shook his head, pressing his lips together. "May I join you?"

He reached for another chair as I nodded, but Izolda stood and stretched.

"Actually, I've got to head back. Lady Heli wants to be at morning prayers tomorrow, and I'll hate myself if I spend all night out."

"Some other time," he replied, but he wasn't looking at her. I could feel his eyes on me as I frowned at my friend.

"Since when do you care about getting to bed early?" I asked.

"'The body is a gift from Otets and should be treated as his Sanctioned dwelling, even in the unSanctioned,'" she quoted. "Last week's homily inspired me."

Liar. She'd slept through most of last week's homily. She was scheming to get me alone with Alexey. I glared at her, but she just winked.

"Make sure she gets back safe, Alexey. Night, Fia." She flounced out of the inn with a wave.

I could still feel the pressure of Alexey's gaze as he took a seat. "How are you?" he asked.

"Good." I rolled the dice over between my hands, watching how they caught the light.

"Did you get my letter?"

I bit my lip. "I did."

He was silent, waiting for me to continue.

"I wasn't—" I started. "I didn't—" I huffed, trying to gather my thoughts. "It wasn't anything you did."

He still didn't speak. I looked up from the dice and found his dark eyes locked on me.

"Did you not want it?" His voice was quiet, raw with emotion.

"Otets' Blood." I rubbed my temples. I'd had weeks to prepare for this confrontation, and I still wasn't sure what to say to him. "You didn't do anything wrong."

He reached across the table and took my hands in his. "I meant what I said in the letter. If there's anything I can do, I will, but don't leave me in doubt. I need to know if you care for me at all."

Otets help me, I did. My throat was too tight to speak, but I squeezed his hands.

"Do you?"

I nodded slowly, not breaking eye contact, and his breath came out in a rush. "My sun." He raised my hands to his lips and pressed a kiss to each one.

"How long have you been back?" I asked, rubbing my thumbs over his knuckles. His hands were rougher than usual, and I didn't know if it was from swinging a sword or riding.

"Not long. I came looking for you as soon as the baron released me."

I laughed quietly. "I thought you looked a little...road-weary."

He leaned back and crossed his arms, a stern expression on his face. "I don't know what you're talking about, Sofia Stepanova. I never look anything less than perfect."

I plucked a piece of mud from his sleeve and held it up. "Is that so?"

He chuckled. "Maybe a touch less than perfect. I would have changed, but I was in a hurry."

"You waited three weeks, but another quarter hour was too much?"

"Yes," he said earnestly. My breath caught at the intensity in his eyes.

"Well, you've found me. Maybe now you'd like to change into something cleaner?" My face heated as I realized the invitation my words implied, but I didn't correct myself. I wanted him.

Amusement and desire flashed across his face. He stood and offered me his hand. "I'd be happy to put on something less offensive to your delicate sensibilities, so long as you'll come with me."

I allowed him to help me into my coat. He took my arm, and we walked out into the frigid night air.

"I couldn't stop thinking of you while I was gone," he said as the lights of the inn faded behind us.

"Me, too." My heart was pounding out of my chest. If he couldn't hear it, it was a miracle.

"I should have come back that night. I was afraid you'd send me away again."

"I was just—"

He cut me off. "You don't have to explain yourself. You said no. That's enough explanation for me."

"I want to." I couldn't tell him the truth, not all of it, but I could tell him a little. "It was just a lot at once. I got overwhelmed. Scared. I wasn't ready."

"And now?" he asked, not looking at me.

"And now..." I bit my lip. And now what? Nothing had changed.

Nothing but me. It had only been a short time since Han died, but our marriage had been dying for months before that, ever since the day Kazimir attacked me. I'd hardly been able to look at Han, let alone let him touch me. He'd smothered me, not letting me heal on my own time.

I knew I shouldn't compare them, but Alexey was everything Han hadn't been. He didn't push me to share things before I was ready. He sat quietly with me when I needed to cry, and he left without argument when I needed to be alone. He recognized that he couldn't always protect me, so he gave me the ability to protect myself.

I loved Han, of course I still loved Han, but he was dead. And maybe even before he'd died, he hadn't been what I needed anymore. Maybe Alexey was.

"And now I think I am," I said finally.

We'd reached the palace. He led me inside, unspeaking, and up a back staircase that ended on a narrow servants' hallway. Tallow candles lined the hall, lighting our way. Alexey stopped in front of a door halfway down the hall. He unlocked and opened it, gesturing for me to go inside.

The room was small, no bigger than my own bedroom. When he stepped in behind me, his presence filled the room. In the dim candlelight from the hall, I had a brief impression of a clean, well-organized space, but when he stepped around me to lay his fur coat on the chest against the wall, everything else went out of my head.

He knelt down to light the fire. The room was cold, but I didn't feel it as my blood ran hot through me.

Once firelight filled the room, he stood to take off his kaftan. "I apologize for my untidiness," he said with a grin. "I hope you can forgive me."

"I'm sure I can." I meant the words to sound teasing, but they came out breathy with desire. My eyes fixed on his body, the sweat-stained shirt that clung to his skin, showing wiry muscles. I took a step toward him and ran a hand down his chest. He shuddered beneath the touch.

When I lifted my face to his and kissed him, he wrapped his arms around me, gentle and tender, as if afraid I would break.

I needed this. Needed him. I deepened the kiss, tugging at the hem of his shirt.

He drew back with an amused smile. "Anxious, my sun?" He stripped off his shirt, then helped me remove my coat.

I shivered. Was I really doing this? I'd never been with another man besides Han. Our first time had been awkward and rushed, a few stolen minutes before he left to join the first uprising. My first time with Alexey would be different.

He gathered me into his arms again. "Cold?"

"No," I whispered, afraid to break the spell of the moment by speaking any louder.

He guided me to the bed and knelt before me. My breathing hitched, but he pulled my shoes and stockings off, set them neatly against the wall, and sat down next to me.

Brushing his thumb over my cheek, he looked at me with a solemn expression. "Before we do this, I need to know that you really want to. If you're not ready, or if it's going to remind you of...whatever happened to you, we don't have to do anything." He took my hands in his. "I won't lie; I want you. But I want you to feel safe with me. I'll wait for you. Forever, if need be."

Was I ready? I looked down at my bare feet, gathering my thoughts. There was no going back after this. I couldn't go back to my old life.

Then again, there had been no going back for a long time now.

I looked into his eyes. "I do. I want you."

The tension melted from his face, replaced with a tender look. He took my face in both hands and kissed me once, twice, three times.

Pulling back from his touch, I stood and slipped off my sarafan. His eyes widened, drinking in the sight of me in only my long linen shirt. "Beautiful," he murmured.

My cheeks blazed at the compliment, and I knelt before him. I pulled off his boots one at a time, then dragged his pants off. His erection, thick and slightly curved, sprang free. I reached for it, a thrill of power running through me.

I ran my thumb over the tip, and he gasped. Looking up at him through my lashes, I lowered my head, intending to take him into my mouth, but he reached down to touch my cheek.

"No."

I stroked him. "No?"

He clenched his eyes shut. "No," he said through gritted teeth. I stopped stroking, and he opened his eyes. "Not the first time, my sun. I want you, all of you."

Heat rushed through me at his words. "Well, then." I straddled him, feeling him against my center. I wasn't ready yet, but he didn't rush me. He kissed my neck, fingers trailing up and down my spine. I squirmed, every touch of his lips on my skin leaving me slicker.

"Please, Alexey." My words were a whimper.

He groaned in response, lifting me up by the hips and sliding further back on the bed. "Whatever you need." He laid back against the pillow. "Take it."

My hand shook as I guided him into me. He was wider, thicker than—no, I couldn't think of him. Not right now. Alexey moved beneath me, just slightly, and I jerked.

He froze. "Did I hurt you?"

"No. You won't." I'd never been more sure of anything in my life.

"Show me," he said. "Show me what you want. How to touch you."

I guided his hands to my hips. "Just hold me here."

I slid up and down on him, relishing the feel of him inside me. He groaned, fingers digging into my flesh, but otherwise didn't move.

I swirled my hips, grinding against him. I was close, so close already. Alexey's eyes squeezed shut, and I placed my hand on his chest.

"Look at me," I whispered. His eyes flew open.

Otets, I felt like a whole new person. He pulled my mouth down to his for a kiss, and I exploded, my climax flooding through me.

A moment later, he followed, spasming inside me as he cried out in wordless release.

32

ATTAINTED

Mila

We lay together tangled in his bed. I rested my head on his chest. "I'm glad you're back safe," I whispered.

His fingers comed through the curls at the end of my braid. "I wasn't in any danger. We didn't even join battle."

Then my message had gotten through to Tsar Borislav in time. "What happened?"

"Either our spy was wrong, or they got word that we were coming. They took a different route. Circumvented us completely and reached the castle before we'd even realized we were in the wrong place. Borislav took the castle without any opposition."

It had to be an important victory, and we'd managed it without bloodshed. A blessing.

"It's selfish," I said, "but I'm glad you weren't in any danger. Even if it means we lost the battle."

He pressed a kiss to the top of my head. "I'd fight a thousand battles if that was what it took to come back to you."

"I'd rather you not have to." I snuggled closer.

A frantic knock at the door made me jump.

"Just a moment!" Alexey dragged himself into a sitting position and reached for his pants.

"Get your ass out of bed!" Izolda hissed through the door.

I looked wide-eyed at Alexey. His expression mirrored my own. I threw my shirt back on and pulled the covers back on as he put on his pants.

Not bothering with a shirt, he opened the door, and Izolda flew inside. Her brows raised slightly as she saw me, but she didn't comment.

My mouth went dry. Something horrible must have happened.

She rounded on Alexey. "Did you know?"

"Know what?" I asked. "What's wrong?"

"Lady Heli's been arrested. And the baron."

Miroslav knew everything. He knew about the rebellion, Lord Ilya and Lady Heli's involvement. They'd be looking for me and Izolda next.

Alexey's brow furrowed. "Did you hear the charges?"

"What else could it be?" She crossed her arms. "Miroslav's suspected them both of treason since the first rebellion."

I clambered out of bed, modesty forgotten in my fear. Alexey wrapped an arm around my waist, pulling me to him, and I curled into his warmth. "Did they arrest the rest of the household? Will they be looking for you?"

"I don't think so, but I should probably lay low for a while."

"I agree." He looked down at me. "If the tsar decides to question Lord Ilya's household, they may remember Lady Heli recommended you for your position and question you, as well. If that happens, just be honest. Tell them you knew the baroness very little, and you know nothing of any plots against the tsar."

If I hadn't been so terrified, I might have laughed. He didn't know how wrong he was, how much I actually knew about the rebellion. I stared at the ground, swallowing hard.

"I'll keep track of things in the palace," he said. "Lord Kazimir may not have known about the arrests before they happened, but the tsar won't keep him in the dark about it. I should be able to get news to both of you if there's any danger." He looked at Izolda. "Do you have enough money for a private room?"

"For a few nights, at least."

"Good. The Frozen Boar should be safe enough. Get a room there, and I'll get word to you if anything changes. And Izolda?" he said as she turned to leave. "Be careful."

She grinned halfheartedly. "Thanks, Alexey."

Once she left, he wrapped me in a tight embrace. "It's going to be alright, my sun."

I didn't answer. He couldn't know that. Not with who I was—what I was.

"I need to find out what's happening. Will you be okay alone tonight?"

I nodded, not trusting my voice. If Lord Ilya and Lady Heli had been discovered, it was only a matter of time before someone found the connection to me. And even if they didn't, I couldn't be sure our contacts hadn't been caught as well. Izolda might know, or at least be able to find out, but I'd have to wait until later to speak to her. I couldn't let Alexey find out about my real connection to Borislav. Not now that he meant so much to me.

We dressed in silence. As he helped me into my coat, he kissed my neck. "You're quiet."

"I'm...worried."

"It's going to be alright," he said again. "The tsar doesn't pay much attention to the lower classes. Even Izolda should be fine. And your connection to the baroness is so minor, he likely won't even consider having you questioned."

I prayed he was right. For all our sakes.

When we reached my rooms, he pulled me tight against his body, claiming my mouth in a hungry kiss. "I know it didn't end the way we wanted, but tonight was..." He trailed off, searching for the right word. "Indescribably wonderful."

"Was it?" My cheeks flushed, and I lowered my gaze.

"Yes! By the Blood, yes." He put a gentle hand under my chin, making me meet his eyes. "You are the answer to every prayer I've ever prayed and every dream I've ever dreamt. Don't ever doubt that." He kissed me again, softly this time. "I'll come by tomorrow evening. Be careful, my sun."

*****

I woke before dawn and hurried through the frozen gray light to the inn to find Izolda. She'd managed to get a private room, and she answered on the first knock.

"Fia! Thank Otets." She ushered me in and closed the door, locking it behind us. "Are you alright?"

"I'm fine. You?"

She was a mess, her clothes and hair rumpled from sleep. Dark circles surrounded her yellowish eyes, and her face was completely colorless, devoid of the vast amounts of rouge she usually wore. She sank down onto the bed. "Worried about the baroness."

"What happened?"

She shook her head. "I don't know. Miroslav's suspected them for years. It could have been anything."

"What about Sevken?" I couldn't regret passing along the information that led to Borislav's bloodless capture of the castle in Sevken, but I would hate to find it was something I had done that led to the baroness's capture.

Izolda shrugged. "Who knows? They were taking them when I got back. Lady Heli was already in her nightdress—practically naked!" Her voice shook with rage. "She was walking on her own feet, at least, stately as any royal, as though they hadn't just dragged her from her bed in the middle of the night. As soon as I saw, I ran back here to find you, but you'd already left. You weren't at your quarters, either." She turned blazing eyes on me. "I went to see if Alexey knew what was happening, and there you were in his bed!"

I cringed, cheeks burning. "I didn't mean to worry you."

She sighed, and some of the anger went out of her. "You didn't do anything wrong. I just—I panicked when I couldn't find you, and then you were there with him, safe, while I was running all over the palace terrified out of my mind. I should have guessed you'd be there, honestly."

Silence fell between us. Below, I could hear the clatter in the kitchen as the inn workers began their morning preparations.

After a moment, she reached for a bag. "Since you hadn't planned to sleep with him, I don't suppose either of you thought about contraception?"

I went cold. I hadn't even thought about the possibility of pregnancy. It had taken so long to conceive with Han. But I wasn't with

Han now. I wasn't even *Mila* now. Who knew how fertile Sofia's body was?

"Your stunned silence is reassuring," she said drily. She rummaged through the bag, pulling out a small glass bottle and tossing it to me. "Drink that."

I peered inside. A viscous green liquid filled it, letting off a sickly sweet smell. "What is it?"

"Potion from a Blood Bastard." She leaned against the headboard. "It'll keep you from conceiving. I keep a couple on hand in case of emergencies."

I dropped it like it was a snake. "I'm not taking that."

"Why not?" She frowned. "The last thing you need right now is a baby."

"I can't—" My chest tightened. Had the room always been so small? I walked to the window, pressing my head to the cold glass. "I—"

"Fia." Izolda's voice was distant. "What's wrong?"

"I can't take it." Was that my voice, weak and pleading?

"You don't have to take it!" Cloth rustled, followed by glass clinking together. "It's gone. *Da?*"

Breathe. In. Out. I forced myself to turn and face her. "I'm sorry."

"I mean, it's your body." Her face screwed up. "Well, you know what I mean. I just thought it would be hard to do what you're doing while pregnant."

Another breath. "I know." The sensible thing would be to take it. I closed my eyes and breathed deep. When I opened them again, Izolda was staring at me.

"My baby died," I blurted.

Her eyes widened. "Spider's Blood. What happened?"

I sat down on the bed, my breathing almost normal. "I was raped."

I'd never said it out loud, I realized. Never told anyone else. My vision was blurry. I touched my cheek; it was wet with tears. Strange. I hadn't noticed I was crying.

"Oh, Fia." Izolda sat down next to me and placed a hand on my back. "I'm sorry. If I'd known..."

"No, it's fine." I wiped my cheeks with my sleeve. "I just—" A sob tore from my throat. "It took us so long to get pregnant. And then those *bastards* showed up and *murdered* my son and took *everything* from me, including my husband. And now I realize I might have a chance to have another baby, and everything's all wrong. He doesn't even know my *name! Fuck!*" I grabbed my head, deep, gasping breaths wracking my body. "Would it even be my baby?"

After a moment, she asked quietly, "You love him, don't you?"

I let out a humorless laugh. "Does it matter? If he ever finds out who I am, he'll hate me forever." I'd deserve it, too.

Izolda was silent. What else could be said, anyway?

I wiped at my face again. "Sorry. I shouldn't have gone off like that."

"Fia." She grabbed my hand. "Really. I'm here for you."

I choked back more tears. "Thank you, Izolda."

"What are friends for?"

I gave her a watery smile. "I came to make sure you were alright, and here you are comforting me."

"I'm fine." She flashed a grin. "I'm worried about the baroness, as I said, but Alexey brought me some of my things a couple hours ago and told me what he'd heard."

I ignored the flutter my heart gave at the mention of his name. "Anything new?"

"No. Lord Ilya's being questioned, which is no surprise, but the baroness likely won't be, on account of her sex and relation to the tsar."

Questioned. My stomach twisted at the word. Lady Heli had warned me what questioning would entail, were I ever to be arrested. I shuddered to think of the tall, commanding baron subjected to Miroslav's cruel imagination.

"Has anyone else been arrested?" I asked. "Will we still be able to pass on information?"

"No, as far as I can tell, everyone else is unaffected. The baron and baroness don't even know the names of most of our contacts, let alone how to find them, so we should be able to go on as normal."

I swallowed. It was hard to imagine going back to normal with Lord Ilya and Lady Heli in Miroslav's power. "There's got to be something we can do."

She fixed me with a stern look, uncannily reminiscent of the baroness's. "We can. We help the tsar win the war. The sooner we win, the sooner they're free."

"Can't we get them out?" Lady Heli was strong for her age, but who knew what the conditions of the dungeon would do to her? The noblewoman was far from young. If there was something I could do to help her...

"Do you have any idea how to do that?" When I didn't answer, she snorted. "I didn't think so. No, you need to pretend nothing has changed. Keep your eyes and ears open, and help us win this war."

I bit my lip and nodded. I could do that.

I had no other choice.

33

BREACH OF ETHICS

Han

"Again!"

Sweat dripping down my back in spite of the cold, I complied with Fyodor's order and executed the series of positions again. The muscles in my arm burned with the weight of the dull practice sword, but I knew better than to complain. I'd made that mistake as a new recruit during the first rebellion, muttering my frustration to the man next to me. Benedikt, my commander, had heard me and given me a caning in front of the entire unit. Ten strokes. I knew why he'd done it; he hadn't wanted to be seen showing favoritism. That knowledge hadn't comforted me over the next week, when I hadn't been able to lie down properly.

Not that Yakovlevich would cane a fellow captain. Still, it was best not to push the man. He was a brutal taskmaster, expecting perfection from me, missing hand or no.

"Who trained you?" The captain's voice cut into my thoughts. "Straighten your spine. Arm up!"

I reached for the gears on my new hand, intending to tighten my grip on the sword, but Yakovlevich knocked my hand away with his own blade. "Fiddling with that on the battlefield will get you killed."

I gave a short nod and stepped back. Though my muscles were so sore I could hardly move each night as I fell into bed, I was surprised at how quickly I had progressed in the two weeks since Tsar Borislav had made me captain. I didn't have as much dexterity as before, owing to the immobility of my new hand, but the basic movements still came naturally to me, the memories buried somewhere inside my muscles.

I'd even managed to survive my first field test with the new hand. We'd had news of a small group of Miroslav's soldiers in the nearby countryside a week earlier, and I had taken some men to flush them out.

The rumored group had turned out to be a scouting party. The fight had been short and nearly bloodless, with only a single injury among Miroslav's men before the scouting party retreated. Our army was on high alert now, with patrols around the camp at irregular—and thus unpredictable—intervals.

Yakovlevich cared little for the fact that I had succeeded with my new hand in battle, however small that battle may have been. He'd pointed out that my sword arm was lacking in muscle strength and had set me to work rebuilding the muscles through constant drills and physical activity. If I wasn't in the sparring ring, I was transporting sacks of wheat or barrels of kvass across the camp. At least when I wasn't in meetings with the tsar and the other commanders.

I'd been so busy, I hadn't even had time to worry. According to the tsar, Mila had been instrumental in ensuring our capture of Sevken, but since then, we hadn't had any word from her.

A voice cut through the bustle of camp. "Captains!"

Yakovlevich and I turned to the castle servant standing on the edge of the sparring ring.

"Scouts caught sight of an enemy unit approaching. The tsar wants all the commanders in the war room, immediately."

*****

The full moon illuminated the snowy battlefield in yellow light. I walked up and down the line, nodding encouragement at my men, saying a few quiet words to the most agitated among them. Only a small portion of Miroslav's army had been spotted; according to our sources, the bulk of it remained in the south. Nonetheless, the tsar had been reluctant to send our entire force to meet the enemy, in case it was a ruse to draw us away from the castle. Most of the units remained behind, while I and two other commanders had been chosen to meet the approaching enemy.

Borislav had ordered us not to allow the enemy time to make camp. We would take advantage of our opponents' exhaustion, engaging them as soon as they arrived. I prayed the other army would arrive soon. My men were growing restless.

This was the worst part, the waiting. Every sound echoed over the snow, and my heart pounded out a staccato rhythm.

At last, the whistling wind gave way to the crunch of snow beneath boots. The enemy crept out of the woods toward us, dark against the white battlefield.

Cannon-fire erupted around me.

The first cannonballs broke apart the enemy lines in a blast of dirt, snow, and screaming men, but they reformed quickly and pressed on.

"Steady," I called to my men. "Steady."

Another round of cannon-fire split the air.

The smell of smoke filled my nose. The enemy marched forward, forward.

I could see the enemy's faces. Grim. Determined. Frightened, even.

I raised my sword. Down the line, I could see the other commanders doing the same. "Charge!"

We ran forward. My arm jolted as my sword met an opponent's. I kicked, knocking the man prone, and thrust my sword through his neck with a sickening squelch. I drew the sword free and turned to meet the next soldier.

They fought fiercely despite their exhaustion, but it didn't take long for their commanders to call a retreat. I breathed a sigh of relief as the opposing army turned and fled. It was over. We'd won.

A cheer went up from our men, but the tsar's voice, magically amplified, echoed over the field.

"Stop them."

I shared a look of confusion with my fellow commanders before I echoed the tsar's order and took off running after the enemy.

I led my men toward the army fleeing through the trees, but the delay had cost us. They were nearly out of sight. How far did Borislav expect us to pursue? He couldn't expect us to overtake Miroslav's men.

Something ahead rumbled, and I slowed, signaling for my men to stay back. It could be a trap. The noise grew, the ground beneath my feet trembling. The hairs on my neck rose as a metallic scent filled the air.

Ahead, the enemy had slowed as well. Part of the ruse?

No, the trees beyond our quarry were falling, one by one. The rumbling grew. My heart, already racing, leapt to my throat. What was happening?

I raised my hand, signaling for my men to stop. Miroslav's men had halted their retreat, looking around wildly. Whatever was ahead of them, it was enough to make them risk capture rather than face it.

I inched forward, closer to the source of the still-growing noise. Then silence fell.

Ahead lay a great ravine.

I'd been over this part of the countryside many times on guard. The land was flat, at times densely wooded, but there were no gorges, no great chasms or ravines.

Had Borislav done this, rent the land in two to trap Miroslav's men? They were trapped now, caught between us and the chasm.

The enemy scattered. I hesitated a fraction of a second before calling for my men to charge ahead.

*****

It was near dawn when I trudged into my room and collapsed on the bed.

"Morning."

I looked up to see Yakov, still clothed, in a chair next to the dying fire.

"Good battle?" he asked.

"We won," I said without emotion.

He raised a brow. "You don't sound pleased."

I sat up, groaning, and pulled off my sweat-soaked clothes. "We took almost a hundred prisoners. Minimal casualties on our part."

Yakov waved his hand. "I know about the casualties. Lada had me working with the wounded all night."

He and the Blood Bastard had resolved their argument over *women's work,* apparently. He'd spent nearly every day for the past fortnight working with her in the med tent. Between Yakov's new work and my responsibilities as a commander, we hadn't seen much of each other lately.

I sighed, taking a cloth from the nightstand and wiping the worst of the sweat and grime. "The tsar..." I shook my head. How could I explain what had happened out there? Borislav hadn't used his power directly on the enemy, but he'd crossed a line. A dangerous line.

I pulled a shirt over my head and sank into a chair next to him. "The tsar blocked off the enemy's retreat."

"Is that supposed to be a bad thing?" Yakov asked. "We took prisoners."

"He didn't order us to cut them off. He did it. Magically."

His mouth dropped open. "How?"

I described the events of the battle, our pursuit and the sudden appearance of the ravine. When I finished speaking, he let out a breath. "Fuck."

"Yeah."

There was silence between us as we stared into the coals. Finally, hardly daring to voice the words, I whispered, "Did we make a mistake, Yakov?"

"No." He clenched his fist. "Miroslav's a monster. We had to do it."

And if Borislav wasn't any better? I couldn't bring myself to say it, but he knew what I was thinking.

"He's better. He has to be."

"You're probably right." It wasn't as though Borislav had used his Gifts to kill anyone. He hadn't interfered with the battle itself, just ensured we were able to take prisoners.

I shook myself. What was I thinking? Of course Borislav was better than his brother. What did it matter if he used his magic to form a ravine during a retreat? It was no different from building a wall before the battle. Not really. I was just tired from the fight. That's why everything seemed so complicated. Everything would be clearer after a few hours' rest.

34

ALLIES

Han

I woke to someone pounding on the door.

I dragged myself from beneath the covers, glancing across the room at Yakov's bed. Empty and unmade—he must have left early that morning. Was it even morning? I glanced out the small window, but the sky was too gray to tell how late it was.

The knocking continued.

"I'm coming," I grumbled. I pulled on a fresh pair of pants and opened the door.

A young servant boy stood there. "Beg pardon, captain, but his majesty requests your presence in the camp. There's an army coming. Drakra."

Yixa na Chekke. At last. "I'll be there," I said, and the boy scampered off.

A short while later, I arrived at the edge of camp to greet our allies. I was the last to arrive; the other commanders already stood around the tsar and the prince. Tsar Borislav and his cousin wore grim looks.

I hadn't expected overwhelming joy, but the arrival of our allies should have been cause for some celebration, however small. At least from the tsar, if not from Prince Radomir.

"Your majesty. Your highness." I bowed. "Is something wrong?"

"We've had news from the capital," Radomir said. "Lord Ilya and Lady Heli have been arrested."

My heart skipped a beat. Mila. Was she safe? Had she been arrested? "And...their retinue?" I asked, afraid of the answer.

Borislav gave a small shake of his head. "Only the baron and baroness have been arrested," the tsar said. "Their household and retinue, to the best of our knowledge, remain free."

Radomir snorted. "'Only.' Ilya alone knows enough to destroy this whole rebellion. If he can't withstand your brother's torture, we could be completely brought down."

My mind reeled. Mila was safe—as far as the tsar knew. But how accurate was his information? News could take days, even weeks to reach us here, so far from the capital. Even if she'd been safe when the baron and baroness were arrested, was she still safe now?

I should have made her stay. No matter what she said, no matter how much she hated me, I should have kept her safe at home. If she ever made it back to me, I was never letting her out of my sight again.

A trumpet blast cut through my thoughts as the Drakra retinue approached. Led by Yixa na Chekke and Xhela na Zanik, the group of women traveled on foot. I recognized a few of them as Drakra I had met during my time in the mountains.

They stopped in front of us, and the priestess spoke. "Greetings, Borislav Vyacheslavovich, Heir of the Sanctioned." She inclined her head respectfully, not enough to be considered a bow. Radomir scowled, but Borislav returned the gesture. Whether or not the prince agreed, the tsar seemed content to allow Yixa to consider him an equal.

"Greetings, Yixa na Chekke, voice of Xyxra. You are most welcome." He swept his arm out toward the castle. "Allow us to show you to your rooms. We've set aside an entire wing for you and your companions. Once you're settled, we can meet to discuss strategy."

She flicked a charcoal-colored hand in dismissal. "No need to see us settled. Our men can unpack for us, provided you have servants to show them where to go?"

"Of course. If you would prefer to meet together first, that can be arranged. Shall we go straight to the war room?"

"Lead the way, Tsar of Inzhria."

With the addition of the Drakra commanders, the enormous war room felt almost cramped. Yixa and the tsar sat at opposite ends of the long table, their seconds in command—Xhela for the priestess, and Radomir for the tsar—next to them. The commanders, me included, filled in the rest of the table, though the humans and Drakra sat apart from each other without prompting. Even when the full table made it necessary for Fyodor Yakovlevich and an ash-skinned Drakra commander to sit next to each other, they subtly shifted their chairs to allow for more distance.

I wasn't surprised. Our two races had been at odds long before the Spider Wars, and relations hadn't improved since the treaty. The fact that the Drakra army had made it to Sevken unmolested was a good sign, though. Perhaps we could learn to coexist.

Once the room quieted, Yixa spoke. "I understand you've made no offensive strikes since your ambassadors," she glanced at me, "reached my territory?"

"That is correct," the tsar said.

"Is there a reason for that?" Her tone bordered on contemptuous. "I wouldn't like to think that I brought my entire army across the country to sit around and wait to be attacked."

"We have the high ground." Radomir's tone matched hers. "Why sacrifice the defensible position of this castle to attack rashly?"

Borislav silenced the prince with a look. "While we were waiting for the details of this alliance to be determined, Lady, we chose to remain here to develop our strategy and allow our men time to rest."

Her lips formed a line. "A single battle and a cross-country march, and your men need time to rest? Are all humans so fragile, or only the males?"

Borislav stood, his eyes flashing. "You may bring necessary soldiers, Yixa na Chekke, but this alliance benefits you as much as it does us. If you wish to continue our friendship, you will not insult my decisions or my men again."

I fought back a groan. Yixa's poor impression of the tsar showed on her face. In the weeks we'd spent in the mountains, I'd learned that the Drakra considered men—of all races, not just their own—to be emotional and rash, ruled by their flesh. They valued logic and emotional control. If Borislav wished to continue the alliance, he would have to restrain his temper in front of the priestess and her people.

"Your majesty, if I may?" I asked. The tsar nodded permission as he sat down. "Lady, the tsar chose this spot, the ancestral seat of the Grand Duke, as his base of operations for a number of reasons, not the least being that it was a suitable place to remain while we waited for our allies to arrive. Abandoning Sevken—which he managed to take without bloodshed, due to the great loyalty the servants of the castle have toward him—would have been a risky decision while we were still limited in number. He was willing to risk being seen as weak while waiting, in order to ensure that when we did attack, it would be from the best possible position. Now that you're here, his patience has paid off, and we can attack without reservation."

Yixa na Chekke appeared to consider my words, staring at me as the room remained silent. Then she looked at Borislav.

"Your ambassador has the mind of a female, your majesty," she said, and I heard the compliment she intended. "All cool logic and consideration, with none of the heated desperation for honor that so many men have. You should ennoble him."

The tsar frowned at her. "Indeed." He gestured toward the large map in the center of the table. "I take it that you have an idea for our next offensive move?"

*****

The rest of the day was spent in talks with the Drakra, determining our next point of attack, what route we would take to get there, what order the companies were to travel in, and various sundry details. By the time they dismissed us, my eyes were swimming. I cast a longing glance down the hall toward my room, but there were orders to be given and plans to be made, so I dragged myself back out to the camp. The high priestess and the tsar had decided it was time to take the fight to Miroslav. We were headed to the capital.

The capital. I'd only be a matter of miles, possibly less, from my wife. It would be over, and I could take her home. We were close, so close to the end. Only a short time, and I could keep her safely chained to me for the rest of our lives.

35

SURVIVOR OF BARBEZHT

Mila

I shifted the bag over my shoulder, hoping my nerves didn't show on my face. I'd been summoned to the Tsarina's Tower to meet both the tsarina and dowager tsarina. I hadn't received any commissions from them yet, but this was my opportunity to make connections. There were bound to be secrets shared within the tsarina's quarters that weren't shared elsewhere. Information I could pass along to Tsar Borislav and his army.

I'd seen the tsarina and grand duchesses on occasion during my time at court, but the dowager tsarina rarely left the Tsarina's Tower. As I approached the ornate golden doors that marked the entrance to the tower, I tried to picture the dowager's face. Miroslav and Tsar Borislav were so different. Which one took after their mother?

The guards standing at attention near the doors let me in, and a footman led me up a narrow flight of marble stairs. At the first landing, the chatter of women's voices came from behind another set of doors, these white with gilded scrollwork along the edges. The footman knocked, then opened the door.

"Sofia Stepanova, the seamstress," he said, bowing to the two women seated on a low purple settee.

The dowager tsarina looked me up and down as the footman left. She had light skin and hazel eyes, and her round cheeks were pink. She looked nothing like her sons, save for her regal bearing. Tsarina Desislava, Miroslav's wife, sat next to her, hands folded demurely in her lap.

I made a low bow and held it.

After a moment, the dowager tsarina said, "You may rise."

I stood, noting the other women in the room. The grand duchesses, Miroslav's young daughters, were nowhere to be seen, but I recognized several noblewomen seated around the room, sipping hot drinks from delicate white cups. Princess Alisa, a simpering smile on her face, sat near the tsarinas, and I did my best not to cringe at the sight of her. Hateful woman. I'd worked for her on several occasions, and not once had I heard a kind word leave her lips.

"I had intended to commission you for a betrothal dress for my eldest granddaughter," the dowager tsarina began, "but it appears that won't be necessary after all. Still, there's no sense in wasting your talents nor our time. I would like to see your designs. I was quite taken with our cousin Alisa's latest dress."

A duchess tittered. "Yes, it was quite wrong of you, princess, to keep the seamstress's talents all to yourself!"

"I could have died over the ermine trim," a countess said.

"Lay everything out." The dowager waved a hand toward an empty table.

I took my design book out and placed it in front of the tsarinas. As I began laying out my fabric samples on the table the dowager had indicated, two noblewomen approached.

"Did you hear about the battle outside of Sevken?" one of them asked the other in a low voice.

"It's all over the palace," the other replied. "I heard the Survivor of Barbezht fought."

I went cold, nearly dropping the cloth in my hands. A survivor of Barbezht? They'd all been killed. Alexey had said they'd all been killed.

Maybe they were talking about someone who fought for Miroslav at Brbezht. But why would they call him a survivor? That term had been reserved for the rebels, the dozen or so men who had survived the decimation of Borislav's troops. Miroslav's men had never been called survivors of Barbezht.

If Alexey had been wrong, if one of the men from Barbezht was still alive... I fought to remain calm. Was it Han? Yakov?

I couldn't give myself away by asking questions. I bit the inside of my cheek to keep from demanding answers from the whispering countesses that stood perusing the table of fabrics.

Princess Alisa, thankfully, couldn't stand being left out of any conversation. "What are the two of you muttering about back there?"

They turned to her. "The Survivor of Barbezht, princess," one said.

The dowager tsarina scoffed. "Traitorous scum. I cannot fathom why anyone cares about him at all."

"I expect it's the scar," one of the duchesses said. "I saw the broadsheets. It does lend him a certain air of mystery."

A scar. Sweat broke out over my body. Han?

One of the countesses lowered her voice to a conspiratorial whisper. "I heard Borislav gave him a new hand, made from wood and magicked to function like a real hand."

"Borislav did no such thing," the dowager snapped. "His Gifts of the Blood are mediocre at best. He couldn't give someone a new hand."

A scarred Survivor of Barbezht. The room seemed to swim around me. That could have been anyone. It didn't have to be Han. But still... He was fighting for Borislav.

I had to know. Swallowing, I focused my attention on the fabrics I was arranging and willed my voice to be calm. "Survivor of Barbezht? I thought they'd all been killed."

Silence fell, and I cursed myself. Servants and trade workers were to be silent in the presence of royalty unless spoken to. I shouldn't have drawn attention to myself.

But I needed to know if Han was alive. If my husband was alive.

After a moment, Tsarina Desislava answered. "It appears at least one evaded capture."

"Yes, and he's made quite the name for himself," another noblewoman said. "I hear he was the one who made the Drakra alliance."

"I thought that was Prince Radomir."

"No, Radomir's been heading the campaign."

The conversation turned to Prince Radomir's movements as my head spun. A survivor of Barbezht.

I had to know, had to discover the man's name. If it was Han, if he was alive...

What would I do?

*****

By the time the tsarinas released me, I barely had time to dash across the palace grounds to meet Alexey for my daily training session.

He frowned t me as I rushed in. "You're late."

"I was working," I snapped. I tossed my coat into a corner and dropped into position. I wasn't in the mood to talk. There was too much on my mind.

He didn't push, just moved into a fighting stance as well, a wooden dagger in his hand. This week, we were focusing on disarming. As he'd told me, I wouldn't always have a weapon. I needed to be able to take down my enemy without one.

He lunged, and I dodged, aiming for his legs, as he'd taught me.

In an instant, he had me pinned, the dagger to my throat. My heart raced, but not with fear. I shook him off and stood. "Again."

He raised a brow but nodded, leaning back into a crouch.

Again he lunged, again I dodged, and again he pinned me.

He stood, holding out a hand to help me up. "Where's your head, Sofia? You're not even trying."

"Nowhere. I'm fine." I flicked my braid back over my shoulder. "Do it again. I'll get it this time."

He overpowered me three more times before finally stepping back, hands up. "I think we're done for the day."

"What?" I scrambled to my feet. "I'm fine. I can keep going."

He narrowed his eyes. "You're obviously distracted. I'm not working with you like this." He took my hand. In an instant, he transformed from the hard-faced trainer to my gentle lover. "It's alright, my sun. We can take the night off. You've been working hard. You deserve a break." He brushed his thumb over my cheek.

I sighed. "I'm sorry. It's been a long day."

"Anything you want to talk about?"

I started to shake my head but thought better of it. I wanted answers, and of everyone I knew, he was the most likely to have them. "I was called to the Tsarina's Tower today."

"Oh?" He leaned against the wall, giving me space. "I'd have thought that was a good thing."

"It was." For Sofia the seamstress, it was wonderful. For Mila the spy, it should have been, as well. "I got several new commissions."

He grinned. "I'm proud of you. But what's wrong?"

I leaned against the wall next to him. "I don't know. Some of the noblewomen were talking about the recent battles." I glanced sideways at him, picking at my sleeve. "They kept talking about some of the men fighting for Borislav. It...set me on edge."

"Did they mention names?"

"Just one. Well, a title. 'The Survivor of Barbezht.' I thought you said everyone from Barbezht had been killed?" I looked up at him, searching his face for the slightest reaction.

He studied me for a moment, likely remembering how I'd responded the day he told me about the slaughter. After a moment, he let out a long breath. "Han Antonovich, the so-called Survivor of Barbezht. Apparently he was already with Borislav before the tsar arrested the remaining survivors."

The blood drained from my face. Han was alive.

He went on, oblivious to my racing heart. "He's high in the Grand Duke's army, which is likely why the tsar couldn't get to him. Apparently he negotiated an alliance with the Drakra." He paused. "You look worried, my sun."

Control. I had to get myself under control. I swallowed. "The war—everything about it worries me." Not a lie.

He drew me into an embrace. "I'm sorry I haven't ended it yet."

I choked on a strained laugh. He'd said something similar before that first battle, when I'd been so afraid for Han. And I'd told him... "I believe you have an inflated sense of self-importance, sir."

He brushed a kiss to my forehead, and the tender touch soothed the ache in my heart. "Anything to ease your mind." He picked up my coat and draped it around my shoulders. "Come. You've had a busy day. You should rest."

As we walked back to my quarters, I clung to his arm, needing the contact to ground me. The large workroom was cold and dark, but Alexey soon had a fire roaring. He turned to me, eyes glazed with desire.

"You're so beautiful." He pulled me into the bedroom

Tears blurred my vision as he sat on the bed and drew me onto his lap. I didn't deserve him. All this time, I'd been falling in love with him, and my husband had still been out there. I didn't deserve either of them.

Alexey wiped the tears from my eyes. "Shh, my sun. I have you. You're safe."

"That's not—I just can't tonight."

"Then we won't." He rubbed my back. "Whatever you need."

"Hold me?"

"Always."

We lay down, and I rested my head on his chest, listening to his heartbeat. He held me until we both fell asleep.

In the middle of the night, a twinge in my stomach woke me. I sat up, extricated myself from Alexey's arms, and rubbed my eyes. The pain was familiar, and it came with a sinking feeling. In the dim light of the fire, I reached for the rags I kept nearby and wiped between my legs.

Blood.

My courses.

My heart clenched. It should have relieved me, but...

I glanced at Alexey, his dark figure limned with firelight. His breathing was deep and even.

I'd known it wasn't the right time for a child. Not with him, not with me in this body. But I'd wanted to be a mother for so long. That dream had been taken from me, first during the years of infertility, then when my son had died, and finally, when I'd thought Han was dead. Wrong though it might have been, I'd wanted to have that chance again.

Otets, what was wrong with me? My husband was alive, and I was mourning the fact that I wasn't pregnant with another man's child.

I closed my eyes and took a deep breath. It wasn't the right time. He wasn't the right man. And maybe—maybe I wasn't the right woman, either.

36

MARCH

Han

Three days on the road. My muscles ached, and not with the pleasant burn of exercise. The plodding pace set by an army redefined the word *tired*. I'd be glad to reach the capital, just to end the monotony of the journey.

And to be near Mila. We'd still had no word. What if the tsar was wrong? What if she *had* been arrested with the baron and baroness? What if something had happened since then? The crawl of information across the country grated on me. At least when we reached the capital, I'd be with her. I'd find a way into the palace and bring her out myself.

The late afternoon shadows cast an eerie look over the snow-covered landscape. Ahead of me, the train slowed, sleighs coming to an unscheduled stop on the road.

The hairs on the back of my neck prickled, and I scanned the trees and bushes bordering each side of the road. The stop could have been due to something as simple as a horse throwing a shoe or a sleigh going off the road, but something felt wrong. This was the perfect place for an ambush. Low hills all throughout this part of the country made it easy to hide the approach of a small group of attackers.

I wheeled my horse around and rode down the line, speaking to the men under my command. "On your guard," I said. Silence fell as we waited for whatever was coming. I hooked my iron hand around the hilt of my sword and drew it, listening for the sounds of approaching enemies.

Shouts rang out from the back of the train, further down the road. Moments later, I heard the clash of steel on steel. Battle had been joined.

"Steady," I called to my men. We couldn't abandon our position. Not until we knew if it was a targeted attack on the back of the line. "Hold." My eyes darted around. Every hint of movement could be one of Miroslav's men, and the trees were too dense to see clearly.

Soldiers darted from between the trees, charging toward us.

"For Borislav!" I bellowed, raising my sword. My men echoed the cry as the enemy reached us.

I swung my sword into the neck of one of the oncoming soldiers, turning just in time to see one of my men fall, then another. I wheeled around, searching for my next target. Further down the line, I could see moving shadows—the Drakra. Darkness swirled around each Drakra warrior, a cloud of black that left carnage in its wake.

I didn't have time to admire the battle prowess of our allies. Someone stepped directly under my horse's nose. The beast skittered to the side, and I was thrown to the ground. I scrambled to my feet, sword in hand, as the man charged me. Too slow. I couldn't get my sword up in time to block him.

Someone shouted, "Down!"

I hit the ground as Konstantin's ax slashed the air above my head.

Hot blood spurted down on me. Konstantin yanked the ax from the body and offered me a hand up.

The big man grinned. "Careful there, Captain. Almost went home a head shorter."

I opened my mouth to answer, but a spurt of hot metallic wetness choked me. Konstantin blinked down at the ax embedded in his chest.

I reacted without thinking. I drove my sword through the attacker's neck, kicking the man down as I took the sword back. Konstantin swayed on his feet, and I grabbed him before he could fall.

"I've got you. Healer!" I half-dragged him back to the sleighs, out of the fighting.

"Han?" His voice was weak.

"I'm here. I've got you," I said again. "Healer!" I roared.

"Don't—" He gasped for air. "Don't bother. I'm not—not going—"

"Don't even think like that." I eased him to the ground. "You're going to be fine."

Lada appeared at my side. Kneeling next to Konstantin, she examined the wound. With tight lips, she shook her head.

"You're going to be just fine," I choked out. "Have to get you home to that beautiful wife of yours, right?"

"Ulyana." His mouth curved in a smile. "Going to—going to have a baby. In the spring."

My eyes burned as I grasped his hand. "You'll have to invite me to the blessing."

"Tell him..." He gasped for breath, every word a struggle. "About me. My son."

"I will."

"Tell Ul—...thought—thought about her." He gasped again. "...love her."

"I'll tell her." I squeezed his hand, cold tears trickling down my face. "She knows, Kostya. She knows."

"I'm going to take the ax out of his chest," Lada said in a low voice. "It's keeping the blood in, prolonging his suffering."

Unable to speak past the lump in my throat, I nodded. Blood flowed slowly from the wound, so slowly, as I watched his final breaths, the chest rising and falling. One final, gurgling breath, and he was gone.

There wasn't time to grieve. I'd left the rest of my men alone long enough. I stood, swallowed hard, and walked back to them.

The enemy was gone, but the army was in chaos. I looked around at dying men and riderless horses. Further up the road, a gap in the line indicated at least one supply sled had been captured. How much had we lost in this one, brief attack?

"How did this happen?" The tsar's face was pale with anger.

We'd limped into camp late that night, once it was clear Miroslav's men wouldn't return, and the tsar had called a meeting as soon as we were settled.

"He knew we were coming," Borislav hissed. "Someone must have told him."

"I doubt that, your majesty." Radomir's voice was casual. I marveled that he could appear so at ease after the events of the evening. "Miroslav knows if he doesn't attack us, we'll take the fight to him. It's no secret we left Sevken, and there's only the one road between there and the capital large enough to easily transport an army. I'm sure he came to the conclusion without the help of traitors."

"Prince Radomir is right," I said. "Miroslav's no fool."

The tsar frowned, seeming unconvinced, but he let the matter rest for the moment. "How did they get past our scouts?"

Xhela na Zanik cleared her throat. "They took a southern road and attacked us from behind. It seems like it was a small unit, no more than a hundred, split into even smaller groups to make targeted attacks and cause as much chaos as possible."

The tsar looked around the tent, face tight with anger. "Losses?"

"First estimates indicate upward of two hundred men lost, possibly as many as three," Fyodor Yakovlevich answered, looking grim. "We also lost two cannons and three supply sleighs."

So many men in such a short time. I gritted my teeth. The loss of supplies could be devastating, if we didn't defeat Miroslav soon.

"Witness, Steward, and Prophet," the tsar swore. Radomir gave him a sharp look at the blasphemy but seemed inclined to agree with the sentiment. "Three hundred men, three sleighs, and two cannons lost to a *hundred men?*"

"We can't take another hit like that," one of the commanders said. "We need to end this."

"What do you think I'm trying to do?" Borislav snapped. He sighed, running a hand through his hair.

"Your man is right," Yixa na Chekke said. "We must make it to the capital before they wear us down."

Borislav stood and turned away from us with his hands clasped behind his back. "We will. Tomorrow morning, we split our forces. The units with the fewest casualties will make a forced march and take my brother by surprise. The other units can join as soon as possible. Once we reach the capital, we give the citizens three days to surrender Miroslav." He turned back to us. "Or we destroy the city."

Silence fell in the tent. I stared at the tsar, mouth slack. I would have expected something like this from Miroslav, but not from Borislav. Not from my tsar.

The Drakra priestess was the first to speak. "You would destroy your own capital?"

Radomir shook his head. "Even if we had the manpower to raze it, what would be the purpose?"

"The purpose," the tsar said through clenched teeth, "would be to set an example. Those who refuse to follow the Heir will suffer the consequences."

"And what of the innocents?" I demanded. Why would Borislav, of all people, propose destroying his own people? "You'd have us kill everyone in the city?"

His response was cool, emotionless. "They will have three days to leave. We won't stop anyone from leaving the city. My brother is too proud to flee in secret."

I couldn't be the only one thinking this was madness. No, I saw, looking around. Even the Drakra stared wide-eyed at the tsar.

"It could take weeks to break Idesk's walls, even with all our cannons," Yakovlevich said. "We don't have enough cannonballs. We don't have enough powder. We don't have enough men. Your majesty, I understand you're frustrated, but—"

The tsar cut him off. "We have all the men we need." He looked pointedly at Radomir.

I frowned in confusion. Glancing around, I saw similar expressions in the faces of others at the table. The prince must have understood, though, because he said vehemently, "No."

"This isn't a request, cousin."

"You would turn the Blood Gifts on the unSanctioned. No." The prince stood, facing the tsar with blazing fury in his eyes. "That has been an abomination since the Gifts first appeared. They are not to be wielded against the unSanctioned."

Comprehension dawned. The tsar wanted to destroy the city by magic. Dread settled in my stomach, low and heavy. This couldn't happen.

"The people will turn on my brother." Borislav sounded so confident, his face fixed in determination. I wanted to believe him. "There will be no need to destroy the city. I'm sure of it."

"And if they don't?" Radomir's fists were clenched, his knuckles white.

"We destroy it, and we take my brother out by force." The tsar's face softened. "It won't come to that, though."

Looking around at the others in the tent, I knew I wasn't the only one who doubted the tsar's assurance.

"Enough of this discussion," Borislav said. "I've made up my mind. In the morning, we leave for Idesk, and by the week's end, this Disinheritance will be complete, one way or another."

In the morning, the tsar left, taking half the army to march on the capital. I stood with Prince Radomir and the remaining commanders, watching them leave.

When the tsar was out of sight, Radomir turned away. "I would speak with you privately, Han Antonovich."

I followed the prince back to his tent. He took a seat, gesturing for me to do the same. His small eyes scanned my face. "You are a man of honor, are you not, Han Antonovich?"

What was this about? "I strive to be, your highness."

"You hold your vows highly?"

"Yes."

"And if you made a vow in error? What would you do about it?"

I swallowed hard. The same question I'd been pondering for weeks. "That would depend on the error in question."

The prince steepled his fingers. "Suppose you gave an oath of loyalty, only to discover the subject of your oath was undeserving."

My heart raced. This was a dangerous conversation. I'd already been labeled a traitor by one tsar; was I willing to risk betraying another? "Undeserving how?"

Radomir narrowed his eyes. "Cruel. Dangerous. Caring more for his victory than for those he has sworn to protect."

"I..." I fiddled with the gears on my hand. "I suppose that a vow made to an unworthy leader could be broken, your highness, without betraying one's honor."

The prince nodded. "My thoughts precisely. And what would make you consider a leader unworthy?"

I considered. The tsar hadn't done anything directly against his people—yet. "I believe," I said slowly, "that words spoken in anger shouldn't be held against a man. But when he goes beyond words, acting against what is right, that's when he becomes unworthy."

"I believe you're right." Radomir stood. "Thank you for your wisdom. I'm glad we can count on your assistance in this Disinheritance."

I knew he wasn't referring to Miroslav's Disinheritance.

37

LAST CHANCE

Mila

The palace buzzed with fear and anticipation. Borislav's army was on the move, heading toward the capital. Miroslav had ordered the nobles to remain at court, but every morning found another household gone, secreted out of the capital in the middle of the night, in fear of the approaching enemy.

They would arrive within two days. *Han* would arrive.

I still couldn't believe it. He was alive. I'd mourned him, healed, and moved on. And now he was alive, and he was coming back for me.

I didn't know if it was excitement or dread that had my stomach in knots.

What would Alexey think? The tsar had promised to get me out of the capital before they attacked. Would I have time to explain, to tell him goodbye?

I'd probably never see him again. I was going back to my husband and my old life. Back to being Mila. Alexey wouldn't *want* to see me again once he found out who I was.

I looked around my workroom, and my gaze landed on Lady Yelena's latest order. I'd planned to have my assistant deliver it tomorrow—provided the capital wasn't under siege by that time—but I needed something to do.

And maybe I'd see Alexey. Possibly for the last time.

I packed the dresses carefully and trekked across the grounds to the main palace. Alexey was nowhere in sight when I reached Lady Yelena's quarters, but the baroness received me in the drawing room, where she lounged on a low couch. Her face was ashen, but her smile was warm.

"Sofia Stepanova. You've finished them already?"

I smiled back. "I made them my top priority, my lady. How are you feeling?"

"Ill. Overwhelmed. Tired." She sighed. "I'm told the illness should stop any day now."

"I'm sure you'll feel better soon."

The baroness gestured for her maidservant to take the dresses. "I'll try them on." She stood but clapped her hand over her mouth. "Excuse me." She darted through the door, followed by her maidservant.

Left alone, I stepped toward the open door, my heart pounding in an odd rhythm. Was Alexey nearby? Most likely he was off preparing for the upcoming battle, but I couldn't help peering down the hall in hopes of seeing him.

The door across the hall was ajar as well. I saw a desk covered with papers, and a crystal decanter of medovukha sat atop the desk next to a half-filled glass.

Kazimir's study.

I looked up and down the hall. It was empty, silent as a tomb.

If I wanted revenge on Kazimir Vladimirovich, now was my chance. I slipped my hand into my pocket, wrapping my fingers around the tiny potion Borislav had given me. I carried it everywhere; he'd told me it was for emergencies only, but what possible use would I have for it after this week? I didn't have to use all of it, anyway. Just a few drops, enough to kill the bastard who had taken my child from me.

Heart pounding, I scanned the hall again and darted over to the study.

This might be my last opportunity to help Tsar Borislav win the war, as well. Kazimir could have left important papers on his desk, something revealing details about the palace security or the army's movements.

I rifled through the papers. Personal correspondence, financial statements...

There. My gaze landed on a stack of sheets bearing the seal of the palace guard. I picked them up.

They were reports by the captain of the palace guard going back at least a month. Perfect. I didn't have time to go through them, but the tsar might find something useful in them. I tucked them into my pocket and pulled out the poison I carried.

This was it. My only chance to kill the monster.

With shaking hands, I reached for the stopper.

"My sun?"

I whirled around, heart in my throat. Alexey stood in the doorway, frowning at me, brows knit together.

"Alexey." My voice came out breathless. "I—" What could I say?

"What are you doing in here?" His eyes flashed between me and the decanter.

I tucked the potion into my pocket and reached for his hand. "I...I'm sorry. The door was open, and I was admiring the glassware. Is it crystal?" A poor excuse, but I prayed he'd believe me.

He pulled his hand from mine and drew the bottle and letters from my pocket. I went cold.

He tucked the letters beneath his arm and opened the potion to sniff at the contents.

"Tell me you weren't trying to poison him," he whispered.

"I—" I began, but he held up a hand.

"No. Don't lie to me." He rubbed his temple. "Don't you think if that was an option, I would have done it already? He's a bastard, I know. I hate how he treats his wife. But he's not worth throwing your life away over." He brushed my cheek. "They will *kill you* for it. Don't ask me to let that happen."

"I'm not—" Tears threatened to choke me. "It's not just her he's hurt." I had to tell him what Kazimir had done to me. He needed to know who he was serving, why I was willing to risk everything for this. I took a deep breath.

Lord Kazimir strode into the study, and my words died in my throat.

"What is this, Grigorovich?"

"The seamstress got turned around on her way to attend your lady wife, my lord. I was ensuring she hadn't seen anything she shouldn't before I returned her to the baroness."

The baron jerked his chin at the papers Alexey held. "And those?" He grabbed them and glanced at them before turning to me, nostrils flaring. "Treacherous little bitch."

I couldn't breathe. I tried to step back, but the wall was behind me. Out. I had to get out.

Alexey stepped between me and the baron. "My lord, I hadn't had a chance to question her yet, but I can do that now."

Kazimir flicked a hand. "Leave us. I'll question her myself."

I turned wide eyes on Alexey. *Don't leave me alone with him.*

"My lord—"

"Now, Grigorovich."

Alexey stiffened, bowed, and left.

The baron walked to the door, his footsteps drowned out by the rushing of blood in my head. He closed it and turned back to me.

Alone with the monster.

I couldn't do this. Not again.

"Now," he said in a voice of deathly calm, "explain to me why my manservant had those papers. Because I know he didn't take them himself."

I took a step to the side, putting the desk between us. Out. I had to get out.

He darted around the desk and grabbed me by the neck. "Answer me."

A whimper escaped my lips, but I didn't speak. Couldn't speak.

He smacked me. "Answer me, bitch!"

Not again. It couldn't happen again. I curled into myself, arms around my stomach.

Quick, heavy footsteps sounded in the corridor, and two palace guards burst into the room, followed by Alexey. I took in a deep, gasping breath. Salvation.

"That's her." He pointed at me, his face void of emotion. "I caught her trying to poison the baron."

Not salvation. Just another punishment. I backed up, but the guards took me by the arms.

As they dragged me from the room, I heard Kazimir swear. "I didn't need your interference, Grigorovich."

I couldn't hear Alexey's response.

The clang of the closing door and the thud of the guard's retreating footsteps echoed in the cold chamber. I blinked as my eyes tried to adjust, but the darkness was absolute. A scuffling sound nearby made me flinch.

"Who's there?" My words came out in a whimper, still too loud in the silence.

A woman's voice, raspy from disuse, answered me. "Sofia?"

"Lady Heli?" I felt my way around the cell. It was small and empty with bars on one side. The baroness's voice came from a nearby cell.

"Why are you here?" she asked. "Were you discovered?"

My face was hot in the cold darkness. Kazimir had seen the papers I'd taken from his desk, but that wasn't what Alexey had told the guards about. Why?

Maybe he hadn't realized what the papers were. Or maybe he hadn't understood why I had them.

No, he was too smart for that. He had to have known. Was it possible he'd done it to protect me? I wrapped my arms around myself, wishing I could talk to him. What was he thinking right now? Did he think I'd betrayed him? That I'd been using him?

"Sofia?"

I had to stay calm, focused. Whatever Alexey thought of me, I was here now. I'd survived Kazimir again. I hadn't killed him, but he hadn't killed me, either. "I tried to poison the baron of Arick." My voice came out steady. Good.

"Why?"

What could I tell her? He hadn't suspected me of working with Borislav, hadn't been suspicious about my connections to Lord Ilya and Lady Heli. There was no reason I should have done it—no reason Sofia Stepanova should have done it.

The truth, then. "He attacked me last year, before I came to court. He killed my son."

Silence met my words, stretching on until it was nearly unbearable. Guilt burned through me, but I raised my chin. I refused to be ashamed about trying to avenge my son.

At last the baroness spoke. "You risked all our lives for revenge?"

My throat tightened. Calm. I had to stay calm. I hadn't risked our lives. Tsar Borislav would be here in a day or two. They would take the palace, find us, and free us.

As if she'd heard my thoughts, she scoffed. "You are a traitor and a fool. Miroslav's jailers torture as a matter of course. You won't be able to withstand it. You'll tell them everything, and then you will beg for them to kill you."

I wouldn't. I didn't have to survive it long, just long enough for Borislav's army to get here. A couple days at most.

Still, I shivered at the thought. "Have you—have they tortured you?" I fought to quell the mental image of the old baroness chained to a wall, her slender body marked with bruises, dried blood streaked down her cheek.

She made a choking sound that resembled a laugh. "No," she said. "No, my sweet cousin may be content to lock me in here and let me waste away, but he doesn't believe women are capable of masterminding conspiracies. He has some reservations about torturing those of the Blood, as well. You don't happen to be a distant relative of ours, do you?"

I didn't think she expected an answer, but I gave one anyway. "No."

"Pity. I suggest you find a way to kill yourself. The alternative is truly unbearable."

"But Borislav is coming!" I said. Of course, she wouldn't have heard. She'd been locked in here for weeks. "He'll rescue us."

"He's finally marching on the capital?" She laughed again. "Take what comfort you can from that, girl. You won't live to see it. Even if he arrives today, sieges take weeks, months. You and I will be long dead before they can get to us."

The chamber fell silent once more, the atmosphere growing thick and heavy. As Lady Heli's ragged breathing grew steady, I struggled to suck in air.

Why hadn't I realized? Just because Borislav was coming to the capital didn't mean he'd capture it in a single day. My chest tightened, and my stomach knotted as I pictured what would happen once Miroslav's men came to torture me. I wouldn't be able to withstand it, not if the stories were true. Water torture, the witch's chair, compression, and other devices too horrible to consider. Whatever they did to me would make Kazimir's attack look like child's play. Even if I could survive for a day or two, Lady Heli was right. By the time Borislav took the city, I'd be begging for death, having revealed everything I knew about Tsar Borislav and the rebellion.

The tsar had given me that potion for emergencies, for a moment like this, and I'd squandered it on a futile attempt at revenge.

The walls closed in around me. I couldn't breathe. The damp dungeon air was thicker than water, filling my lungs. I gasped, tearing at my clothes.

Out. I had to get out.

I'd betrayed them all. Han was alive, and I was going to get him killed. Han, and Izolda, and the tsar, and everyone else whose survival depended on my knowledge remaining secret.

Silent, gasping sobs wracked my body. I curled up in the corner of my cell, the stone floor frigid against my cheek, and let my despair consume me.

38

BORISLAV'S ARRIVAL

Mila

I woke to darkness and damp. I had no blessed moment of oblivion, no moment to wonder where I was, before the day's events came crashing back to me.

Alexey had had me arrested. Why? Was he trying to save me from the baron's assault, or did he think I deserved prison for what I'd done?

I sat up and wiped at the wet streaks from my face, hoping they were tears. Given the state of the cell I was in, the rancid smell permeating the air, I didn't want to think what foul, half-frozen liquids could be on the floor.

"Lady Heli?" My whisper came out hoarse.

"I'm not dead yet," she said wryly. "Much though I might wish it."

Silence fell, the only sound a steady drip of water—I hoped—somewhere nearby. Lady Heli spoke again, her usually stern voice strained with emotion. "Was there news of my husband?"

For all her rigidity, she truly loved the man. I'd seen it in her eyes, the way she looked at him. I swallowed, my stomach tight as I delivered the bad news. "The last I heard, he was ill." Gravely so. "That's all I know."

There was no response. I stared ahead, unable to see even the wall I knew was in front of me, and eventually drifted back off to sleep.

The next time I woke, it was to the sound of a door opening. Footsteps neared, setting my heart racing. Had they come to collect me for execution? Torture? Keys jangled, followed by the scrape of my cell door opening, and something clattered on the floor. The door closed again, and the sound repeated in the baroness's cell. The dungeon door opened, letting in a sliver of light from the torches in the hall. The guard left, footsteps fading in the distance.

I crawled over to the cell door, reaching for what the guard had left. A tin cup and plate. I drank the contents of the cup—warm, slightly musty water, but I wasn't in a position to turn it down. On the plate was something wood-like. Old bread, maybe? I nibbled at it. Yes, it was bread, but hard enough to break my teeth. I held it in my mouth, hoping it would soften enough to swallow.

"You ought to soak the bread in the water," Lady Heli said. "It's impossible to eat otherwise. Or you can leave it to the rats, I suppose."

Unsure what to say, I didn't respond.

She let out a humorless chuckle. "I thought when you were brought in, it might be nice to have a companion, but you seem as inclined to conversation as the rats."

"I apologize, my lady."

She scoffed. "Apologies mean nothing to me now. Tell me something. News from the world beyond my cell."

"Borislav should be here in a day—maybe two." Not that it would do us any good. "Most of the nobles have fled the capital." I relayed everything that had happened since her arrest.

When my stores of news were exhausted, I listened, waiting for her to speak. Her breath came deep and even. She'd fallen asleep.

How long had I been in this dungeon? The guards had brought food five times, but with nothing else to indicate, I couldn't begin to guess how much time had passed. It felt like weeks.

The door to the dungeon creaked slowly open, and I froze. I still had a small crust of bread in my cell. Surely they weren't bringing another meal so soon—if the hunk of bread and small crust of water could be considered a meal. Maybe they were ready to torture me. If so, should I make a run for it? Fight? I wouldn't make it far, but maybe they'd kill me by mistake. Death was preferable to torture.

A figure entered the room, shrouded in darkness. Darker than what was natural, with the torchlight from the corridor.

"Fia?"

"Izolda!" Relief coursed through me. "What are you doing here?"

The darkness dropped away, revealing my friend. "I'm here to get you out. We have to hurry. The guards'll be back soon." Keys jangled as she unlocked my door.

"Lady Heli's asleep in the cell behind you." I scrambled to my feet. Pins shot through my legs from disuse, but I ignored the pain.

"I'm awake," the baroness said.

Izolda freed her as well. "Follow me."

Lady Heli took a shaky step and almost collapsed. I reached out. "Let me help you." She pulled back, but I grabbed her arm. "If you can't make it, none of us will. Let me help you."

She nodded stiffly.

The guards were nowhere to be seen. We crept along the hall, slipping out a side door.

Night had fallen. The sky was clear and moonless, and I took a deep breath of the crisp, fresh air. I'd expected to die in that dungeon; the air filling my lungs felt like I'd been born again.

We rounded the back corner of the building, and I stopped dead, nearly knocking Lady Heli to the ground. Alexey stood there, a hand resting on the sword at his hip. His eyes passed over me like I wasn't there, but he looked at Izolda.

"Thank Otets. No problems?" he asked her.

"None."

He was helping us escape?

He pulled a thick, full-length coat from the large pack he carried and handed it to Lady Heli, who was shivering in her nightdress. "I'm sorry, my lady, but I couldn't get you any of your own clothes."

She shrugged into the coat. "Don't apologize. Where is my husband?" Already, she sounded almost like her old self.

Izolda and Alexey shared a look. "I'm sorry, my lady," Izolda said, her voice thick. "He didn't make it."

The baroness's face went blank. She swallowed audibly. "Get us out of here."

Alexey looked at me for the first time. His eyes scanned my body. I wasn't sure what emotion lay behind his blank face. Anger, maybe? Concern? He turned away. "Borislav's men are camped outside the city. They're expected to attack at dawn. There's an unused door in the palace wall I can get you through. It hasn't been used in years, so it's not guarded. Once you get to the main city gate, you'll be able to join the crowd that's fleeing."

Borislav. The battle. My heart did a flip. It would all be over soon.

Alexey led us across the palace grounds, careful to walk only where the snow was packed, so we left no footprints. I flinched at every flickering shadow. An icicle fell, tinkling as it hit the ground, and I gasped. Alexey turned to me at the sound, his face unreadable. He put his finger to his lips and jerked his head, indicating for me to keep moving.

The door he led us to was behind the stables, half-covered with dead vines. Positioned as it was, I never would have noticed it, had Alexey not led us directly to it. He pulled the vines aside and grasped the handle. The door came open with a loud crunch, and we all held our breath.

When no one came to investigate, he told Izolda, "Follow the wall down until you reach Telezhnaya Doroga." Wagon Road. "Follow that to the main gate, and try to blend in with the crowds." He pulled open his pack and took out another coat and hat, then handed the pack to Izolda, nodding for her to go on.

She took the baroness's arm from me. "Thank you, Alexey. For everything."

He gave her a bow, unsmiling, and she led Lady Heli through the door.

Once they were through, Alexey held the coat out to me. I reached to take it from him, but he didn't let go. "You were spying for Borislav."

I couldn't look at him. "I was."

"Was any of it real?" His voice was husky. "Or were you just using me to get closer to Lord Kazimir, to the tsar?"

I could feel the heat of his hand on mine through the coat. What could I say? It was selfish to tell him how I felt. We didn't, couldn't have a happy ending. He fought for Miroslav, and I fought for Borislav.

And I was married.

He'd asked me before to break his heart cleanly if I had to break it. But I couldn't lie to him. Not anymore. I opened my mouth, still unsure what I was going to say. "Alexey—"

Izolda appeared in the doorway. "What are you doing, Fia? We need to go."

"Coming."

She disappeared again. Alexey shook his head, pulling the coat from my grasp. He wrapped it around my shoulders. My heart raced at his nearness, my stomach churning with guilt and grief. When he placed the hat on my head, his hand brushed my cheek. My breath caught, eyes filling with unwanted tears.

"Go," he said.

I reached up to touch his face. "I'm sorry."

His eyes were tight with pain. He clenched his teeth. "Go," he repeated.

I stepped through the door, and he closed it solidly behind me. The sound echoed through my head with striking finality. Would I ever see him again?

Probably not in Sofia's body. Not ever, if we didn't make it out of the city alive. I tamped the emotions down until I couldn't feel them anymore and followed Izolda.

When we reached Telezhnaya Doroga, the sounds of a crowd grew. The gate came into view as we rounded a corner, surrounded by a throng of people jostling to get out of the city.

"Wait here." Izolda passed Lady Heli's arm to me, and she walked up to a sleigh driver near the edge of the crowd.

A few moments later, she returned. "He's agreed to let us ride on his sleigh until we leave the city. On account of my grandmother's poor health." She grinned at us.

"Izolda, no one on earth could possibly think she's your grandmother."

"Well, then, I guess you'll have to take the part," she said, winking at me. I rolled my eyes, grateful for the familiar banter to ease my nerves. She helped Lady Heli adjust her hat and coat to hide the baroness's face. "Come along, Babushka."

"Where are you headed?" the sleigh driver asked as we approached.

"My brother lives in Cadmist," Izolda said. "He's going to meet us outside of the Grand Duke's camp—provided we can get that far."

"I would have pegged you for an easterner," he said, scratching his beard. "As it happens, I'm heading to Cadmist myself. My wife went on ahead, and I'm meeting her there before heading home to Kolteshko. I'd be happy to take you the whole way."

"Thank you for the offer, but my brother would be furious if he couldn't collect us. He's terribly protective of his wife." She jerked her chin at me where I'd climbed onto the back of the sleigh next to Lady Heli. Izolda took the baroness's other side just as the crowd started moving.

My chest tightened as we crawled slowly toward the gate. City guards in their red kaftans stood on either side, scanning the crowd. They weren't stopping anyone, but—

"You there!" The booming voice of a guardsman cut through the chatter of the crowd, making me jump. He was looking at us, at our sleigh. "Pull over here."

The driver guided his horses to the side of the road where the guard waited.

"Destination?" He glanced at the three of us women, then turned to the sleigh itself, peering inside. I pulled my coat tight around me, as if to protect myself from the cold night air. My gaze remained fixed on the ground, and I could hardly hear what was said over the pounding of my heart.

"Cadmist, if you please, sir." The driver's tone was cheery, unbothered by the guard's brusqueness.

"Purpose?"

"Be with family, sir. Rather not be here when the fighting starts, *da*?"

The guard rolled his eyes as he lifted the cloth that covered the driver's belongings. "It's all bluff and bluster. Borislav wouldn't destroy the city, not when he's gone to all this trouble to take it."

Destroy the city? Why would they think Tsar Borislav would destroy the city?

"Still," the driver said. "I'd rather not have an army between me and my wife. I'm sure you understand."

"Best be on your way, then." The guard stepped back and nodded for us to drive on.

We were past the worst of it, but I didn't take a breath until I could see the camp. The tents of Borislav's army faced the city, illuminated in the winter night by their fires. The tents bordered the road; anyone who wanted to pass would have to go directly through the center of the camp. Doubtless they were checking all the travelers, ensuring none of Miroslav's army—or Miroslav himself—escaped.

As we neared the tents, I bit my lip. Was Han in there somewhere? Did he know I was coming? I still couldn't believe he was alive. Wouldn't be able to believe it until I saw him.

"We'll get off here," Izolda said.

"You sure?" The driver frowned at her as he pulled to a stop. "I'd be happy to see you through, at least to the other side of the camp."

"My brother wanted to take us through himself." She shrugged, the picture of nonchalance. "Protective, as I said."

"If you insist."

We climbed off the wagon, and Izolda pulled a handful of coins from the pack Alexey had given her. "Our thanks, sir, and may Otets bless you."

He inclined his head. "Stay safe." He made a clicking sound with his mouth and drove on.

We watched as a guard stopped him at the edge of the camp. The wind carried their words away, but the guard looked briefly in the back of the sleigh and waved him on.

Izolda waited until he was out of sight before starting forward. She took the baroness's arm. "Let's go." We walked the short distance to one of the guards, who watched our approach.

"Names?"

Lady Heli drew herself up to her full height. Despite her disheveled appearance, her bearing was unmistakably noble. "Baroness Heli Fedorova of Tsebol, cousin to Borislav, who is Heir of the Sanctioned and rightful Tsar of Inzhria. I wish to see my cousin." Izolda held out a ring as the baroness said, "My seal, if you require proof."

The soldier blinked several times, stunned, as he accepted the ring. Recovering himself, he said, "Wait here, my lady."

He strode to another guard and spoke animatedly, too quiet for us to hear. In a moment, he returned and bowed to the baroness, handing her ring to her. "Welcome, Lady Heli. We didn't know to expect you. I'll escort you to his majesty, if you'll follow me."

He turned to leave, but I cleared my throat. "I'd like to see the Survivor of Barbezht first, if I may," I said, more bravely than I felt. My whole body was shaking, and not from the cold.

The soldier looked to Lady Heli for confirmation. She nodded.

He led us past the first tents and into the camp. A young man sat in front of a fire, sharpening an ax. He jumped to his feet at our approach.

"Show this woman to Captain Han Antonovich's tent," the guard said.

Captain Han Antonovich. It was him. He was alive.

And a captain. What had happened while I was gone? Was the gossip true? Maybe the tsar had given him a magic hand. He couldn't lead soldiers one-handed. Could he?

"Miss?" The young man looked at me expectantly. Izolda, Lady Heli, and the guard were already gone. "This way, please."

I'd never be able to find my way back to the road, I knew, as he led me through the maze of tents. Despite the late hour—I wasn't sure what time it was, but it had to be late—there were still a large number of fires, with men sitting around them, talking and eating. We walked a long way into the camp before my guide finally stopped.

"Here we are. I don't know if the captain's back yet, though. I think the commanders were meeting with the tsar."

I looked at the tent before us. The soldier could probably hear my heart pounding. Otets' Blood, the whole camp could probably hear it. "That's alright. I'll wait."

He gave me a curious look, undoubtedly wondering what a young woman wanted with the commander so late at night. I looked a mess, covered in filth from my time in Miroslav's dungeon. My hair was still uncovered, a single braid down my back, marking me as an unmarried woman. *What could an unmarried, grimy woman like this want with the Survivor of Barbezht?* I could almost hear him thinking.

I was beyond caring. Han was alive. He was here.

"There's no need to wait with me. Thank you," I said, dismissing him.

"Of course." He made a slight bow and walked off, giving one last questioning glance at me over his shoulder.

I took a deep breath and put my hand to the flap.

Darkness and silence filled the tent. He wasn't back. I felt my way around the tent until I found a lantern and tinderbox.

Lighting the lantern, I looked around the tent. A cot, a trunk, and a small table with a pitcher and washbasin. Simple provisions, far less cluttered than his room at home. He'd finally learned to clean up after himself. The thought made me smile.

The pitcher was filled with water. Thank Otets. Disgusting as I felt, I was in no state to greet the husband I'd thought was dead. I cleaned myself as best as I could with the half-frozen water, then took a seat on the cot.

Footsteps approached, and I sprang to my feet.

39

REUNIONS

Han

Still no word from Mila. As I walked back to my tent, I looked up at the city. Somewhere in there was my wife, possibly facing imprisonment and torture at the hands of Miroslav's sadistic followers. The tsar still wouldn't agree to let me go to her, nor would he send someone else. *Wait,* he cautioned me. *Be patient. We can't spare the men right now, but once the time comes, we will find her.*

I was done waiting. The tsar was ready to attack the city, and he still hadn't made a plan to rescue my wife. It was time to take matters into my own hands. I'd cover the scar on my face, strap my old bean-filled glove to my wrist, and tell the city guards that I was a resident of the city coming back to collect my wife. Tonight, one way or another, I would be with her again. Even if they refused to let me in, and I had to scale the city wall. Even if Borislav labeled me a deserter for it. I'd deal with those problems once my wife was safe.

I just had a few provisions to gather from my tent first.

I pushed aside the tent flap and stopped. A woman stood there, illuminated by lantern-light. She looked at me with wide eyes, biting her lip.

Mila.

It was Mila, in that stranger's body she'd taken on before she left.

I crossed the tent in two strides, and she was in my arms. "Milochka."

"Han." She breathed my name as I pulled her close.

"You're here." I couldn't believe it. I'd been planning to mount a rescue, but here she was waiting for me.

"I'm here." She took my face in her hands, her eyes filling with tears. "I thought you were dead."

"I'm not." I ran my hands over her body, searching for signs of injury. Her clothes were dirty and rumpled, but she seemed unharmed. "Fuck, Mila, I thought *you* were." I clutched her to my chest. She was whole. She was safe. She was alive.

"I heard Miroslav killed all the survivors from Barbezht." Her voice was muffled against me.

"Not all of us." I stroked her back. "I'm fine. Yakov is fine."

"Yakov?" She pulled back, looking into my face, her own streaked with tears. "Yakov is alive, too?"

"He is." I touched her cheek, needing to reassure myself this was real. "We're all safe." I kissed her, soft and slow, tasting the tears that covered her face. She was here. Really here.

I deepened the kiss, grabbing her face with both my hands, but she pulled back again and touched my iron hand.

"What's this?"

"A gift from the tsar. He gave me a command and had it made so I could join the men on the field." I showed her the gears, moving the fingers. "I can hold a pen and a sword, now."

"You fought?" Her brow knit together with concern.

I shrugged. "Just a couple times." No need to worry her. "But where have you been? We haven't heard from you in weeks. We heard Lord Ilya and Lady Heli were arrested, but..."

She looked away. "I was, too."

Borislav was wrong. She *had* been arrested with the baron. All my tears from the past months welled up again, and I held her tight. "Did they hurt you?"

"I'm fine," she said, still not looking at me. "Some friends got me out, along with the barones."

I ran my hands over her body again. She was whole. She was safe. I took a deep breath, calming myself. "I'm glad you're back."

She nodded. "I—I should probably go see the tsar. He'll want my report on everything that happened in the past few weeks."

Reluctantly, I released her from my embrace and took her hand. "I'll take you to him."

She reached for her coat. "You don't have to come with me. I'm sure you need your sleep."

"I just got you back, Milochka." I kissed her hand. "I'm never letting you go again."

Mila

My heart was oddly calm as I followed Han through the camp to the tsar's tent. Shouldn't it have been pounding out of my chest? But the sight of him, alive and safe, didn't set me ablaze like I'd expected. I was relieved, of course, but not overwhelmed with joy and excitement.

Everything about this felt wrong.

We reached the tsar's tent in the middle of the camp, and Han stopped outside. "Ready?"

I nodded, and he opened the tent flap.

A small-eyed man stood in the middle of the tent. Not the tsar, though he had the high cheekbones and straight black hair of the Blood. Prince Radomir, perhaps? Lady Heli and Izolda were nowhere in sight.

Han bowed, and I noticed the tsar seated in a chair further back in the tent. He stood and smiled warmly at me.

"Mila Dmitrievna. I'm glad to see you returned."

A flash of shame filled me. He didn't know how much I'd endangered us all with my foolish actions.

Tsar Borislav turned to the other man in the tent. "Radomir, allow me to introduce Mila Dmitrievna, Han's wife and one of our primary informants in the capital. Mila Dmitrievna, my cousin, prince Radomir Demyanovich of the Blood."

The prince inclined his head. "Thank you for your work. You've been most instrumental in our successes thus far."

I bowed, but the twinge of guilt remained. "I apologize for not coming directly to you with Lady Heli," I said.

The tsar waved his hand. "I quite understand the desire to be reunited with your husband. And you're here now." He smiled warmly and gestured to the table in the middle of the tent. "Please, sit."

As we sat, the tsar leaned toward me. "My cousin and her maidservant already told me their perspectives, but I would like to hear what you saw when you escaped. What was the situation on the other side of the gates?"

I gave a brief summary of our escape, leaving out Alexey's name. I couldn't talk about him, couldn't even think about him without my throat closing up and tears threatening in my eyes.

When I finished, Han pressed a kiss to my hand. "I'm grateful for your friends," he said in a voice intended only for my ears.

I couldn't meet his eyes. Would he say the same if he ever found out what Alexey meant to me?

The tsar picked up a sketch of the palace grounds. "Do you remember where, exactly, this hidden door was?" When I pointed, he looked at the prince. "Perhaps we can compromise. We can dispense with breaking down the city gates, and I can lead a small group into the palace through this door. I'll confront my brother myself, to limit the bloodshed."

Radomir frowned. "Miroslav won't fight you. He knows you'll win. He'll surround himself with guards as he always does."

"He can try." The tsar's face was grim, his lips pressed together in a line.

Warning filled the prince's voice. "Using your Sanctioned Gifts against the unSanctioned is an abomination, Borislav."

It didn't sound like the first time they'd had this conversation. Before it could go further, though, Han cleared his throat. "How would you get into the city?"

"Draw them out," the tsar said. "They'll be focused on the main gate, on defending against the siege. We'll take a dozen men around the city in a boat, climb into the city here," he pointed to a spot on the map, "and travel to the hidden door from there." He traced the path with his finger. "Their focus will be on our attack from the land. They won't notice a small group coming from the sea."

"A few minor points," Prince Radomir said dryly. "First, and perhaps most important, you are the tsar. We can't risk you entering combat. Second," he went on as the tsar opened his mouth to respond, "once you reached the palace, Miroslav would have the entirety of the palace guard there to protect him. A dozen of our men against the hundred in the palace guard won't stand a chance."

"I agree with the tsar," Han said.

I stared at him. The two royals fell silent, looking at him as well.

"If there's a chance to limit the bloodshed, whatever the risk, I think we need to take it." He frowned, tapping his fingers like he always did when he was deep in thought. "A dozen men might be too few, but if we add to that number a dozen Drakra... I think it's worth the risk."

He'd changed since I'd been gone. The Han I'd married would never have been so bold. Would never have spoken so freely to royalty.

Tsar Borislav and Prince Radomir didn't seem to find anything strange in Han's behavior. The prince looked at his cousin. "It's an unacceptable risk. We can send the men, if you think it's necessary, but you cannot go with them."

"This is between me and my brother," the tsar said. "I have to face him."

"This is between Otets and His chosen Heir," the prince retorted.

"If Otets has chosen me to be His Heir, He will protect me. If I die, it will be clear He's chosen you."

They stared at each other, locked in a silent battle of wills. Finally, the prince loosed a breath. "This war isn't about you, Borislav, but if you choose to throw your life away on a fool's errand, I won't stop you."

"Good." The tsar picked up a bell and rang for a servant. "Mila Dmitrievna, you must be exhausted after your trials. I have need of your husband, still, but I'll return him to you as soon as possible." He smiled warmly at me. "Is there anything else you need for your stay here in the camp? I will have someone deliver fresh clothing to your husband's tent, of course."

I glanced down, my face heating. I was standing before a tsar in a sarafan that was stained and wrinkled from days in a dungeon. "Thank you, your majesty. I don't believe I'll need anything else."

Han clutched my hand tight in his. "I'm sure Mila could be of some help," he said. "There's no need to send her away."

"The lady has been trapped in my brother's dungeon for days, Han," the tsar said sternly. "I'm not so selfish as to deny her a full night's rest."

Han swallowed and nodded once. "I'll be back as soon as I can, Milochka." He took my hand and held it to his lips, closing his eyes. Then he glanced at the tsar. "Would you change her back to her own body now, your majesty?"

My breath caught. I'd grown comfortable in this body, living as Sofia. I'd known it would have to change once I returned home, but was I ready for that yet?

"Later." The tsar had already turned away. "For now, you can remain the seamstress. Once the battle is over, I'll return you to your own body, Mila Dmitrievna."

I breathed a silent sigh of relief. At least I would have a day or two to prepare myself. "I'll bid you goodnight, then, your majesty."

I squeezed Han's hand and let it go. He caught my eye and mouthed, *I love you*. I gave him a tight-lipped smile in return, but I couldn't bring myself to say the words back to him.

40

BEFORE THE STORM

Han

I was aware of my wife even before I fully awoke the next morning. She was warm and soft, pressed against my body. I opened my eyes to see her strange, familiar face on the pillow next to mine, illuminated by the gray pre-dawn light.

She stirred, blinking sleepily.

I pulled her closer and kissed her forehead. "Good morning, *dorogusha.*"

"Hm." Then her eyes flew open, and she sat bolt upright. "The battle!"

"It's still early," I said, wrapping my arms around her from behind. "We have a little while."

She glanced at the light creeping into our tent. "Where will you be?"

"I'm going with the tsar."

"With the tsar?" She stiffened, turning to look at me. "Into the city?" Fear filled her eyes.

I'd give anything to erase that fear. I stroked her cheek. "It's no more dangerous than being in the battle."

"You're taking a dozen men into the palace to confront Miroslav directly," she snapped. "How is that less dangerous than the battle?"

"I didn't say 'less dangerous,' I said 'no more dangerous.'" I sighed. "I don't want to fight with you today, Mila." I didn't want to fight with her ever again. We'd done enough of that before she left. Now all I wanted was to keep her safe. "It's dangerous, yes, but it has to be done."

"But why you?"

"The tsar asked me to. He wants the Survivor of Barbezht with him when he takes the throne."

"I thought you weren't the only survivor," she said, resting her head against my chest.

I raised a brow, looking down at her. "You'd prefer Yakov go?"

"I don't want either of you to go. I just don't understand why it has to be you. Why you're *the* Survivor of Barbezht."

"I don't know." Somehow, in the few small battles I'd fought, my popularity had grown. My name—or at least my unofficial title—was spoken across the country, and while most of the rumors about me were entirely false, the tsar wanted to exploit my popularity among the unSanctioned. *Your loyalty lends legitimacy to my claim, Han.*

The people see something of themselves in you. They'll support who you support.

It discomfited me, taking on the mantle of *Survivor of Barbezht,* but the tsar insisted. I sighed. "I won't be alone, Milochka. The tsar asked me to go, but we'll have a dozen of our best soldiers and a dozen shadow-melding Drakra."

"Just be careful." She took a deep, shaky breath. "We should get ready." She reached for the clean clothes someone had delivered to the tent overnight.

We? "Ready for what?"

"The battle. Isn't the tsar expecting you?" She stripped off her old sarafan and replaced it with a new one as I tried to ignore the twitch of my cock. Now wasn't the time or place to be lusting after my wife.

"Expecting *me,* yes, but you're staying here." I wasn't risking her. She was going to be safe if I had to tie her to the tent pole to keep her here.

"Don't be ridiculous." She tied a belt around her waist. "I'm not trying to come with you. There's plenty for me to do. I'm not sitting in the tent the whole time you're gone."

"It's not safe. I need to keep you safe." Here, in my tent in the center of camp, she'd be protected from any stray cannonballs or rogue soldiers. On the edge of the battlefield, tending to the wounded or transporting the dead, anything could happen. I'd almost lost her twice now. I wasn't losing her again.

Mila

I could see by the stubborn set of his chin that he wasn't going to give in on this. Han rarely made demands—at least the Han I'd married rarely did—but he'd changed in the past few months. I didn't know if I could convince him to let me go.

But I did know that I could distract him. I cupped his face with my hands. "I'm not in any danger, Han."

Before he could answer, I kissed him. He responded immediately, pulling me against his body. His tongue slid along my bottom lip, and his cock pressed against my stomach. A jolt of desire went straight to my center, followed by a hot flash of guilt.

Why did that feel so wrong? He was my *husband*, by the Blood. I grabbed fistfuls of his shirt and straddled him.

He moaned, grinding against me. "I want you, Mila. I need you."

I needed him—needed this—too. I tugged my skirts upward, trying to remove some of the fabric between us. Han, thankfully, wore only his long shirt. He pulled it up, then grab me by the hips and slid inside me.

I wasn't ready; his entry stung, but he slid his hand between us, massaging my bud.

"You're so tight," he groaned, burying himself deeper as I grew wet. Not deep enough. Not hard enough.

What was I doing? I'd moved on, fallen in love with another man. I shouldn't be making love to Han like nothing had changed. Shame choked me. I swallowed it down and met him thrust for thrust.

Before long, his movements quickened, his breath coming in pants. I kept my frantic pace, driving him higher. When he stiffened, I smashed my lips to his, less a kiss and more a claiming, our teeth clashing together. I tasted blood—his or mine, I didn't know.

He pulled back first, looking at me through heavy-lidded eyes. "I missed you, Milochka."

I looked away. I was despicable. He'd been risking his life, fighting a war, and I'd given up on him. I'd left him for dead and turned to someone else for comfort, for love. I didn't deserve his affection.

A voice came from outside the tent. "You better not be naked, Han. I'm coming in."

Han pulled the covers over us as Yakov burst into the tent, still talking.

"Ready for today?" He took in the scene before him and froze. His eyes widened, and he turned red, clenching his fist.

I couldn't help the grin spreading across my face. Yakov was here. He seemed to have grown, adding a couple inches to his height. His freckles were somewhat faded—though it was hard to tell with the angry scarlet splotches on his cheeks.

Han scrambled to a sitting position and reached for his pants. "It's not what it looks like."

"It better fucking not be." He glared between us. "Because it looks to me like you just bedded some whore while your wife's off risking her life."

That was just like him, to defend my marital integrity. My grin widened, and I stood, brushing the wrinkles from my sarafan. "Grateful as I am for your concern, Yasha, I don't appreciate being called 'some whore.'"

His face went from red to white in an instant. "Mila?"

"In the flesh. Well, not my flesh, but still." I stepped toward him, arms open.

"Prophet's balls!" He grabbed me and swung me around. "Han said you'd been changed, but I didn't think... I didn't expect to see you here."

"You're not the only one." I jerked my chin toward Han. "I think he just about collapsed."

Yakov smirked. "He seems to have recovered well. You must have...revived him."

"I think that's enough." Han grabbed his arm as I laughed. "Get out of my tent, *durachok*."

Much as I would like to leave you two to 'reviving' each other,"—he waggled his eyebrows at us—"the tsar's waiting for you."

"Shit." Han shoved his feet into his boots and grabbed his new iron hand. "Mila, stay here. Yakov, don't let her leave this tent." He fixed us both with a stern look. "Stay safe."

I had no intention of placing myself in danger, but I also had no intention of waiting here in the tent for him to return. "You, too," I said.

He pressed a quick kiss to my lips. "I'll be back as soon as I can."

Once he was gone, I turned to Yakov. "Obviously I'm not staying here all day. What are we doing?"

He twisted his face in a grimace and glanced after Han. "I was on my way to the med tent."

"Med tent?" I reached for the headscarf that had been delivered with the rest of my clothes.

"The Blood Bastard asked me to help out." He tucked his hand into his pocket and shrugged. "Might as well be useful, since I can't fight."

Yakov Aleksandrovich was working for a Blood Bastard. I never would have believed it. From the reddening tips of his ears, I could tell there was more to the story, but now wasn't the time.

"Could you use extra hands? I'll go out of my mind if I don't have something to do during the battle."

"Never enough hands." He waved his arm, and I laughed. "Come on, we'll find you some work."

41

BATTLE

Mila

The med tent sat on the edge of camp, nearest to the city. Despite the early hour, by the time Yakov and I arrived, people were already bustling around. Outside, cauldrons of water boiled over large fires. Cauterizing irons stood next to the fires, ready to be heated at a moment's notice.

As we stepped into the tent, Yakov thrust an apron under my nose. "Put this on."

"Bossy, aren't we?" I took it and tied it around my waist.

He rolled his eyes with a grin as he guided me toward a bronze-skinned young woman with a long black braid. "Lada, this is

Han's wife, Mila Dmitrievna. Mila, Blood Bastard Lada Radomirovna. Mila's here to work during the battle."

Ah. This was the missing piece of the story, the reason Yakov was working in the med tent. He had feelings for the Blood Bastard. I smirked at him. His ears turned pink, and he scowled.

I gave the Blood Bastard a bow. "Pleasure to meet you."

She gave him a questioning glance, but he shook his head. "I'll explain later."

"Pleasure to meet you, Mila Dmitrievna." She bobbed her head. "I've heard a lot about you. I wish we had time to get better acquainted, but that will have to wait until after the battle. For now, Yakov can get you set up."

I followed him to a table filled with linens. "Tear those into strips while we're waiting," he said. "I hope we've already got enough, but once casualties start coming in, we won't have time to make any. The more we have, the better."

I saluted, and he laughed.

"I missed you, Mila." He gave me a quick hug, then pointed at the linens. "Now get to work!"

The next hour crawled by. Outside, the armies gathered, the clanking of metal and the tramping of boots intermingling with shouted commands. Inside, it was quiet, tense. Why wouldn't the fighting start already?

It was almost a relief when the cannonfire began.

The first thunderous crack echoed through the camp, making me jump. Yakov and Lada, sitting together nearby, snapped their heads up at the sound. Several of the other men and women in the tent flinched, and one young woman screamed.

Relative silence followed the blast. "It won't be long now, Mila Dmitrievna." The Blood Bastard leaned toward me. "The waiting's the worst part. Once the wounded start coming in, there's no time to worry."

I tried to smile. "Call me Mila, please."

"If you'll call me Lada." She slouched in her chair, relaxed, a striking contrast to my tightly wound insides. "I take it you've never waited at the edge of a battlefield?"

"No."

She opened her mouth, but a pair of soldiers appeared in the doorway, carrying the first casualty, a young man missing most of his left arm. Someone had tied a belt around it, just below the shoulder. The wound was still dribbling blood. I froze, but Yakov and Lada jumped into action.

"Put him on the cot here." Lada reached for a pile of linens. "Yakov, I need the—" He handed her a bottle before she could finish speaking. "Yes. Mila, I'll need the largest cauterizing iron, and while you're waiting for that to heat, bring me a bucket of cool, clean water. I need to get this cleaned out."

Running outside, I placed the iron directly onto the fire and scooped a bucket of clean water from the trough next to the tent.

Back inside, Lada took the bucket and ladle from me, pouring a scoop directly onto the open wound. She did that several times, then took the bottle Yakov had given her and poured a little of the green liquid onto it. "I'm ready for that iron now, Mila."

I ran to fetch it.

When I came back in, the Blood Bastard was barking orders. "Hold him down tight—he's going to fight this." Taking the iron from me, she spoke to the wounded man in a soothing voice. "Now, I have to get the wound sealed. The potion I gave you should numb the pain a bit, but you'll still feel most of it. Yakov will give you something to bite down on."

Yakov loosened the belt around the man's arm, and blood spurted; he tightened it again. "We have to hurry," he said through gritted teeth. Positioning a wide strip of leather in the man's mouth, Yakov put both his arms on the man's chest, holding the wounded arm down.

The soldiers who had brought him in took his remaining limbs. Breathing hard through his nose, the wounded man nodded at Lada, who held the iron to the raw flesh below his shoulder.

He bucked and thrashed as the smell of burning flesh filled my nose. Bile rose in my throat, making me glad I'd forgotten to eat breakfast.

Finally, it was done. The wound was sealed, a disgusting cluster of burns stemming the flow of blood. The soldier slumped onto the cot, his face bloodless.

Two more soldiers hobbled into the tent, both wounded—one with a vicious head wound, the other with his leg bent at an odd angle. One of the other workers, a tall woman, moved to assist them.

"Back to the field," Lada ordered the uninjured soldiers. "Mila, clean off his wound—gently, mind—then pour a bit more of the numbing potion on top. Yakov can show you how to bind it when you're done." Leaving the two of us alone with the patient, she rushed off to treat the new arrivals.

Han

Unnatural shadows surrounded us, leaving us nearly invisible as we crept toward the shore. The sound of crashing waves and the smell of fish and saltwater filled the air. In the distance, the first cannon blasts rang out.

Beneath a low cliff up ahead were two long, narrow boats, left there by one of our contacts inside the capital.

We stopped. A shadow peeled off from the group—one of the Drakra—and approached the boats, circling them to check for traps. The rest of us remained in formation around the tsar.

After a moment, the shadow in front of us disappeared, and the Drakra beneath it, a woman with skin the color of snow, nodded once before wrapping herself in shadow again.

We climbed into the boats and pushed off the shore, into the waves. Mist sprayed into my face as we began rowing, keeping close to the jagged rocks that jutted out over the water. The Drakras' shadows swirled around the boats, hiding us from view.

We stopped at a small wooden dock at the base of a cliff. A steep set of stairs, carved into the cliff-side, led upward from the dock; we tied off the boats and began our ascent, single file, into Idesk.

The steps led us to the road that ringed the city. It was empty as ancient ruins, though I could hear in the distance the sounds of battle as our army laid siege to the walls of the city. Somewhere high above us, a loon let out a keening wail. I shivered and reached over to tighten the fingers of my iron hand where it held my sword.

We fell into position around the tsar again. Turning away from the battle, we began our journey to the palace.

Two city guards were still patrolling the road. Miroslav's attempt to prevent his own people from looting the city, I assumed. They stopped as they caught sight of the unnatural cloud of darkness, exchanged frowns, and approached, drawing their swords.

Without a sound, two of the Drakra leapt toward them, shadows swirling. A moment later, the guards were dead, blood pooling on the packed snow beneath them.

I swallowed my rising bile as the Drakra fell back into formation.

At last we reached the hidden path Mila had told us about. We turned off the main road and followed the overgrown cobblestone alley, two by two, with the tsar in the center and me next to him.

The path ended with a small, ancient wooden door. The Drakra in the front of the line shoved it open, and a loud crunching sound marked our arrival.

We flooded through the door and found ourselves, as expected, behind the palace stables. I took the lead, and we formed ranks around the tsar once again. We made our way around the stables and into a courtyard in front of the main palace. A fountain flowed with something thick and red—blood? I shuddered.

Just beyond the fountain stood several men wearing the black armor of palace guards. The Drakra dropped the shadows around us, but the guards saw us a moment too late. They met their fates at the edge of my men's swords.

Inside, the halls were empty of any other guards. Eerie silence filled the palace, broken only by the sound of our footsteps.

We didn't have to go far before we reached the throne room, where Tsar Borislav expected his brother to be holed up, surrounded by his guards and whatever nobles hadn't managed to flee. Judging by the low murmur of frightened voices on the other side of the door, he was right.

Two of my men tried the doors. Bolted shut from the inside. We'd anticipated this, though. The same men placed two black bottles on the floor against the doors. I pulled the tsar back down the hall, and the rest of the group followed.

My men removed the corks from the bottles and ran for cover. I blocked my ears and turned away.

A second passed. Two. With a sound that shook the whole palace, the bottles exploded.

Exploding potions. Lada was either a miracle worker or a witch. Either way, it was a blessing from Otets that she wasn't working against us.

I waited for the smoke to clear before stepping toward the doors that were surely demolished in the blast.

But the smoke and dust from the explosion faded, and the doors still stood. In front of them, two craters remained where the potions had been, but the doors were untouched. Someone had protected them by magical means.

"Step back." Before I could move, the tsar strode forward and touched his staff to the doors.

There was no blast this time, no explosion, but they crumbled at the touch. In a moment, they were nothing more than a pile of ash on the ground.

On the other side, facing us, stood approximately a hundred palace guards. Behind them, nobles and their attendants filled the room, and Miroslav sat on a dais at the end of the hall, atop a giant golden throne. A woman and two young girls stood on his left, and another, older woman, stood on his right. His wife, daughters, and mother, I assumed.

Borislav surveyed the room coolly as he stepped over the rubble. I muttered to two of the Drakra to keep watch, then scrambled after him.

Ignoring the crowd of guards, Borislav looked across the hall. "Mother. You're looking well."

The dowager tsarina didn't respond.

"It's over, Miroslav," the tsar said. "You can give this up now."

Miroslav sneered. "You come with a dozen men and some beasts to claim victory? I have five times your numbers."

Despite the size of the throne room, neither man had to raise his voice. No one made a sound.

"I wish to avoid unnecessary bloodshed. You know you can't win." Borislav was confident, unbothered by the hundred men with weapons pointed in his direction. After everything I'd seen, I understood why. With a wave of his staff, he could wipe out the entire room. I shuddered, saying a silent prayer for protection. "Face me yourself," he said. "Let's end this."

"Do I look like a fool?" Miroslav's voice grew shrill, hysterical. "You've always been able to best me with the Blood Gifts."

"Perhaps that's because Otets favored me." Borislav's tone, calm and emotionless, sent a chill through my bones, though I couldn't say why.

"You were favored, certainly, but I can't speak to Otets' favor."

"Jealousy doesn't suit you, brother."

"Enough!" Miroslav shrieked. "You won't manipulate me. Guards, kill them!"

The first few guards stepped forward. I raised my sword, but Borislav lifted his staff and touched it to the ground. A rumbling grew beneath our feet, accompanied by a cracking sound, and I stumbled backward. A split appeared beneath the staff, spreading and widening toward the oncoming guards. With cries of terror, they fled as the crack became a yawning chasm, but it sped onward, consuming them all.

Still Borislav didn't stop the magic. The chasm grew wider, cutting a path through the crowd of nobles. Most of them scrambled out of the way, but a stout, black-haired man let out a piercing scream as he fell in. A woman with splotches of white across her brown face grabbed the steel-clad arm of the man next to her. They both slipped toward the edge. He wrenched his arm free, grabbing a column for purchase, and the woman fell into the abyss below.

"Stop!" I screamed, but the tsar couldn't or wouldn't. He stared at his brother, his face like stone, as the steps of the dais began to crack. Miroslav flinched, and Borislav raised his staff.

The chasm stopped spreading.

Stunned, I looked at the chaos around us. My men wore wide-eyed, open-mouthed expressions that reflected my own horror.

"Face me," Borislav said. His voice was like ice. "There's no one left to defend you. Face me."

Miroslav looked around at the nobles, and his gaze stopped on the man who had let the noblewoman fall. Large and red-faced, with a shock of orange hair, the man wore an expression of disdain as he looked up at Miroslav, who nodded.

The nobleman and his servant drew their swords and charged forward. I elbowed the tsar aside and stepped in front of him as my men joined me.

The nobleman reached me first, and our swords met, sending a jolt of pain through my arm. He came at me with a ferocity that seemed fueled by a personal hatred, though I'd never seen him before. I backed up, letting the other man take the offensive, searching for weaknesses.

There. As he raised his sword for a high strike, I spotted a chink in his armor. I jabbed my sword under his arm, into the gap.

He clutched at the wound, eyes wide, and stumbled backward. He was almost to the edge of the chasm—his foot slipped. He fell, and a scream tore from his lips, cutting off in the middle as he hit the bottom of the chasm with a sickening thud.

I looked around. The tsar was safe. The nobleman's servant had been dispatched as well, not killed but disarmed. He lay on the ground, panting, with a sword at his neck.

"Face me," Borislav insisted once more.

Miroslav's defenders had all been defeated. His mother handed him a black staff, the twin to Borislav's white one. He took it and lifted it into the air as Borislav touched his own to the ground again.

In an instant, the throne was gone.

It took a moment for my mind to process what I saw. The chasm, which had grown quickly but steadily before, had expanded in a flash as soon as Borislav touched his staff to the ground. With barely a movement, the tsar had killed his brother.

The screams of the dead, of Miroslav and his wife, mother, and daughters echoed far longer than I thought possible. The surviving nobles, what few there were, didn't move. Didn't make a sound.

He'd killed them. And not just that, he'd committed the greatest abomination. He'd turned the Gifts on the unSanctioned.

I dropped to my knees as the contents of my stomach splattered on the ruined palace floor.

"Captain," the tsar said when I'd collected myself enough to stand, "please send someone to inform Grand Duke Radomir and Yixa na Chekke of our victory."

42

CONFRONTATION

Mila

The battle was long over. The afternoon stretched into evening, but still people filled the med tent. New casualties had stopped arriving, thank Otets, but the wounded were numerous. My head pounded, the tent swimming around me.

"Go, Mila." Lada's voice was firm. "You're going to collapse. You're no good to me like this. Get some sleep and come back in the morning."

I opened my mouth to argue, but Yakov, binding a chest wound several cots over, met my eyes and shook his head. I sighed. "Fine. I'll be back in a few hours."

The Blood Bastard had already turned away. I navigated the crowded tent and made my way to the slightly less busy camp outside.

Lada was probably right. I hadn't slept much, and I hadn't eaten all day, either. Otets, I was tired.

I hadn't seen Han since the battle, but he'd sent word that he was safe.

And Miroslav was dead.

I sank down onto the snow with my back to a tent pole. It was over. We'd survived. I closed my eyes and took a deep breath, drinking in the stench of the camp, the blood, sweat, and snow, the unwashed smell of an army on the move. I hadn't breathed properly in months. But I could breathe now. It was over.

"Fia!" My eyes popped open as Izolda called my name. "There you are! I've been looking everywhere."

Something was wrong; I could tell by her tone. I scanned her for signs of injury. "What's happened?"

She waved a hand in dismissal of my scrutiny. "I'm fine. It's Alexey."

My heart filled my throat. Had he been injured? Worse? "What happened?" I choked out, scrambling to my feet.

"He's been captured."

Alive. He was alive. "He's safe? He's not hurt?"

She grimaced. "Yes, but... The Drakra are taking the prisoners when they go back east."

"As slaves?" A pit opened in my stomach.

"It's...complicated."

I gritted my teeth. "Uncomplicate it. What's going to happen to him?"

"He'll be a bondservant. Eight years of service to the Drakra, and he'll be free to return home. Or to stay, if he chooses."

Eight years. That would be an eternity to him. And who knew what might happen to him during those years? I had to get him out. "Where is he? He's not injured?" I'd already asked, but I needed to hear the words.

Izolda shook her head. "He's not injured. He's in the temporary cells outside the camp, until we move into the palace."

"Take me to him." I had to see him. Han was still with the tsar, dealing with the aftermath of the battle. He didn't have to know that I'd gone to see the prisoners, or one specific prisoner. He didn't have to know why.

The wooden cells outside of the camp weren't crowded. Izolda approached one of the guards. "We'd like to speak to one of the prisoners."

I didn't hear his response as I scanned the cells for Alexey's familiar face. There were so few people in the cells. So few prisoners. Had so few survived the battle? Or had they fled?

"Fia." Izolda grabbed my hand and pulled me toward the furthest cell.

I almost didn't recognize him. He sat in the corner, spattered in dust. Flecks of something—gravel, maybe?—covered his shoulders and hair. He stared toward the city, so we could see his profile, missing its characteristic cocky grin. A shadow of the man I'd come to know.

"Alexey." The name, barely a whisper, slipped past my lips before I could stop it.

His head snapped around so hard he must have strained his neck. When his eyes met mine, they tightened with some unidentified emotion. Anger, perhaps? Anger would be reasonable, given what I'd done to him. Betrayal, maybe, or sadness? He stood, never removing his gaze from my face. I opened my mouth, then closed it again.

"I'll give you two a minute," Izolda muttered. I turned to stop her, but she was already out of reach. When I tried to call her back, my throat didn't work.

I turned back to Alexey, willing myself to say something. Anything. I opened my mouth again, but no sound came out.

"Why are you here?" he bit out. It was anger, then, that I saw in his eyes. When I didn't respond, he stalked closer, until we were barely a foot apart, only the bars of his makeshift prison between us. "Did you come to gloat?"

"I'm sorry," I whispered. "I'm so sorry."

"Was any of it real?"

He'd asked me that same question the last time I saw him. Had it only been a day? So much had changed.

Was any of it real? I'd thought it was. He'd helped me heal. I hadn't planned to, but I'd felt something for him I'd never felt before. Not even with—

"I'm married."

He flinched. "I see."

"Alexey, I—" I reached through the bars to touch his face, but he stepped out of reach.

"Don't." His voice was flat, emotionless. "Who is he?"

I didn't want to talk about Han with him. I didn't want to talk about Han at all. "A commander in the tsar's army."

"Not Tsar Miroslav's, I take it," he said wryly.

I shook my head. "Miroslav is dead."

"I know. I was there."

He'd been in the palace?

"He was a monster," I whispered.

"And your tsar is so much better."

He was mocking me, but I answered him anyway. "Borislav doesn't kill innocents."

"Doesn't he? I'm sure Lady Yelena would be happy to hear that. As would Count Andrej and the dowager tsarina."

Cold shock filled my veins. Were they all imprisoned as well? Had Borislav decided to execute them? "What do they have to do with this?"

"Why don't you ask your husband?" he sneered. "I'm sure he knows all about the carnage your tsar wreaked in the palace."

My head spun. What had Borislav done? "Where is Lady Yelena?"

"She's dead. Along with her husband, Tsar Miroslav, and nearly a dozen other nobles killed at the hand of the man you call tsar. Tell me, Sofia, what crime did the grand duchesses commit to deserve death?"

I couldn't believe it. Wouldn't believe it. Borislav wouldn't do that. He championed innocents; he didn't slaughter them. Miroslav was the one who allowed his men to rape women, kill their children. Borislav wouldn't, couldn't have killed all those people. Lady Yelena, the sweet young woman who'd been forced into marriage with that monster Kazimir. The grand duchesses, whose only crime was being born to the wrong father. "No."

Alexey laughed, but there was no humor in it. "You don't believe me? No, of course you don't. I'm the villain here, just another mindless follower of Miroslav the monster."

"I never thought that!" He had to believe me. He was a good man. I didn't want to leave him hating me, thinking I hated him.

"No? You didn't use me? Didn't take advantage of my position in Lord Kazimir's household? Didn't pass on the information I shared with you to your husband and your tsar?" When I didn't respond, he scoffed. "That's what I thought."

"I didn't mean to hurt you." My voice was small. "I didn't mean for any of this to happen."

He didn't look at me. "What did you think would happen? What did you want?"

"I wanted to go home!" My eyes filled with hot tears. "I wanted my husband not to be branded a traitor. I wanted to raise my son. I wanted to live somewhere I didn't have to fear for everyone I loved." The words poured out of me as fast as the tears rolling down my cheeks. "I wanted to live a quiet life with my family. But Kazimir and Miroslav took that away from me. Miroslav crippled my husband. Kazimir killed my son. They turned my home into a battleground. So yes, Alexey, I went to court to spy on Miroslav. And yes, I passed on what you told me. But I didn't mean to hurt you, and I certainly didn't mean to fall in love with you." The last words came out in a sob, and I leaned against the cell, grabbing the wood for support.

In the aftermath of my outburst, all I could hear was the ragged sound of my breathing. I closed my eyes, willing the tears to fade.

A hand brushed my face. "I did." I looked up to see Alexey staring at me, his own eyes glistening. "I meant to fall in love with you," he said.

A sob escaped me. He'd loved me, and I'd betrayed him. "Alexey, I—"

He placed a finger over my lips, cutting me off. "I told you I didn't care how long I had with you, that every moment was a blessing. I lied." He slid his hand to the scarf I wore on my head, slipping a finger under the edge. "I want every moment of the rest of your life. I want to help you move on from whatever happened before me, and I want to protect you from whatever comes next." He slipped the scarf from my head, voice lowering to a growl. "And I don't want to send you back to the bastard of a husband who sent you to court to do his dirty work."

He kissed me, a hungry, possessive kiss that set my heart racing. My forehead pressed against the wood planks between us as he pulled me closer, holding me to him with his hand on the back of my head. I could taste my tears on his lips.

"Don't go, Sofia," he murmured when he finally pulled back.

My breath came in pants, forming clouds in the air, and my tears still flowed. "Mila." He searched my eyes, questioning, so I clarified. "My name is Mila Dmitrievna."

He let go of me and stepped back. All emotion on his face disappeared once more. "My apologies, Mila Dmitrievna."

"Alexey, no." I reached for his hand, letting out a breath when he didn't step away. Something flickered in his eyes as our hands touched. "I didn't mean to feel what I do for you. I'm married."

"Yes, you've said that." I could hear the hurt behind the anger in his voice.

"I thought he was dead." Fuck, this was hard. I swallowed the lump in my throat and pressed on. "But he's not. And when I found out he was alive, I had already fallen in love with you." I shook my head. "I just wanted to know that you knew me, not Sofia."

"I do. Or," he shrugged. "I thought I did."

I deserved that. I'd lied to him for months. Tears welled in my eyes again, and I wiped furiously at them.

He brushed his thumb against the back of my hand, watching it as he did. "But your name doesn't matter to me. Who you are, that doesn't change. No matter what you did, what you felt like you had to do, that woman is still the same, whether you call her Sofia or Mila."

I blinked up at him. I'd heard that somewhere before. Maybe not those words exactly, but the sentiment. Izolda had said it, maybe?

No. A stone settled in my stomach. Han had told me something similar the day the tsar changed me.

"I fell in love with you. I don't know what's going to happen to me now, but whatever happens next, knowing you loved me, however briefly..." His words trailed off into silence. He turned my hand over and pressed a kiss into the palm. "You're my sun, and my life will be dark without you."

I gave him a weak, teary smile, but he returned my gaze solemnly. "Go home, Mila. Go be with your husband. Raise your children, serve your tsar. Be happy."

"And you?" I fought to hide the tremor in my voice.

He shrugged. "Exile if I'm lucky. Execution if I'm not."

I shuddered at his casual tone. I should tell him what Izolda had said about the Drakra, but I couldn't bring myself to say it. He wouldn't be executed, surely. But after eight years of laboring for the Drakra, what part of who he was would remain? "I want to help you. I can talk to my husband—"

He cut me off. "No. I don't want his charity."

"And mine?" I clenched his hand tight in mine, wishing for...anything. "Can't I do something?"

"Go home," he repeated. "Go home and be happy." He trailed a finger down my cheek, and I closed my eyes.

My tears were back in full force now. He dropped his hands to his side and stepped back, out of my reach. "Goodbye, my sun."

I took a step back. Another. I stumbled, still watching him, and he flinched.

"Easy, Fia." Izolda, coming from nowhere, put a steadying hand on my arm. "It's late. We should get you back."

I looked up. The sky was nearly dark. Odd. I hadn't noticed the time passing. I staggered back toward camp, directed by the pressure of Izolda's hand on my arm. What was she saying? I couldn't understand the words. I took another step, and the ground came up to meet me.

Then I was being lifted up. Someone had strong arms around me. Alexey? No, Alexey was in a cell. "Han?" I struggled to open my eyes.

"Sorry, Mila. Just me."

That voice was familiar. Who was it? "Yasha?"

He laughed, the sound vibrating against my cheek. "I hope so. Who's Alexey?"

A friend, I wanted to tell him. My tongue was too thick. I leaned into his chest and let sleep drag me under.

43

DISINHERITANCE

Han

I stared down at my wife in the dim morning light. Her breathing was deep and even, her face peaceful in sleep.

I'd been so worried.

When she hadn't been in the tent on my return, I'd gone to the med tent, sure that she would be with Yakov. He might not have made her stay in our tent, but he wouldn't have let her wander off.

Neither Mila or Yakov had been in the med tent, though. Lada had sent Mila to get some rest over an hour before my arrival, and I had just missed seeing Yakov leave.

In a near-panic, I'd gone back to my tent to pace and think of where she could be. Nothing had come to mind; she knew next to no one in the camp, and the battle was over, so she hadn't been caught up in the fighting.

It hadn't been long—though it felt like ages—before Yakov strode in, depositing an unconscious Mila on the cot.

She'd been with Izolda, her friend from court who'd helped her escape from the palace dungeons. Yakov had come across Mila and Izolda on the edge of camp, Mila barely conscious and her friend half-dragging her along. She'd said three things. "Alexey," "Han," and "Yasha."

I'd managed to move her, still sleeping, to the palace. Nearly a mile riding in the small cart I'd found, and she hadn't budged. Now she lay in the middle of the large bed, untroubled in sleep, as though she hadn't ripped my heart from her chest when she went missing.

I propped myself up on an elbow and frowned down at her sleeping form. What had she been doing outside of camp? I'd told her to stay where I left her, and not only had she disobeyed by spending the entire day working in the med tent, she'd disappeared after Lada sent her back to me. My blood heated. How dare she put herself at risk like that? Hadn't she seen enough danger for a lifetime?

She stirred, and I reached out a hand to her. She opened her eyes, blinking blearily.

"Prophet's balls," she swore. "I feel like I've been run over by a horse. What time is it?"

"Well past dawn."

"And you're still in bed?" She feigned a look of shock. Then she looked around, taking in our surroundings. "We're in the palace?"

"Yes, when my wife goes missing after a battle and is deposited unconscious on my bed an hour later, it tends to put me off my schedule." I scowled at her.

"I wasn't missing."

"You weren't in our tent, and you weren't at the med tent. Yakov found you half-conscious on the edge of camp. What was I supposed to think?"

"Oh." She chewed her lip, avoiding my eye.

"What were you thinking, Mila?" I sighed, taking her hand. "I was terrified something had happened to you."

"I was perfectly fine. The battle was over, and I was with Izolda the whole time. She had a friend from court who was captured in battle. She wanted to go see him."

"And after only getting a couple hours of sleep and working from dawn to dusk, you had to join her, I suppose." She had no concept of self-preservation. "I swear, Mila, you're going to be the death of me. Did you even eat yesterday?"

The guilty look on her face was answer enough. Thankfully, I'd had the foresight to find some food. I reached for the tray on the bedside table. She gave me a grateful smile and tucked into the bread and cheese.

"Who's Alexey?"

She froze mid-bite, looking up at me with wide eyes.

"Yakov said you mentioned him last night. You weren't making much sense."

"Oh." She turned back to her food and shrugged. "The friend Izolda wanted to go see."

"Someone you know well?" I struggled to keep my voice nonchalant. She'd been tired. She'd just seen the man. The fact that she'd called his name didn't have to mean anything.

She shrugged again. "As well as anyone, I suppose. Izolda's known him for years. He got us out of the capital."

I blinked, guilt overtaking the misplaced jealousy. If this Alexey had helped bring Mila back to me safely, I owed him a debt of gratitude.

"I'm glad he was there. I can't promise anything, but maybe I could speak to the tsar—"

"No."

The vehemence in her voice took me aback. "Oh."

"I'm sorry. He just…he's very proud. He wouldn't want any special treatment."

"Not even to thank him for bringing back my wife?" I couldn't read her expression. I'd always been able to tell what she was thinking. I didn't like this separation between us.

Her eyes grew distant. "No. Not even for that."

"I see." I didn't, but she was safe now. She was with me. Whatever else had happened, it didn't matter anymore.

She shook her head and refocused. "So, the war's finally over." She sat up and wrapped her arms around her knees.

"It's over," I confirmed. "Miroslav is dead, along with the entire palace guard."

"I heard it was bad in there," she said softly. "What happened?"

Images from the previous day flashed through my mind. "It was horrible." I told her what I'd seen from the moment we reached the palace, trying not to dwell on the more gruesome aspects. Still, by the time I finished, she'd pushed away the plate of food, cringing.

"Borislav did that?" Her eyes were wide with horror. "He was supposed to be better," she said, as if saying it could make it true.

I thought about Matvey Il'ich, his response to the desertions, his use of magic in the battle outside Sevken. "He's done some awful things in this war, but not like this. I think I made a mistake." It pained me to admit that I'd been so wrong about Borislav, but after what I'd seen in the throne room, this couldn't be allowed to stand.

"We both did," she said.

"But I'm not responsible for just me." I ran a hand over my face. "I convinced other men to fight. By the Blood, I convinced the *Drakra* to join us! And what did we get? We traded one monster for another. And I let you put yourself in danger to make it happen." I wouldn't make that mistake again.

"We both should have known better. But we didn't." As always, she was practical to a fault. Yixa na Chekke would love her. She was all logic and reason.

"So what do we do now?" she asked. "We didn't go through all that trouble to remove one tyrant, just to put another on the throne. We have to stop him while the country is still disorganized, before he can consolidate his power."

We would be doing nothing. I wasn't risking my wife, or allowing her to risk herself, on another rebellion. But I humored her. "Radomir." Radomir would already be planning Borislav's Disinheritance. He wasn't as charismatic or likable as his cousin, but he was next in line, and more importantly, he regarded the title of Sanctioned with the reverence it deserved. He'd been against Borislav at all the key points—sending slaves to the Drakra, Il'ich's execution, the hanging of the deserters, even Borislav's insistence on stealing into the capital before the battle was over.

"Would he take it?" She didn't question my decision at all. She trusted me implicitly. I squeezed her hand. What would I do without her?

"Yes. He won't let this go. He's said from the beginning that he would do what was right, even if it meant going against Borislav. You should have seen him in the palace yesterday. He was horrified."

"Han? Mila?" We both jumped as Yakov's voice came through the door. "Cover up. I'm coming in."

He strode into the room and took a seat on the bed, swiping the bread from Mila's plate. "What were you two talking about before I improved your day with my presence?"

Mila gave me a small, encouraging nod. We had to tell Yakov.

"Did you hear what happened in the throne room yesterday?" I asked.

His face twisted into a grimace. "Rumors. I can't believe it."

"All true," I said. "Every bit as bad as Miroslav, if not worse."

"Fuck. What have we done?"

"We messed up," Mila said. "Badly. We have to fix it."

"Radomir." Yakov caught on quickly. "Will he do it?"

"He's already suggested it." I told them about my conversation with the prince after Borislav had left for the capital.

We were all silent when I finished speaking. Were we really considering this? If I was wrong, if I failed, or if I'd somehow misunderstood Radomir's intentions, we'd be executed. Borislav would show no mercy. He wouldn't spare Mila just because she was a woman. My stomach twisted at the thought of her on the gallows, slaughtered like Matvey Il'ich.

"We've got to move fast. Find out who'll support us, get them on board. I'll go to Prince Radomir right away. Yasha, the commanders know I trust you. Go feel them out, see who we can count on. Mila..." I looked at my wife. She'd been through so much. Could I drag her into the rebellion against Borislav, too?

No. No, I wasn't risking her. No matter what she wanted, I had to keep her safe. "Just stay here," I said finally.

Her mouth dropped open. "Stay here? I just spent six months risking my life. You're not casting me aside now. You need me."

I did need her. I needed her protected, here for me to come home to. "Not for long. Just until things settle down." I stood, backing toward the door. We needed to get out of here, put plans into motion before Borislav caught on.

"You're not going anywhere without me." She rose from the bed, stepping toward me. "We've had this discussion before. I have just as much right as you to see justice done."

"I won't put you at risk. Not again." I grabbed the key to the room from the desk and jerked my head at Yakov, indicating that he should follow me. "I'll be back soon."

Her face contorted in anger, and she lunged toward me, but too late. We were already at the door. I slammed it shut and locked it.

"I'll be back soon," I said again, putting a hand on the wood.

"Han Antonovich, come back here!" she shrieked, but I turned away.

Yakov grabbed me by the shoulder, brow furrowed with concern. "You sure about this?"

"She'll be fine." I shrugged him off. "I need to make sure she's safe. And since she won't stay where I tell her…"

"She's never going to forgive you for this."

"If I want your opinion on how to handle my wife, I'll ask," I bit out. "Just go."

He opened his mouth, but with a guilty glance at the door, he closed it again without speaking. He let out a long breath and left me alone.

The door shuddered as Mila threw something heavy at it—a chair, probably—but it held. She wouldn't get out of that room. Not until this was all over. "I'm sorry," I whispered. Sorry for hurting her. Not sorry for keeping her safe.

I found the prince—Grand Duke? Tsar? His title would depend on the events of the next few hours—with his daughter and a couple of the commanders in Radomir's new rooms in the palace, deep in conversation. At my entrance, he looked up. From the steely look on the prince's face, I knew he was already set on his course of action.

"I need to speak to you, your grace."

"He has to be taken down." His eyes flashed. I'd never seen him so full of righteous anger. "My cousin's reign ends today, before it begins in truth. He's broken every edict Otets gave the Sanctioned."

I glanced at the others in the room, but he waved a hand. "They will join us."

I nodded. "Yakov is gathering the other commanders."

"Thank you. We have perhaps an hour until Borislav returns. I would prefer not to do this in the presence of the Drakra. They are an...unnecessary complication."

"Yes, your grace. Your majesty," I corrected, but he shook his head.

"'Your grace' until my cousin's Disinheritance is complete. I am not Borislav. I will not use a title until it is mine in truth."

"Yes, your grace."

He gestured for us all to sit. "We'll meet the tsar in the courtyard when he returns."

"And if he fights?" Lada asked. A fair question. I couldn't imagine Borislav stepping down quietly after all he'd done to get here. He'd managed to cause so much destruction on his own. What would be the results of a battle between Borislav and Radomir? They could turn the palace to rubble between them.

"Otets willing, he won't." The prince placed his wand on the table. "But I'll be prepared if he does."

Fyodor Yakovlevich cleared his throat. "If he doesn't fight, will you allow him to step down peacefully?"

"I will allow him to step down, yes, and I pray he does." His tone was sincere. "But if he refuses to accept his Disinheritance, even if he doesn't fight, I will see justice done."

My eyes widened in alarm. I'd seen Borislav's version of justice.

Radomir noticed my distress and clarified. "Beheading. A swift, painless death. I won't slaughter traitors."

"Of course not, your grace. I didn't mean to imply otherwise." I knew that. Radomir was an honorable man, if not as charismatic as his cousin.

A knock sounded at the door, and Yakov stepped into the room, followed by most of the remaining commanders. He quirked a brow at me, and I nodded.

Yakov bowed. "Your grace, we're yours to command."

"Thank you, Yakov Aleksandrovich." He rose. "We should adjourn to the courtyard, in case he returns early."

My sword knocked at my side, a comforting weight, as we followed the prince through the palace halls. As we stepped outside into the cold air, I tightened my metal fingers around my sword hilt, leaving it sheathed. Things could happen quickly, and I didn't want to be caught unawares.

The sky was clear over the palace, the sun glinting brilliant gold off the onion-shaped domes. In the center of the courtyard was the sickening fountain I'd seen the day before, viscous red liquid pooling around the feet of the two figures in its center. The liquid didn't bear the metallic tang of real blood, but the sight still made me shudder. Would blood run over the cobblestones this morning?

I bowed my head in silent prayer that the transfer of power would be peaceful.

As time crawled by, I couldn't stop my thoughts from dwelling on Mila. She'd understand, eventually, why I'd made the choices I had. Even if it took weeks, months. Her anger would be worth it, as long as she was alive to be angry.

An eternity later, the palace gates opened. Borislav approached, staff in hand, flanked by the remaining commanders.

His eyes narrowed as he caught sight of us waiting for him, armed and standing at attention. As he entered the courtyard, he stopped by the fountain. "What is this?"

Radomir took a step forward. "You've gone too far, Borislav."

"Treason." His nostrils flared, and he clenched his staff tighter. "After all I've done for this country, you turn on me." He met the eyes of each person in the courtyard, ending with me. "And you. I made you, and you're betraying me."

"Only Otets can make someone," Radomir said. "Han Antonovich is doing what he feels is right. As am I. As is every man here."

"You would make a Disinheritance of me?" The tsar's voice was deadly calm, but I could sense the roiling fury beneath it. My mouth went dry as I remembered what he'd done the last time I saw him so composed, so angry. Remembering the massacre in the throne room. I glanced at Yakov, but his attention was fixed on the scene before us. He stood next to Lada, their hands clasped together.

"I told you I wouldn't hesitate to do what was right for Inzhria." Radomir took another step toward his cousin. "Will you accept your Disinheritance?"

"I will not."

I drew my sword, moving to stand next to Radomir. Behind me, the other commanders drew their swords as well. Borislav glanced at us, his lip curled, before returning his gaze to Radomir.

"You cannot win, Borislav." Radomir's words sent a chill through me. Similar, so similar to what Borislav had told his brother.

"You cannot take what is rightfully mine. Inzhria is mine," he hissed.

"Inzhria belongs to Otets," Radomir said. "Surrender. Accept your Disinheritance, and end this." He raised his wand.

"Never." Borislav raised his staff, and the not-blood from the fountain shot toward us, sharpening into frozen spikes.

"Back!" Radomir roared. He waved his wand, and the spikes hit an invisible wall. They crashed to the ground amidst the sound of rushing wind.

Borislav attacked again, thrusting his staff forward, and a wall of rock rose in front of the prince, who waved his wand. The wall shattered into large stones, which flew toward Borislav. The men with him scattered, diving to the ground.

Borislav pointed his staff, and the stones became sand that blew past him. He slammed the butt of his staff on the ground, and a rattle echoed through the courtyard. Radomir stumbled as the ground beneath him grew uneven. He fell to the ground, and my heart skipped a beat. If he lost, if he died, we would all be killed.

With a wave of Borislav's staff, the statue of the Prophet shattered into pieces, all of them flying at once toward Radomir.

The prince rolled out of the way and with a flick of his wrist, shot a dagger of ice out as he rose to his knees. Borislav dodged, but it caught his cheek. A thin line of blood bloomed in its wake.

Borislav let out a guttural snarl and dragged his staff in a line on the ground. A set of icy spikes sprang up in front of Radomir. One caught him beneath the chin, knocking him sideways. His head hit the ground, and he lay unmoving.

Lada screamed. "Father!"

A roaring filled my ears, and I darted forward as Borislav pointed his staff toward his cousin.

Steel met wood, and Borislav's staff cracked in two. His eyes widened. It was over—he was powerless without his staff.

But he wasn't done fighting. He dropped the broken pieces of his staff and drew his sword. The blow clanged through my bones as steel met steel.

"I gave you that hand." He forced me backward, the full force of his strength behind each thrust. "I made you what you are today. You dare turn your blade on me?"

I didn't answer him. I wouldn't let him goad me. He was impatient, his movements hastened by fury. I feinted an opening, and when he struck toward it, I slashed at his sword hand. Blood dripped from the wound, and his sword clattered to the ground.

I met the gaze of my former tsar, the point of my sword at his chest. "Surrender."

"Well done, Captain." Radomir's voice cut through the rush of blood in my head.

I glanced back to see the prince on his feet, eyes glazed. He swayed but remained standing as he said to his cousin, "Accept your Disinheritance."

"Never." Borislav's chest rose and fell with heavy breaths.

"If you won't abdicate, I'll have no choice but to see you executed."

"So bloodthirsty."

Radomir turned away, ignoring the taunt. "Fyodor Yakovlevich, Han Antonovich, please escort my cousin to the palace dungeon." He glanced back at Borislav. "I'll give you three days to reconsider your position. If not, you will be executed for crimes against Otets and against the Blood."

I dropped my sword to my side and stepped forward to take Borislav's arm, but he shook me off. "I am unarmed. You will not manhandle one of the Sanctioned."

I looked to Radomir for confirmation. When he nodded, I gestured for Borislav to go ahead. The tsar—former tsar—held his head high as he walked through the assembled crowd, followed by me and Yakovlevich.

Over. It was over.

I'd forsworn myself and ended the rule of my tsar.

I'd helped ensure not one, but two Disinheritances over as many days.

Only time would tell if I'd made the right decision.

44

EXECUTION

Han

I stared at Borislav through the iron bars of the cell. "Please, reconsider. You made the wrong choice—many wrong choices—but you don't have to die for it. Radomir respects you. He would give you a position of honor, listen to your counsel. You can still lead this tsardom, even if you don't wear the crown."

"Whether I die tomorrow or not, he'll have to kill me eventually." He didn't look at me from his seat next to the tiny window. "Radomir is no fool. My claim is stronger than his. He knows that if I remain alive, I can become a focal point for future rebellion. Oh, yes," he said before I could contradict him, "legally, if I accept my Disinheritance,

I can make no future claim on the throne, but what does the common man care for the finer points of religious doctrine? Radomir is unpopular, and I was their chosen tsar. I was *your* chosen tsar."

"You were my tsar until you betrayed your people. You turned your Gifts against unSanctioned. You attacked citizens, nobles in your court." He opened his mouth to answer, but I cut him off. "And before that, you betrayed your army. Matvey Il'ich deserved mercy. Maybe he deserved to die for his betrayal, maybe not, but he still deserved mercy, and you had him slaughtered like an animal. Worse than an animal. And the men who had flocked to your cause, believing you would set the country to rights, you betrayed them, too. When their families were threatened, when they were afraid of the consequences of their actions and tried to return home, you didn't offer them the reassurances they so desperately needed. You murdered them. And you agreed to sell your people, men who had done nothing but fight for what they thought was right, into slavery. You became no better than the man you were trying to overthrow."

I paused, taking a breath. "If you had shown mercy in just one of those instances, you might have been able to hold our trust. But every opportunity you had to show kindness, you insisted on showing strength. You're no better than your brother was."

"I'm not the only one who betrayed the trust of our people, Han." He turned to me, his eyes cold. "Do you think the people will respect you when they learn the agreement you made with the Drakra? The heathen creatures from the mountains, unleashed by you on their lands. And you gave them free rein to take slaves from among our people. Do you think they will remember that I gave that order? Or will they blame you when their brothers, their fathers, their sons are forced to serve for years under those pagans, tortured and brutalized with unholy magic?"

My stomach clenched, but I shook my head. I couldn't allow myself to be baited. I hadn't made that decision. I'd followed orders, done what I thought was right. I could do my best to mitigate the effects of my actions, but I couldn't regret what I'd done.

"This is why you'll never be tsar, Borislav." My voice was quiet but firm.

"Otets will judge between us."

I turned away. "Make your peace with Him tonight. Your execution is scheduled for dawn."

My heart weighed like a stone in my chest as I left the dungeons. I hardly noticed the guards saluting as I passed. Mila. I needed to see Mila.

I found her in our room in the palace, writing something. She didn't look up at my entrance. Her eyes were trained on the paper, and she worried her bottom lip between her teeth. I watched her in silence. How could she be so strange and so familiar at the same time?

She'd be back in her old body in the morning. I'd almost forgotten. Borislav had told her the spell would last until he removed it...or he died.

She flinched when she caught sight of me. It wrenched at my heart, seeing the fear and betrayal on her face, but we would heal. She would realize that everything I did, I did for her. She'd understand that I had no other choice.

I wrapped my arms around her and pressed a kiss to the top of her head. "I'm glad you're here with me, *dorogusha*."

She tried to pull away, but I held her tight to me. She was mine, and I was never letting her go.

*****

I woke in the early morning darkness. Mila lay in my arms; even in sleep, I held her close, though she faced away from me.

But I had an execution to attend now. I extracted my arm from beneath her, careful not to wake her. She didn't need to see Borislav's death. She'd seen enough carnage to last a lifetime.

The day was relatively warm, hinting at the coming spring, though gray clouds covered the sky. Despite my heavy fur coat, I shivered. The air felt oppressive, like Otets was angry.

I shook off the thought. I'd done what I had to do. Otets knew that. This execution was merely justice being served.

I found Radomir waiting in the small, enclosed yard behind the palace dungeons. "Captain." The new tsar nodded a greeting as I approached.

"Your majesty." Strange, to think of Radomir as the tsar, after knowing him for so many months as prince.

A raised platform stood in the center of the yard, a discolored block of wood in the center. The yard was empty except for me, the tsar, and a couple other commanders. Radomir had insisted on a private execution. "The death of a tsar is nothing to be gawked at," he'd said.

Two guards led Borislav out of the prison and onto the platform. The executioner followed, his ax by his side.

Borislav knelt before the block without prompting. He wore a simple linen shirt and black pants, and he shivered with the cold, though his expression held disdain.

Radomir approached the platform. "Even now, you can repent, cousin. Accept your Disinheritance, and I will spare your life."

Borislav merely looked at him, unspeaking.

He pursed his lips. "If you have any last words, now is the time."

"Otets will condemn you for this." Borislav's voice came out calm and clear. Venom filled his eyes. "All of you."

The executioner approached, taking the ax in hand. "When you are prepared, place your head on the block."

The two cousins stared into each other's eyes, unblinking. Borislav laid his head down on the block without breaking eye contact, and the executioner swung the ax.

Mila

I woke with a jolt. Sitting up, I looked around the room. What had woken me? Han was gone, and the dim light coming through the window told me it was only dawn.

As I swung my feet over the side of the bed, I paused. My skin was lighter, a tawny brown that was new and familiar all at once. I touched my hair—long and straight, no longer the tight, textured curls I'd become accustomed to.

Borislav was dead.

Prince Radomir—Tsar Radomir—had had him executed. After all we'd sacrificed to bring Borislav to the throne, he was dead.

He'd earned his death. Still, we'd given up so much for him, only to see his cousin on the throne instead. Borislav wasn't right for the tsardom, but would Radomir be any better?

And with Borislav's death, Sofia died, too. The woman I'd been for half a year, the name and body I'd worn, was dead. I'd more than taken Sofia's body; I'd become a whole new person at court.

I dressed quickly, slipping on my shoes. They were loose. All my clothes were, but they'd have to do. Izolda would be with her mother in the trade quarters, where the Drakra had been housed following the battle. I needed to talk to my friend.

If Izolda was still my friend. She'd been Sofia's friend, but Sofia was well and truly dead now. How would Izolda feel about the sudden change?

I stopped at the door, heart pounding. It was closed. What if Han had locked me in here again? I couldn't bear that. Not again. I didn't know what I would do if he'd trapped me in here like he had when he went to face Borislav.

I put a hand to the latch and pulled. It swung open, and a wave of relief crashed over me. I was free.

Two gray-skinned Drakra women stood at the entrance to the trade quarters, fur coats draped over their shoulders. They held their spears upright and watched me as I approached.

"I'm looking for Izolda. Izolda...na Xhela?" That was her Drakra name, right? She'd told me once.

One of the women disappeared into the building. She returned with Izolda.

"Can I help you?" my friend asked.

I bit my lip. "Can I speak with you privately?"

She nodded, her brow knit together, and walked with me in the direction of the gardens. "I don't believe we've met before."

I took a deep breath. "It's me. Sofia."

She stared. A grin split across her face. "Tia! Or should I bow and use your full name now? Spider's Blood, I didn't even think about you getting your old body back. Is it weird?"

I could have wept with relief at the normalcy in her tone. "You have no idea. And my name's Mila. If you bow, I might vomit." I looped my arm through hers.

"But your scarred stud is Han Antonovich, the Survivor of Barbezht, right? You're practically married to royalty!"

I cringed. Han was the last thing I wanted to think about right now. "If you start calling me Lyudmila Dmitrievna, wife of the Survivor of Barbezht, I'll have to start calling you Izolda na Xhela, daughter of the Mandible."

She groaned. "Please don't. I get enough of that from them." She jerked her thumb in the direction of the Drakra quarters. "I think I'll still call you Fia, if that's okay. It suits you."

A rush of warmth spread through me. "Please do. I feel like..." I sighed. "I think I wasn't ready to give up being Sofia. The last time I was me—the last time I was Mila, I mean—I was so broken. Being Sofia helped me heal somehow. And then everything got so complicated with Alexey, and we left, and I don't even know who I am anymore."

We'd reached the gardens. She stopped next to a snow-covered shrub and gave me a look that was half amusement, half exasperation. "You have a real penchant for drama, you know?"

I blinked at her, stunned. Whatever I'd been expecting her to say, that wasn't it. "What?"

"You're still you, you idiot. You were you when you were Mila, you were you when you were Sofia, and you're still you now." She sighed heavily. "It doesn't matter what body you're in or who you're with. Yes, being at court changed you. People change; it's what we do. But you didn't become another person entirely. You just need to find out what you want now."

"What if I don't know what that is?"

I might have, once. At one time, I would have gone through anything to come back to Han. I'd chosen him, despite his injury, despite my family's objections, despite his status as traitor. But something had changed in those months we were apart. *He'd* changed. And I had. When I'd discovered he was alive, my first reaction hadn't been joy—it had been dread. Dread for what it meant for me and Alexey.

And now he'd broken my trust. After so many months apart, after all I'd faced for him, for us, when it mattered most, he'd left me locked in that room. He'd gone to face Borislav without me, imprisoning me. He'd treated me like a child.

"I think you do," Izolda said softly.

My eyes flashed to her face and away. "And what if I do, but I can't have it?"

"Why not?"

I brushed snow from a bench and sat. "He doesn't want me anymore." If he did, he would have let me help him, let me free him somehow.

"Are we talking about Alexey, or your captain?"

"Alexey." Whatever had been between me and Han was broken. Perhaps forever. "He told me to go back to my husband."

Izolda laughed, the sound irreverent and strangely comforting. "He's an idiot. A well-meaning idiot, but an idiot nonetheless. He's trying to protect you."

"He wouldn't let me try to get him released. Even when I told him I could talk to Han..."

"Can you blame him? If you found out he was married, would you want any help from his wife?"

The thought of Alexey with another woman was a fist around my heart. "No. I'd hate her."

"You understand how he feels, then." She took a seat next to me. "Does your husband know?"

I gave a hollow laugh. "How do you think that would go over? 'Oh, by the way, I fell in love while I was gone. He was fighting for Miroslav and got captured, so I'll never see him again, but I thought you should know anyway.'" I shook my head. "Han doesn't know anything about Alexey, and he never will."

"Eight years isn't forever."

"Feels like it." It probably felt longer to Alexey.

"You know," she said after a minute, "my mother asked me to go back east with her. I was thinking about saying yes. I don't know how much I'll be able to do for him, but I can at least be there. If nothing else, he'll need a friend."

"You would do that?"

She nudged me with her elbow. "As I said, I was thinking about going already. I'm not in love with him, but I do care for him."

I nodded absently, my mind swirling. "Do you know when you'll leave?"

She shrugged. "Probably in a day or two. I think the high priestess has some things to work out with the new tsar, but she's anxious to get home before the snow thaws." She patted my leg. "I need to get back. I'll write when we get there, *da?*"

"Find me before you leave. I want to say a proper goodbye." I hugged her. "I wasn't sure we'd still be friends now that I'm me again. I'm glad we are."

She pulled back and shook her head, lips pressed together with exasperated amusement. "I told you before, I'm not your friend because I knew the old Sofia. I'm your friend because of you. And as I said, you never changed who you were." She rolled her eyes. "Ugh, now you have me spouting cliches. Go on, I'm sure you've got your scarred stud waiting to see the old you."

I swallowed hard. I did need to find Han.

"Well, try not to look so excited about it." She laughed. "I'll see you later, Fia."

As she left, I stood. I wasn't ready to go back to Han. Not yet. I wandered slowly to the palace. Izolda was right; I wasn't a completely different person, not really. But I wasn't the same, either. Could I become the person I was before?

Han had changed while I was gone. He was more sure of himself, more confident. A leader, not just of our small group of servants and tenants, but a real leader now. People looked up to him, respected him. By the Blood, the *tsar* respected him.

Not all his changes were good, though. He didn't trust me anymore. Didn't see me as an equal. He'd grown possessive, controlling.

But hadn't I earned his distrust? I'd lied to him, left him, and done things while I was gone that would tear his heart in two. I'd fallen in love with someone else.

What would that mean for our marriage? In some ways, Alexey knew me better than Han did. In the brief months I'd known him, he'd seen what I tried so hard to keep hidden, how broken I was. He'd seen my walls and broken them down, stone by stone. He'd helped me put myself back together, even while I used him.

Han and I had been through so much together. His recovery after Barbezht, the years of struggling to make ends meet, the joy and anticipation of the birth of our son.

He would never be Alexey. He could never fill the hole in my heart that Alexey left. But Alexey wasn't here anymore. He'd told me to go home, told me to be happy. After all I'd done to him, to both of them, I owed it to them both to do that. I couldn't walk away from my husband to chase an unattainable dream.

Han had broken my trust, but I'd broken his, as well. Maybe we could heal from that betrayal. Maybe we could find a way to come back from this war. Together.

I was back at the room before I realized it. I pushed open the door, and Han was there. His eyes swept over my body, drinking me in, and I was in his arms, his lips on mine.

"Mila," he said. My name. Not a stranger's. "Mila."

"I'm back," I whispered. "I'm home."

EPILOGUE

Alexey

I stared at the not-so-distant city between the slats of wood that made up my prison. The sun was getting low behind the palace, lighting up the white stone and golden domes in a brilliant shade of orange. If I hadn't been inside it that afternoon, I could almost imagine it hadn't changed.

But I had been there, and it had changed. A giant chasm split the throne room floor. The bodies undoubtedly still lay at the bottom of that pit where they'd fallen. I shuddered to think how close I'd been to becoming one of them. Then again, how unwelcome would that death be compared to what awaited me? Death by hanging was a strong possibility for my future. Exile, possibly, if I was particularly lucky. I didn't want to be exiled, but I supposed, when considered with detachment, it was preferable to death.

I heard footsteps approaching, but I didn't turn. More guards, or possibly more prisoners. It was too early after the battle for executions to begin. No one would be coming for me yet.

"Alexey."

I heard my name, half-whispered, and turned so quickly something in my neck cracked.

Sofia.

She stood there watching me. Izolda stood next to her, I noted in the back of my mind, but I only had eyes for Sofia. A scarf was tied around her head, and my fingers ached to tear it off, to see her beautiful hair.

She wore an apron, too, and I saw smears of blood on it. Her own? My eyes narrowed as I scanned her for any wounds. Nothing obvious. She wouldn't have been in the battle. She'd probably been working in the med tent. Unsurprising. She wasn't the type to sit quietly and wait for things to happen. She had to be involved somehow.

Izolda muttered something I couldn't hear and turned to leave. Sofia looked after her as though she wanted her to stay, but she didn't say anything. After a moment, she looked back at me.

"Why are you here?" I asked, more harshly than I intended. Not that I didn't intend it to be harsh. She was the reason I was here, at least in part. When she didn't answer, I stepped closer, pressing her for an answer. "Did you come to gloat?" Vicious, beautiful woman. She'd used me, played me like the fool I was. And I'd gone along with it willingly.

"I'm sorry." Her voice was breathless. "I'm so sorry."

Something in my chest cracked. "Was any of it real?" I'd asked her the same thing yesterday morning, when I'd helped her escape from the tsar's dungeons. She hadn't answered then. I watched her face, searching for a response. She couldn't have fabricated everything. The taste of her lips, how she felt in my arms...those were tools she'd used against me, yes. But the tears she'd shed in front of me, the laughter, the admiration in her gaze. I couldn't have imagined all of it. She had to feel something for me.

The first time I'd kissed her, when she fell apart with fear from some remembered trauma; that had been real. As had the rest of the evening, when she let me hold her as she cried away her pain on my chest, sitting out in the frigid air overlooking the ocean.

And the tears of fear and shame in her eyes when she'd let me take her to bed the first time, before I left for battle? That was the most real of all. I'd never understood her. Loved her madly, needed her desperately, but never understood her. I watched her face, wishing she would answer my question, or at least give me some sort of a sign.

"I'm married."

I flinched as the words left her lips. Married? She couldn't be married. She'd given herself to me. She was mine. Fully, completely, in every way. She was *mine*, dammit!

Father's Blood, I'd lost my mind over this woman. She'd used me so skillfully, I hadn't even noticed I was being used.

"I see," I said, praying my emotion didn't show in my voice.

"Alexey, I—" She reached through the slats of wood, but I stepped back. If I let her touch me, I'd be well and truly lost.

"Don't." She couldn't touch me. Talk. I needed to talk. "Who is he?"

She pursed her lips, and I glanced away, trying not to remember the feel of those lips on mine. "A commander in the tsar's army."

"Not Tsar Miroslav's, I take it." Of course not. I'd been making love to her, telling her all about Tsar Miroslav's strategy, trying to impress her, so she could pass it all to her husband, a commander for Borislav. What a damned fool I was. A besotted, idiotic fool.

"Miroslav is dead."

"I know. I was there." After the pit had opened up in the floor of the throne room, after most of the tsar's court was dead, Miroslav and Borislav had faced each other. Tsar Miroslav hadn't had his right-hand man to protect him anymore, no Lord Kazimir to keep him safe.

"He was a monster," she whispered.

I could have laughed at that. Miroslav was no saint, I knew, but after the carnage from that afternoon, it was hard to imagine anyone thinking Borislav was an improvement. "And your tsar is so much better."

She straightened her spine at that. Never one to back down from a fight, my Sofia. Or, not mine. Someone else's. Possibly not even Sofia. She'd lied about everything else, why not her name?

"Borislav doesn't kill innocents."

By the Blood, she sounded so sure of herself. I could picture Lady Yelena, though. The look of terror on her face as she'd fallen through the floor of the throne room. She'd been expecting her first child. Lord Kazimir, abusive bastard that he was, would have been a terrible father. But Lady Yelena was a sweet girl. An innocent. She hadn't deserved to die like that. She hadn't deserved to die at all. "Doesn't he?" I asked coldly. "I'm sure Lady Yelena would be happy to hear that. As would Count Andrej and the dowager tsarina." And all the other victims in the throne room.

I saw the blood drain from Sofia's face and instantly regretted my words. I hadn't meant to frighten her. "What do they have to do with this?" she asked.

Regretful or not, I couldn't stop the next hateful words from leaving my mouth. "Why don't you ask your husband? I'm sure he knows all about the carnage your tsar wreaked in the palace."

"Where is Lady Yelena?" Her usually husky voice bordered on shrill.

"She's dead. Along with her husband, Tsar Miroslav, and nearly a dozen other nobles killed at the hand of the man you call tsar. Tell me, Sofia, what crime did the grand duchesses commit to deserve death?"

"No."

I laughed humorlessly. "You don't believe me? No, of course you don't. I'm the villain here, just another mindless follower of Miroslav the monster."

"I never thought that!"

"No? You didn't use me? Didn't take advantage of my position in Lord Kazimir's household? Didn't pass on the information I shared with you to your husband and your tsar?" When she didn't respond, I scoffed. "That's what I thought."

She was silent for a moment. When she spoke, I had to strain to hear her. "I didn't mean to hurt you. I didn't mean for any of this to happen."

What game was she playing? I couldn't look at her. "What did you think would happen?" She'd used me, broken my heart, and now that I was captured, imprisoned, she came to say she didn't mean it. "What did you want?"

"I wanted to go home!" Her outburst surprised me, and my gaze was pulled to her face like a magnet. "I wanted my husband not to be branded a traitor. I wanted to raise my son. I wanted to live somewhere I didn't have to fear for everyone I loved. I wanted to live a quiet life with my family. But Kazimir and Miroslav took that away from me. Miroslav crippled my husband. Kazimir killed my son. They turned my home into a battleground. So yes, Alexey, I went to court to spy on Miroslav. And yes, I passed on what you told me. But I didn't mean to hurt you, and I certainly didn't mean to fall in love with you." She gasped out the last words, clinging to the wood of my cell to keep her upright.

I stared at her, processing everything she'd said. Her husband, a crippled traitor. A commander in Borislav's army. Father's Blood, she was married to the Survivor of Barbezht. The man who'd negotiated the Drakra alliance. I'd seen him that afternoon, next to Borislav in the throne room. He'd looked appalled at what was happening, but he hadn't done anything to stop it, either. Of course, it wasn't like anyone unSanctioned could stand against the Sanctioned. Not if they wanted to live.

Lord Kazimir had killed her son. I hadn't known that she had a son. She wouldn't have told me, but I wished I'd known. I could have—I didn't know what I could have done. But I wished I'd known. It explained why she'd been trying to poison the baron. She'd wanted to protect Lady Yelena and her child from Kazimir. There had been times I'd wanted to kill the abusive bastard myself, but Sofia had actually tried. Not just to help her tsar win the war, but to avenge her loss and stop others from facing the same horrors.

And she'd fallen in love with me. I turned that thought over in my head, examining it. It could be another lie, I knew, but what would be the point? Why tell a prisoner, one likely to die soon, that she loved him?

I looked over at her. She leaned against the wall of the cell, tears streaming down her face. She was so fragile. She needed me. I would regret this, but I reached out and brushed a tear from her cheek.

"I did," I told her softly. She looked up at me, and I was surprised to feel my own eyes fill with tears. "I meant to fall in love with you."

She let out a sob that shattered whatever part of my heart wasn't already hers. "Alexey, I—"

I cut her off with a finger to her lips. "I told you I didn't care how long I had with you, that every moment was a blessing. I lied." I took a deep breath to steady myself. My hand moved to the scarf on her head, and I slipped a finger under the edge. "I want every moment of the rest of your life. I want to help you move on from whatever happened before me, and I want to protect you from whatever comes next." I pulled the scarf off, relishing the sight of her beautiful rows of braids. I hated myself for whatever part I'd played in causing her pain. But I hated the Survivor of Barbezht even more, for sending her to court to spy for Borislav. He'd sent his wife into danger. If she hadn't escaped, she could have been tortured, even executed. My next words were little more than a snarl. "And I don't want to send you back to the bastard of a husband who sent you to court to do his dirty work."

I couldn't restrain myself any longer. I kissed her, pouring every emotion I'd felt over the last week into that kiss. I unleashed all my fear, anger, betrayal, hurt, holding her in place with a hand on the back of her head. She didn't pull back, though, and she kissed me just as fiercely. I silently cursed the cell that held me, wishing I could run my hands over her body.

Too soon, always too soon, I pulled back. "Don't go, Sofia," I whispered against her lips. She was still crying. My face was wet with tears, and I didn't know if they were hers or mine.

"Mila," she said in a breathless voice. I searched her eyes, trying to parse out the meaning of the word. "My name is Mila Dmitrievna."

Fuck. She hadn't wanted me to kiss her. I dropped her and took a step back. She wanted me to remember who she was, really. Another man's wife. I schooled my features into a cool disinterest. "My apologies, Mila Dmitrievna."

"Alexey, no." She reached for my hand, and I let her take it, too confused to pull back. "I didn't mean to feel what I do for you. I'm married."

"Yes, you've said that." Was she deliberately trying to hurt me?

"I thought he was dead." She stopped, swallowed hard, and went on. "But he's not. And when I found out he was alive, I had already fallen in love with you." She shook her head. "I just wanted to know that you knew me, not Sofia."

"I do," I said, confused. Then I shrugged. "Or I thought I did."

She wiped at her tears. Fuck. Was that because of me? She still held my hand, and I looked down, watching my thumb brush against her skin. "But your name doesn't matter to me," I said, surprising myself. As soon as I said it, I realized it was true. "Who you are, that doesn't change. No matter what you did, what you felt like you had to do, that woman is still the same, whether you call her Sofia or Mila. I fell in love with you. I don't know what's going to happen to me now, but whatever happens next, knowing you loved me, however briefly..." Overcome with emotion, I couldn't continue. I turned her hand over and pressed a kiss into the palm. "You're my sun, and my life will be dark without you."

She smile she gave me was weak, tear-filled, and I couldn't bring myself to return it. She wasn't mine. She'd never be mine. "Go home, Mila," I said quietly. "Go be with your husband. Raise your children, serve your tsar. Be happy."

"And you?" Her voice was pained.

I shrugged. "Exile if I'm lucky. Execution if I'm not." On the whole, I thought I'd prefer execution. Hanging wasn't dignified, but it would mean an end to the whirling hole of despair that had opened inside my chest when I realized she'd been using me. A world without the sun wasn't worth living, and though I'd called her the sun first as a flirtatious joke, it had quickly become true. She was everything warm and light in my life.

She shuddered at my words, and I wished I hadn't mentioned execution. I should have comforted her somehow. "I want to help you. I can talk to my husband—"

"No," I said sharply. Father's Blood, I didn't want to owe the Survivor anything. I already had to give him the woman I loved. I couldn't stand giving him anything more. I didn't have anything more to give. "I don't want his charity."

"And mine?" She looked up at me, her brown eyes hopeful. "Can't I do something?"

If I kept looking into those eyes, I would get down on my knees and beg her not to leave me. "Go home," I repeated before I lost my nerve. "Go home and be happy." I trailed a finger down her cheek, and she closed her eyes.

I forced myself to drop my hand to my side and stepped back out of her reach. "Goodbye, my sun," I said.

She took a step back, her eyes still locked to mine. Then another. She stumbled, and I flinched, wishing I could catch her. Izolda was there, though, taking her arm to guide her. I felt a rush of gratitude toward Izolda for doing what I couldn't. She would see Sofia—Mila—safely back to her tent. And back to her husband, the bastard Survivor of Barbezht.

I watched as the two women walked back toward the camp, and I said a silent prayer that Borislav would execute me in the morning.

To Be Continued

ACKNOWLEDGEMENTS

Once upon a time, a little girl dreamed of being an author. Doubts crept in, life got in the way, and she gave up that dream. Then she had kids, and she remembered how important dreams are. On January 1, 2019, she opened up her laptop and started writing again. That's when *A War Apart* was born.

It was the first novel I ever wrote, and I was afraid to let it go. But my friends, family, and colleagues kept pushing me to step out of my comfort zone, and I finally gave in. (Mostly because I knew my sister would never let me hear the end of it if I didn't publish "her book.") Here it is, Lane. It's always been yours—I'm just the one telling the story. And I promise I'll fix all the awful things I did to them! ...Eventually.

Aly, my PA, thank you for keeping me on track. With my pseudo-ADHD brain, I wouldn't be able to get anything done without your check-ins and encouragement. Or at least not in a manageable time frame. Lexie, thank you for creating this beautiful cover that brought *A War Apart* to life. Aunt Ammy and Andrew, you were my first and loudest cheerleaders with this book. I couldn't have done it without you. Thank you.

To my wonderful alpha and beta readers: Kelly Keith, Sarahbeth Nedwed, Stephen E. Seale, Zara J. Black, Kaylin Barlow, Nisha J. Tuli,

Alex Sembach, Kari Robinson, Everly Wright, Nicole Marie Peck, Matthew Connor, Gabrielle Goodloe, Harmony Friedman, Elizabeth Myrva, Yuy Ren, and Alina Rubin. You made this book what it is today.

I also want to thank everyone in the countless online communities who gave me advice and support: Fantasy Writers Critique & Support Group; Project X; Moms Who Write; Trauma Fiction; Write Like a Mother; my Facebook, Instagram, TikTok, and Threads friends; and more that I've probably forgotten. You answered all my questions, from "how long would it take to bleed out from a battlefield amputation?" to "what type of underwear did they wear in 16th century eastern Europe?" All the little details that hold the book together are thanks to you.

Mom, I can't wait for you to read this one! (But you've got a couple other books to finish first, so get on that.) Dad, thanks for answering my weird questions while I was writing it, even if you won't ever read this. Dyami, Dalton, and Kayla, I know you don't approve, but [insert obligatory acknowledgment here]. Keaghn, I hope I did a better job of writing the male POV this time.

There isn't time or space to thank everyone who made this book a success, so I'll end this with a general thanks. To my family, to my friends, to my colleagues, and most importantly, to my readers. I do this for you, and I look forward to many more. Be back soon!

Milton Keynes UK
Ingram Content Group UK Ltd.
UKHW041629240924
448733UK00002B/48